D0012230

ILLUSIONS

Charlotte Vale Allen

IVY BOOKS • NEW YORK

Ivy Books
Published by Ballantine Books
Copyright © 1987 by Charlotte Vale Allen

Library of Congress Catalog Card Number: 86-25956

ISBN-0-8041-0190-6

This edition published by arrangement with McClelland and Stewart.

This novel is a work of fiction. Names, characters, places and incidents
are either the product of the author's imagination or are used fictitiously.
Any resemblance to actual persons, living or dead, events or locales,
is entirely coincidental.

Manufactured in the United States of America

First Ballantine Books Edition: March 1988

For Shirley Van Wagener

One

She'd known Joel was going to die. They'd all known it for a very long time. But when it finally happened Leigh was shattered. She couldn't seem to absorb it, even though she was there at the end, and saw for herself how, with dreadful ease, Joel simply ceased to exist. While there was a certain, hateful rightness to his death, there was also a terrifying simplicity to it at the last. And she kept thinking it should have been a larger, grander moment somehow. The ease and simplicity distressed her. If he could die this way, after such a long, valiant battle, she had to wonder if there'd been any point to his having struggled as long and as hard as he had.

She was frightened, exhausted, and angry, and the only thing she wanted to do was go to visit her father. She admitted it was an arbitrary idea, even probably irrational. Nevertheless, she was determined to go. She was in sudden, desperate need of a destination.

Once in her aisle seat in the first-class smoking section of the 747, she put a tape into the Walkman, adjusted the volume and the ear phones, opened a book, and tried to ignore everything going on around her. She didn't want to have to speak; she had no desire to communicate with anyone except her father. And she had no notion whatever of what she wanted to say to him, or what she hoped he might say to her.

"You're off on a fool's errand," her mother had declared earlier that day. "No one's ever been able to hold anything remotely resembling a conversation with your father. He'll undoubtedly be up to his thighs in manure; he'll likely give you one of his typical blank stares while he huffs and puffs a bit about the weather; then he'll offer you a glass of cheap sherry and tell you about the cost of seed, or something equally captivating. I *wish* you'd reconsider, Leigh. This is truly ridiculous."

"He's my *father*, and I haven't seen him in almost thirty years. I *want* to see him!"

"I know you're upset, dear"—her mother took another tack—"but do you really think this is wise?"

"I can't give you straight answers," Leigh told her. "I don't *know* if it's *wise*. I don't *know anything*."

"It's just that I do worry about you . . ."

"I know that. I worry about me, too. I'll call you from London."

"Please don't do anything foolish," her mother had begged.

"I will try my very best not to."

"It's all madness," Marietta had sighed. "Take care."

"I will try," Leigh had promised.

She'd no sooner finished the conversation with her mother than the telephone had started ringing again, and she'd wanted to ignore it, let the machine answer for her. But she thought it might be her mother again, with some last-minute thought, so she'd picked up the receiver to give a wearied hello.

At once, Miles had made his pitch. "The last thing you

2

should be doing is flying off this way, leaving your mother to cope with all the arrangements."

"You just talked to her, didn't you?" Leigh had guessed.

"Yes, but—"

"And if you talked to her, I'm certain she told you she has *agreed* to cope; she *volunteered* to cope."

"Yes, but—"

"Miles, this is one of those times when I wish you were agent for one of us, but not both. I loathe all this back-and-forth business, with you rushing between the two of us. It's unfair to everyone."

"Speaking of which," he'd said, "I know it's probably not the best time, but at the risk of life and limb, dare I ask when, if ever, you intend to work again, to get on with your life?"

"It is *not* the best time. I may *never* work again. And I especially loathe it when you start impersonating my mother, sounding like her and trying to browbeat me with good intentions. Miles"—she had tried to overcome her exasperation—"I know you mean well. I know you care. But I don't want to talk to you now."

"All right," he'd backed down. "I know the timing's dreadful. It's just that we're very concerned about you, Leigh."

"I know that. I thank you for that," she'd said, and put down the receiver.

Giving up now on her attempt to read, she raised the volume on the Walkman so that her eardrums throbbed achingly as she looked around the cabin. A few more minutes to takeoff and, with luck, the seat next to hers would remain empty. She'd barely completed the thought when one of the flight attendants touched her on the shoulder. Leigh switched off the music and simultaneously slipped sideways into the aisle so the latecomer could get to his seat.

"Sorry to disturb you," he apologized, passing his overcoat to the waiting attendant.

Leigh gave a slight nod in response, sat again, fastened her seat belt, turned the cassette back on, and closed her eyes. Please, she prayed, not a chatty executive; please not one of those pin-striped wonder boys flying on a company ticket for a few days' business in London.

Finding her place in the book, she tried to force herself to read. It was like being back in school, at a time in childhood when words had been individual entities that hadn't seemed to want to be joined together to make sentences. Simply recognizing random words had been a significant accomplishment, worthy of parental applause. Hopeless. She couldn't make sense of the neatly printed blocks of letters set so reasonably on the page. She closed the book and stared at the back of the seat ahead.

The only reason she'd married the Good Doctor, in whom she'd had only a minimal interest initially, was because she met and was at once taken with his twelve-year-old son. At their first meeting, Joel had made coffee for them and then sat and talked with her about a production of *The Pirates of Penzance* in which he was playing the lead. He'd been so self-possessed, so wise and witty and charmingly confident, that she'd known she'd involve herself with his father in order to spend more time with the son. She'd been open about the selfishness of her motives, and had told Joel about the son she'd lost. He'd loved her anecdotes about Stephen, and had encouraged her to tell all about him. Joel had no jealousy. He was so firmly entrenched in his own identity, even at age twelve, that he was able to hear stories about another twelve-year-old boy and find only pleasure in them.

In view of how little interested the Good Doctor had

been in the son of his late wife, Leigh had taken the position that, at the very worst, she and Joel would benefit from one another. And they had.

For just shy of ten years she'd had not only a new model for her books, but also the privilege of watching Joel grow to become even wittier and wiser. Not even his father's eventual outrage had daunted Joel's confidence. Despite the hurt, despite the brief span of the marriage, despite everything, she and Joel had remained close. When Joel "came out," revealing to his father what Leigh had sensed intuitively almost from the start, the Good Doctor threw him out, and refused to see or speak with him even after Joel became ill.

It still infuriated her to think that anyone could be so stupid, so rigid in his thinking that he'd sever himself from his only child simply because that child had not turned out to be interested in girls. It meant nothing to the Good Doctor that Joel had been generous, gifted, and giving. He'd preferred his lovers to be male, and not female. He was, therefore, in his father's eyes, a sickening aberration, a degenerate, a pervert, a disgrace.

Now Joel was dead, and she doubted his father would even attend the funeral. She wouldn't be there either, but Joel would have understood that. They'd been saying goodbye for three years—from the initial diagnosis, through the two remissions, until just two nights ago, when his hand had gone limp in hers and he'd exhaled one long, slow, final time. She'd held her own breath, waiting for him to inhale again, to go on living. But he hadn't. His eyes had ceased to see; they'd gone opaque and visionless. With that final exhalation the humor and inventiveness and energy that had been Joel had left his body. She'd imagined his essence blending invisibly with the air of the room, and she'd breathed deeply as if, if she took in enough of that air, she might take in some significant part of her stepson.

Ten years of running out to catch a late showing of some old movie Joel insisted they had to see; of afternoon concerts at Avery Fisher Hall; of Sunday brunches, and dinners he prepared; of weeks at a stretch in the country where she worked and he tried to do something with the hopeless old furniture, by means of new arrangements, or painted the kitchen a bright grass green, or came into her studio, with coffee and sandwiches, to keep her company while she took a break; of celebrating when an audition turned into a job and he had three days' work on a commercial for a soft drink, or six weeks in an Off Off Broadway production that gave him an opportunity to demonstrate how immensely talented he was. He'd brought his friends along to meet her; he'd come racing across town in a cab, popping in on his way to a party to show her the clothes he'd bought with the residual check from his second commercial. There'd been occasions when he'd stopped by late, after some outing, to have coffee with her and to tell her how angry he was with Jeff over some misunderstanding, or how delighted he was about their reconciliation, or, finally, how exhausted and ill he felt. "I just hope I haven't got the plague," he'd whispered in the waiting room when they'd gone together for his tests. "I've been so goddamned careful."

He'd actually been relieved when the doctor had called them in to give them the results. He'd laughed, and the doctor had stared at him quizzically. "It's a respectable disease," Joel had explained. And when he'd been admitted to the hospital to begin chemotherapy, he'd said, "People have been known to beat it, Leigh. I intend to beat it." But his blood had turned to water, and he'd died.

She swallowed to ease the knot in her throat, and looked around the cabin. Why, with so many empty seats, had they put someone beside her? She felt suddenly furious. They should have known better than to put someone beside her. But at least he hadn't made any attempt to draw her into conversation. And he was, she saw peripherally, wearing an attractive Cartier tank watch and fragrant cologne. A briefcase sat unopened on his knees. The instant the no-smoking sign went off, he lit a cigarette. It smelled wonderful, and she realized it had been quite some time since her last cigarette back at the airport.

Just as she held one to her mouth, a gold DuPont lighter popped up in front of her to light it. She said, "Thank you," hoping she wasn't shouting. Joel was forever accusing her of bellowing when she tried to talk with the Walkman on. She said the words without turning, hoping to discourage further courtesies. She felt very edgy, dangerously full of untapped negative energy. Anything might set her off, and the next thing she knew, they'd be making an unscheduled stop, to put her into restraints before removing her from the plane. She could see herself being dragged, screaming, from her seat. There was a kind of jagged wedge of anxiety inside her chest, just behind her ribs, and when she indulged in imagining the darkest possible scenarios, it felt about the same way it did when she pushed the nail of her little finger into the flesh behind the nail of her thumb: a keen minor pain with the potential for considerable growth.

She'd heard the Albinoni twice, and ejected the tape, assaulted at once by noise—of the aircraft itself, of conversations, of pages turning in books and magazines, of ice cubes and liquids in glasses, of a wailing infant. Airplanes were so damned noisy. Just like hospitals. Hospitals were the noisiest places on earth, what with the announcements echoing up and down the corridors, the efficient-sounding squeak of rubber-soled shoes, various trolleys wheeling here and there, some with medications, some with food, some with mystifying loads of arcane equipment. Joel had never complained, though, about any of it; not when his hair came out, not when the medicines made him violently sick, not even when an acute toxic reaction to the drugs turned his face scarlet. "I'll beat it," he'd told her. "I'm going to beat it." Ah, Jesus! she thought, pushing through the tapes in her carryon bag. I believed you would, Joel. If anyone could have beat it, I believed you would. No one's meant to die a few weeks before his twenty-second birthday. It's too bloody young.

She gave up trying to find a tape, removed the earphones, and at once felt robbed, as if of armor. Why was privacy something one had to erect between oneself and others, like a barricade? It was simply horrendous the way people refused to recognize one's desire to be left alone unless it was clearly signposted by an open book, or headgear hooked up to music, or work arrayed on the tray table. If you simply sat gazing straight ahead, someone was bound to intrude. She was indulging in misanthropy, knew it, and didn't care. Since Joel's death, she'd had to fight an all but overwhelming desire to tell absolutely everyone to fuck off and get the hell away from her. Beneath this desire, rather like the bottom sheet on a well-made bed, was her knowledge of the transitional nature of her present feelings, as well as an ungrudging admiration for the completeness of her alienation, no matter how temporary. She was so deeply, pervasively angry, so utterly, desperately grief-stricken, that she wanted, from one moment to the next, to lash out at anyone who inadvertently crossed her path.

She'd only just finished a cigarette and already she wanted another. Why couldn't she quit? Joel had been nagging her for years to give up the habit. It should, she'd long reasoned, have been possible to go to bed one night and wake up the next morning as someone who didn't smoke. If she quit, her lungs would clear in time, her breath would turn sweet as a newborn's, her teeth would stay clean, she'd add years to her life. What for? Who cared?

She turned slightly to take a look at the man with the cologne and the Cartier watch. Late thirties, an impeccably tailored navy suit, crisp white shirt, gold tie pin; clean-shaven, good skin, dark hair, eye color unknown due to lowered gaze, hands resting motionless atop the still-unopened briefcase; no glaring abnormalities, ears and chin well proportioned. He looked young.

Quickly, she lit another cigarette, inhaled, then let her head fall back against the padded rest, considering the issue of age. There was hardly a day, recently, when she didn't, with mild confusion and disbelief, wonder how she could still think and feel as young as she did, yet be as old as she was. Even her mother didn't seem all that old. How did it happen? Eighteen one minute, forty-five the next. It wasn't like catching a cold; it wasn't something that would lay you out for two or three weeks, then be gone. It was there for good, and progressing at an astonishing rate: facial lines and wrinkled knees. Every morning when she ritually bent to touch her hands flat to the floor, if she cared to look, she could have an alarming closeup view of the crepey flesh sagging over the knobs of her knees.

"You're nuts!" Joel had laughed. "You look sensational. You worry about the dumbest stuff. What'll you do, Leigh, when you've got something really serious to worry about?"

"It depends on what you consider serious," she'd replied then.

Well, she certainly knew what was serious now. And she had handled it well. She'd held in the anxiety and uncertainty and fear; she'd been cheerful and optimistic

9

and encouraging with Joel right to the last. They'd even discussed it once, rating each other on how badly or well each had dealt with his illness. "We're both terrific at it," Joel had told her. Now it was over. He was dead, and congratulations for having dealt well were not in order. Now she had moments when the slow decay of her own flesh seemed so ominous she could have sworn she actually smelled it.

The man beside her wore a simple gold wedding band. She had three diamond rings on the third finger of her left hand, two diamond bands on the middle finger of her right, and a large solitaire on the finger beside it. He did have attractive hands, wide and strong-looking. They were the sort of hands she'd always imagined surgeons must have, until she'd married the Good Doctor and relegated that particular fantasy to the trash heap along with the dozens of other fiction based notions she'd entertained in her lifetime. The Good Doctor had pale, narrow hands that were softer than her own, and almost as small, and far, far cleaner.

"Are you on holiday?"

She turned. She could kill this dead at once, "cop an attitude" as Joel would have said. But she simply couldn't do it, not when she had hours left of having to sit beside him. And she lacked the energy to move elsewhere. Plus, his blue eyes were unexpected.

"No," she answered, her mouth rusty as if she hadn't used it in too long. "Are you?"

"No. I was just," he pointed, "admiring your rings."

She looked at her hands. "Oh. I get married a lot," she said, and then emitted what sounded to her like a grating bark of laughter. He didn't seem bothered. He actually smiled. What was it about his eyes? She was so tired it was difficult to home in on specific thoughts.

"What's 'a lot'?"

"Twice."

"That's not a lot. Four, five, that's a lot." He had a slight accent, but she couldn't place it. The plane was running into some mild turbulence, and he went suddenly sober, saying, "I hate flying. It terrifies me." He gazed at her, as if prepared for either her scorn or her support.

"And of course," she said, fascinated by his visible fear, "you have to fly constantly."

He nodded, still awaiting her ultimate reaction.

"I don't think I've ever met a man who admitted to being afraid to fly," she said, as taken with this thought as she was with the evidence of his fear.

"It's only fair to admit it," he said, looking relieved that she'd chosen not to display scorn, "in case I faint in your lap, or jump up and start screaming uncontrollably."

"You do that kind of thing?" she asked.

"Not so far," he allowed, "but you never know."

"Well, I will consider myself warned."

"You're not afraid?" he asked seriously.

"I'm not fond of turbulence. But afraid? No." Afraid? If anything, she'd gone so far beyond fear she scarcely valued her own life. Take the other night, for example, after Joel died, when she'd been driving around town after leaving the hospital. Some fool in a little car was beside her at the stoplight, just panting to race her. She was in the inside lane; there was a car parked about two hundred yards dead ahead. The lights changed, and she did it: she hit the kickdown switch, and the turbo-diesel shot off, but the guy in the Honda was gunning it for all he was worth and he wasn't going to let her into the left lane; he was hanging in there, nose to nose. Raining, the street icing over, and there they were, the two of them, doing sixty down Park Avenue. She missed the parked car with about six inches to spare, shot ahead and then, in delayed reaction, checked the rearview mirror for police while asking herself what in hell she was doing, while the adrenaline surged nauseatingly through her system and she eased back on the accelerator. The Honda zipped over in front of her before the next red light and stopped, to sit there, its rough idle making the thing shake like a big wet dog. The hot-shot behind the wheel had raced the middle-aged woman in the Mercedes, and lost. So now he'd teach her some manners, irritate her thoroughly by just sitting there after the light went green, then crawling ahead perhaps six feet, stopping, then a few feet more, and then, at the last moment, flipping his turn signal and shooting off to the right. Giving her the metaphoric finger. She'd sat through another red light and laughed mirthlessly, thinking they were both idiots. But he was a bigger one because *she* didn't care if she died; he, however, she'd have wagered, cared a great deal, but just didn't know how much. Like most arrogant idiots driving ancient Hondas and trying to prove his social equality and male superiority by having late-night drag races with people who, he believed, considered themselves at least financially above him, he thought he was immortal. She, on the other hand, knew better. She certainly did know better. Periodically, during the past two days, she found herself running that race again, but losing. She could see the Mercedes rear-ending the parked car; she could see and feel the heat of the resulting fiery crash; she could see herself sitting calmly, hands on the steering wheel, as she was immolated.

"There's nothing to be afraid of," she now told the man seated beside her. "You can only die."

He literally blanched, and she felt dreadful for speaking the truth because this man had no doubts about his mortality. "That isn't funny," he reproached her.

"I wasn't trying to be funny," she said. "Just try not to think about it," she advised.

"The more I try not to think about it, the more I think

about it. It's a conundrum. I don't suppose you play back-gammon?'' Again he gave her that open gaze.

There was something about him that was too vulnera-ble, she thought. It was as if he'd never quite mastered the skill of concealing his feelings, or his need to have those feelings approved. Did she want to spend time over a game with him? They'd be bound to talk. ''We could,'' she said at length, ''go up to the lounge. I am assuming you have a board.''

''*Would* you?'' he asked almost feverishly, as if she were consenting to far more than just a game.

''Backgammon's my weakness,'' she confessed. She and Joel had, at the last, played daily for hours, until he'd been unable to roll the dice or move the pieces. She'd ended up owing him two million, eight hundred and twelve thou-sand dollars. ''Consider it a gift,'' he'd grinned at her. ''I'm tearing up your markers, toots.''

''I am Daniel Godard.'' Her seatmate extended his hand to her. ''This is very kind of you.''

''I dislike telling people my name,'' she said, placing her hand in his. ''Call me Leigh.''

''What's wrong with that?'' he asked, bringing a port-able set out of his briefcase.

''I'll tell you after I've had eight or ten drinks.''

''You'll be too drunk to tell me then.''

''Exactly!'' She stood and headed for the staircase lead-ing to the lounge.

''We've got the whole place to ourselves,'' Dan noted, as they sat on opposite sides of one of the tables. ''Couldn't be better. The only thing worse than flying is having to be sociable in forced circumstances.''

''I agree. Where are you from?'' she asked as he handed her the brown dice and cup. ''You have a faint accent.''

''I was born in France. My family came to the States

when I was nine. And what is *your* faint accent?'' he asked with a smile.

"I grew up in England. My mother and I left when I was twelve."

"I think," he said, rolling one die to open—a four to her six; she took the first move—"you sound far more English than I do French."

She shrugged, intent on the game, grateful for the distraction.

An attendant came up to ask if they wanted drinks. Leigh ordered gin and tonic. Dan asked for vodka on the rocks. Neither of them paused in their playing. She couldn't concentrate, though, and lost three games in succession. Conceding the last game, she studied her companion while he cleared the board, and decided he was as bored as she.

"Shall we take a break?" she suggested. "My mind's not on this."

He pushed the board to one side, picked up his drink, and said, "Tell me about your name. I'll have the stewardess bring you nine more drinks."

She lit a fresh cigarette and drew hard on it. "Why are you going to London?"

"I have absolutely no reason. It's merely a delaying tactic. I'm supposed to be traveling in the other direction, but that route means seventeen hours nonstop in the air. By this route, I can fly in fits and starts, and it doesn't seem quite so nightmarish."

"But where are you going?" she asked, curious.

"Thailand." He smiled. "I'll spend a day, or two, or three in London, then pick up a flight to Zurich, or Stockholm, or Frankfurt, wherever; pick up another flight, and then another, until I get to where I'm meant to be."

"It must take forever."

"It does," he agreed. "But at least I don't faint, or

14

jump up and start screaming." He laughed self-mockingly.

"And what will you do in Thailand?"

"I own—owned," he corrected himself, "a mail-order business. I was conglomerated two years ago, but I contracted to stay on for a time to do the buying. What were you listening to before?"

"Albinoni."

"Ah!"

"Ah what?"

"Ah, good. If you'd said Barry Manilow it would've been terrible."

"Why?"

"You know why," he said.

Games, she thought. I'm not up for games. "You tell me."

"Barry Manilow represents a case of mistaken identity," he explained.

"I see. That happens to you often, does it?" Was he some kind of fool who went around judging people by their exteriors and their cassettes?

"It doesn't happen to you?" he countered. "Someone seems a certain way and then, when you become acquainted, they're not at all what they seemed. It was either contrived, or you were seeing what you wanted to see and not what was really there."

"And I seem to be one thing," she said, holding down her sudden anger, "but I may be something else, depending either on my skill at contrivance, or the flaws in your perception?" Another goddamned game, she thought, determined to put a stop to it.

"You seem," he said carefully, "to be many things, none of them contrived. I can't comment on the quality of my perception. It varies, depending on the situation. So," he took a deep breath, "tell me your name."

Because she felt he'd won that round and put her nicely in her place, she told him. "Stanleigh Dunn."

"It's a good name," he said judiciously.

"Oh, *please*! Everyone calls me Leigh."

"I thought you were a man," he said, drawing a leg up and wrapping his arms around it.

"I beg your pardon?"

"My daughter, when she was little, was one of your biggest fans. Still is, as a matter of fact. They're incredible, your books. The illustrations are—phantasmagorical. If I don't get your autograph before we land, Lane will never forgive me." Some doubt touching his smile, he said, "There couldn't be *two* Stanleigh Dunns, could there?"

"God forbid! Phantasmagorical," she repeated. "What a wonderful compliment! Thank you." Since she was predisposed toward people who knew of her work, she found herself relenting in her hasty assessment of this man as a potential games player.

"I've always admired people who could paint, draw."

"How old is your daughter now, Mr. Godard?"

"Lane is almost twenty, *Mrs. Dunn*," he teased. "Do you have children?"

Had he not asked the question, she would have corrected him about the name. Instead, she shook her head, at once reaching for another cigarette.

"You smoke too much," he observed.

"Cigarettes," she said wryly, keeping a grip on her temper, "are my personal punishment and reward." She knew if she sat there one minute longer she'd tell him precisely what she thought of people who liked to comment on the habits of other people they'd only recently met. "If you'll excuse me," she said, "I think I'll try to take a nap." She put out the just-lit cigarette. "I haven't

16

slept in two nights . . .'' She stopped, wondering why she'd begun explaining herself to this stranger.

"I'll just sit here, enjoy the quiet, if that's all right with you."

"Of course." She headed for the rear of the lounge where blankets and pillows were stacked. Halfway there, her conscience struck. She stopped and looked back, pitying him for his fear. She considered telling him how little there was to fear, how easily life could leave a person. "Thank you for the game," she said instead.

Distractedly, he replied, "Oh, you're welcome. Thank you."

She stretched out on one of the seats, her handbag on the floor beside her shoes. The instant her eyes closed, she saw Joel, and her anger at the unfairness of it all engulfed her. Pulling the blanket up over her head, she gave in both to the images and to the pain they created. She curled in on herself, her fists wedged against her teeth.

Two

He dawdled over his vodka and waved away the attendant when she returned, indicating with a finger to his lips the sleeping figure at the rear of the lounge. The attendant smiled her understanding and went away, leaving him gazing over his shoulder at the narrow form, hidden beneath a blanket, of the woman with the man's name. It disarranged his preconceptions to learn that someone with whose work he'd been familiar for so long wasn't the brawny male he'd always envisioned but a thin, crop-haired female with large, suspicious green eyes, a squarish stubborn chin, and an aura of sadness and anger.

It hardly seemed possible, when he thought of those elaborately detailed, otherworldly illustrations populated by nonmenacing monsters, that the woman asleep back there had not only conceived of them, but had executed them with such energy. There were only five or six books altogether, but he was certain that every one of them had won awards. And even though Lane had been sixteen or so when the last one came out, she'd bought it anyway, telling him, "They're not just kids' books, Dad. I'll bet half the people who buy them are grownups. And anyhow, someday I'll have kids and I wouldn't want them to miss out on these. This is *exactly* the kind of stuff kids think about.''

Pajama-clad, elfin-faced little boys pushing through the yielding walls of their bedrooms straight into the heart of nightmares that, when confronted, were actually conquerable. Exhausted but victorious, these children returned through their bedroom walls to sleep peacefully, having defeated their worst fears. Sturdy little boys, they slept in rooms chock-full of treasures: mica-glinting pieces of rock, pet turtles, bubble gum cards, rubber bands and crumpled candy wrappers, Matchbox cars; posters and pennants on the walls; dresser drawers gaping open to reveal the chaos caused by small hands searching for favorite T-shirts; heaps of abandoned, inside-out clothing on the floor; bedding half off the mattress; and well-worn sneakers kicked aside, peeking from beneath the bed alongside a battered but much-loved teddy bear.

The completeness of the images was as compelling as their content. And somehow not only the boys, but the monsters as well, were recognizable; all of it rendered so finely, with such an eye for detail that each new book had caused a rush at the stores and received not only review space in the national magazines but a high ranking on their best-seller lists as well.

Dan had never tired of sitting with Lane at bedtime, reading the few lines of text that accompanied each miraculous illustration. The two of them had discovered something new, some previously unseen detail, in the paintings with each viewing. He'd liked the books as much as his daughter had. And now his mental picture of the person who'd created them had been invalidated. Instead of some burly, bearded guy, there was this woman dressed like a diminutive man. Yet the clothes, rather than detracting from, actually heightened her femininity. He reacted strongly to the hint of lace behind the silk shirt, and to the thin wrists emerging from the sleeves of the severely tailored jacket. He found her attractive altogether, with her very pale skin, auburn hair, and angry eyes. It gave him a jab of satisfaction to think that circumstances had put him in the seat next to someone famous. And it was curious to consider that people were merely people until you came to know certain facts about them. Fame, it appeared, didn't necessarily leave a visible stamp.

Lane would be thrilled to find out he'd met Stanleigh Dunn. He smiled, and moved to light another cigarette, thought of the way Leigh had been chain-smoking, and pulled back his hand. He could go days without a cigarette, and usually only had a couple with his morning coffee and one before bed. But flying always had him smoking. There was simply no way he could climb into a plane without a full pack of cigarettes in his pocket and a spare pack in the briefcase. What had she said? Reward and punishment? Interesting way to put it. It used to infuriate Celeste that he could take cigarettes or leave them alone. "It's not fair!" she protested repeatedly. "I smoke thirty and you have one. Why can't *I* smoke just one?"

"I'm not addicted," he'd answered routinely, in time fatigued beyond measure by the conversation. His ability to stay away from cigarettes had evolved into a simile for their marriage: she was addicted, he was apparently uncommitted. Yet they'd remained married, hadn't they? Long after he'd lost interest, in every way, he'd stuck with the marriage. But his presence, his faithfully returning home every night, proved nothing to Celeste. When she failed to derive any satisfaction from taunting him, she turned to taunting Lane, successfully obliterating from her own mind any recall of the teenage antics she'd got up to once upon a time or of the emotional gusts that had turned her into a human storm that raged over anyone who came near.

By comparison, he'd always considered himself bland. He loved his parents, had had a storybook childhood. There'd never been anything to react against, and so he'd merely pretended rebellion for Celeste's sake because she'd been so violently dedicated to destroying whatever bonds existed between her parents and herself. He'd found her entrancing in her role as fifteen-year-old rebel. He'd admired her formidable anger; he'd admired even more her determination to wound her parents by taking risks with her person, with her very life. She had once, to his paralytic horror, jumped out of his car while they were stopped at a railroad crossing and run wildly across the tracks only seconds before a train came roaring through. And he'd never really understood what sort of punishment might be wrought on her parents by the giving of her virginity at age sixteen to Dan. But at that time he hadn't cared in the least about her motives. He'd only been interested in continuing to prove worthy of her time, and in the extraordinary opportunity she gave him to satisfy his cumbersome sexual curiosity. She allowed him to make the transition—in his own eyes—from sordid, hulking adolescence to self-confident young manhood. She gave herself to him in angry awkwardness, and he'd accepted the gift with astonished gratitude and a bursting sense of protectiveness toward her. Inevitably, Celeste got pregnant, and he honored his responsibility by marrying her. He'd been twenty-one; she'd been eighteen. In no way did this honorable act seem to gratify or appease her, and with time he began to see she was incapable of either gratification or appeasement.

He'd been Lane's father for close to half his life and it was one role he'd never regretted. Yet it was his absolute love for his daughter that Celeste had used most successfully against him. She'd mocked him for it, even questioned his manhood; she'd picked and prodded and poked at his love for their child, as if hoping to reveal him either a fraud or a failure. The result was that father and child pulled even closer together. This, in turn, fanned the flames of Celeste's frustration. He'd married a woman who seemed to lack some genetic faculty that would permit her to be happy.

He sighed, then clutched at the rim of the table as the 747 lurched suddenly. He hung on, panicked, for several minutes, anticipating more alarming midair shudders. When none seemed to be forthcoming, he slowly let go of the table and turned to look at the sleeping form in the rear of the lounge. He'd never before confided his fear to a stranger. But he wasn't sorry, even though she'd made that cryptic reference to death. It wasn't death that frightened him, but the thought of those three or four or five minutes *before* death, when the plane dropped from the sky and panic galvanized the passengers as they realized they were trapped. Imagining that unstoppable descent made him start to sweat and caused his heart to thud sickeningly against his ribcage. He knew that statistics proved he was far more likely to lose his life in a road accident, or at the hands of several infuriated youths in the subway, or even simply crossing the street. But those statistics were nowhere near as terrifying as the prospect of falling through space, sealed inside a huge metal lozenge.

"We'll be serving dinner in a few minutes," the flight attendant said quietly from the top of the stairs. "Will you and your friend be eating?"

"I'll ask her and let you know."

He walked to the rear of the lounge, debating whether or not to disturb her. The other thing about air travel that mystified him was the way one's encounters with people seemed magnified, heightened. Up here, marooned together in the inky sky, people could draw close and exchange the most privileged details of their lives with no fear of criticism or repercussion. As soon as the plane touched down on the tarmac, you pulled away and slipped back into the separateness you put on along with your shoes and your overcoat.

She was entirely concealed by the blanket, except for her right hand which rested motionless at the very edge of the banquette on which she lay. Slowly, he bent to look at her hand, fascinated by the fragility of her wrist. He could span it easily with his thumb and forefinger. It was so fleshless and narrow, so *exposed*. A bracelet would slip right off. He stared close-to at the exposed inner area, thinking he could almost see a pulse beating gently beneath the skin.

He placed his hand gingerly on her arm, saying, "I hate to bother you, but they want to know if you're going to have dinner."

The blanket came away from her head and he saw that she'd been crying. Seeing the evidence of her recent tears struck him in the chest like a blunt-tipped dart, causing him to sit down abruptly while he waited for her to orient herself. She shifted onto her back and looked up at the roof of the cabin as she moistened her lips.

"You probably should eat," he said, studying her. He could see the signs of age in the laugh lines at the corners of her eyes and in the softness of her skin. When she'd smiled earlier, he'd gained an impression that was diametrically opposed to the one he'd had upon first sight. Awake and unsmiling, her eyes were those of a skeptic. But when she'd smiled, she was suddenly younger, impulsive and good-natured. He looked at the slow rise and fall of her breasts and thought she would be astonishing in bed—changeable and surprising and ardent. He wasn't sure why he thought this; it was no more than a hunch. He was finding her increasingly appealing. Part of it had to do with the isolated feeling he had about the two of them alone in the darkened lounge.

"I probably should," she said finally, turning her eyes to him. "Are you always so concerned about the well-being of strangers, or are you relying on me to help get you through this flight?"

He thought a moment, taken aback by her directness. "Probably both," he answered. "Does that make me a pain in the ass? Would you like me to take a hike?"

"It makes you unusual," she said, looking surprised by his strong tone. "Why would you think it makes you a pain?" She leaned on her elbow and gazed at him. Her hair was sticking up on one side in small spikes, and her mascara had blurred the undersides of her eyes. He dropped his defenses, thinking she looked adorable.

Folding his arms across his knees, he said, "I've been known to bring out the worst in people. Good intentions are no guarantee of favorable reactions. We're all supposed to stay inside our stereotypes. If we venture outside, well . . ." He looked at the neckline of her shirt, then away, down at his hands. "There are things we're not supposed to say to people, at least not in casual circumstances. You're supposed to save up your observations for private, persuasive moments. So when it comes to the crunch, you can whip out your most profound thoughts, like American Express Gold Cards, to wow the crowds, and prove you had secret resources the whole time."

She smiled, approvingly, he thought. "I'll tell you something," she said. "Ninety-nine men out of a hundred would've let me sleep here until we landed. And not one of them would ever admit to anything as potentially damaging as your fear of flying." As she spoke, she sat up and pushed her feet into her shoes. "Thank you very much. I have to go repair my face," she said, retrieving her bag from the floor.

While he zipped closed the backgammon set, he thought about the disparaging expression she'd worn while talking about herself. He realized she didn't think she was good-looking, and was again taken off guard. Naive, that's what he was. He could never get over the fact that women had such objections to themselves. Lane was a beautiful girl but she just couldn't see it. And Celeste was the same way. She'd always laughed at his compliments, so that eventually he stopped making them. And years later she'd managed to become almost as unattractive as she believed herself to be. But she'd been a lovely-looking girl, with long, silky, brown hair and wide-set dark eyes.

"You're very pretty," he told Leigh, when they were again seated downstairs. "And when you smile," he forged on, "you're beautiful."

She stared at him for so long he pulled himself tight inside, prepared for an attack. Fear did the damnedest things, made him blurt out whatever was on his mind. Yet she didn't appear angry. If anything, the compliment seemed to make her sad.

"Are you considered legally blind?" she asked at last, with a suspicious little laugh. "You really *are* afraid, aren't you? Or are you simply in the habit of being kind to middle-aged women?"

"You talk as if you're a thousand years old," he said.

"I'm forty-five."

"Never!"

"I'll be happy to show you my driver's license," she told him, still smiling.

"You sure don't look it."

"You haven't seen me first thing in the morning," she quipped.

"I'm sure you look fine. And anyway, it's not that old. I'm forty-two, and I don't consider myself over the hill."

"You're forty-two?" She now stared.

"Uh-huh. A couple of months ago."

"You are living proof that men age better than women."

"Poop!" he said, and laughed.

She continued to stare at him, wondering what could possibly be written on his hidden agenda. The silence held while the attendant served the food, then poured wine.

"This looks above average," Dan said, touching the tip of his knife to the steak. "A lot of times, on short flights, I bring my own food. I'll stop at a deli on the way to the airport and get a sandwich, something I know will taste halfway decent."

"Do you live in New York?" she asked, looking without appetite at the chicken breast on her plate, still mulling over the possible reasons behind his compliments, still working to control the emotions aroused by his compliments. If she wasn't careful, this man's apparent kindness might gut her.

He shook his head. "My office is in the city. We live in Bedford."

"I have a house not very far from there, over the Connecticut line. Mostly for the weekends." She kept talking in order to cover the fact that she wasn't eating. "During the week, I'm usually in the city. My mother detests the country place. She insists the co-op in the city is where I'm most myself. Whatever that is. I've never been especially interested in decor, you see, but since it's such an integral part of her image, she's convinced it has to be part of mine, too."

"What's her image?" he asked, intrigued.

She laughed. "Mother's image is almost as important as her work. My mother, you see, has moments of supreme silliness. She's Marietta Dunne, with an *e* because the *e* lends a certain something to the overall image. You don't know who she is, do you?'' He shook his head again, and she continued. "My mother left my father and brought me to New York thirty-three years ago, without a penny to her name. After pawning her jewelry to get us set up in a flat, she rented a typewriter and wrote the first of her romance novels. She sold it, bought back her jewelry, as well as a secondhand typewriter, and started writing as hard and fast as she could. All her heroines are headstrong young virgins between the ages of nineteen and twenty-three. All the heroes are tall, dark, broodingly handsome types with strong jaws who fall instantly, hopelessly, in love with the virgin, and then go through a convoluted series of ill-timed misunderstandings. There's lots of traveling to far and exotic places—which Mother researches personally, sometimes—lots of near-broken hearts, and so forth. They sell by the trillions, and she's become the queen of the romance set—which is where her image comes in. The clothes she wears for publicity appearances are always yellow, and so are the limos hired to take her to speaking engagements. Privately, she lives a life that would give her readers coronaries. She has men from here to there; she looks way better than I do; she enjoys herself to the hilt. She's just simply incredible."

"Do you get along well?" he asked.

"I adore her," she said. "I truly adore her. I think she's the only reason I haven't—" she stopped abruptly, wondering if Miles was right and it was unfair of her to run off, leaving her mother to deal with the funeral.

"Haven't what?" Dan wanted to know, seeing she looked sad again.

"Nothing," she said. "Nothing. Are your parents still living?"

"Both alive and well. My father's a professor at NYU. And my mother just gave up her job last year. She was

27

one of the head fashion buyers for Bloomingdale's. Years ago, in Paris, she was a model.''

''What does your father teach?'' she inquired, eager to keep the conversation going. She didn't want to have to think about what she'd left behind.

''French, naturally.''

''Brothers and sisters?''

''Nope. Just me. And you?''

''Just me.'' She aligned the knife and fork across her untouched plate of food and picked up her wineglass.

''What about your father?'' he asked.

''The last time I saw him was on a visit the summer I was fourteen. I'm on my way over to try to see him again.''

''That's a hell of a long time. What was he like?''

''I'm not sure I know. My impression—reinforced in steel by my mother—is of a gentleman farmer. Inherited money, but the house was always dark and stone-cold. I picture him in a tweed hacking jacket and hat, with his trouser legs pushed into a pair of mud-covered Wellingtons; his face and ears bright red from the cold, and his hands permanently chapped from being outdoors in all weather to supervise the farm activities. Tenants and hired staff did the actual farming.'' Had he really been soft-spoken and reticent, or was her memory faulty? Describing him had expanded her need to see him.

''So, he has an image, too,'' Dan suggested.

''Perhaps he does.'' She looked at him again. ''You may be right. And two people with images probably couldn't survive together under the same roof. It's very clever of you to see that.''

''Your mother never remarried?''

''Never. She enjoys her gentlemen friends far too much. They give her fabulous presents, take her off on marvelous trips, wine and dine her as often as she'll allow them. And she accepts every bit of it with perfect equanimity. If I had one-tenth of her ability to handle things as they come, my life would be . . . let's just say I envy her that.''

''Where does your father live?'' he asked, aware that her attention was fading in and out, rather like the reception on a short-wave radio.

''In Warwickshire.''

''And you're going up there, when we land?''

''I have to write or phone first. I couldn't just drop in on someone I haven't seen for so long. No, I'll stay in London for a few days while I test the waters.'' She lit a cigarette, then asked, ''Do you ever do things and then wonder why you did them? Dangerous things, stupid things, I mean.''

''I'm not sure I follow. Give me an example.''

''All right.'' She paused for a moment, thinking. ''I once picked up a man in an airport.'' She paused again, then went on. ''I was married at the time. Well, this airport fellow was unexceptional really, except for his interest in me which, of course, elevated his status enormously.'' She laughed ruefully. ''My interest had to do with reaffirmation of my desirability, et cetera. So, I went with him to a seedy motel, and we did it. Or rather, tried to do it. He couldn't, and tried everything he could think of to persuade me to let him call his wife and have her come make up a threesome. I said, no, thank you very much, and went to the bathroom, had a wash, got dressed, and went home. Later, when I thought about it, I decided I'd been very lucky. He could've been insane, or a murderer.''

''I think everyone's done something like that,'' he said.

''Oh? Have you?''

''Along those lines, uh-huh.''

''Did you feel guilty?'' she asked interestedly.

''As sin. But for my daughter's sake. It didn't seem to

have anything to do with Celeste and me. It felt as if it had everything to do with Lane and me, though.''

"I see." She took a sip of wine, thinking. The man had stepped out on his wife, but his qualms had been about betraying his daughter's trust.

"What do you see?" he challenged her.

"I see there's trouble in paradise," she said, and then began laughing so hard she spilled some of the wine down the front of her shirt. Appalled at herself, she went quiet as Dan grabbed his napkin, dipped a corner of it into his water glass, and began blotting the stain.

Realizing what he was doing, he stopped, his eyes meeting hers. He couldn't read her eyes, or gauge her reaction to his small incursion past the invisible wall of her privacy. Jesus! he thought, he'd put his hands on her without even stopping to think about it. Silently, she took the napkin from his hand, and continued dabbing at the stain.

"What's wrong?" he asked quietly. "Is something the matter?"

Her eyes liquid, her voice soft, she said, "If I went slamming out of a room, the good Doctor Jacobson wouldn't dream of coming to ask if there was anything wrong. He would assume it was my problem, and if I wanted him to be aware of it, I'd tell him. You can't imagine how many futile gestures I've made in my life in the hope of getting the right, the needed reaction, just once. And here you are, wanting to know if I'm hungry, if something's wrong; giving compliments, being kind. Are you really real?"

"Sure I'm real," he answered automatically, but without much conviction. He considered asking for her definition of real. Perhaps it wouldn't coincide with his interpretation. Philosophical discussions, even of the most rudimentary kind, were like concentric circles. It made him tired just thinking about trying to define one's "realness,'' one's state of being. Or was her question simply her way of trying to fend him off? "I'm real," he repeated, then wondered for a moment why she'd chosen to ask if he was real, rather than if he was honest.

"This is ruined.'' Dropping the napkin on the tray table, she sighed and said, "I think you're the sort of person who always manages to find things to value in other people. Your wife and daughter are very lucky to have you.''

"I think the doctor's lucky to have *you*," he replied with utter sincerity, touched deeply by the remark.

Her hand, when she took hold of his, was startlingly cold. "We'll land in London," she said, "and probably never see each other again. But I'm glad you happened to be seated here." As she spoke, she drew closer to him. Then she touched her mouth to his, sat away from him, and released his hand.

Electrified, he sank back in his seat, all his senses thrown into chaos. "I'm glad, too," he managed to get out. It was the truth. She was the surprise reward for an unwanted journey. He'd met this strange, sad woman who'd just kissed him. And he was powerfully attracted to her. His eyes on her hands, he wished he could stop lying, telling her silly, inconsequential lies one after another. But it was too late now. Besides, what harm did they do? A man had to protect himself whatever way he could.

Three

After the meal, the cabin was darkened so the movie could be shown.

"I always watch," Dan said. "It helps me pretend I'm not thirty-odd thousand feet up over nothing but water, with nowhere to go but down."

Leigh gave him a vague smile, then fussed with her blanket and pillow, all the while covertly watching as he located the channel for the sound track, his eyes on the screen.

"The most dangerous thing about you, Stanleigh," her mother had once stated, "is your capacity for caring. It's a weapon you use primarily against yourself, to calamitous effect."

Years ago, when her mother said this, Leigh had laughed. Now it seemed to be one of the single most accurate observations her mother had ever made. Because here she was now, inches away from someone she found so attractive she was having trouble thinking of reasons why she shouldn't just put out her hand and stroke him. If only, she thought, ideas and feelings were tangible, items you could look at and turn and touch, life would be so much simpler. You could stack up the blocks and cubes and triangles in such a way that no one could argue with their reality.

She was near exhaustion, and told herself sternly that the affection she seemed to feel for this man was due solely to her state of wearied susceptibility. She was interpreting his complimentary kindness as more than it actually was. And so she closed her eyes to block him out.

Every few minutes throughout the film he turned to look at her. She'd scored a perfect bull's-eye in her observation about his willingness to find good in others. But he couldn't stop himself from seeking it. He was forever seeing hints of treasure where none existed. It was like those rocks in the illustrations of the elfin boys' bedrooms, with glinting bits of mica. Did she really know about that? he wondered. Did she understand the perennial hope that the fool's gold might just once be the real McCoy?

He couldn't stop thinking about that moment when he'd gazed into the disturbing depths of her eyes just before she'd put her mouth to his. For those few seconds, he'd been suspended, caught between pragmatism and his life-long desire to believe all things were possible. Upon review, he was flabbergasted by how much aspiration one could cram into such a small fragment of time. Yet he'd felt so many things—fondness and anticipation and pure, undiluted hunger. Why was he such a cluck that a demonstrative gesture from an attractive woman could push him to the brink of believing in miracles?

He drank the last of his wine, disgusted with himself. Put him on a plane and he became needy. He was too old to waste his time on daydreams. And yet he was prepared to buy wholesale into a fantasy because an interesting woman had expressed her approval of him with a kiss. Not just any woman, either, but a successful, famous one.

* * *

When she awakened, the cabin lights were back on and, beyond the window, a spectacular sunrise was taking place. His passport open in front of him, Dan was completing his landing card. She went to the lavatory to try to do something with her hair, and to add more makeup to the several layers already caked on her face. She looked at her reflection in the mirror and burst into tears, covering her eyes with her hand while her body shook from the force of her weeping. Why had she hacked off her hair? What good had it done anyone to return from the hospital one night and go directly into the bathroom to start chopping off her hair? Nothing proved, no good done; another mess.

She blotted her face with a handful of tissues, then did what she could to fix herself up.

"I thought you might want some coffee," Dan said upon her return. He had a cup waiting for her.

For several seconds she was tempted to ask him if he was trying to kill her with his thoughtfulness and generosity. She felt utterly victimized by his kindness. She managed to thank him, and got herself organized to drink the coffee while filling out her landing card. "How was the movie?" she asked, copying her passport number onto the card. Strive for normalcy, she told herself. Keep all the balls in the air, woman.

"You'll be happy to know Sylvester Stallone is single-handedly killing off the bad guys who menace our lives. Between him and Charles Bronson, it'll soon be safe to ride the subways and go for walks in the woods."

She laughed, finishing the card, then put it and her passport back into her bag. "I keep wishing we could go back to black and white, with plot lines and fade-outs instead of full frontal nudity. There are only so many ways you can show people doing it, and after you've seen those two movies, there's nothing left."

It was his turn to laugh. And then it seemed they'd run out of conversation. She lit a cigarette, then wondered why. Her throat hurt already and another cigarette was making it worse.

Dan tucked his hands into his armpits and looked out the window as the plane began its descent. There was a sudden rumbling in the underbelly, and he swallowed hard, afraid.

"It's just the landing gear being lowered," she said, seeing his fear.

"I know that," he got out hoarsely, unable to look away from the window. "Knowing doesn't make any difference."

She wished she could think of something to say, but you couldn't stop someone from being afraid, just as you couldn't prevent someone from dying, or from behaving badly, or from hating herself. The most anyone could do, ever, was to keep going forward alone. Everyone was separate, for all time. No one fit permanently to anyone else. But she had this goddamned dangerous capacity—or so her mother liked to say—for caring. So she reached over and took hold of his hand, saying, "Listen to me! Nothing's going to happen. We'll land safely, and that'll be that. Don't be afraid just for the sake of being afraid. It's a criminal waste of energy. It's not your time to die. Keep telling yourself that on all those other flights you have to take!"

He held on to her hand in grateful silence, looking away from the window to see that she'd closed her eyes and let her head fall back. He looked out the window again, rescued by her enclosing hand. Once the plane was taxiing toward the terminal, she gently pulled free of him.

He caught sight of her in the terminal, as she was leaving. A porter was carrying her bags and she followed several

35

yards behind. She moved along as if unaware of the people crowded around the baggage carousels, of the others headed toward the exits. To Dan it appeared as if she was dawdling, in no hurry to reach her destination. She opened her purse, got out a cigarette and paused for a moment to light it, then dropped the lighter back into her purse. It was like watching a movie, he thought, and he was the only one aware it was playing.

She arrived at the exit. The porter held open the door for her. She drifted through it. And was gone.

It wasn't the right ending; no movie was meant to end this way, with someone simply going away.

He turned back to the carousel in time to see his own bag come tumbling down the chute, and pushed through the others waiting in order to grab it before it started off on its journey around the treadmill.

In the early afternoon, having bathed and napped for an hour, in clean clothes and fresh makeup, Leigh put on her coat and went out for a walk. She moved through the crowds feeling as if she were pushing her way through fast-drying cement. Loneliness was like cancer eating its way through her system. It was so potent she thought, not for the first time, that it might just be possible to die from it. All those years after she'd divorced Joel's father, she'd never suffered from overexposure to her own company. She'd traveled, spent weeks alone doing this and that, meeting with friends and publishers. Now, she'd plummeted into darkness and only time could bring her out of it. Time, however, was unreliable. It could be weeks, or years, if ever, before she once again found a point to living. She'd come out of it the first time because of Joel. He'd been someone to care about, not a replacement for Stephen, but someone wonderfully unique who'd needed the caring she'd had to offer. Now there was no more Joel, and it seemed too unjust that she should, for a second time, lose a child.

She walked until she grew tired, then returned to the hotel thinking to have a late lunch, but the dining room was closed. She went instead into the lounge, took one of the armchairs by the window, and lit a cigarette as soon as her drink arrived. The gin went directly to her brain. She shouldn't have had it. It had been so long since she'd eaten or slept properly that not only were her clothes loose but the idea of food made her queasy. She was going to have to eat or she'd become ill. And while it was one thing to consider death, it was something else to be ill. She had no patience with her body at those times when it crumbled beneath the onslaught of some virus. So, she would eat. Soon. In the meantime, she'd have another drink, which she would consume more slowly, and she would try to formulate some plans for the coming days.

She glanced around, seeing she was separated from the only other people in the lounge—a quiet foursome—by a wall. It would be some time yet before the room filled for tea. God! she thought, experiencing a resurgence of the agitation that had periodically overtaken her since Joel's death. It was a kind of internal trembling that made everything inside her feel disconnected. What was she going to do? She was utterly devoid of ambition. Eating was too much trouble, as was telephoning her British publisher, as was contacting her father just now, or letting her mother know she'd arrived safely, as was almost everything she could think of. She was going to have to get past this. She couldn't go to pieces now. But God! It was terrible, sitting there with her eyes on the window, hoping no one would come in and find her going out of control. This wasn't some imagined horror, some made-up conflagration to punish her for her failures and omissions. This was real, wasn't it? Sitting alone in the lounge of Brown's Hotel, disintegrating. There had to be something she could do.

Dan looked around his room at the Hilton, depressed. He decided he'd go out, buy something for Lane. He'd take a taxi to Covent Garden and walk through the shops, browse at the outdoor stalls, see all the outrageous kids. When he'd been there a few months earlier, he'd been entranced by the kids with their hair partly shaved and the rest Krazy-glued into astonishing shapes, with clown-white makeup and outfits of studded black leather and chains, skinny black pants and army boots. He'd sat with a drink at an outdoor table, wondering where these people worked, and what their employers made of them.

He went out, got into a taxi, but instead of Covent Garden, he said, "Brown's Hotel," and the driver craned around to give him one of those looks.

"You could walk it in less time than it'll take me to get you there, mate," the man told him. "Five minutes, straight along Piccadilly."

Embarrassed, Dan gave the man fifty pence for his trouble, then strolled the few blocks over to Albemarle Street. Lack of sleep was catching up with him. He knew where the hotel was. He'd been coming to London regularly for years.

There was no answer from her room and he felt absurdly let down. He'd imagined them celebrating the elevation of an airline encounter into an actual friendship. He wrote a note, inviting her to dinner, and handed it over to the concierge. Then he stood looking at the brochures on the concierge's hatch, trying to think what to do next. Like a child, he had a totally groundless urge to cry. Shoving one of the brochures into his pocket, he crossed toward the lounge. He'd go to the bar, have a drink, then head on to Covent Garden.

He stepped into the lounge and there she was, sitting over by the windows with her mink coat puddled around her. She'd changed out of the man-tailored suit into a dress, and the difference was phenomenal. She was attractive now in an entirely different way. She appeared taller, thinner, and somehow less approachable.

As he crossed the room he expected she'd look up and see him, but she was so absorbed in her thoughts she didn't raise her head even when he sat down in the chair next to hers. He unbuttoned his coat, sat back, and openly stared at her. The dress was of soft-looking caramel-colored wool, very simple, and flattering. It emphasized the width of her shoulders and the tapering length of her torso. It also brought out the red in her hair. He decided he liked the pale angularity of her face. And her features, he saw, were slightly asymmetrical, so that, in repose, her mouth had an unusual tilt.

"I tried calling your room," he said, "but I got no answer, so I came in to drown my sorrows, and here you are."

She looked at him finally, and it seemed as if she couldn't decide how she felt about his turning up this way. He stopped smiling in view of her as yet unknown reaction. "I cheated," he told her, "and watched while you were filling out your landing card. Curiosity, I guess. Anyway, I thought I'd call you and we'd get together for a drink, or dinner. Then I thought that was a pretty silly idea because you can't push situations so they'll be the shape you want them to be. I mean, for all I know, you got off the plane hoping you'd never have to see me again as long as you lived." He leaned forward and waited for her to say something.

She shouldn't have been angry, she thought, but she was. Here she'd been praying for something to salvage her emotions, and it came in the form of this man. But he was dressing it up, pretending he was after something more noble than he was. "Men are such dogs," she said with a sigh, "always sniffing around looking for some bitch in heat. I suppose you'd like a drink. We could save time and order from room service." She began pulling her coat out from under her, but when she saw he hadn't moved, she stopped. "You don't want to come upstairs, Mr. Godard?"

"That isn't quite what I had in mind," he said uncomfortably.

"Oh, come on," she chided. "You were so wonderfully honest on the plane. Now you're going to be dishonest, and that's a great pity. You came here because you want to go to bed with me, but you're going to lie and say you only meant to be sociable. Mr. Godard, I'm tired and hungry, and a little drunk from two gins on an empty stomach. I'm so tired that I can't be bothered playing games. If you want to do it, we'll do it. I'm flattered you'd be interested."

He wanted to escape. He also wanted to defend his good intentions. Spotting the waiter peering around the corner, Dan beckoned him over. "We'd like a pot of coffee and some sandwiches, please." The waiter went off, and Dan turned back to her. "Is it possible you could be wrong?" he asked her.

"You have a wife," she reminded him.

"You have a husband."

Pause.

"You don't give a damn that I've got a wife," he said, his eyes narrowing slightly.

"I think perhaps," she said astutely, "*you* give a damn that I've got a husband." What was she doing? she asked herself. Why was she reviving a long-dead marriage? Protection, she decided. However slim, she felt she needed it. There was no need, though, for her to behave the way she was. Had she already gone so far out of control that she no longer recognized the boundary between acceptable behavior and craziness?

"What are we doing that's so terrible?" he wanted to know, his expression innocent.

"We haven't done it yet," she answered, thinking she was bound to drive him away if she kept this up. And she really had no reason to want to be rid of him.

"Jesus!" he exclaimed, starting to feel overheated, and wishing he'd gone to Covent Garden.

"Why don't you admit it? You want someone to sleep with."

He was saved from having to reply by the swift return of the waiter bearing a tray with coffee and a plate of crustless sandwiches. Dan pulled some notes from his pocket, gave the waiter ten pounds, and waved him away.

"That was good," Leigh said confusingly.

"What was?"

"That bit with the waiter. You care more about people than you do about money."

"Well, of course . . ." he began.

"Don't get defensive," she cut in. "It's a refreshing change."

"From what?" he asked, placing several triangles of sandwich on a plate before passing it to her.

"I've met quite a few men who thought the direct route to either my brain or my money was between my legs."

The remark seemed to him so graphic and so intimate that he had an image of her spread naked on a bed with her legs parted, while some faceless man's hand searched inside her. The image was upsetting but arousing. It stayed with him, gradually fading as their conversation continued.

"What about your husband?"

"He's very successful. My money has never been of any interest to him."

"It doesn't interest me, either. Let's agree to something," he suggested. "You won't talk about your husband, and I won't talk about my wife. Could we agree to that?"

"It may not be possible," she said, rapidly losing her anger. "I'm sorry," she said, looking doubtfully at the sandwiches. "I'm being hateful. It has nothing to do with you."

"You really do think I've got ulterior motives, though."

"Yes, I do," she said quietly. "Because everyone does, and you're no exception."

"You should eat," he said. "Maybe it'll improve your mood. In my experience," he said, pouring the coffee, "most women nowadays want to be conned. They look forward to the familiar little conversational minuet we all know is the prelude to a sexual encounter." He glanced at her, read her objection, and hurried to retrench. "Maybe," he elaborated, "they don't actually *want* to be conned; they've simply learned to expect it. I think a lot of women really dread finding themselves locked up in a traditional situation. Marriage, I think, has become the prerogative of those young enough to believe they can defy the established code of failure. Their marriages will last; they're more gifted at commitment than our generation; they have more talent for life, for careers, for success, for any goddamned thing you can name. And I have to admit that any group that can come up with the idea of wearing tennis shoes to and from work in order to save themselves from possible lower back pain definitely has the world by the balls. Wouldn't you agree? Would you wear a pair of Nikes with that dress?"

At this, she laughed, and put her cup down in order not to ruin a second outfit while in his company. "I don't actually know what that little speech was about, but you are very funny.''

"Why are you giving me such a hard time?'' he asked.

"Because I'm old enough to know better.''

"I think you play for shock value.''

"I don't have the energy to play.'' She retrieved her cup and drank some of the coffee.

"You have the energy to be pretty goddamned angry.''

"I don't think you realize you're dealing with someone who's not entirely *compos mentis*,'' she told him. "That's the truth.''

"Fine. So what do we do now?''

"I don't know,'' she said, rattled. "What were you going to do if I wasn't here?''

"I planned to go to Covent Garden, pick up something for Lane, have a look around.''

"I could go with you.''

"Would you like to?'' He brightened at once.

"I'll have to change my shoes.'' They both looked down at her brown leather high heels.

"I can wait here,'' he said.

"Come with me. You can remind me what I'm doing. I keep forgetting things.''

Fatigue was doing strange things to her perception. One moment she felt very tall and terribly thin; the next she felt small and rotund. Daniel remained fairly constant. What altered was her view of him. He was never unattractive, but different features caught her attention each time she looked at him. His eyes were very blue, very clear; then his mouth appeared generous and well shaped; next time, he had good teeth, and fine, dark skin. In the length of time it took them to ride up in the elevator and walk along the hallway to her suite, she came to a decision, so that once they were inside her room with the door shut, it was inevitable that they should embrace. She closed her eyes and held him. Nothing was ever quite so consoling or more potent than holding another body close to one's own. She lifted her head to look at him, and he did something that removed her completely from the darkness of her mood. He slipped his hands inside her coat, placed them on her waist, and lifted her straight up so that she found herself looking down at him. So pleased was she that she put her hands on his face and kissed him.

"You're so tiny!" he said, holding her aloft. "You weigh nothing at all."

She laughed with pleasure, only a bit disappointed when he lowered her down.

Another kiss, and then they were dispensing with their clothes; an activity punctuated by further kisses and brief, tentative caresses. The laughter was gone. Revealing herself was too serious, too risky; it made her hands shake and her heart flutter. She felt imperiled, put at risk by tidal forces within her over which it seemed she was never going to have any viable control. She had to look away from his eyes, because she despaired of seeing anything but approval there. She had no talent for temporary blindness; even at her most casual, she'd always been horribly serious. That damnable talent for caring was at work again. Because of her seriousness, she most often remained totally silent while making love. Or, to her dismay, she'd say something unintentionally absurd. In this instance, daunted by the firm, healthy-looking body in front of her, she said, "Oh, you're circumcised," and watched him wilt instantly as, with a surge of defensiveness, he declared, "Of course, I am. My father is Jewish. Did you assume because I'm French I'm also Catholic?"

"Not at all." Was this happening? *Why* was this happening?

He pointed at her belly and said, "I thought you said

44

you didn't have any children. That looks suspiciously like a Caesarean scar to me."

She turned her back, bent to retrieve her clothes, then straightened, holding them to her as she faced him again. "I didn't say," she spoke almost inaudibly, "that I'd never had a child."

"Oh, hell! What're we doing? I'm sorry . . ."

"I'll change. If you still want to, we can go out."

"I really am sorry. I don't know what . . ."

"*Please!*" she cried. "Neither one of us managed to draw blood. Do you still want to go?"

"Well, sure . . ."

"I'll only be a few minutes." She escaped into the bedroom and closed the door.

Not sure what had happened, or why, he stepped into his shorts, pulled on his shirt, and stood doing up the buttons while his eyes remained on the closed bedroom door. He saw and heard himself accusing, and felt sick. He'd overreacted wildly to an innocent observation. Christ! He was going to have to watch himself very carefully.

Dressed, he perched on the edge of the sofa. She was taking more than a few minutes, and the longer she was out of the room, the worse he felt. If she didn't reappear in two more minutes, he'd go over there, knock on the door, and try to explain.

Once the door was closed between them, she found herself folded over her armload of clothing, feeling a complete fool, and trying to tell herself she had no cause. But were they both crazy? She dropped the clothes on the bed, and went to get fresh underwear from the chest of drawers. Her legs felt rubbery as she at last walked over to open the door, fully expecting to find the sitting room empty. But he was still there, seated on the edge of the sofa, with a cigarette.

"That whole thing was ridiculous," he said, the moment she opened the door. "You have to let me apologize."

She leaned against the door frame and said, "If I let you apologize, then somehow I'm obligated to explain, and I can't do that. Let's just leave it be."

"I don't understand what's going on," he said. "I do like you, an awful lot."

"I like you, too. Let's get the hell out of here."

As she was handing her key to the concierge, the man said, "There's a message here for you," and gave her Dan's note.

She read it, then said, "Perhaps by dinnertime, I'll have figured out which of us is really crazy."

"Probably me," he said with a low laugh. "Probably me." He drew her arm through his, and she had the distinct feeling, for a moment or two, that she'd metamorphosed into something rather like a house cat, an animal with nerve endings so close to the surface that the most casual gesture or caress gave satisfaction and reassurance.

"Are you very clever?" she asked, so that he turned and smiled at her. "I have the idea that you are."

"If I was very clever," he replied, "my life would be far less fucked up than it is. I'm not especially clever."

"I think perhaps you are."

"We got so close back there," he said, as the taxi flew around a corner, causing him to slide over against her. "Are we going to have another chance?"

"You're saying you'd like to go through that comedy of errors again?"

"I'm very attracted to you. And if you want the truth, it's been a while."

"You don't sleep with your wife?"

"I don't *anything* with my wife," he confided with a hint of bitterness.

"Daniel, doesn't it ever seem risky to you to admit the

things you do? You're afraid of airplanes; you get lonely; you don't sleep with your wife. People just do not go around telling other people things like that.''

"I don't think of you as 'other people.' Anyway, I always thought I knew who you were. I had a very detailed mental picture of you.''

"You thought," she argued, "that I was a *man*!''

He laughed, shattering the tension, and tilted his head to one side. "I'm so glad you're not. I'm really glad you're not.''

She applied a slight pressure to his hand, wanting him to know she was growing fond of him.

"Before or after dinner?" he asked in a whisper.

"Probably before," she answered, able to feel his body's warmth.

He smiled. She closed her eyes. His lips touched against her throat and she started, colliding with his chest. He sat away slowly. "It feels as if I've spent most of my life looking at people going by, seeing things other people never seem to notice, watching the parade from the sidewalk. Every so often, I get the feeling that I'd like to be a part of the whole thing and not just someone stuck on the sidelines noticing all the details.'' He thought again of the way he'd stood watching her leave the baggage claim area, and that sense he'd had of viewing a movie. The camera could have been anywhere—in someone's briefcase, say, or fitted cleverly into a suitcase.

"Do you always say how you feel, what you're thinking?" she wanted to know.

He retreated a little, his features firming. "It's boring, right?''

"It's definitely *not* boring. Do you find *me* boring?''

"Hell, no!''

"Well, that's something, don't you think?''

He gazed at her for a moment, for the second time aware

of a pulse beating—this time, in her throat. Then, as he gazed at her, that image returned of her naked, on her back with her legs parted. "I'm sorry about what happened back there," he told her. "I was way out of line. It was stupid." Everything he said seemed to have an internal echo, so that the words bounced off the interior of his skull.

"It doesn't matter." It was true, she thought. It really didn't matter. She wasn't alone. For a few hours she didn't have to be alone. And perhaps tonight she'd sleep.

Four

They looked in shops on the periphery of Covent Garden, then in those of the garden itself. Leigh asked to try on a pair of shoes in one place but when the young woman returned with them, apologized and said she'd changed her mind. She didn't want or need any more shoes; she couldn't think why she'd asked to try them, and apologized as well to Daniel who seemed quite content to go along with whatever she decided.

They moved outdoors and wandered from stall to stall, pausing to study rubber stamps at one place, dried flower arrangements at another. Leigh felt they were simply killing time, that he wasn't actually looking to buy a gift for his daughter. But then he stopped by a display of hand-knitted sweaters and began examining them in earnest. Although he asked for her opinion before he bought the sweater, it was plain he knew his daughter's preferences and required no assistance. She watched him pay for his purchase and then moved to one side to wait while it was wrapped, glancing at her watch before pushing her hands deep into her coat pockets. It was almost five o'clock.

She'd arrived at a point in her exhaustion where, at present, she felt quite calm.

"If you wouldn't mind," she said when he joined her, "I'd like to walk."

They set off, and she marveled at her body's ability to function even when pushed to its absolute limits. "I haven't been awake for this long," she told him, "since I was a teenager."

"How long has it been?" he asked.

"Several days. I've lost track."

"What happened, Leigh?"

She knew she couldn't talk about Joel. It was too soon. If she attempted to describe what the past three years had been like, she'd break down. And, besides, it would mean revealing her true status, which she had no desire to do. "I'll tell you a story," she said, and linked her arm through his. "A true story," she qualified, glancing over to see she had his attention. "I got married when I was nineteen. I was madly in love, so I got married. It was very nice. We bought a place in the country. My husband commuted into the city to his job with the brokerage. I stayed at home and sketched a lot, did a few paintings, cooked occasional meals that were inedible, and generally enjoyed myself. We socialized with other young couples; we sometimes had weekends in the city when we stayed at my mother's apartment and went dancing and drinking half the night. We had fun, and I wasn't at all unhappy.

"I had Stephen when I was twenty-one. The timing was right, because I was beginning to get bored, and with Stephen to look after, I didn't have much time to be bored. From the start, everything about him fascinated me. He was so perfectly complete within himself.

"When Stephen was four, I started the illustrations for the first book. I wanted to find some way to capture forever everything about him that was, to my mind, the quintessence of little-boyhood: his prized possessions, his funny habits, his hiding places, his dreams and nightmares, everything. And he was my model, of course. I'd take photographs of him, dozens of them, and then, at night when he was sleeping, or during the day when he was away at nursery school, I'd work him into the illustrations. He was such an imp! And that face! God, he had the dearest face, pointy features and a great, wide smile, sandy hair and freckles and wise-old-man brown eyes. He was forever falling down, coming home with new bruises, cuts scabbing over. While he had his bath every night, we'd take inventory of his latest injuries.

"The two of them wrote their names in the snow in the garden the winter Stephen was six. I'll never forget the way they came in, redfaced and sobbing with laughter, to drag me out and show me what they'd done. Stephen had run out of 'ink,' so Carl had had to do the last three letters for him." She laughed.

"By the time Stephen was nine, if he and his dad went out in the car and were a little late getting home, I'd imagine they'd been in an accident and were never coming back. One part of me was actually relieved at the prospect. I wouldn't have to be responsible; I could go where I wanted, do what I wanted, without having to account to anyone. I had a career, my own money, I'd be able to live unencumbered. I imagined the two of them dead, and my reactions when the police came to tell me, and how I'd dispose of my husband's possessions, and what I'd do with the insurance money. All of it. That was one part of me. The other part of me couldn't breathe. I was so afraid of losing them, of losing Stephen primarily, that I knew my life couldn't possibly continue beyond the moment when I'd be informed they were gone for good. I despised myself for being capable of thinking such thoughts, of imagining them dead. But I couldn't help it. It seemed like something that could very possibly happen. And in a way, it was like preparing myself for the worst, in advance of its ever happening. That way, you see, if anything did happen to them, I'd be ready. I reasoned that you couldn't love anyone as much as I loved Stephen and not, at some time, consider what sort of life you might have without that person.

"So, life went on. I did a second book, and a third, and was working on a fourth. They take quite a long time," she explained. "The actual paintings are two or three feet high by four or five feet wide. That way, when they're reproduced and the color separations are done, you don't lose too much definition. I'm digressing," she said impatiently. "The thing is, I'd become tired of the marriage, tired of being a wife and a mother. If I was going to have to choose, I'd choose being a mother. But sometimes I felt it was miserably unfair to have to choose at all; sometimes I felt as if I wanted to be rid of *every* responsibility to *everyone*. No one running to me to ask where this was, or that was; no one to pick up after; no mounds of laundry waiting to be done; no meals to cook or lunches to prepare. So, I'd daydream, and then I'd feel guilty. And on we went.

"We never had disagreements in front of Stephen. In fact, Carl and I rarely disagreed. I simply wasn't in love anymore; I'd outgrown Carl, as well as the limitations imposed on me by the marriage. I was biding time, seeing other men occasionally on the sly to prove to myself that I was still young, still desirable; I directed most of my energy into Stephen, and the books. We managed to get through another two years, with me hiding out in my studio, living another, different life entirely in my head. I was free-floating, letting my energy and imagination flow unchecked directly onto the canvases.

"I was hardly paying attention when they went out after

an early dinner that night. I was putting the finishing touches to the last painting for the fourth book, and didn't want to be separated from the work any sooner than I had to be. So they went out, to the ice rink, to skate. We exchanged kisses, I reminded Stephen to take his earmuffs and his mittens, I smiled, they smiled, we said goodbye, and they left. I worked for another forty minutes or so, and then the phone rang. It was Stephen, calling to say he and Carl had decided to drive into town to see a movie. I said have a good time, hung up, and worked a while longer. At eight, when I imagined the movie was halfway through, I made a pot of coffee, fixed a sandwich, and sat down in the kitchen to eat. Then I took a fresh cup of coffee back to the studio to have another look at the illustration.

"I hope you're not finding this tedious," she said suddenly, and looked at him searchingly.

"No, not a bit," he said, dreading what he sensed was coming.

"It's just that every last detail is so clear, you see. All of it. It's clearer, more detailed, than anything else has ever been. There isn't one minute of it that I don't remember, not a second.

"I started getting ready for bed just before ten. Taking into account that the movie had probably finished at nine, and that Stephen had probably begged to go to Baskin-Robbins for ice cream after, and that it was a twenty-minute drive from the theater, I guessed they'd be arriving home any minute. By ten-thirty, I was sitting in the living room in my nightgown and robe, watching television with the sound turned low so I could listen for the car pulling into the driveway. I chain-smoked, jumping up every few minutes to look out the front window, then went back to sit in front of the TV.

"At eleven, I changed back into my clothes, then called

the Playhouse to find out what time the feature ended. I couldn't imagine Carl taking Stephen to the nine o'clock show on a school night, but it was possible. It wasn't likely, though, that they'd stop to have ice cream at that time of the night. So, given that the second showing ended at eleven, I expected them home by eleven-thirty at the very latest.

"By eleven forty-five I began anticipating either a telephone call or a policeman coming to the door. I didn't know what else to do, so I walked back and forth, and went to look out the window every few minutes, and as more time passed, and they didn't come home, I began to feel despair like acid hollowing out my bones so that I got lighter and lighter until the only things holding me anchored to the floor were my Dunhill lighter that my agent had given me one Christmas—it's silver, and quite heavy, you see—and the pack of cigarettes in my other hand. I went back and forth, back and forth, stopping to look at the telephone, then at the window, rehearsing the way it would go, what they'd say when they came to tell me, how I'd react, what I'd say and do; I wouldn't break down or become hysterical. I'd take in the news; I'd do what had to be done step by step. By twelve-fifteen, I had no doubt at all they were dead. I knew it. I *knew* it. They were dead. I was never going to see them again. My heart was triple and quadruple beating, and I couldn't catch my breath, and the slightest noise in the house had me jumping and rushing and exclaiming out loud. The house got smaller and smaller until it was about the size of a refrigerator, and the only two points of reference I had were the telephone and the door, and I was waiting, listening so hard that my ears hurt, and so did my throat from all the cigarettes. I had this dreadful, nonspecific, nonlocalized pain because I knew they were dead and any moment someone was going to confirm it and I didn't know what to do except light another cigarette and keep hurrying back and forth, going over to look out the windows, then to open the front door and stand at the top of the driveway staring out, wanting to see the car come turning in, the headlights swinging in an arc the way they always did, and then Stephen slamming out of the car not wearing his ear-muffs or his mittens, while Carl gave his usual lengthy explanation of all the things that had fouled up their plans.

"The call came at one thirty-eight precisely. A very quiet voice on the other end asking me was I Mrs. Dennison. At first I couldn't answer. And then all I could say was, 'Are they dead?' and he said, 'I'm afraid so, ma'am,' and I asked where they were and what I was supposed to do, and he told me. I thanked him and hung up, put on my coat, and went out to my car to drive over to identify them. All the way there, I kept hearing myself asking, 'Are they dead?' and hearing him answer, 'I'm afraid so, ma'am,' and I tried to convince myself I'd misheard; that wasn't what he'd said at all. But he'd said that; it was what he'd said all right. All those daydreams were catching up with me; this was what happened when you had moments of wishing for freedom. If you wished for it, you just might get it.

"The lights bothered me more than anything else. It was so *bright*; there was such a glare in the place. I thought it would've been easier somehow if it had been dimmer, less unrelentingly, garishly, bright. Anyway, I got it done, said yes they were who they were, who they'd been, and they wanted to know if I'd be all right, driving home. Did I want someone to drive me home? I hardly heard them. All I could think was, 'How am I going to live? What am I going to do with my life? I don't have a life anymore. Everything's gone. How am I going to *live*?' I never *wanted* them dead; I'd merely imagined the worst possibilities.

Just because you thought of something, because it occurred to you, didn't mean it had to happen.

"Well, one of the officers had the wits to keep me there, get my mother's name and number. They called her and told her, then gave me the telephone to talk to her, and I was like some sort of idiot robot, saying the same bloody thing over and over, How am I going to live? What will I do? My mother said she'd come at once; she'd call my agent and he'd bring her; she'd come as quickly as possible, she said, and asked me to wait for her. Which almost made me laugh, because where was I going to go? Downstairs there were two unbelievably, horrifically shattered bodies. I'd forced myself to look at their faces, because I had to be sure. But I only recognized them by their clothes. You know what happened, Daniel?" Again she looked at him.

"What?" he asked, dry-mouthed.

"It seems there was a young woman from Bedford who'd been seeing a young man from New Canaan, but they'd had a falling-out and split up. So the young lady in question took herself off to a bar to have a few drinks and forget her misery. She had many more drinks than a few, then said goodnight to everyone and got up to go out to her car to drive home. No one thought to stop her. One or two people rather half-heartedly said something to the effect that she was in no condition to drive. But no one took away her car keys, or pulled out her spark plugs. They let her go even though later, at the hearing, half a dozen customers as well as the bartender—who was found guilty of some kind of negligence, I forget whether it was contributory or criminal—admitted she was in an extremely depressed and drunken state.

"She went out, climbed into her car, and drove, at close to a hundred miles an hour, headlong into another car coming in the opposite direction. Everyone died. Instantly, they told me. But what I've wondered for years now is what constitutes the length of an instant. There have been times when I've tried to clock it, to see how long an instant could possibly be, how much I could see and hear and feel and recognize in an instant. Anyway . . ." She cleared her throat, opened her bag, halted briefly while she lit a cigarette, then went on. "I was incredibly controlled. I didn't carry on, or break down at having to see them. I think it was because it had happened in my mind so many, many times that there was a sort of block between what was happening on one level and any possible reaction I might have to it on another. I got through it. One thing after another, I got through it. The funeral, with Stephen's class from school there, singing a hymn. All Carl's friends, and mine. I felt like a witness at the proceedings, wrapped up entirely in the gross unfairness of it: that they could get killed, be dead, leaving me behind to oversee the disposal of their remains. I had to go home and see all the things that had belonged to the other people who used to live there. Stephen's clothes and toys, bits and pieces he'd squirreled away because they'd had some special, secret significance to him, notes from classmates, and notes he'd written. I'd go into his room again and again, determined this time to strip it bare, get rid of every last thing in there so I wouldn't have to see any of it, so I wouldn't have to keep on feeling the sick, sick feeling I had finding his favorite shirt, or three pairs of mittens he'd hidden because he hated having to wear them, so he'd tell me he'd lost them, and I'd go out and buy more, but he'd merely hidden them. I kept finding things, and I'd start feeling hollow again, purposeless, useless, and I'd have to go out and close the door.

"Then, when I thought at last I'd managed to clear out every last thing, that there was nothing left, I'd come across a pair of Carl's cuff links at the back of a drawer, or one of Stephen's socks would turn up in the dryer, and I'd sit down holding the cuff links or the sock, and when I moved to get up again, it would be three hours later and the kettle had burned itself out on the stove, or I'd left the bath water running and it had overflowed. Time had become an immense, elastic vacuum, and I was trapped in it. Oh, hell!'' she said, throwing away the cigarette. ''You don't want to hear all this. I can't think why I'm telling you.''

''I used to try to imagine what it would be like,'' he said somberly, ''if something happened to Lane. I couldn't stand to think about it. I think you're very brave to admit you thought about those things before the accident. Most people wouldn't admit that, even if it was something they'd thought about.''

''There's nothing brave about it,'' she disagreed. ''It's simply what I thought.''

''Do you blame yourself?'' he asked. ''I mean, do you feel there was some kind of wish fulfilment?''

It was a good question, she thought. ''No, I don't do that,'' she answered. ''I couldn't see that I'd been negligent, or that my daydreams were so potent they could transcend reality. In a way, imagining the loss made me very attentive. There wasn't a day of his life when I didn't tell Stephen I loved him. If I let him go off to school in the morning without saying it, I'd be waiting when he came off the school bus in the afternoon. I'd drag him into the house and we'd wrestle, roughhouse, while I asked him about his day and told him I loved him. He was almost twelve when he died, but he was quite a bit bigger and heavier than I. And very gentle. He had a lovely awareness of his strength, and he didn't want to hurt the Little Mother—that's what he called me. Can't go hurting the Little Mother, he'd say, and then chortle down his shirt front. He had a way of ducking his chin down, and looking up at you through his eyelashes while he went ho-ho-ho down the front of his shirt; or he'd pull the neck of his sweater up over his nose and laugh into the neckline. He had a splendid sense of humor. He needed it, living with me. I was distracted much of the time, my mind on my work, and I'd snap at him if he interrupted, or get angry for no good reason, and then he'd snap right back at me, mocking the way I stood, the expression on my face, the way I articulated each word when I was in a bad temper. He never failed to make me laugh. He knew exactly how to bring me around, jolly me into seeing I was behaving like an idiot.

"My telling the truth doesn't have one goddamned thing to do with bravery," she said, returning to his point. "I've never been brave. If anything, I look for things to hold on to." She became aware that he was holding her hand, and had been for some time. Here she was again, holding on. She wondered if it was obvious to him that he'd inadvertently become the latest of people, things, she instinctively swam toward in the hope of staying afloat just a little while longer. "I almost never talk about any of this," she said apologetically.

"I can understand that," he told her. "I'd probably be the same way. While you've been telling me, I've been having little flashes—you know how that happens?—between words, sort of. I keep trying to put myself into your place in the picture. It's too rough. I can't do it. I *hate* that story. I really hate it. I mean, what about that girl? Weren't you outraged?"

"I felt sorry for her," she said quietly. "I kept thinking about her parents having to come to identify her . . . I don't suppose this is what you had in mind when you came to the hotel."

"I told you: I didn't have anything special in mind. I don't mind listening."

She looked at his profile, and was suddenly apprehensive. He was just a little . . . what? Too good to be true. "I should," she said slowly, "Probably be very careful with you."

"Hell! Don't do that!" he said quickly. "Let's just say fuck it, and be reckless; we'll say and do whatever we want." Why did everything have to have predetermined beginnings and endings? Why couldn't things just happen in their own space and time? Was there really a need for protection?

"I don't trust either one of us enough to be reckless . . ." She trailed off, caught for a moment in the giddiness of fatigue. Everything around her seemed to have come free of its moorings; buildings wavered, people drifted, the pavement undulated.

"Are you okay?" His hand tightened around hers and she looked at him again.

"I need a drink. There's a pub over there." She pointed to the corner. "Buy me a drink. And after that we'll go to your hotel, or to mine. That is, if you still want to."

He didn't move at once; he stood and stared at her, recalling the intensity of his disappointment when he'd telephoned her room and there'd been no response. Nothing ever happened the way you imagined it would. He'd thought of the two of them talking generalities over a drink, followed by dinner; he'd imagined seeing her spread in naked invitation on a bed. He hadn't considered the possibility that she might tell him anything as awful as the story he'd just heard. He'd certainly never considered telling her any of his own true stories. But just now he wanted to throw down hunks of truth in front of her, to see how she'd react to someone else's story. It was an impulse he couldn't bring himself to act upon, yet he could clearly see himself heaving slabs of his own truth around like sides of beef. It made his jaws clench in resistance. He looked away from her to the pub on the corner. There *was* a need for protection.

"Will you buy me a drink?" she asked.

Again, his eyes came back to her. "Sure," he said, in an instant deciding she wasn't someone who overindulged as a matter of course. "Why not?"

As they crossed toward the pub, he asked himself what it was about this woman that had prompted him to pursue her. Her blunt directness irritated him one moment, charmed him the next. Part of the irritation he felt was due to the way she pushed pieces of her personal truth around, possibly as if she sensed his little lies when he told them. And that worried him slightly, because she was clever enough to sort fact from fiction. Of course it was everyone's right to shield himself in whatever fashion he chose. He happened to do it with fairly harmless distortions of the truth, lies that he saw as misleading clues that wouldn't give him away. He hadn't always done it. In fact, now that he thought about it, it was quite a recent habit. Bits of camouflage for concealment. He used lies. And he had a hunch Leigh did it with sex; she used it to sidetrack a man when he seemed to be getting too close to things she didn't want revealed. Fair enough. He varnished facts in one way, she did it in another. Who cared? He didn't. If anything, they balanced each other. All right, she'd thrown him completely by confronting him with the specifics of why he'd come looking for her. He did want to take her to bed. She'd guessed that, and forced him to retreat. He still wanted to take her to bed. She wasn't easy, and the challenge of winning her over was both tiresome and increasingly compelling. He wanted her to capitulate. The odd thing was he was beginning to care. And he couldn't help thinking that caring was potentially the riskiest enterprise known to man. Yet how did you stop yourself?

Five

She smoked one cigarette after another, and drank the gin very quickly, trying to figure out what she was doing, and why she'd told this man about Carl and Stephen. She was divided between an inclination to tell him all the rest of it, and an impossible desire to retrieve every last word she'd spoken. Staring at her empty glass, a fresh cigarette between her fingers, she examined her feeling of having betrayed two people she'd loved by talking about them to someone she scarcely knew. The worst part of all this was that she wanted to get into bed with this man, to have him put his arms around her, to have him distract her with his body. It was such a hateful cliché, she thought, wanting, in the face of death, to make love, to find some degree of peace no matter how brief-lived it might be. A simple ceremony, an exchange of caresses, and then they'd go their separate ways. There was a decidedly selfish aspect to it, but since they'd both get what they wanted, it would be fair.

"Are you mad at yourself?" he asked. "Do you wish you hadn't told me any of that?"

He was anything but stupid, she thought, her eyes still on the empty glass. "Actually," she said, lifting her head to look into his blue eyes whose dark perimeters looked exactly as if someone had taken a pen dipped in India ink and carefully drawn a fine line around his irises, "I am mad at myself, furious."

"You shouldn't be. Maybe you needed to talk about it."

She opened her handbag, pulled out a five-pound note, and laid it on the table. "Will you buy us more drinks?" she asked, feeling suddenly volatile. One wrong move or word, and she'd go off like a rocket.

"No," he said. "I won't. I'll be more than happy to buy you wine with dinner, even something after dinner, but nothing more now."

"May I ask why?"

"Because you're out with me, because I'm responsible for you *while* you're out with me, because I want to get you safely back to your hotel . . ."

"Where you can safely be rid of me because it's not turning out the way you expected. You came around hoping to get laid, but here I am forcing you to make conversation, instead of just shutting up and doing what you want me to do."

"Jesus! What's wrong with you?"

"You want to be in control of the situation . . ."

"No! I won't buy you more drinks right now because if we *do* do it, I'd like us *both* to remember the occasion. It's too goddamned depressing making love with someone who's drunk."

"Your wife drinks?"

"She *invented* it."

"I'm sorry."

Pause.

"I don't know how we keep managing to do this," she said sadly. "It's my turn to apologize. If I'd had an entire night's sleep recently, I wouldn't be saying or doing any of this. It feels as if my skin's been removed and I'm walking around with the raw flesh exposed. Even the air hurts.''

He winced at the description. ''I know the feeling,'' he told her, giving his head a shake, as if to clear it. ''Way back when, it was once in awhile. We'd go out to dinner, or to a party, and she'd drink too much, and I didn't mind, to tell the truth, because those were about the only times she'd be interested. But then it got to be . . . she had this prodigious capacity; she could drink so much . . . Christ! She'd sweat booze. And it was like making love to a god-damned duffle bag. And what did it make me, what was I, if I could . . . I felt like a shit because I was still sexually interested in my wife. I'm tired too, Leigh. I haven't slept in a couple of days, myself. And why should either one of us be pissed off if we seem to want to be together? I can't make any sense of that. The way I see it, if I can feel good for half an hour or an hour, if the two of us can have some pleasure, why shouldn't we. *Why shouldn't we?* More and more, I keep thinking maybe that's all there's going to be. Maybe half an hour or an hour's all I'm ever going to get. And if that's it, then I want it. I don't want you to have another drink because I don't want you to turn into Celeste on me. Okay? I don't want to deal with a woman I want who has to be half in the bag before she can do it. Okay?''

''Yes, okay,'' she relented.

In the taxi, on the way back to her hotel, she remembered and said, ''I have to call my mother. I should've called hours ago. She'll be worried.''

Once inside her suite, she threw her coat across the arm of one of the chairs, saying, ''Help yourself to something, if you want a drink. I'll try not to be too long,'' then went through to the bedroom and shut the door.

He got himself a Coke from the minibar, popped it open, and sat on the sofa to drink directly from the can. It was one of his habits that drove Celeste wild. So many things he did drove her wild. It took him a lot of years to realize that even if he performed strictly to her specifications there'd always be something that failed to please her, because what bothered her most was his continuing to care about her. Just thinking now about all the years of effort that had gone into keeping Celeste happy made him feel battle-worn and stripped; he felt as if all the blood had been drained from his body by the countless small wounds inflicted by the marriage. As a direct result of so much time spent on failed acts of appeasement, he'd evolved into a man who now told lies for reasons of self-preservation. At best, he gave most people only snippets of truth. He served up concoctions fabricated with great care, stews made of gristly bits of truth hidden by chunks of colorful distortions. He'd become a master chef when it came to preparing entire meals that would fill those with appetites for details and leave them groaning, satiated, and temporarily beyond craving more. He'd come to know the caloric value of items others would discard. And when he stuffed a conversation full of self-protecting camouflage, he almost invariably remembered his father commenting one time on the fact that spare ribs had always been thrown away until the Orientals had turned them into delicacies. Dan had done something similar in turning the lesser details of his life into canapés. He'd been doing it so often, and so well, that even when there seemed no obvious need, he kept on with it. The result was his present inability to deliver up even the smallest portion of the truth without feeling mildly imperiled. Yet he'd told the woman in the other room more about himself than he'd ever told anyone. He'd kept back certain facts, but he'd revealed a great deal to Leigh, and he didn't know why. His interest in her had been minimal until she'd revealed who she was. And learning who she was, discovering he was in the company of someone he'd long admired, had prompted him to be truthful. It was, he thought, very damned strange.

"Oh, Leigh," Marietta exclaimed with a slight quaver in her voice, "I've been frightfully worried about you. You promised you'd ring me as soon as you arrived."

"I'm sorry. I intended to call, then I got sidetracked."

"It was a most distressing day. It really was."

"I'm sorry," Leigh said again, close to tears.

"Are you all right?" her mother asked. "This is not the best connection."

"I'm still functioning."

"Have you been in touch yet with your father?" Marietta's tone was wary.

"Not yet. I'm working up to it. Were there many people?"

"Quite a number. Some lovely young people, really. It went well, all considered."

"I don't suppose Jacobson came?"

"Did you really think he would? No, he didn't come."

"It wasn't a horror show, was it? I'd hate to think I ran off and left you to cope if it was a nightmare."

"It went very well. Jeff read a very moving piece, and several other young people spoke. It was quite a lovely service."

"I should have been there," Leigh said. "I feel guilty."

"Don't!" Marietta said. "There's no need for that. No one could possibly have done more than you did. No one! But are you sure you know what you're doing, darling? This business about seeing Philip . . ."

"I honestly have no idea. I'm just going to get through this, one way or another. Actually, I met someone. He's helping to keep my mind off everything."

"Well, I suppose that's for the good. Try to get some rest. And, please, ring me in the next day or two to let me know what you're doing. I worry, Leigh. You know I do."

"I know. And I'm sorry about not calling sooner."

She had to sit for a few minutes after the call ended, to collect herself. Joel was no more. Jeff had agreed to scatter the ashes into Long Island Sound. "You know how much I love swimming," Joel had laughed. "Don't look that way, Leigh. It's what I want. It really is."

She got up at last, and went out to walk across to the sofa where she leaned down and kissed Daniel on the forehead. "I hope that didn't take too long. We could have dinner downstairs, try for a table close to the fire. Shall I phone and ask if they have one available?"

"How is your mother?" he asked, catching hold of her hand and directing her down beside him.

"Ah, my mother. If only they'd give her the chance, she could run the world. It would be beautiful—legions of unblemished virgins and hardy heroes, concerned only with love. There'd be no wars, no political intrigue, no nuclear weapons, nothing but people earnestly fretting over whether Gregory truly loves Helena, or if he is in fact a cad and simply leading her on. I grew up on my mother's books. Until I was well into my twenties, I honestly believed I would be rescued, like Helena, and Victoria, and Constance, and the others. When I realized that wasn't the way it was going to be, I was very angry, for a time, with Mother. I became most indignant and argued horribly with her because I felt she was simply encouraging generations of girls to believe in fairy tales. It was stupid," she sighed. "If she didn't write them, somebody else would. I suppose the fact is there's a need for those fairy tales." She got the words out, then went silent, menaced again by tears. After a moment, she rose and went to put the Do

Not Disturb sign on the outer doorknob, while Dan watched from the sofa. Halfway to the bedroom, she stopped and looked over at him, then continued on into the room. The creak of the sofa springs indicated he was following, and she reached with an unsteady hand to turn off the overhead light. She stood just inside the door, and waited. He came up behind her, and she turned. His hands moved indefinitely, wavered, then settled lightly on the edges of her shoulders, his brows drawing together as he studied her face.

"What?" she asked.

"You seem different every time I look at you."

"So do you to me. We're both punchy. It's probably the best condition to be in." She waited for him to make a move; she didn't think she could take the initiative. She stood there, assailed by slow inner contractions of expectation, and a twisting sensation in her chest that was perilously close to anguish.

"I like you," he said, looking somewhat surprised. "I'm, uh, just having a little trouble getting started."

"Oh," she said, sympathetic. "So am I."

They gave each other shaky smiles, still not moving, and she could no longer bear the tension, so she offered her mouth against his, going forward with the last of her energy and courage, amazed at having found the resources to take the initiative after all.

It was what he'd needed—some evidence of her interest—to begin his cautious examination of the length and breadth of her back. They proceeded, he thought, with an unusual lack of haste. Languorously, she attended to the removal of his jacket and tie, then to the unbuttoning of his shirt. Her motions so mesmerized him that he had to hold her still so he could push his hands past the layers of her clothing to make contact with the sleek warmth of her flesh. Then, again, she stole his attention away with her hands, and with the potency of her mouth. Kissing her was very like drowning; he sank into a stirring darkness wherein he discovered the depths of her appetite and his own. Two minutes, three, then he held her captive to his chest. "Just don't move for a moment, and let me do this," he murmured, taking her out of her clothes before clasping her to the length of his body until she was light-headed and breathless.

It occurred to him—a few seconds' illumination like the flash of a flare—that this half-naked woman he was touching was Stanleigh Dunn; she was *someone*, and he was being allowed to caress her; he actually had his hands on her breasts. He'd never felt remotely like the way he did now, as if he'd been accorded a privilege of exceptional magnitude. He wanted suddenly to be able to touch her everywhere at once, avid for the most intimate knowledge of her. Yet even his greed couldn't force him to move any less slowly. His hands investigated her spine, the flesh tight over her ribs, the tidy span of her waist, the backs of her thighs, while he kissed her throat, her arm, her mouth once again. The pleasure of learning her was too extreme. He frightened himself with the intensity of his desire. He shouldn't have cared about the texture of her skin, or its fragrance; it shouldn't have mattered that her inner thighs were rounded and yielding, and that he was thrilled at having access to her. He'd lost his detachment and was being affected by absolutely everything about her.

This wasn't casual, she thought, stunned by the way he was making love to her. She couldn't move; he held her captive. He appeared to be perfectly content to have her remain as she was—motionless, compliant, open to his inspection. He had control; he could turn her this way or that, do anything he wished. Perhaps he hoped she'd remain passive. The idea frightened her. She freed herself of his embrace to stand pulling air into her lungs in huge gulps. Then she flew at him, to put her hands, and then her mouth, on him. He seemed frozen for a time, almost as if no one had ever done this to him before. Then his hand began to stroke her hair, and she thought frantically, We're too naked. We shouldn't be this naked.

He raised her up and looked slowly at her, his eyes as questing as his hands had been. She found it agonizing to have to stand beneath the weight of his gaze, with a wall of cooling air between them. This was nothing like previous collisions she'd had with near-strangers when, with little or no preamble, she'd closed her eyes and accepted their bodies into hers. Perhaps it was fatigue, or sorrow, or her age, but she was being undone by something she'd thought would bring no more than temporary comfort. It seemed as if she'd lost her prior adeptness at taking without question what was being offered sexually. All at once she was too aware of nuance, of her own dreadful needs and those of this man who was either as dreadfully needy as she, or a consummate artist at manipulation. She suffered his slow, visual examination, powerless to put a stop to it.

Her long pale body, her breasts—fuller and heavier than he'd anticipated—her vulnerability, made him feel both sad and enormously potent. He couldn't think how this had happened, how they'd argued, and laughed, and talked, and now were skin to skin, exchanging caresses. The pleasure penetrated all his defenses. No one had ever made love to him with such aggressive abandon or such skill. Who was this woman with her spiky hair and grieving eyes, her adroitly experienced hands and mouth? He watched her eyes as his hand moved between her thighs. Her eyelids lowered. He could see a pulse beating strongly in her throat. She swayed slightly, her lips parted. He was astonished to think she'd allow him to touch her this way. But she did allow it. She opened to it.

He maneuvered her to the bed and put her down, then breathed in the perfume, strongest between her breasts. He examined the fine, long bones that formed the cradle of her hips, setting it to rocking gently, undulating beneath his hand. Her arms reached for him, and he let himself be drawn into their circle, sheltered at their apex. He sank into the scented cavern of her embrace, her perfume and motion obliterating everything; he sank into her irreverent ardor, and felt as if he loved her. So quickly, so readily, all sense was lost of where one began and the other ended; definition had no significance. All that pertained was the pulse, maintaining the meter limb to limb, eyes and hands joined; an homage to symmetry.

He was shaken by her continuing silence; she was stricken by his unfeigned interest. Just a short time and each knew the taste and scent of the others flesh; there was nothing withheld. He rested, still inside her, making no sign he was anxious to be on his way now that he'd had what he'd been seeking. Her body expanded and contracted in slow aftertremors; she lay motionless, savoring the lassitude, her heart gradually finding its more temperate rhythm.

"You can't stay," she said at last. "This can only be for tonight."

"But why?" he wanted to know, unwilling to be separated from her. "We're both on our own. There's no reason why we shouldn't have a few days together."

"There's every reason. We'll have this evening, without complications."

"I have no say in this, do I?" He pulled away, but hung over her as he asked his questions.

"I *can't*. please take me at my word. I simply can't."

"Do you want me to go now?"

"Oh, not yet," she said, and wound her arms around

him to bring him close again. "It's still early. And I did promise you dinner."

He thought of a number of arguments, but had to dismiss them. That's what happened when you told lies; they invalidated your arguments. He gave it up and with a sigh, touched the back of his hand to her cheek, saying, "You have no idea, none at all, how lovely you are. You don't see a bit of it. And you don't believe me, either. I can tell by the way you're trying not to hear what I'm saying."

"Don't," she said. "Let's not say anything." She distracted him again, her clever hands searching, stroking. She wanted only to feel the hard edge of his hip, and the articulate muscle in his thigh; she wanted to trace the deep veins running the length of his arm, and then fold herself into his embrace, seeking oblivion.

Six

"Lane, it's me."

"Daddy! Where are you? I've been so worried. Are you all right?"

"I'm fine, sweetheart. I'm sorry about . . . I should've let you know, but I just didn't have a chance."

"But where are you?"

"London. On my way to Bangkok."

"But, Daddy, I thought you weren't going to . . ."

"I know, but I changed my mind at the last minute and decided I should go after all. How are you, sweetheart?"

"Oh, me. I'm okay. It's you. Boy, you can't believe the kind of stuff I've been thinking, not hearing from you for so long. And why London? Isn't that out of your way?"

"Yes and no. You know me." Daniel gave a laugh. "You know I never fly anywhere direct."

"No, I know. I just didn't think you were going, that's all."

"I changed my mind. It's been known to happen."

"Well, as long as you're all right. That's what really matters."

"I'm just fine. How's school?"

"I'm surviving. This semester's a major yawn, except for . . . *God*, Dad! I don't want to blow this call talking about school. How long're you going to be in Bangkok? And when're you coming home?"

"I don't know for sure. A couple of weeks at the outside, maybe less."

"You promise? A couple of weeks and then you'll come home?"

"I promise. I'll be back in plenty of time for Christmas, tons of time. We could go somewhere, if you like. Take a couple of weeks in the sun, the Bahamas or someplace, whatever you'd like."

"If we do go away, would it be all right if Cathy comes with us? I kind of promised her, because her folks're taking a cruise and she'll be alone otherwise. You wouldn't mind, would you?"

"Whatever you like," he repeated.

"Daddy, what's going on?" She sounded suddenly younger, not quite so sure of herself. "I really was getting scared. I kept calling and when I couldn't reach you, well . . ."

Dan could almost see her shrugging, and smiled at the image. "It was very last-minute, babe. I do have one interesting thing to tell you. You'll never guess who I met on the flight over!"

"Who?"

"Stanleigh Dunn."

"Dad! You're joking! You actually met him?"

"Stanleigh Dunn's a woman, Lane. And I not only met her, I got her autograph for you."

"That's amazing! What was she like? Was she nice? Young, old, what?"

"My age, and very nice. I'll tell you all about it when I get back."

"God! Wait till I tell Cath! She'll die! That's too amazing! And you got her autograph?"

"I sure did. Listen, sweetheart, I'd better go. I just wanted to check in. I had a hunch you might be trying to reach me. Call your grandparents, will you? You know they like to hear from you."

"Dad," she said with strained patience, "I've only spoken to them about *sixty* times in the last two weeks. We've *all* been worried."

"Well, now you know I'm alive and well, so you just think about where you'd like to go for Christmas. Okay?"

"Okay."

"Take care of yourself, and call your grandparents anyway. I love you, sweetheart."

"Love you too, Dad."

An officious-sounding woman answered the telephone, and for a moment Leigh couldn't think how to ask for her father. The woman again said hello, and Leigh had to speak or hang up.

"Is Mr. Reid available?" she asked.

"May I ask who's calling?"

"Stanleigh Dunn."

"Oh! Just one moment, please."

Leigh heard the receiver being set down, then the sound of receding footsteps on wood flooring. After several moments there was the distinct click of a door opening, an indecipherable exchange of words, then the return of the footsteps.

"Sorry to be so long," the woman said. "Could you leave a number? He's not able to come to the telephone just now."

"Actually, I was hoping to come to see him."

"Oh, yes? And when did you think you might do that?"

"Well, when might be convenient?"

"Almost anytime, I should think. Had you some specific date in mind?"

"To whom am I speaking?" Leigh asked finally, puzzled by the woman's proprietary tone.

With a laugh, the woman said, "This is awkward, isn't it? I'm Delia, Mrs. Reid. I do apologize for not introducing myself at once. I think Philip would like very much to see you. Are you nearby?"

"I'm in London. I thought if it was convenient . . . how would tomorrow be?"

"You'll come for lunch?"

"If I may."

"We'd be delighted. You know the directions?"

"I'll manage."

"Splendid! Tomorrow then," Delia said. "Looking forward," she said, and rang off.

Leigh made arrangements for a car and driver for the following day, then phoned room service for toast and coffee. In her dressing gown, she went to the window to see what kind of day it was. Rain. She stood looking down at the dull, greasy-looking street, her chest tight from too many cigarettes, her entire body stiff from the previous night's activities.

I'm Delia, Mrs. Reid. Her father had remarried. Delia, Mrs. Reid. Judging by her accent and careful diction, she sounded like the tall, too-thin, bony-chested type who'd wear sensible brogues, tweed skirts, and twin sets; no makeup, long wispy gray hair done up in a bun.

The tray from room service came quite quickly. She signed for it, then sat on the sofa to drink some of the coffee and consume one piece of the toast. She lit a cigarette, refusing to think just yet about last night. If she did, she might relent and telephone Dan at the Hilton. She poured more coffee, smoked the cigarette, feeling the not unpleasant ache in her thighs. Her eyes went to the telephone. Last night had been fantastic; last night had been orgiastic; last night had been such a sexual extravaganza that she could feel heat rising into her neck and face just thinking about it in the light of day.

She hadn't made love so hard, or for so long, or with such *intent*, in years. And now that she thought about it, recalling moments when she'd felt she might literally expire beneath the engulfing waves of almost too much pleasure, she couldn't quite believe she'd actually given herself so absolutely. But she had. She'd made love with someone she scarcely knew, in every conceivable fashion, until she could no longer move and had watched from the bed, through slitted eyes, as he'd crept around the room gathering up his clothes before leaving. And then she'd slept, falling into blackness as silent and unpopulated as a desert in the dead of night. For almost nine hours, she'd slept.

Now it was nearly noon, and it appeared Daniel was going to keep his word. She looked again at the telephone. She smiled, thought of Joel, and was suddenly sad. She tried not to think about him. If she thought about him she'd begin to slide, the way she was now, into an adhesive, cottony substance that threatened to suffocate her. Setting her feet on the floor, she dropped the cigarette into the ashtray, bent her forehead to her knees, and folded her arms over her head. Losing it, I'm losing it, she thought, sitting quite still but floundering. Joel. I miss you. You were so wonderfully special. Every time I opened the door to find you there, waiting, smiling, I had a sense of occasion because you had qualities that radiated; you glowed with youth and optimism and that so enviable belief in yourself. All the dozens of times I opened the door to find you there, with flowers, or a bottle of wine, or a clipping from some magazine, or a plate of something you'd cooked. And you came inside smelling of fresh air and limitless possibilities and you allowed me to enjoy you, the sight of you, your smile, and your audition stories, tales of the cattle call.

She sat up and looked again at the telephone, her arms now wrapped around her midriff. If he'd meant a word of what he'd said, he'd have called, and never mind that she'd said not to. If he'd been sincere, if his feelings had genuinely been aroused, he'd have gone past her words, to make another attempt to convince her.

The telephone rang, and she snatched up the receiver.

"I know we were supposed to hum 'Strangers in the Night' and just walk away," Dan laughed, "but I can't stop thinking about you. Don't be mad. I really did try not to call, but knowing you're there . . . are you mad?"

"I'm not mad." She reached for the still-burning cigarette in the ashtray.

"I can't get a flight out of here until tomorrow morning. Have you managed to get in touch with your father? Did you sleep, by the way?"

"I'm seeing him tomorrow. And yes, thank you, I did sleep."

"Spend the day with me!" he said eagerly. "We'll have lunch, go shopping, or take in a movie, a show, anything you want."

"You're ignoring everything we agreed on."

"Who cares! Let's spend the day together."

"Daniel," she began, then stopped.

"What?"

"I have to care," she said. "I *have* to. I'm glad, though, that you called." Gently, she put down the receiver. Then, her eyes still on the telephone, she had to ask herself what she was doing. He'd offered, for a second time, an escape route, and she'd refused it. All at once the remainder of the day spread itself before her like a road into infinity. It didn't have to be that way.

She found the number of the Hilton, and called him

back. There was no response from his room. She didn't bother to leave a message. Perhaps it was for the best. He could only be a complication in her life. And the last thing she needed, she told herself, going to the bathroom to start the water running in the tub, was an involvement with a married man.

She put the phone down on him, just like that. He was staggered. She'd really meant what she'd said, and intended to stick by it. He'd been so certain, after last night, that she'd change her mind. But she hadn't. With no idea where he was going, he pocketed the room key, made sure he had his wallet, and left.

Tell enough lies, you wind up losing track, not sure what you've said, or why. Sometimes the lies and the truth got hopelessly mixed up, and he couldn't remember which was which. They were thousands of miles away from home; she was the only person he knew nonprofessionally in London; they'd spent hours naked together, but she didn't want to see him. Maybe the previous night hadn't been as exceptional as he'd thought; maybe he was mediocre in every way and was no longer able to differentiate between mediocrity and excellence. Christ! he thought angrily, pushing out of the hotel, to stop on the pavement for a moment before heading down Park Lane.

He stomped along, ignoring the rain and the passersby and the traffic, reviewing the events of the past day and night, deciding that for once in a very rare while he'd told more truth than lies, that he'd given the very best of himself to their lovemaking, and that it was his right, at the very least, to be allowed to state his case. He marched up to Piccadilly, did a complete circuit of the Circus, made an impulsive stop in one shop and then another, then headed determinedly for Albemarle Street.

Outside the hotel he paced back and forth for several

minutes before pushing his way inside, going directly through the lobby to the elevator. The Do Not Disturb sign was still on her door. He knocked, breathing hard through his nose, and waited. He heard her call out, "Just a moment," and squared his shoulders, set for a confrontation.

She opened the door, saw him, and tried to shut the door.

"I want to talk to you!" he said, holding open the door with the flat of his hand.

"I don't want to talk to you!" she replied, with both hands trying to push it shut.

"Well, that's too goddamned bad!" He shoved open the door, causing her to reel several feet back into the room. He stepped inside, closed the door, and threw the box of flowers at her. "A little something," he snapped, as instinctively she caught the box. "A token of, as they say, *affection*. What the hell's the *matter* with you? I'm just trying to be nice and you're treating me like . . . I don't know what . . . a customer or something."

"Can't you take no for an answer?" she wanted to know, a bit frightened by his determination and his irate energy. He was larger and stronger and younger than she, and capable, from the looks of it, of fairly violent behavior.

"Obviously not. I could buy this, maybe, if I believed you didn't like me, but you do. Like me. You did last night. I know you did."

"Last night has nothing to do with today."

"Yes, it does. Listen, Leigh, who's to know if we spend another day together? Who's to know or care?"

She didn't answer, but stood glaring at him, and now he felt like a complete asshole. She looked tired, and her eyes didn't seem quite so large without makeup. She was still in her dressing gown, her hair damp. Somehow, she appeared more accessible than at any time since they'd met. And he was behaving like an ox. She kept staring at him, not moving, not speaking, and he couldn't make the connection between the woman of the night before and the woman now. They seemed completely unrelated.

"You didn't have to hang up on me," he said, hearing how feeble that sounded, and wishing he could disregard the signals and take hold of her. "That's all. As if I didn't even deserve a goodbye. Okay." He started for the door.

"I'm sorry for hanging up that way."

He stopped and turned to look at her.

"I don't want to hurt you," she said, her eyes softer. "I just don't have anything to give you, and you seem to be in need . . . of something." She moved finally, and set the box of flowers down on the coffee table before reaching for her cigarettes. She lit one, then crossed her arms in front of her. "You don't want to know me, Daniel," she said quietly. "People don't really want to know other people. They just want to see new reflections of themselves, or get lost temporarily in someone else. We did that last night: we got lost. That's all there is. That's all I have to give. And surely you have no problem finding willing women to get lost in. You're a very attractive man, and the world is crawling with unattached women."

"How do you know what I want?" he asked. "You don't even give people time to get a word in."

She got sidetracked for a few seconds by his looks, and by the simple fact of his being there. On a purely esthetic level, she was captured by his dark hair and unique eyes; he was a fine-looking man and she couldn't imagine why he was being so persistent, or what it was about her he found so appealing. Her inner voice cautioned her that she couldn't possibly have any sort of a future with someone whose physical appearance made her so self-conscious about her own flaws.

"Go away, Daniel," she said imploringly, tamping

down her sexual response to him. "Please. You're a complication I simply can't handle. I do like you. And last night was wonderful. Okay? It was terrific. Truly. I'm sorry I was rude on the telephone. Thank you for the flowers. Please, go away now."

"Could I call you sometime in New York? just to talk, or maybe for lunch?"

"Daniel! Don't *do* this, to either one of us! I was rude, and I'm sorry. But you're looking only at the surface of the matter, and not at everything that's underneath. Please, go away."

"This morning," he said thickly, his hand on the door, "I woke up thinking about you. It was the best thing that's happened to me in years." He got the door open, and left. Head down, deflated, his feet and legs heavy, he trudged along the corridor, down the stairs, and out of the hotel. He felt almost sick with sudden fatigue. The one time in his life he'd gone along with his impulses, he'd blown it skyhigh, made a fool of himself. What he wanted now was to go back to the Hilton, have a couple of drinks, and then go to sleep until it was time to head to the airport.

"A goddamned caveman," Leigh said under her breath, watching the door close. She stood finishing her cigarette, then opened the box to gaze at the dozen long-stemmed red roses inside. "A sensitive caveman," she amended. Leaving the flowers on the table, she went to the bedroom to dress, oddly energized by the confrontation.

As she put on her makeup, she reviewed the scene, laughing aloud at the way the two of them had pushed at the door before he'd succeeded in bulling his way in. They were both idiots, she told the mirror.

The rain had stopped. She was just passing Ryman's, had second thoughts, backed up and went into the stationer's to buy a small sketch pad, several fine-point felt-tip pens, two 4B pencils, and a sharpener. With a paper cup of coffee and her supplies, she arranged herself on a bench in Green park, and began to sketch a bench nearby and, in front of it, the rounded sections of dirt, created by restless feet, that looked to her like bathmats; she went on to a naked tree, its bark oddly dappled; a discarded pack of 555s on the sodden brown grass; a piece of the sky inhabited by restless clouds.

When she stopped, having filed half a dozen pages of the book, her coffee had gone cold, her hands were numb, and the inhalation of a cigarette made her dizzy. She'd spent more than two hours on the first freehand sketching she'd done since her days as an art student. Throwing away the cigarette, she turned to a fresh page and quickly roughed in Daniel's face, the dark hair and light eyes, the assertive chin, the Gallic slant of the bones beneath the flesh. She studied the hasty rendering for several minutes, then decisively closed the book. It was getting dark; the sky was thick with unshed rain. She remained, looking up at the sky, for several minutes more, wondering, as she had done increasingly of late, what possible point there was to her having two homes—both filled with furniture and possessions—and closets full of clothes, some of which she'd never worn, and a life with no purpose. There had to be something, some goal, some interest, someone, to validate one's existence. As always, she returned full circle to her point of mental departure without an answer and only the hope that the visit to her father might provide her with a piece of history, or an incentive, or merely a welcome. Get through this hour, and then the next, and the next, until you've lived out the day.

At Fortnum & Mason she had a gift box prepared of several kinds of tea and coffee and jam, then carried her purchase out into the rain. By the time she got back to the hotel—only a few blocks—the mink was saturated and many pounds heavier. She hung it on a hanger from the showerhead to drip into the bathtub, dried her hair, then went down to the lounge for afternoon tea. And there was Daniel, sitting where she'd sat yesterday, looking like a naughty schoolboy. She couldn't help herself. She laughed, and went to give him a kiss—standing back from herself as she did, amazed by this display that so contradicted her earlier remarks to him—and then to sit with him.

"You're such a fool!" she laughed, pleased by his dogged persistence. "What are you doing here?"

"I was hoping you're a creature of habit. I left another note for you with the concierge, too."

"Inviting me to dinner?"

He shook his head. "Nope. Saying goodbye. I managed to change my reservation, get a flight out tonight."

"Oh!" She opened her bag for a cigarette, unreasonably disappointed.

"I want you to know I'm aware I'm behaving like an asshole," he told her. "You have to believe I don't usually do things like this."

"I believe you," she said. It was true. She did believe him. "Will you stay for tea?"

"If you really don't mind."

"What time is your flight?"

"Seven-forty. I'm going from here directly to the airport. I left my bag with the concierge. Very nice staff here," he said, looking around, as if for examples. "Next time I'm over, I think I'll book in here."

"Well, good," she said awkwardly.

There seemed so much to say that neither of them was able to say much of anything. He stayed an hour, then she went with him while he claimed his bag and the doorman began looking for a taxi. They stood by the foyer doors gazing out at the doorman, natty in his brown frock coat, watching as a cab slid to a stop and the doorman turned to signal Daniel.

Daniel took hold of her shoulders, saying urgently, "For however long it's been—what? Twenty-four hours?—I've felt as if I love you. I know I've been a pain in the ass, but for what it's worth, I'll be thinking about you." He kissed her on the mouth, and she held on, for a few seconds thinking perhaps she was making a serious error in letting him go without so much as her telephone number. But he released her, said, "Goodbye, Leigh," and hurried out through the rain to the waiting taxi. He waved as the taxi drove off and, automatically, she waved back. He had courage, she thought; certainly more than she did. She'd never have been able to admit that, at the last, holding on to him, she'd felt very much the same way. And now there was no possibility of thanking him for rescuing her from the emotional quicksand that had been much reduced simply because he'd given her something else to think about; because, for a few hours in the dark, he'd allowed her to forget everything.

Seven

Delia, Mrs. Reid, materialized in the sitting room doorway seconds after the housekeeper had taken Leigh's coat. Delia, Mrs. Reid, was, in every way, the antithesis of Leigh's imaginings. Fiftyish, naturally blond, and generously endowed—above average height, ample of breast and becomingly broad in the hips—even her hair seemed incredibly thick in its Gibson girl upsweep. Behind modishly large glasses, her eyes were round and clear and of a perfect cerulean blue. Altogether sunny and stunning, she stood framed in the doorway, looking somewhat cautiously at Leigh. The woman's blatant good health made Leigh feel wizened and haggard. Delia was an older version of the classic example of British beauty Marietta was so fond of using as the heroine in her novels.

"Do, please, sit down," said Delia in a rich plummy voice, having apparently satisfied herself that, physically at least, Leigh represented no menace. "I thought we might have a moment together before you see your father."

Leigh pressed the gift box into the woman's hands with

an uncertain smile, saying, "Just a little something. I'm terribly nervous. Do you mind if I smoke?"

"Not at all." Delia slid an ashtray along the top of the square-cut mahogany coffee table until it was within Leigh's reach from the sofa, then sat in the wing chair situated diagonally opposite. She crossed her long, shapely legs, adjusted the silk of her daintily printed dress over her knees, then placed her large, long-fingered hands carefully on the arms of the chair. Her hands, Leigh thought, were somehow out of keeping with the rest of her. They were unadorned but for a plain gold wedding band, the nails short and scrupulously clean. Those hands represented a significant clue to the woman, and Leigh wished she had time enough to decipher it.

"You're not as I expected," Delia said, chancing a smile. "You don't strongly resemble your father, and you look really very young."

Leigh returned the smile. "You're not what I expected either," she admitted, briefly wondering what life would be like for a woman with perfect skin, lapis eyes, Nordic bone structure, a long aristocratic nose, and a mouth that hinted of depthless sensuality. "You must be wondering why I've turned up this way, out of the blue."

"Your father's been hoping for quite some time that you'd contact him."

"He has? I was under the impression he had no interest whatsoever in me."

Delia shook her large, exquisitely molded head. "Nothing could be farther from the truth," she asserted. "However, it really isn't my place to discuss it." Indicating the Fortnum & Mason box on the table, she said, "So good of you. Will you be in England long?"

"I don't think so," Leigh answered, taking a hard drag on her cigarette. She was so nervous her stomach was constricting unpleasantly, and her hands were damp.

"And your mother? She's well?" Delia asked, her pale eyebrows lifting.

"Do you know her?"

"We've never met. I do, of course, know who she is. I've even read several of her books. Not quite my sort of thing, but fairly interesting. I understand she's hugely successful."

"Hugely," Leigh agreed.

"I'd best take you along to your father now," Delia said, watching Leigh put out her cigarette with an interest that suggested she seldom had an opportunity to watch someone hold a burning tube of shredded leaves to her mouth and greedily suck in quantities of poisonous smoke.

"I scarcely remember him," Leigh said in a rush. "The last time I saw him was just before my fifteenth birthday. I came for a month's stay, but he was never here." She glanced around the room. "He was busy with the farm, busy with the tenants, busy with this and that. I was deeply disappointed. When I left at the end of the month, we hadn't exchanged more than a few sentences during half a dozen meals we'd taken together. I thought somehow it was my fault, that there was something about me he disliked. How long have you been married?"

Delia was standing now, patiently waiting for Leigh to come with her. "It's dreadful, isn't it," she said, "the way children will hold themselves responsible for the attitudes of their parents. I'm certain there was nothing about you to which he took exception. Twenty-six years we've been married. You had no idea," she said rhetorically.

"None. No one told me. Twenty-six years. Do you have children?"

"Come along," Delia said pleasantly, as if to a recalcitrant child, her hand extended to show the way. "We weren't lucky enough to have children," she said, leading Leigh along the hallway to the rear of the house. "And I was getting rather long in the tooth when your father and I met. He's in the garden room,'' she explained. ''I'll leave you to visit, join you for a cup of coffee in a bit.'' She paused with her hand on the door, her eyes on Leigh's. ''Don't be nervous,'' she said kindly. ''He's really a very dear man.''

During the second or two before the door opened fully, and Delia dematerialized as silently as she'd appeared, leaving behind a fragrant floral scent, Leigh was gripped by panic, wondering why on earth she'd come here. She had an intuition that this reunion was going to have unimaginable repercussions.

The so-called garden room had been added since her childhood. Three of the walls were of glass. The perimeters were filed with enormous potted plants, and in one corner was a grouping of rattan furniture with pillows covered in a green and white leafy-patterned fabric. From an armchair, her father rose and came across the room to greet her. Leigh was staring again, as she had at Delia, searching for something familiar about this man. He was taller than she'd remembered, and attractive in ways she hadn't recalled until this moment when she discovered that she did know those deep-set hazel eyes, and that squarish face, and the stubborn jaw so like her own, that shy smile, and even the tentative strength of his hands as they enclosed hers. It was overwhelming. She had the feeling, suddenly, that her ribs were curved inward over a clean, empty expanse that might be filled by the things this man, her father, could say to her.

Keeping hold of her hands, he studied her wordlessly for some time before he spoke. And when he did, his voice too was familiar, low and resonant, the words shaped with precision and delivered with care. ''One thought one wouldn't see you again. Then, so unexpectedly, here you are.'' He didn't smile, but she could see he was genuinely pleased. He was a man, she realized, who rarely smiled, who didn't use what amounted to a facial tic in so many people to illustrate his pleasure. He chose instead to use his eyes, and words. And she couldn't help thinking that if she'd understood this as a child, all their lives might have been very different.

"Come sit down, Stanleigh. Unless," he stopped moving to say, "you find the atmosphere in here overpowering." He gestured at the massed plants that so visibly thrived in the moist warmth of the room.

"No, no, it's fine. This is a lovely room."

"Oh, good," he said, and returned to his chair, his rather stiff, slow gait reminding her of his age. Several newspapers sat on a nearby table, along with an ashtray in which rested a pipe and a number of spent wooden matches. He glanced out at the sodden garden, frowning slightly at the rain splattering against the glass. "You look very well," he said, turning back to her. "Very well indeed. Handsome woman. You've grown to resemble your mother."

"I didn't know you'd remarried," she said, touched increasingly by his diffidence. How could she have forgotten, or failed to know, so many things about him? Or was the truth that, beyond certain fuzzy details retained from childhood and remarks made by her mother, she knew very little about him?

"Years now," he responded, his features lifting with satisfaction at the reference to Delia. "Remarkable woman, your stepmother. Remarkable." Again, he looked out at the rain. "One is most fortunate. Were you aware," he continued in the same tone, "of my efforts to contact you? Was there some specific reason you chose to visit now?"

"No specific reason," she answered. "What do you mean about trying to contact me?"

"One never dreamed," he said quietly, "when you left here that summer that one wouldn't see you again for thirty years. One thought the next summer, or during some school break. Beyond conceiving that you wouldn't return. Mean to say, quite one thing for your mother to do as she would with her life; her prerogative, after all. Quite something else to return my letters to you unopened, refusing me contact with my own child. Can't think why the woman despised me so, although given the circumstances . . ." He trailed off, his eyes somehow magnetically drawn to the rain beyond the glass walls.

"What circumstances?" Leigh asked, bewildered, and remembering now how, when she was a child, her father's manner of speaking had constantly confused her. She opened her bag for a cigarette and lit it. Then, without knowing she was going to do it, she said, "There is a reason, in a way. My stepson, Joel . . . he died a few days ago." She had to stop in order to firm up her grip on her emotions. "We were very close," she went on. "He'd been ill, with leukemia, for nearly three years. When it was over, when he finally died, all I wanted was to come see you. I don't know why. Perhaps it had to do with the dreadful sense of loss . . . I don't know. I wondered, you see, if it was what you felt . . . it suddenly seemed very wrong not to have seen you for so long. As if perhaps a terrible mistake had been made and, unwittingly, I'd helped it happen. Thirty years. We don't know each other. You're married again. The house is completely different from the way I remembered it. I felt," she said inadequately, "I had to see you again." She put out her cigarette and sat back. The only sound was of the rain against the great sheets of glass that were the walls of this hothouse room.

"That was your stepson, you say," her father spoke at last.

"From my second marriage," she elaborated.

"I see. I hadn't known of your first. But I believe I felt fairly much as you say you do." He referred to himself directly as I, not as one, and offered her a slightly apprehensive smile meant, she knew, to be encouraging.

"My first husband and our son were killed in a road accident," she told him, then busied herself getting another cigarette lit. Her throat felt dry and raw, but she knew it was going to be one of those occasions when she smoked nonstop, clinging to illusory support.

"How very tragic," her father said. And there followed another, longer silence while she reviewed that piece of her own history, and he absorbed the impact of gaining and losing both a son-in-law and a grandson all in the space of seconds.

"What's happened to the farm?" she asked at last.

"Came a time when it got to be too much. It's been broken up, parts sold. Retirement," he added unnecessarily. He was seventy years old, after all.

"You must miss it," she said, flooded with sudden sympathy—for both of them. "I do recall how busy you used to be, how much there always was to do."

He nodded, and reached for his pipe, to hold its bowl in the palm of his hand. Leigh thought she knew, all at once, what it was about this man that two so very different women had been drawn to. Certainly he was attractive enough, with his lean height, his plentiful white hair, his Irish tweeds and Scottish woolens; he had the bearing of a man born to wealth and position, as well as that forgivable upperclass affectation of referring to himself as "one." But what appealed about him overall was his aura of kindness. It showed in any number of ways—the prudence in his words and gestures was self-protecting but also intended to spare the sensibilities of others; the intelligence and acuity of his gaze was rescued from harshness by the crinkling of the flesh around his eyes, so that the effect was one of good humor. The smiles he failed to offer with his mouth he gave quite generously with his eyes. Seeing all this, Leigh tried to think why her mother had such tremendous long-lived and ongoing antipathy toward him. He was, very clearly, someone incapable of intentional cruelty. Of course she knew from her own experience how hurtful the unintentional cuts could be.

"What did you mean before about 'circumstances'?" she asked him, certain since he'd created that particular opening he intended to tell her.

"One didn't mean to create a mystery," he said, his diffidence apparently intact. "It was a bit of unpleasantness a very long time ago." He'd no sooner finished saying this when he visibly reconsidered. "That is not strictly the truth," he said, his eyes seeing the window. "It was a frightful jolt, completely unexpected. She confronted me one day, with no warning. Not a hint, prior to then, of what was to come. I was an impediment to her desires, an obstacle standing between her and the life she preferred to live. I was insensitive to her needs, obsessive regarding the farm, less than a satisfactory partner in every area." Meeting Leigh's eyes again, he said, "Perhaps I was rather wrapped up in the farm. Very likely, I was. But I'd gone along believing our life here was a good one. Throughout our marriage, I took my cues from your mother. I realized then that one can live very closely with someone else and be quite unaware of the thoughts and feelings of that other person. I never was terribly good socially, lacked the conversational skills, the dinner table airs and graces that were, by her sights, important. Any number of sins of omission of which I was guilty. Tried and convicted without benefit of what one might call a courtroom appearance. She announced she was leaving and taking you with her. Nothing I could say or do would dissuade her. She wanted an end to the marriage; an end to the 'boredom and bondage' as she called it; she wouldn't hear any argument; one was not allowed to state one's case.

"The agreement stipulated you were to be with me on all your school holidays, but she'd write to say this or that had come up. And, as you know, after two years the visits came to an end. I wrote many times, as did my solicitors. I even made a trip to New York to confront her, but somehow she managed to learn of my presence and left the city in order not to have to see me. There was nothing to be done, so I came home. We tried every means, including a number of threatening letters from the solicitor, but nothing came of any of it. I wrote to you. The letters were all returned. At last I conceded defeat and hoped you'd seek to contact me. And now you have. For that I am grateful."

"Did something happen? I mean, it doesn't make sense. I'm not sure I understand."

"There was a chap in London she was terribly keen on. Perhaps she hoped he'd marry her." He shrugged. "She brooded a bit after that episode. Then she began taking weekends in London, and there were other chaps. One simply couldn't ignore it. It was the sort of thing—rather blatant, and much talked about—that was, after the fact, most embarrassing. I was completely in the dark. I thought we had a good marriage. Then one morning she decided every last bit of it had to be destroyed, so that it could never be resurrected. To this day I cannot think what I did to so turn her against me. As I said, there was no discussion."

"Perhaps," Leigh ventured, "she decided she *couldn't* be married." She hesitated, gauging her sense of loyalty. "My mother," she went on, "likes men, likes to be liked by them. She's always thought I was ridiculous for wanting to be married. She has great contempt for marriage. It feels as if we're talking about someone neither of us knows. I don't think I know *her*, or *you*, for that matter. I didn't know about your letters, or about your wanting to see me. Perhaps things might have been different if I'd known. But in many ways I'm very like her.''

''And in many ways, very *un*like her. Understand, please, that I bear your mother no malice. Certainly not at this late date. It's simply that some areas remain puzzling. She refused a financial settlement, yet she left with a number of pieces that had been my grandmother's. They were meant to come to you. Family heirlooms, that sort of thing.''

He spoke of the jewelry and Leigh thought of her mother pawning valuable items in order to get the two of them established in New York. Had her mother redeemed those things as she'd said? Just as Leigh was about to assure him her mother still had those heirlooms, the door opened and Delia came smiling in, followed by the housekeeper pushing a trolley bearing a full silver coffee service.

''We've rescued your driver,'' Delia said, ''and installed him in the kitchen. He put up quite a fight, according to Anne here. Insisted on showing her his bag of lunch. Anne, however, has prevailed.'' As she spoke, she glided across the room to position herself behind her husband's chair. Her hands slid over his shoulders and, in a tellingly protective gesture, she bent to rest her cheek briefly against the top of his head before crossing to seat herself in the chair next to Leigh's. ''I know,'' she said, ''the two of you haven't had near enough time alone together, but I'm far too curious to stay any longer in the sitting room alone with my imagination.'' She gave Leigh a wide, girlish smile. ''Has he told you yet how we met?''

Leigh said he hadn't.

Delia looked fondly over at her husband, then laughed. ''Men,'' she told Leigh, ''are such fools when it comes to their health. He'd been feeling unwell for quite some time, but kept putting off doing anything about it. I'd just opened my surgery a few months earlier, and it was terribly slow going, everyone apprehensive about the new female GP. In any event, he finally dragged himself in one morning, coincidentally placing his stamp of approval; you know, the country squire seeing fit to put himself in the care of the new physician. Poor fellow had pneumonia. Slung him straight into hospital, and made sure he stayed there. Which, I promise you, was quite a feat. The cows were waiting." She laughed. "The fields were waiting; the tenants were waiting. We kept him tucked away for three weeks, then he went off home grumbling, to see to all those waiting cows and fields and what-have-you. Then, not a week later, he was ringing up to invite me out for a meal."

"She decided," Phil put in, "I needed looking after on a full-time basis. Full time," he qualified, "outside surgery hours, emergency calls, hospital visits, and a week-long spur-of-the-moment trip to the Edinburgh Festival. Fortunately, these days she has a partner, so one sees rather more of her. Of course the telephone still rings at three in the morning, and off she goes to see to someone's granny who's fallen off the loo." He chuckled at this.

The housekeeper, Anne, offered cups of coffee. Then she positioned the trolley for easy access and went out. Leigh lit another cigarette and tried to picture her stepmother in a white coat with a stethoscope around her neck. It was a fairly glamorous image, but one with a lot of appeal. Those hands were a significant clue, after all. Leigh would never in a hundred years have guessed Delia's profession.

"I don't suppose you could come stay with us for a few days?" Delia asked, her hand on Leigh's arm.

"I'm afraid I have to get back to New York," Leigh

lied, alarmed without knowing why at the prospect of a long visit.

"There's been a death in the family," her father explained solemnly. "Stanleigh's quite anxious to return."

"Oh, that is too bad," Delia said. "I'm sorry."

Leigh sipped her coffee, wishing she knew what to do, and why she'd lied. She was seated opposite her father, and the feeling she had was of watching an old film with actors who had been familiar to her once but who now seemed slightly mannered. There was this very beautiful blond woman sitting so close that Leigh could almost feel the woman's flesh closing around her. Under other circumstances, these two people would have seemed foreign in every way, but the fact was that the white-haired seventy-year-old retired farmer was her father. And the sweet-natured blonde was his clearly devoted wife, as well as Leigh's just-acquired stepmother. Her long-held view of this man was a concoction fabricated in part by her own time-tempered memories and in part by her mother's ongoing animosity. Both her view and her mother's animosity seemed unwarranted. Setting down her cup, Leigh put out her cigarette, guiltily aware that she'd fogged and contaminated the air of this charming house.

"I'll remember to ask Mother about the jewelry," she told her father, "and let you know. She did pawn some items when we first moved to New York. But I'm almost certain she redeemed them. If they were meant for me, she wouldn't have risked losing them. She's not at all irresponsible."

"One didn't mean to imply . . ."

"It's all right," Leigh cut in. "I know what you meant. It's very difficult," she said, looking to Delia for assistance. "I can't discuss her with you without feeling disloyal. She's been a wonderful mother . . . I mean she's silly and eccentric, and she often talks too much, but she's always done her best for me. And whatever went wrong between the two of you . . . well, it really didn't have anything—I don't think—to do with me. I felt I had to see you, to know you before it was too late . . ."

"We quite understand," Delia came to her aid. "No need to explain, no need at all. But if you should find your plans have changed, we'd very much like to have you here. For as long as you'd care to stay."

"Why?" Leigh asked.

Delia looked momentarily startled by the question. Then she smiled and said, "Because it's your home, after all."

"Oh!" Leigh exclaimed softly, then looked over to see her father nodding his agreement.

After lunch, her father embraced her, said, "Please do come back again very soon, Stanleigh. It's been good, seeing you," then excused himself to go upstairs for his lie-down.

Delia said, "Come chat with me for a few minutes before you go," and led Leigh back to the sitting room, where she picked up a thick manila envelope from the coffee table. "This is for you to look at at your leisure," she said, giving the envelope to Leigh before sitting with her on the long sofa. "I know it's been difficult for you, coming here today, but it's meant such a lot to your father. I hope you'll forgive my saying so, but you seem terribly angry. I realize that happens when there's the death of someone close to you, but I can't help sensing there's more to it than that. Please, don't be angry with Phil. Whatever went on between him and your mother, it was a very very long time ago. And, as you said, it didn't really have anything to do with you. You and I may never know what actually happened. Time has a tendency to distort things, even to change the way we believe certain events actually played themselves out. I know it's affected you, but I think you're able to see for yourself what a good man he is.

"I do see that," Leigh concurred. "And I know marriage can do strange things to people. I know that from firsthand experience."

"Well, then." Delia smiled, relieved. "So long as you don't hold him entirely responsible. And if I may offer one small piece of advice, go gently on your mother. In all likelihood neither one of them is the same person they were thirty-odd years ago."

"I *am* angry." Leigh was mildly taken aback by the woman's astuteness. "Is it that obvious?"

Delia smiled. "There's no harm to being angry. And I quite like angry people. They have such exceptional energy. I do wish we were going to see more of you. I would like to get to know you better."

"I'll come back," Leigh promised.

"Good," Delia said decisively. "Good!"

Eight

It was one of the very infrequent occasions when he flew in a fairly direct line: from London to Hong Kong, from Hong Kong to Bangkok, and from Bangkok to Chiang Mai. He used his stopover hours in Hong Kong to arrange for his usual interpreter and driver in Chiang Mai, and they were there waiting when his Thai Air flight landed. A quick stop to deposit his luggage in his room at the Orchid, and then he was off in the air-conditioned car to make his visits to Sankamphaeng and Bor Sang. An hour at each factory to accept the politely offered fruit juice while he examined the silks and cottons, the paper umbrellas and fans, the lacquerware and teak carvings, the silver and brassware. He ordered brass boxes with enameled tops or inset with mother-of-pearl; he ordered sets of brass cutlery and ornamental spoons; he ordered legions of small, carved wood elephants, and black lacquered boxes with intricately painted floral designs in a variety of shapes and sizes; he ordered bolts of densely woven silk, as well as silk-covered wallets, picture frames, and notebooks; he ordered the wonderfully smooth boxes whose tops were decorated with fragments of brown and white eggshell painstakingly set piece by piece in free-form patterns; he ordered fans and umbrellas of all sizes, and silver bangles by the gross. He did it all in the space of six hours on the first day, and another five on the second. He was driven from place to place through the lush countryside, absently noticing lines of religious men walking single file along the road in their gauzy saffron-colored robes, and black-clad women in their oddly shaped straw hats working on a construction site, and young people driving recklessly everywhere on their omnipresent motorcycles. He gazed through the car window at the vast rice paddies, at the astonishing temples—wats—some in ruins, some intact. It all flew past the car windows, somehow both familiar and first-time new. By the evening of the second day, having spent a restless night in his room at the Orchid, he was at the airport to catch a flight back to Hong Kong.

Once in Hong Kong, installed in a large room at the Peninsula—having gone through the ritual of accepting the welcoming bottle of champagne, the bowl of exotic fruits, the pot of tea; having selected the soap of his preference from the cart wheeled in by one of the bellboys—he was annoyed with himself for leaving Thailand in such a hurry. What he should have done, he told himself, was to spend several days at the Oriental in Bangkok. He thought longingly of the superb hotel and its spectacular view of the river. Dumb. He should have gone there. He could have seen again the Emerald Buddha and the Grand Palace; he could have gone on one of the motor launch cruises down the river to the Floating Market, or to the ruins at Ayutthaya. There were endless wats all over the city he hadn't yet seen, and stores he'd never investigated, strange foods in the street stalls he hadn't tasted. But he'd come hurrying back to Hong Kong as if there were something waiting for him here and, of course, there was nothing.

He'd go out and do some shopping. He wanted a Mont Blanc pen, and he'd find some new electronic gizmo for Lane, and some jewelry, do a little leisurely wheeling and dealing. The best part of shopping in Hong Kong was the bargaining, minidramas in which the vendor played his part with absolute conviction and credible rue at being bested on his price.

He drank some of the green tea, then lit a cigarette and wondered if many people had killed themselves in this hotel. It seemed an improbable place for a suicide. Too many people ringing your doorbell, popping in and out to bring fresh flowers, more hot tea, this-that-and-the-other. He thought of Celeste as he'd last seen her, and immediately sat up to hold aside the curtains and look out at the street, thick with people all with destinations. He looked again at the room and knew he had to get out of there.

He turned right out of the hotel and walked along Salisbury Road, headed toward the harbor and the immense indoor shopping precinct at the Ocean Terminal. He liked Hong Kong, had always enjoyed the multinational crowds, the ceaseless traffic, the countless shops, the tidy good looks of the Chinese, and the music of their unexpected laughter.

Instead of going directly inside to look at the dozens of elegant shops, he went up to the roof of the outdoor parking garage atop the terminal and stood first on one side by the wall and then on the other, gazing at the ultramodern skyline, and at the many ships in the harbor. It was a fantastic city, jammed with people; clothes drying on poles outside the windows of high-rise buildings; double-decker trams zipping along on the Hong Kong side; cars rushing back and forth between Kowloon and Hong Kong. And over in Aberdeen—he'd gone there only once out of curiosity—there were thousands of people living on junks that looked pretty picturesque until you got close enough to see and smell the sea of garbage in which they floated. The smell was revolting. Dogs and cats sunned themselves or prowled the decks; lines of laundry and people playing mah-jongg. The stench had overcome his curiosity, and he'd left there bothered by the difference between the look of the place from a distance and the upclose decay.

He didn't go into the terminal after all, but retraced his steps to Nathan Road where the crowds were even thicker and the sky was filling with neon as the afternoon faded. The signs themselves were art; hundreds of multicolored invitations to buy, to eat, to come look, to see and hear and smell the ceaseless motion of the city. He felt better, and wandered down narrow passages to look into out-of-the-way stalls and tiny shops offering everything from expert instant tailoring to antiques and calculators and cameras and jade and diamonds; anything conceivable. Gold and ivory and pearls; perfume and stereo equipment and Swiss watches. Kowloon was one gigantic shopping center; you could overdose on it.

He bargained in six different shops for the Mont Blanc Diplomat, and finally returned to the first shop to tell the proprietor of the last, best offer, allowing the man to perform his bit of theater as he shook his head, gazed balefully at his merchandise, then with an expression of disgust, said, "Ninety U.S. dollars," and looked as if he'd weep as the words left his mouth. "Cash only," he added.

Dan said, "Sold," and pulled out his money while the proprietor now smiled as he lovingly polished the pen, showed Dan the guarantee papers, then returned the pen to its box and slid it into a padded silk bag. Only then did he accept Dan's money, and write up a receipt.

Farther along the road, Dan sat down with the owner of

a jewelry store, accepted the man's offer of a soft drink, and then looked at the ropes of unstrung pearls, the gold chains, the diamonds—set and unset—and the earrings. At a leisurely pace, Dan studied the merchandise before deciding he liked a handmade, unusually set diamond pendant. It was far too sophisticated for Lane, and not something his mother would wear. But he could clearly see himself giving it to Leigh. He could see it so clearly that he began to bargain in earnest for the piece. It was serious haggling, with the owner asking twenty-two hundred American, and Dan coming in at six hundred, an offer that caused the man to reevaluate his initial impression of Dan as another malleable tourist. In the end, they agreed on nine hundred, with the owner providing an appraisal showing the true retail value at just under three thousand dollars. Dan did only token haggling for a fine strand of pale pink pearls for Lane and a seed-pearl choker with an ornate gold clasp for his mother.

When he emerged from the shop it was almost seven and he was hungry. He debated whether to continue shopping for something for his father or to eat. He was too hungry. He'd give his father the pen, and that would solve that problem.

There was a restaurant nearby that he knew from previous visits, and he had a sudden craving for a good Szechwan meal. He worked his way through smoked duck marinated in rice wine and ginger, with crisp rice and many small cups of tea.

By the time he got back to the Peninsula, pleased with his purchases and sated with food, he was ready to try for some sleep. He sat on the side of the bed for a time, examining the pendant. The fact that he'd bought it had to mean he'd see Leigh again. He had enough information to go on. It shouldn't, he thought, be too difficult to find her.

* * *

The day was sunny but very cold, and she was glad of the mink as she headed toward the park carrying the package Delia had given her. She still felt drained from her visit with her father the afternoon before, and thought it remarkable that so momentous an occasion had been treated by all of them—on the surface, at least—so quietly, so very socially. They'd all been so damnably British, restrained and polite; very little emotion on display. It had been most civilized, but with undercurrents of not readily identifiable feelings. She knew well enough what she had felt, but she couldn't have begun to state for certain that her father or Delia had felt this or that specifically. It was, she told herself, probably because nothing whatever seemed clear just then. Her feelings were so subject to instant change, so wildly unpredictable, and so extreme, that things she might have found amusing at another time now grieved her.

Seated on the same bench where she'd sat sketching two days earlier, she pushed her hands deep into her pockets as she surveyed the area. Then, turning, she looked behind her at the busy street a few hundred feet away. She did love this city. There was a feeling she had in London that she never had anywhere else. It had to do with the narrow streets, and the monstrously snarled traffic, the double-decker London Reds, the entrances to the undergrounds with their steep escalators, the venerable old shops—and the sense, above all, that rightfully she belonged here. She was of this country; trace elements of its dirt and grandeur and nobility resided in her cells. She was not foreign here as she was everywhere else in the world; this place had been home to her parents and their parents, on and on, back into time. This rambling, architectural surprise package of a city was a part of the heritage she could claim along with her dual citizenship, whatever remained of her accent, her philosophical regard for dismal weather, and her last-gasp sense of humor. Maybe she'd just stay here, she thought, picturing herself installed in a cozy flat somewhere, with a telephone that gave off double rings; picturing herself out to do the marketing with a basket slung over one arm and a scarf to guard her head from the rain; picturing herself climbing into her car at the weekends to drive up to see her father and stepmother. She'd have a coal fire and a cat, and potted plants lining her windowsills. She'd have chilblains, bronchitis, and rheumatoid arthritis. She'd die without central heating; she was allergic to cat hair; and she was a notorious killer of houseplants. So much for that.

She lit a cigarette, then opened the package. It was filled with letters. Across the front of each one, in her mother's hand, was written "Return to sender." They were in date order, all still sealed. She held the rubber-banded packet, profoundly upset by this proof of the small crime her mother had committed against her. She knew that once she opened and read these letters she was going to have to go directly back to New York, because she would be in need of a firsthand explanation from her mother as to why she'd deprived her in such cruel fashion of her father's influence, her father's company, her father's affection.

In advance of the event, she could see and hear herself shrieking at her mother; could see her mother pulling back. Perhaps it would be best to leave it alone, not open these envelopes and see the evidence of a caring she'd been led to believe didn't exist. "Why the hell did you do it?" she could hear herself demanding of her mother. "What right did you have to do that to me, or to him?"

The cigarette tasted foul. She took a last puff, then dropped it on the ground and stepped on it. When she'd come here before, she'd sketched Daniel from memory. He seemed to have been a part of her life for far longer than just a few days. He stood very clearly in her mind;

she could see and hear him; she knew his facial expressions and certain habitual gestures he made; she knew the ways in which he made love and the feel of his body under her hands; she knew the sound of his voice and the faint, underlying foreign lilt to his Americanized accent. If she'd asked him to stay on, he'd have done it. Overall, she'd enjoyed his company; she'd liked bantering and arguing with him; she'd liked the look and feel of him. She was right: he represented a complication. Cardinal rule: never become involved with married men. Yet nothing about him suggested the usual guilt and deviousness of a married man. She was aware of the signs and signals. No, this was best. Still, she had to laugh recalling his line about "Strangers in the Night." And there had been that moment when, after they'd made love a second time, they'd stared at each other and then burst out laughing. He'd made her laugh. It seemed noteworthy.

She found her reading glasses—she hated them, convinced they were proof of her decline into old age, and so rarely wore them—put them on and, using her nail file, slit open the first of the envelopes.

It was a voyage back in time, one that took her through the ages of fifteen to twenty-six. Some of the letters contained checks, birthday and Christmas gifts. Undramatic, newsy letters, they represented too many years of thwarted caring. Never once did he make any negative reference to her mother; never once did he express any of the frustration and anger he must have felt. He simply said he hoped she'd receive this particular letter, and that he looked forward to seeing her at any time she'd care to return home for a visit. And if finances were a problem, he'd be more than happy to wire funds. The very simplicity of his declarations undid her. She sat and wept, feeling betrayed by the one person she'd most loved and admired, unable to comprehend her mother's motives. The woman had deprived Stephen of his grandfather, of visits to that great, echoey house and the acres of farmland with the stream he might have fished in the company of his grandfather. And Joel. God! Joel would have gone mad for every bit of it. He'd have checked the plants for spider mites; he'd have admired Delia's decorating; he'd have been out in the kitchen whipping up special tidbits for afternoon tea; he'd have had everyone laughing with his Ethel Merman routines. All the visits that had never taken place; all the emotions that had never known a proper outlet; all the seasons missed. She could only be glad her mother wasn't with her just then, because her rage had murderous proportions.

She put away her glasses, found a tissue to dry her eyes, lit a cigarette, and gave thought to what she wanted to do. It was all fine and good getting from one hour to the next, one day to the next, but she couldn't continue on indefinitely that way. She had too much curiosity left about life, and too much anger—as Delia had so accurately pointed out—to give up and die. So, she was going to have to begin living her life again. But she couldn't merely kill time in the city during the week, then kill more time in the country at the weekends. She had to *do* something. Perhaps Miles would have some suggestions. He was forever calling up with ideas that had popped into his head. Maybe, for once, she'd encourage him.

God damn it! she swore silently, shifting again to look at the city behind her. She wanted to hang on to her anger, yet well in advance of a showdown, she knew her mother would have any number of reasons for what she'd done. And already, a lifetime of actively loving the woman was killing off her anger with her. It was ridiculous. Forty-five years of a life lived with the most dreadful, tenacious optimism. She felt like some uncommon, ridiculous creature, something like a pack rat that hoarded and scrounged, saving up bits and pieces for no discernible reason. Except that in her case the bits and pieces she collected and tucked away all had to do with emotion, and with using those emotions—filips of varicolored feeling—like set dressing. She'd spent her entire adult life attempting to adorn the invisible walls of her existence with portraits of the people she'd loved who'd loved her, as if this documentation could validate an otherwise meaningless era. Plain white cotton she'd turned into embossed brocade by collecting love and weaving it into the fabric spooling off the loom of her life. And what frightened her, now that Joel was gone, was her doubtful ability to find something to substitute for the caring she could never have again. The people she had loved had died, and she was left with big empty spaces all around her that she didn't know how to fill.

Maybe her mother had been right all along in saying how dangerous was her capacity for caring. Getting through the days would have been so much easier without the emotional excess baggage. But how the hell did you stop caring, stop wanting to care? She was such a bloody optimist she even had hopes for some man she'd gone to bed with who was not only married to someone else but who didn't even know her telephone number. What kind of stupidity was that?

And there it was, already happening: She'd shifted her anger from her mother to herself without missing a beat. It wasn't what she wanted. What she wanted was . . . what? *I want my sons back!* she shrilled in mute protest. *I want to keep the love alive.* To lose one son once, all right; it happened. But to lose two! The gross unfairness of it, and now the proof of what her mother had done, had her weeping again. She wasn't sorry she'd made this little pilgrimage. She wished she'd never made the trip. Anger, grief, anger, alternating, taking her up and down, back and forth, like some bizarre circus ride. She jumped up to hurry back to the hotel. She was going to get on the first available flight to New York, to see her mother.

Flying home, Dan berated himself for placing so much importance on a chance meeting, a chance bedding, with this woman. Why was he so bent on pushing the thing beyond its imposed limitations? Buying an expensive gift with the vague notion of tracking her down to give it to her; in the giving, he'd prove the sincerity of his intentions. Crap! All it would prove was his interest. The lies had put him in a no-win situation. It was where he'd thought he wanted to be. Now he wasn't so sure of that. How could he be sure—of anything—when unbidden images of the woman kept insinuating themselves into his consciousness? The images he had of her were so potent, so commanding. All he had to do was half-lower his eyelids, and there was a picture of her, standing in front of him with her shell-shocked eyes and her startled expression as he touched her. What she couldn't have known, of course, was the strangeness he'd felt at discovering this new flesh, so dissimilar to Celeste's. Celeste's bones had hidden themselves beneath overfolding layers of doughy rolls. It had seemed as if her skeleton had been growing smaller while the density of her flesh had been increasing. But Leigh. He'd instantly achieved a sense of the entire woman because of her physical composition, because of the bones lying just beneath the surface of age-softened skin still adhering tightly to its frame. He'd been awed by the delicate weight of her breasts, and the rapacity with which she'd accepted him. And it hadn't been merely a physical acceptance; it had been her emotional appetite to which he'd responded most. Because she'd been right: It wasn't hard to find women. You could find them anywhere you looked. But how often did you come across a woman who could laugh and argue; who was completely her own person and yet, mysteriously, heart-stoppingly, gave access? He admired her talent and her success; he admired her. And she'd removed her clothes, allowed him to see and touch and taste her. Christ! It excited him simply thinking about her.

While he killed time in the San Francisco airport, waiting for his United connection back to New York, he wondered again what he was doing. Those images of Stanleigh Dunn alternated with an image of Celeste as she'd been the last time he'd seen her. It was as if his recall of these two, so different women was doing battle against itself. Right there in the middle of the airport, he felt like breaking down. He didn't want to go back to Bedford; he didn't want to think he was *going back*, and had to keep telling himself there *was no* going back. But prove that to his brain! Convince his memory of that! Impossible! And here he'd paid duty on a diamond pendant he was determined to give to Leigh. Goddamned perverse, going through so much crap with a gift for a woman whose address he didn't even know. To find her, he was going to have to play detective. Or, he could save himself the trouble and just give the damned thing to Lane, or to his mother, and to hell with its lack of suitability. That's what he'd do, all right. He didn't have the time or energy to track down a woman who'd likely be furious—if and when he did find her—not only at having her privacy invaded but at his having disregarded her wishes. They'd agreed they wouldn't meet again, but he was spending half his time planning how he'd find her and the other half pissed off with himself because of the first half.

He was so wrought up over the whole stupid business that he actually arrived in New York having paid no attention to the flight. He'd flown three thousand miles in so preoccupied a state that he hadn't bothered to be afraid. And realizing this as he waited to claim his baggage, he wanted to call Leigh up and say, Look what you've done! I was so busy thinking about you, caring about you, that I forgot to be afraid. He wanted to call her up and say, Listen! I fell in love with you and it's not something I do every day of the week, it isn't even something I've done before, never mind every day, so let's not argue about it. Just see me, talk to me, come to bed with me, and to hell with everything, everyone else. The Good Doctor can go fly; the whole world can take a hike, just don't hang up, okay? Don't hang up.

Christ! He looked around at the other people waiting for their bags to come off the carousel, grateful that thoughts didn't show, that no one could tell he'd really gone over the edge, was into it up to his goddamned neck because he'd sat next to a woman on an airplane who not only happened to be famous but who, a few hours later, had been willing to undress and let him fall into her as if she was the atmosphere and he a sky-diver.

Nine

Leigh let herself into her mother's apartment with her own key, and walked through looking for her mother. Pausing in the living room, she saw two half-finished drinks sitting in wet rings on the glass coffee table. If her mother had gone out, Leigh didn't know what she'd do with the immense parcel of anger she'd brought along here with her. Continuing on down the hall, she arrived at her mother's bedroom. The open doorway, like a picture frame, contained the image of her mother, nude, sitting astride Laurence whose hands were fastened to her breasts.

Leigh leaped out of the doorway and sagged against the wall, whispering, *"Jesus!"*

The two in the bedroom continued their slow ride, unaware of anything but each other. Leigh couldn't stand it. From just outside the door, she said loudly, "Ask Laurence to leave, please. I want to talk to you!"

Startled sounds from the bedroom, frantic murmurings. Leigh listened for a few seconds before stalking shaky-legged back to the living room to wait, trying to steady her breathing.

Marietta appeared in a silk peignoir two or three minutes later. Six thirty-five in the evening and here she was, damp at the hairline from her activities, flushed in the face and chest, in a peignoir, of all things.

"You really must ask him to put his clothes on and go," Leigh said. "You and I have some matters to discuss."

"What on earth do you think you're. . . ?"

"If you don't mind having him listen in on our conversation, that's fine with me! I need a drink." Leigh marched over to the built-in bar in the far corner of the room and snatched up a bottle of Chivas, the nearest thing to hand. She could feel her mother's eyes boring into her spine, could sense Marietta's deliberating.

"I will be back in a moment," Marietta said stiffly, and Leigh turned to see her sweep away, the peignoir flowing around her like water.

"Love in the goddamned afternoon," Leigh muttered, turning back to the neat Scotch she was pouring into her glass. A swallow, the acid burn, and then, fortified, she threw off her coat, dropped her bag on top of it, and positioned herself in the middle of the room, holding the glass with both hands. "Jesus!" she whispered again, seriously rattled at having caught her mother at the apex of a sexual encounter, telling herself she should have had the doorman ring upstairs to warn Marietta she was on her way up. But who would have thought she'd be engaged in pre-dinner lovemaking?

Five minutes and Laurence came through, paused to collect his coat from the foyer closet and, without a word either to Leigh or Marietta, let himself out.

Her features still flushed, Marietta returned to stand in the living room archway, keeping the peignoir closed with both hands. Striving to maintain self-control, she said, "I am prepared to take into consideration the tremendous strain you've been under recently, but barging in here unannounced to start issuing orders is positively unforgivable. How dare you . . . ?''

"Oh, shut up, Mother," Leigh sighed. "The affronted duchess routine's not going to wash. I want to talk to you. Don't you think you should put on something sensible, like a dress? My God! I always wondered who bought that stuff. I never dreamed it could be my own mother. You look like something Tennessee Williams wrote on an off day." With every nasty word she spoke, she could feel a mounting dismay and guilt at her terrible disrespect; she could also see clearly the effect this was having on her mother. And despite the justification she'd felt upon arriving here, she didn't understand why she was behaving as hatefully as she was. But she'd seen her mother engaged in a sexual act, and the recollection of what she'd seen made her quake. She wanted to scream; she also wanted to heed the inner voice that was insisting it was most unfair of her to carry on this way when her mother had no idea of the reasons why. And on top of all that, the sheer physical presence of the woman was, as ever, monumentally distracting.

Marietta's looks had always managed to sidetrack Leigh, sometimes to Leigh's extreme disadvantage. Because she was an artist both by training and disposition, the way someone looked, the way he or she fit into his or her environment, was an integral part of Leigh's overall vision. She couldn't merely absorb people and settings into her awareness, she had to analyze and dissect those people and settings, breaking them down into their component elements to see how well or badly everything fit. Leigh found her mother alarmingly close to perfect. It was hard to be at odds with someone who so pleased her visual and esthetic senses. Marietta was a Botticelli woman, tall and angular but with surprising voluptuousness. Her skin was so opaline and her hair such a fiery shade of red; her eyes were so large and of such a rare emerald hue; her neck was so long and delicate, supporting the aristocratic sculpting of her well-shaped head; her shoulders were so wide and her waist so narrow; her breasts so fully symmetrical and her hips so tautly inviting that, altogether, even in her mid-sixties, she could literally stop pedestrian traffic. She had been so magnifcently created, from top to bottom, that she'd never in her life worn makeup or had to have anything more done to her hair than a regular trim. And her hair was as rich and red now as it had been at age twelve. Her eyes were as clear and revealing as undoubtedly they'd been the day they'd first opened to the air. Her skin was that of a woman half her age. Leigh had believed for a very long time that she'd have becn far less critical of her own self had she had someone less blessed, less physically prepossessing as a mother. She'd never been able to accept anyone's compliments on her appearance because she knew she was merely an inadequate, less vivid, copy of the original.

A mother, for example, who'd had a blemish or two during her own adolescent years might not have been quite so vocally horrified when, at age fourteen, Leigh had developed acne. A mother, for example, who as a teenager had spent a few weekend nights at home alone might have been less impatient, more tolerant of the countless Saturday nights Leigh had spent moping about the apartment, praying for the miraculous advent into her life of an admiring teenage male. A mother, for example, who'd had a less than thrilling sexual life might have been more understanding of a daughter who'd confessed, addled with letdown and apprehension, to surrendering to her curiosity one night on the sofa in the living room of the family apartment on Seventy-third Street of a nineteen-year-old boy whom she'd seen only that once and who had never called again. "It is not the end of the world," Marietta had calmly told the then sixteen-year-old Leigh. "Everyone must begin somewhere." It hadn't been what Leigh had wanted to hear; she'd hoped for words of encouragement, reassurance that the future would be brighter and better.

Now here was Marietta holding closed her pale yellow peignoir with a fair, freckled hand, the fabric rising and falling to the cadence of the heaving breasts beneath. Here was the still ravishing Marietta, purveyor of romantic fiction and frequent speaker at conventions of giddy women, with her hair spilling over her shoulders and her bare toes curling into the carpet; Marietta with her ageless face wearing an expression of deep consternation.

"You're a bloody painting!" Leigh cried with reluctant admiration, already halfway undone simply by the sight of her mother. "Why couldn't you have wrinkles and gray hair like other mothers? *I* look older than you do, for chrissake!"

"Is that what this is about?" Marietta asked, a throb in her voice. "You've come here to embarrass me, to rant at me because I don't look like other mothers?"

"No," Leigh conceded, then tossed down the last of the Scotch. "I went to see him," she said, gripping the empty glass as if it offered warmth.

"And he told you scores of sordid tales about me, no doubt, all of which you believe now to be true because you've come pushing in here and discovered me in damning circumstances." The reference to what they both knew she'd seen caused the color to flood upward from Marietta's chest into her neck and face. Leigh thought she looked as if she might actually burst into flames.

"Truthfully, when he spoke of you at all, it was without rancor." She glared at her mother, feeling that morning's reactions gushing back up into her throat. "Why did you return his letters?" she cried. "How could you do that?

They were mine. You had no right . . . to let me go all those years thinking he didn't care. He was . . . very dear . . . he was . . . oh, damn!'' She was succumbing to tears and couldn't stop herself. "I don't know if I can forgive you!'' she got out, choking. "I'd like to know what you thought you were doing, depriving me of my father, deciding for me that he had no place in my life. And what about the jewels? I hope for your sake you still have them. And why, if you *do* still have them, haven't you given them to me? You knew they were intended to be mine.

"God, I wish I could let it all go, just give up and go crazy. Have you any idea how many times I've wished I'd lose my mind so I wouldn't have to be responsible, conscious and responsible, all the goddamned time?'' In a plaintive tone, she asked again, "*Why* did you do it?''

Marietta had stopped clutching at the sides of her fussy robe and wrapped her arms around herself. "I knew there'd be trouble if you went to see him,'' she said recriminatingly. "I *asked* you not to go.''

"Tell me why!'' Leigh insisted. "This is not the time to play the silly, helpless female.''

Marietta's head tilted back and she looked up at the ceiling. The move accentuated the long line of her milky throat, and Leigh understood anew why men lined up for days for the chance to go out to dinner, or to the theater, or into the bedroom, with this woman. It didn't even really matter what she said, or how silly she could often make herself appear. Just to be in her company, to be free to watch her eyes, or to see her smile take form, was something of a privilege.

"I should hate,'' she said slowly, eyes still on the ceiling, "to think we would find ourselves at permanent odds because of your impulsive decision to go see your father. I should truly hate that.''

"Then answer me,'' Leigh pleaded. "Can't you see I've

finally managed to get myself right to the edge? Can't you see that? Maybe I think I'd like to fall into it, just go mad once and for all, but for some reason I keep fighting it, even when the last thing I *want* is to fight it. Can you *see* that?''

Marietta dropped her head and directed her eyes at her daughter. "I can see it," she responded in a tone that signified Leigh had managed to get through to her. "I see far more than you think."

"It's all going to go down the toilet if you don't give me answers. And I'd hate it to happen as much as you. Why? Just tell me why. All I want is to hear your side of it."

"I've never *been* so humiliated!" Marietta railed. "Couldn't you have had the good grace to pretend you hadn't seen? Did you *have* to stand right at the door and begin bellowing? I may be your mother, but I deserve as much respect and privacy as anyone else." The color in her face was growing darker. "You break into my home filled with indignation over events that happened thirty years ago, and begin making demands. Perhaps you've already gone mad. You're behaving as if you have." Her arms reflexively tightened around herself, as if in an effort to hold herself together. "How hateful of you!" she declared. Her eyes filling, she glared a moment longer at Leigh, then crossed the room to slide into an armchair, tucking her feet up under her.

Leigh followed, to stand directly over her so that Marietta had to lean back to look up at her. "One straight answer," Leigh said. "That's all I want."

"Don't hang over me!" Marietta ordered. "I refuse to allow you to bully me in my own home." Putting her hand on Leigh's hip, she gave her a push. "Sit down and try to be rational!"

As Leigh backed away, her mother bent her head into

her hand, covering her eyes. Seeing this, Leigh had a moment of panic, believing she'd gone too far. Then, straightening, her mother looked again at her. "He never displayed any affection for you," she said brusquely. "He had no time for either one of us. Whatever it was he felt, he managed to keep it entirely to himself. And when the three of us were together, he seemed to think he had to vie with you for my attention. It was dreadful. I tried many times to make him see, but he wouldn't, or couldn't. Who cares, at this point? I spent thirteen years with him on that godforsaken bloody farm; thirteen years of either being taken completely for granted, or being taken at his whim. At the end, I felt like one of the dairy cows, something he could milk, or straddle, when the mood took him. Don't look shocked! You asked. I'm *telling* you. He saw either one of us only when it suited him, regardless of how much we clamored for his attention. Then, suddenly, after I'd brought you here, he wanted to be your father. I believed he'd forfeited that right.

"You've been deprived of nothing. No one prevented you from contacting him. You could have been in touch with him at any time over the years. You chose not to."

"How could I?" Leigh wanted to know. "How could I when all you've done since the day we came to this country has been to tell me what a worthless joke he was? You killed off any interest or desire I might have had in contacting him. I believed you," she said mournfully. "I believed you, and you were wrong. He did care about me. And obviously he's capable of showing affection, or he wouldn't have the wife he does. He's been married for the last twenty-six years."

She flung this fact into the air like an arrow and saw it hit home.

A moment of widened eyes, parted lips, then Marietta regained herself. "People change," she said.

Leigh went to the bar to pour more Scotch into her glass. She hated whiskey, didn't even know why she was drinking it.

"Don't overdo it," her mother said. "I'm not up to dealing with you inebriated."

"You make it sound as if I drink too much regularly," Leigh countered, replacing the bottle top before lifting her replenished glass. "Unfortunately, I'm not any better at being a drunk than I am at going crazy."

"I loathe self-indulgence," Marietta said. "You're alive and healthy. You have a successful career, when you care to work at it. I know Joel's death has been a great blow, but . . ."

"Don't bring side issues into this," Leigh cut her off. "We both know I've seen better days. I need you to give me a reason not to hate you."

That had the desired effect. Marietta looked so stricken that Leigh's guilt instantly trebled.

"Nothing I've done warrants that," Marietta said, her composure cracking. "I returned a dozen or so letters. Not such a terrible thing, really."

"*I think it is!* I think it was a monstrous thing to do. You *know* I'm not like you, not fabulously self-contained like a Fabergé egg."

Another silence. Then, to her horror, Leigh saw tears begin to slide down her mothers cheeks. "Whatever I am," Marietta protested, deeply wounded, "it's more than mere decoration. How cruel you're being! How horribly unkind!"

"*You* were cruel and unkind, returning those letters."

"Give me one of your filthy cigarettes!" Marietta flung out her hand.

Leigh opened her bag, found the pack, and tossed it over. Then she watched her mother pick up the table lighter, knowing she'd traded hurt for hurt. Her mother smoked only when the stress of a given situation was mounting to intolerable proportions. She lit the cigarette now and inhaled deeply, turning her profile to Leigh as she looked over at the fireplace, tears still sliding down her cheeks.

"You would like to believe that having Philip in your life would have altered events. But you're wrong," she insisted, "completely wrong."

"And what about the men," Leigh pushed on, "the one in London you thought would marry you, and the others?"

Marietta's response took the form of furious laughter. "Is *that* what he told you? How bloody predictable! He couldn't make me happy so there had to be other men in the picture. There *were* no other men. People talked because I escaped for weekends in London. Rumors. There was one man before I married Philip, and none after until I came here. The two of you can't turn me into a trollop just because he failed as a husband and father, and because you've been foolish enough to be intimidated by what you see when you look at me. You've always been duped by the *look* of things. You've spent your whole life in a state of fascination with *appearances*, and *surfaces, veneer*. I can't help the way I look. And why you should feel inferior, God only knows. You're a very handsome woman; you've got style and appeal. How you view yourself has nothing at all to do with me, and I will *not* be blamed for things that are beyond my control! I wanted to be free of that man, and I wanted you to grow up without feeling torn between your parents. I wanted my own life. I gambled, and I won. I made a decision to restrict your contact with your father. He was a parent in name only who rarely, if ever, contributed to your upbringing.

"As for my scandalous behavior, it's a fiction. I took up men, on my terms, when I was well into my thirties and had no need of them financially." She took a final puff on the cigarette, then leaned forward to stub it out in the ashtray, the movement revealing to her daughter her bare breasts under the robe. "Why are you doing this, to either of us? I'd have discussed the matter with you at any time, but you never chose to ask. Joel died, and you went off to see that pathetic farmer. Then you come flying back here to make scenes, heaving accusations like crockery. Thirteen years is a very long time to try to make a go of a bad marriage. As you, better than most, should know. Everything I've done here has been with definite ideas in mind. And I rather enjoy being silly. If one is a silly woman, one doesn't have to contend with male competition. I like men well enough, but not so well that I'd be willing, ever, to repeat the experiences I had with your father." She brought her legs out from under her, and sat very erect. "I am well aware you consider me frivolous and essentially lightweight, but I've always been available to you when you needed me. I even, if you will recall, only recently attended to the details of a *funeral service* because you were unable to deal with it. I also loved Joel, but that's not relevant. If I am unlike 'other people's mothers' it is by choice. I've never had any great desire to be like other people. And I cannot for the life of me think why, given your most unique attributes, you'd aspire to be anything but yourself. Excuse me just a moment," she said, and got up and left the room.

Leigh remained where she'd been standing, holding the drink in one hand, and wiping her eyes with the back of the other. She'd been given the truth, which is what she'd demanded. But she'd said and done things she knew were all but unforgivable. She'd made a complete mess of everything.

Her mother returned carrying a small wooden box. "I believe you want this," she said, her words rimed with frost as she placed the box on the coffee table. "I've been intending for some time to give it to you but the occasion somehow didn't present itself. And then, quite simply, I forgot. I apologize for that. As for the rest, you have no legitimate complaints,'' she said, her arms once more winding themselves around her. "You've been deprived of nothing, nothing. I am too angry to spend any more time with you now, Stanleigh. When things go wrong—as inevitably they do, in everyone's life—you do dangerous, dreadful things. If you're not rushing headlong into marriage with some totally inappropriate buffoon, if you're not sleeping with strangers in between times, then life has no meaning for you because for reasons known only to you, talent and intelligence and good looks aren't enough. To you, Nirvana is a nervous breakdown. And, invariably, after you've done something especially dangerous, you come round here longing for madness. For someone of your considerable intelligence, it's ludicrous. I've always accepted your eccentricities; I've even found many of them charming. But when you invade my privacy, and try to shame me for being merely human after all, you go too bloody far. It's all too obvious you've done it again. You did have a man with you in your hotel room when you rang me. I wish to God you had some equanimity about your sexuality, not to mention some discretion. Don't you think you're getting rather too old for picking up strangers? I think I might prefer it if you did go mad. I suspect it would be a good deal less expensive emotionally for all concerned. I want you to leave now. I've had more than enough of you for one evening. I love you, Stanleigh, but I think all your sleeping with fools has managed to turn you into one.'' She turned away, then turned back. "And don't forget the family heirlooms,'' she added caustically. She waited as Leigh put down the glass, collected her coat and bag, picked up the box from the table, and then came across the room. "Don't say another word to me!'' Marietta warned. "I am deeply sorry Joel died. He was a lovely young man, and I shall miss him. I am sorry if you feel you lost out on some fairy-tale friendship with your father, and I am especially sorry you felt you had the right to do what you did here this evening, because it is the single most offensive thing you've ever done! We've each had our losses, but not all of us choose to strike out, as a result, at the people who care most for us. Go away now. I need to bathe."

Ten

Leigh was so ashamed of herself, so filled with disgust for everything and everyone, that all she wanted was to get away and be completely alone. She stopped at the apartment long enough to transfer her bags from the taxi to her car; she dashed up from the garage to clear her mailbox, then returned down to the car, headed for the country.

The driving was fine until she was about halfway home on the Merritt. Snow blew in blinding gusts across the road, reducing what little traffic there was to a crawl. Hunched forward over the steering wheel, she strained to see the road ahead, dizzy with apprehension at the idea of rear-ending some vehicle she couldn't see.

By the time she found her exit, her head, neck, and shoulders were aching. The road conditions were only fractionally better as she headed across Route 124 to New Canaan. Everything was white; the snow reflected the headlights' glare. Her concentration was so intense she nearly continued on through town, but remembered in time that there was no food in the house. She found a deli that was still open, ran inside to buy a few basics, then hurried back out to the car, the wind cutting up inside her sleeves and down the back of her neck as she put the groceries in the trunk.

The driveway was close to a foot deep in snow. No one had come by to clear it. The house itself looked forlorn, alone and dark beneath an unblemished froth of snow. A run inside to turn on the lights and the furnace, then she battled the wind carrying in her luggage and the groceries. Just as she got the door closed the telephone rang, and she rushed to answer thinking it might be Marietta. But when she said hello, whoever was on the other end hung up.

The message light was blinking on the machine. She jabbed the PLAY button and, while she put the food away, listened to a lame explanation of why her driveway hadn't been plowed, followed by a solicitation from *TV Guide*, then three requests in succession from Miles's secretary asking her to call, four hang-ups, a prerecorded solicitation from an insurance company asking her to respond to the following three questions—she fast-forwarded the tape past this—two more requests please to call Miles, an inquiry from a local real estate company asking if she'd be interested in listing the house, another hang-up, and a final urgent request from Miles himself that she call him. She erased the tape, then called the apartment in the city with the remote control, retrieving the messages from that line. Six entreaties to call Miles, an Avon solicitation, three hang-ups. She used the remote to erase and reset that machine, then lugged her bags to the bedroom.

Outside, the wind pushed against the house, and she could hear it creating blow-backs in the fireplace. She'd gone off and forgotten to close the damper. As a result the house was drafty and cold but, luckily, no pipes had burst. Still in her coat, she sat down on the side of the bed and picked up the telephone extension. Marietta answered after the first ring, and Leigh said, "Don't hate me. I hate myself enough for both of us."

"That is not going to do it," Marietta said, enunciating slowly and carefully, as if addressing someone severely perceptually handicapped. "You've mortified me, not to mention Laurence."

"If it's any consolation, I've mortified myself."

"That is *not* a source of consolation. I don't think you need aspire to madness, Stanleigh. I do believe you've finally succeeded in achieving it. I think you're out of control, and if tonight is an example of where madness has taken you, I want no part of it. Just having this conversation with you is upsetting me all over again. I'm going to ring off now."

"You know I didn't really mean any of it," Leigh told her.

"You meant every last bit of it! You may be regretting it now, but you came here determined to create pain, and you did precisely what you set out to do." With that, her mother put down the receiver.

At once, Leigh called back.

Again, Marietta answered after the first ring. Without bothering to say hello, she said, "You're merely compounding the felony. Leave matters alone for now. Have some more to drink, go to bed, take a hot bath, ring Miles, but don't ring *me* again tonight."

"I do love you," Leigh said.

"The only reason I'm even considering speaking to you at some future date is because I believe that. Now, goodbye."

Leigh hung up, then folded in on herself on the bed and closed her eyes.

Dan simply couldn't make himself go to the Bedford house. He went instead to the apartment in the Village he'd rented six months before but had stayed at only half a dozen times. He wasn't appreciably happier in the city than he was in Bedford, but the apartment did have the advantage of being unknown to his family. He had an unlisted telephone there as well as a bed, a table, two chairs, an AM/FM radio/cassette player, and two lamps. The place was tiny, two small rooms, a kitchen and bathroom, but it did have a working fireplace, and the walls had been taken back to the brick. For these six hundred and twenty square feet of secret living space, he was shelling out thirteen hundred dollars a month. On one level it struck him as ridiculous that anyone should pay so much for so little. On another level he was completely unconcerned. It was only money, and so far money hadn't been able to do anything more than offer basic security and relieve him of the tension of earlier years when he'd worked ceaselessly to build up the business. Now the business was no longer his. He'd been rewarded with more money, and reduced to a glorified buyer. Thinking of that, he couldn't imagine why he'd told Leigh his mother had been a buyer for Bloomingdale's. It was such an absurd fabrication.

He threw his suitcases on the bed, then went to investigate the contents of the kitchen cabinets. Pretty well stocked. If he didn't care to, he wouldn't have to go outside this apartment for weeks. There were rows of cans lining the shelves, and even a big stock of booze.

He put a pot of water on the stove to boil for coffee, then went to get the Manhattan directory, looking first under Dunn, with an *e* and without, then under Jacobson, and finally under Dennison. Useless. Hundreds of listings. He had several Connecticut directories, and reached for the Stamford one, flipping through to the New Canaan listings—the town closest to Bedford—to check the three surnames. An S. Dennison on Crooked Creek. He noted the number, certain it was Leigh's. It sounded like her.

While he poured water through the coffee in the filter, he considered what would happen if he called that number. If she answered, what would he say? He'd hang up, not say anything. But he'd know where she was. Leaving the water to finish dripping, he dialed the number and listened to it ring. Someone elderly—he was unable to tell whether it was a male or female voice—answered, and Dan apologized for the wrong number. Berating himself, he went back to his coffee making.

Carrying a cup of the good, strong French roast, he went to sit down on the floor with his back against the wall to call his parents.

His mother answered in English, but upon hearing his voice switched at once to French, saying, "Daniel, we have been most concerned for you. Have you returned?"

"I'm in town. I got back about an hour ago."

"Is this the way we should anticipate it will be in the future?" she asked. "Do you intend to disappear and then reappear without warning? Lane has been most distraught, telephoning every evening after her classes. Have you any idea what it is you're doing, Daniel?"

"No," he answered honestly. "I can't say that I do."

"Ten days is too long to disappear when one is a parent with responsibilities."

"Lane's hardly an infant," he defended himself. "And I called her from London. She was supposed to tell you."

"She told us. But you only called after being gone four days, with no one knowing where you were. What is going on?" she asked, lowering her voice.

"I told you: I don't know. I went to Thailand, did the ordering. My last official act. I'm not used to having days with no office to go to, no work. I'm not Papa. I haven't retired to my chair and my books and my classical albums. That shouldn't be too difficult to understand."

"No one is accusing you of anything, Daniel," she reminded him. "It's just . . . you are not without options."

"I know, Mama. I just don't know if I want to exercise any of them."

"Are you remaining in the city, or will you be going to Bedford?"

"I'm giving serious thought to getting rid of that house."

"But where will you live? And Lane?"

Patiently, he said, "I'll buy something else, something smaller and more manageable. Maybe a condo. And Lane isn't home anymore, except during school breaks." Having to explain himself exasperated and wearied him.

"Will you talk to your father? He's insisting I give the telephone to him."

"Sure I'll talk to him." At once, he began gearing up to answer more questions.

"When will we see you?"

"How's tomorrow? I'll come for dinner."

"Good. Here's your father."

"Daniel," his father bellowed, "what is it you're doing? Could you explain it to me? Six months ago, I might have understood this, but now. . . ?" Typically, his father ran out of steam and words simultaneously.

"Am I supposed to be keeping to some kind of schedule, Papa?" he asked his father. "Is there a specific time allotted for specific acts and emotions?"

"No," his father backed down a bit. "That isn't what I mean. But you've never done anything like this before. Therefore you must expect we would be concerned. If you tell me all is well, I will accept that. All is well?"

"All is completely fucked up, Papa," Dan answered, feeling like a kid again, and out of his depths. "I can't go back to that house. I, um, I've got a place in town where I'm staying right now. Tomorrow or the next day, I intend to go up and list the house with a local broker. And maybe have a look around, while I'm at it, for something else. That's my first and only priority right now,'' he said. ''Once that's taken care of, I'll have a look, see where I am.''

''Have you spoken yet to Lane?''

''Not since I got back, no.''

''Don't be upset, Daniel, but she decided she'd like to come with us to Palm Beach for the holidays. Of course,'' he added, ''you know you are welcome to join us.''

Dan covered the mouthpiece, turned his head aside, and swore.

''You are upset,'' his father guessed. ''But there's no need. Come with us. We don't leave for another two weeks. That's enough time for you to make arrangements for the house.''

''I'll think about it,'' Dan promised, ''but I'm not in the mood for Florida.''

''You may change your mind.''

''I might. I'll see you tomorrow evening, Papa. I have to go now.''

''Daniel,'' his father said with some urgency, ''you know you need only come to us if there is something you want.''

''I know that, Papa. I know.''

They exchanged goodbyes, and Dan hefted the Yellow Pages into his lap, to skim the listings of publishers. He found the right one, dialed, and asked for the contracts department. Simple. He requested the name of the agent listed on the contract for Stanleigh Dunn's last book, and was given it. He looked up the agent's number, dialed, and said, ''I'd like to speak to whoever in your organization represents Stanleigh Dunn.'' He was put on hold, and then a man with the melodious voice of an actor rather than an agent said hello.

"I understand you represent Stanleigh Dunn," Dan said.

"Quite correct. I have that honor."

"I'd like to get in touch with her. How might I go about that?"

"If you would care to write to her and address the letter to me, I will make certain she receives your communication. Might I enquire as to what this is about?"

"We're old friends," he ad-libbed. "I'm back in town and thought I'd get in touch with Leigh."

"Well, send along your letter and I'll be happy to forward it to her."

"One last question," Dan said. "Is she in town now, or does she still have the house in New Canaan?"

There was a brief silence on the line. Plainly the agent was mulling over the fact that Dan knew about the country house. "I'm afraid I can't say where she is at the moment," he answered. "But you have my assurance I will see to it she receives your letter."

Dan thanked him and broke the connection, dissatisfied. A letter wouldn't do it. It was too easy to ignore a letter. He would have to come up with something more, something that would guarantee him either an address or a telephone number.

All the while he sat sorting through various ideas, a segment of his brain was standing back taking note of his behavior and wondering what it was meant to accomplish. He was avoiding his parents, reluctant to resume his responsibilities; he'd developed an obsession and didn't really want to be free of it because it seemed like the only positive thing he'd felt in far too long. The rest had been performance by rote; doing what had been expected of him; but all the while he'd been going around like a human grenade with a wobbly pin that could be jarred loose by any action that deviated from the expected. He recalled his father's remark about the length of time that had passed and, reviewing his response, he decided it had been truthful. He had no frame of reference, no "priors" as the police liked to say, no previous experience with anything remotely like what Celeste had done, so how was he to know how to behave, or what to do when? He hadn't known six months ago, and he didn't know now. All he did know was that he felt free now from all restraints. And that was because of his meeting Leigh. He didn't give a damn that she was married to someone else. All he cared about was seeing her again. And the more time that elapsed between their last meeting and the present, the more strongly he needed to see her again. It had been six days since he'd left her in the lobby of Brown's Hotel. It felt like months. It felt wrong. It felt like deprivation from some vital substance he required in order to survive.

There was something else he knew, and that was that he was out of control. Instead of sitting there on the floor cradling an empty coffee cup, he should have been calling his daughter. But he had to rein in his emotions first, deal with the small feeling of betrayal he had at Lane's changing their plans without first consulting him. He'd been looking forward to going somewhere tropical, snorkeling clear water with his lithe young daughter and her companion, lazing on a white sand beach while the sun dazed them all into somnolence. Instead, she was going to go with her grandparents to their Palm Beach condominium. And he couldn't go there. He wasn't up to prolonged exposure to his mother and father and their relentless-seeming need to question everything he said and did. They and Lane were the only people to whom he tried never to lie. He omitted, he distorted on occasion, but he rarely lied to them. He just couldn't cope with two or three weeks of being forced to dredge up bits of harmless truth to give to them.

They would have been flabbergasted to learn he'd transformed his mother into a former department store buyer, and his father into a professor. Most likely, they'd have found his choice of careers humorous. His mother was as devoted to Bloomingdale's as she was to his father, but she'd never worked a day in her life. And the only subject on which his father might have been qualified to lecture was Daniel's present inability to perform to standard. International bankers were among the most didactic people on earth, and his father was no exception. Having made a career in money, predicated on the mathematics that accompanied money everywhere it went, his father saw all things on plus or minus scales that in the end were obliged to balance. His emotional life ran along similarly disciplined lines and the closeness of the family had been achieved as a result of his mother's talent for arousing the passion and humor that luckily lay not too far beneath the surface of his banker father's glacial calm. Given all that, there was no way possible Daniel could explain to his father that his recently acquired obsession had managed to shift him out of his six months of suppressed emotion into an active state of feeling. His mother would understand, and so would Lane. But Dan had nothing concrete to tell them. And any discussion of Leigh would not only be premature, it might also jinx the potential he found in the situation.

Leigh had given her mother a week to recover, but it wasn't time yet to call her again. And every time she thought of how they'd gone at each other that night, she wondered if the right time would ever come. That evening seemed to attain more horrific dimensions with every passing day. She could no longer discern which grieved her more, Joel's death or that last encounter with her mother.

She loathed herself so thoroughly she couldn't bear to

eat, or to sit still for more than ten minutes; she slept only a few hours a night and when awake devoted herself to splitting the last of the logs and then stocking the woodpile outside the mud room door. She hadn't bothered to go into town for food, and burned occasional pieces of toast which she ate standing at the kitchen counter as she stared at the wind-driven snow that had been falling intermittently since she arrived. She let the machine answer the telephone, and kept the volume at minimum in order not to hear who was calling.

Her isolation was broken by the arrival of the mailman, who trudged up the unshoveled walk from the unplowed driveway with an overnight express letter that required her signature.

"Oughta get that walk cleaned," the man observed, after she'd signed his form. "Someone's gonna go ass over teakettle and sue you good. Wouldn't want that, would you?" He said it pleasantly enough, and she had to agree. After he'd driven off, she put on boots and a jacket and some sheepskin gloves and went out to clear the walk. Two hours later, she parked the shovel beside the front door and came in with her face frozen and her sweater saturated with perspiration. Lighting a cigarette, she remembered the letter, and read it. Then she went to the telephone to call Miles.

"Perhaps," he stormed at her, "you'd be good enough to tell me why you haven't bothered to return my calls. I happen to know you've been there for an entire *week*."

"I didn't have anything to say to you," she replied.

"Oh, lovely! I don't suppose it occurred to you I might have a thing or two to say to you?"

"No, it didn't."

"Dolt!" he said affectionately. "There are several items on the agenda, as fate would have it."

"Miles," she said quietly, "if you want to talk to me,

and you want me to respond, you're going to have to be you, and not my mother. I can tell every time you've been talking to her because you start aping her intonation, her expressions, even her attitudes, until I want to start screaming. It is *not* what I like about you.''

He didn't comment, or argue. He simply took a breath and, in the voice he seemed to reserve solely for use with her on those occasions when she demanded it, said, ''I have to remind you you accepted an advance for a book you haven't delivered. They're getting shirty, insisting they get either a book or their advance returned.''

''I'll send you a check to forward to them. Anything else?''

''You do realize, of course, that it means I have to add back my ten percent?''

''I'll make the check out for the full amount of the advance. What else?''

''No,'' he said rather angrily, ''Just make the check out for the amount you were paid, payable to the agency. I'll have the bookkeeper draw a check for the full amount. Next. You will recall the two gentlemen who took an option on the dramatic rights for *Percival* and subsequently made an outright purchase?''

''I do recall.''

''They have put together a book, complete with music and lyrics. And they have called to ask if you would consider designing the production. They feel since you created Percival, you would be the appropriate party to design the sets, costumes, and what-have-you. May I risk interjecting a personal comment?''

''What?''

''I think you should meet with these people. It might be a project that would interest you. If you're not going to do any more books, this could prove an intriguing new direction. What you're doing isn't healthy, my darling.

You'll lose your tiny marbles if you don't do *something*. And you've nothing to lose by having a lunch or dinner with these people. They're most anxious to have you work with them.''

"I will think about it.''

"To assist your thinking, I'm sending you a copy of their book and a tape of the music. It's great fun, Leigh,'' he said enthusiastically. "I think they may just make it to Broadway.''

"Is there anything else?'' she asked.

"As a matter of fact, yes. I have here a missive from an old friend of yours. I promised to forward it.''

"So, why don't you?''

"Obviously I wasn't about to send along a package insured to the tune of twenty-eight hundred dollars without knowing your precise whereabouts. Also, it came addressed to me with a cover note enclosing cash to pay for the cost of a courier. Furthermore, it would be a waste of everyone's time and money were I to ship this off while you were into playing hermit and refusing to answer doorbells and telephones and the like.''

"Who is it from?'' she asked, curious.

"Doesn't say. Just some initials on the note and an address downtown. Whoever he is, he's been calling the office first thing every morning for the past three days, asking if the package has been forwarded yet. Diane says he's very pleasant, very to the point. He's also, obviously, very persistent. She offered to take his number and let him know when it was on its way to you, but he declined, said something about it being easier for him to call in.''

"Well, I'm here, so you might as well send it along.''

"Will do. For fear of sounding like a nag, may I have your word you'll consider this offer? Or are you trying to tell me our splendid relationship is at an end, and I'll have to make do paying homage to your lovely mum?''

"For the time being, you'll have to make do with Mother. I'll let you know when I plan to be in town. And I will listen to the music and read the book and let you know."

"That's all I ask. I'll send the package off tomorrow morning. Take care of yourself, my darling. I miss your aging little pixie face."

"I'm *so* glad I called," she laughed, and hung up.

Talking to Miles had given her a lift. She was actually hungry, and went to the kitchen to look into the near-empty refrigerator. Time to go buy some food and pick up some newspapers. And perhaps later, after she'd eaten, she'd phone her mother.

His plan worked beautifully. The woman who answered the agency telephone was quick to tell him that the package was sitting right there on her desk, waiting to be picked up by Federal Express. He thanked her, replaced the pay phone receiver and turned to scan the lobby. The first two times he'd called from the apartment. But yesterday and today he'd placed his calls from the lobby. Now all he had to do was wait. He bought a newspaper and positioned himself where he could keep an eye on the building entrance, glancing over at regular intervals until he saw the Federal Express van pull up in front. Then, casually, he refolded the paper, tucked it under his arm, and strolled toward the elevator.

Upon emerging at the right floor, he again opened the newspaper, poked the call button, and waited. The Federal Express man arrived moments later, entered the office, and came out again in not more than a minute with the package in hand. Under the pretext of being so engrossed in his reading that he was unaware of the driver, Daniel collided with the man as they both moved to enter the elevator. The collision was sufficiently forceful to knock the package from the man's hands. Dan at once bent to pick it up and, fumbling both with the newspaper and the package, had enough time to read the address before saying, "My fault. Sorry. Here you go."

Dan smiled ingratiatingly and made a show of folding the paper into a tight tube as they rode back down to the lobby. He told the driver, "Have a nice day," and left the building to return to the apartment in the Village where he looked up the address on the New Canaan map he'd bought. Then he took a taxi to the garage on the pier at West Twenty-first Street to get his car, and had no difficulty finding his way to the private road off Route 124 on the far side of New Canaan. He drove on and parked just past the road—which was really only a very long driveway—to look the place over for a few minutes. Then he turned around and headed back to the city.

She lived on Moonstone Lane, in a house he coveted, with a steeply pitched roof and multipaned windows and a fieldstone chimney. And she now had the diamond pendant he'd wanted her to have. He sang along with the music on a Golden Oldies station he found as he drove, right at the speed limit, toward his evening with his daughter.

Eleven

"Daddy, will you *please* tell me what's going on?"

"Sweetheart"—Dan smiled at her—"I'm just getting rid of the house. I want to find someplace smaller, maybe a little closer to town." His smile held. The sight of his daughter gave him a pleasure so intense it bordered on pain. Everything about her was so cleanly, fragrantly, sweetly young; her eyes were such a perfect blue and so clear; her hair was so glossy and abundant; her skin had such tone, such resilience. She was his baby girl grown quick and slim and strong; she was the infant he'd held in one hand in proud amazement; she was the stocky six-year-old who played the morning glory in the school play; she was the fourteen-year-old whose room had vibrated with bass-heavy rock music; she was the miraculous end product of his encounters with a woman whose strongest emotion, ever, was self-hatred. "You look terrific," he told her.

It was Lane's turn to take a long look at her father. Nothing showed really, but something was definitely wrong. He was different, had changed in ways so subtle she couldn't pinpoint them. Mostly it was just a feeling she had, a nebulous kind of intuition that alarmed her a little. He didn't appear outwardly altered. His clothes were the same kind he'd always worn; nothing new there: a pair of gray flannel slacks, a pale-blue shirt with white collar and cuffs, red tie with pencil-thin diagonal stripes, charcoal cashmere sports jacket. She loved the way he dressed. He looked like a preppy businessman. There was always something he wore that felt great to touch, like his cashmere jacket today, or a camel's hair sweater she borrowed from time to time. She liked the way he smelled, and his skin, like a baby's, so smooth and pink and perfect. Sometimes, just looking at her dad, she'd get so emotional she couldn't talk because she loved him so much, and she knew the kind of grief he'd put up with from her mother for as far back as she could remember. If she'd ever been asked to choose between her parents—which, in a way she had been, but not directly—she'd have picked her father every time because he was so *for* her, so totally on her side in all the matters that really counted. He'd been the one, her whole life, to sit down with her and talk about the important things, her ups and downs, her confusion, was she too fat or too thin, what schools she'd go to, her boyfriends, everything. He was a really nice man, and he'd always shown her how much he cared about her, how much she meant to him. No matter what was happening in the house—he and her mother could be smack in the middle of one of their horrible fights—he never brought any of that stuff into his dealings with her. He'd even tried, loads of times, to explain what made her mother tick and why she acted like such a spaz most of the time. In a way, it was as if the stuff that went on with him and her mother was a kind of coat, and he'd take if off when he was with Lane. Every so often, growing up, she used to think she could see him putting on that coat, getting ready to deal with something else her mother wanted to fight about. And a few times she'd tried to explain to him how it made her feel to see him shrug his way into that ''coat'' in order to deal with her mother, how hurt she felt at seeing how hard it was for him. She'd asked him over and over why they stayed together, why they just didn't get a divorce and be done with it. And every time he'd talked about honoring commitments, about moral obligations, about responsibilities. But she'd never been able to convince him that, from her viewpoint at least, he'd done all those things and then some, and there was no need for him to keep on being honorable and obligated and responsible when it wasn't doing any of them one bit of good. She'd known almost all her life that there was no way to please her mother, so there wasn't much point to trying, and that if she had anything important she'd better take it to her father because important things set her mother off in a major way.

''Why won't you come with us to Florida?'' she asked again. ''You look so tired. You could relax for a couple of weeks and take care of selling the house when you get back.''

''You're such a marshmallow,'' he said fondly, taking her into his arms. ''You've been a big softie since the day you were born. You worry too much. You know that?''

''No, I don't, Daddy. I don't worry about anything else the way I worry about you.''

''That's my point. I'm an old man, Lanie; I've been around a while. I know how to take care of myself. Just you worry about you. You'll have a great time in Florida. They'll spoil you rotten, as usual, and you'll come back with a great tan and twenty-three new boyfriends.''

She laughed and leaned away to look at him. ''You're

not an old man," she said. "I hate it when you talk about yourself that way. Half my friends think you're the most gorgeous thing they've ever seen."

"So how come they're not all calling, asking me out?"

"Come on! You know what I mean."

"Okay. I'm not an old man."

"Tell me about Stanleigh Dunn," she asked eagerly, and saw an amazing change overtake him. He seemed to glow very brightly for a few seconds, like a camera-flash. Then he pulled back, and said, "You'd have liked her, sweetheart."

"Come on," she said, dragging him by the hand over to the sofa. "I want to hear all the details. How old is she?"

"Forty-five."

"Oh! That's pretty old."

Dan laughed. "Trust me. It's not very old. Aren't you the one who just finished telling me I'm not over the hill?"

"I guess. Go on. What else?"

"She's taller than you, maybe five-seven, very thin, auburn hair, green eyes, English accent."

"She's English? I didn't know that."

"Her mother brought her over here when she was twelve."

"That's amazing. What else?"

"You find everything 'amazing,' " he teased.

"Yes, I do. What else?"

"She's got a good sense of humor." He went on describing Leigh, while an internal voice track simultaneously recited for his private benefit details of a more intimate nature. She's got lovely shoulders, a beautifully tapered back, and her breasts are incredibly soft and full; her thighs are long and smooth and rounded just there; and there's a thin scar that starts below her navel and travels down the exact center of her belly, right the way down; when you kiss her at the base of her throat you can hear her breathing change, just the way it does if you stroke the backs of her knees, or run your fingers very lightly down her sides; her eyes freeze to green ice when she comes, but she doesn't make any sound at all.

"I think you're in love with her!" Lane exclaimed with scary incisiveness, nailing his attention flat to the present tense. *"Daddy!"*

He shook his head, quickly trying to shuffle together a suitable argument.

"You *are*!" she insisted. "I can tell! When are you seeing her again? Will I get to meet her? God! Cath will *shit* when I tell her!"

"Lane," he said sternly, "you can't tell anyone, because it's just not true. It's not happening. Sure I liked her, a lot. But that's all there is to it."

He looked so suddenly tired, so terribly worn out, Lane felt afraid again.

"Talk to me," she said quietly. "We've always talked. I'm not a little kid anymore. I'm almost twenty."

He put his arm around her shoulders and drew her against his side. After a time, he smiled and said, "Do you remember that time when you were three?"

"The Jesus story," she said, and smiled, too.

"Your mother had put you down for your nap, and I came to get you a couple of hours later. And while I was getting you dressed, I asked did you have a nice nap? And you said, 'I didn't nap,' and I said, 'Oh, didn't you? What did you do, then, Lanie?' And you said, 'I went to see Jesus.' And I said,' You did, huh? And where did you go to see him?' and you said, 'Heaven,' as if it was the most natural thing in the world. So I said, 'What was heaven like, sweetheart?' and you got this indescribably ecstatic look on your face and said, 'It was like cook-

145

ies.' " He paused and they both laughed. Then he went on. "I said, 'What did you do in heaven, Lanie?' and you said, 'I saw Other Gramma there,' and I said, 'You did? What did you and Other Gramma do?' and you said, 'She gived me ice cream.' And then I said, 'How did you get home, baby girl?' and you said, 'Jesus drived me,' and I said, 'He did, huh? How come he did that?' and you said, 'Because Other Gramma told him to.' " Again they laughed, and his arm was tight around her shoulders. "You've always been the most . . ." He had to stop because he was going to cry.

Lane gave him a minute, then said, "Talk to me, Dad. I can tell this is serious, whatever it is." When he didn't speak, she asked, "Did you spend time with her in London?" He nodded, and she asked, "Did you sleep with her?"

"Lane, I can't *do* this!" he protested.

"I don't see why not. The two of us talked when I started getting serious with Steve. You never once made me feel wrong about it, not the way Mom did. You were the one who got me to go to the Family Planning Clinic; you were the one who discussed the whole abortion issue with me. You're the one I've always come to when something was important. You can trust me, Dad. Maybe I could help."

He withdrew his arm from around her shoulders, and she thought maybe she'd really blown it, trespassed on some kind of parental territorial thing. But he took hold of both her hands and shifted around so he was facing her; he kept his eyes down, looking at her hands. "There are problems," he admitted. "She's married. It sounds like a lousy marriage, but she's married." He finally met her eyes as he went on to tell her some of the lies he'd told Leigh.

"*Why* would you *tell* her stuff like that, Dad?" she asked, flustered.

"I honestly don't know why," he confessed. "I was afraid, I guess. *I don't know*. It doesn't matter anyway. She's married."

"Shit!" she said softly, trying to piece it together. "You actually told her Grandmother had been a *model*, and Grandfather was a *professor*?" She began to laugh. "God, wouldn't they just freak if they knew? It's kind of perfect, in a way. I mean, if I didn't know them, I'd guess maybe Grandmother had had that kind of an exotic past. She has that sort of look. But a professor? That's really reaching, especially the way Grandfather dresses." Her amusement ebbing, she asked, "What are you going to do?"

"Nothing. Not a thing. We met; we spent some time together; it was anything but dull; it's over, and that's that. I want to get the house sold. Once that's out of the way, I'll start thinking about what I want to do with the rest of my life. As for Palm Beach, I'm not in the mood for it, Lane; the cocktail parties every night, the seniors' tennis matches, that whole scene. You don't really mind if I don't come, do you?"

"As long as you're not pissed off with me for wrecking your plans. It's just that I thought about it, Dad, and I really felt I should go with them. They're getting so old, and if I don't take the chance to be with them when I can, I know I'll be sorry later on, when they're not around anymore."

"You're a nice person, Lane," he told her. "I really like the hell out of you."

"Me too you, Daddy," she said, and hugged him hard, worried.

Leigh sat down at the kitchen table with a cup of instant coffee and a cigarette, to examine the package before opening it. Inside was a heavy gold open-ended circle, and affixed to the lower part of the curve, held securely in wide gold claws, was a brilliant-cut half-carat diamond. The pendant was suspended from an unusual gold chain that was heavy and smooth and somehow liquid to the touch. She sat looking at the necklace for quite some time, experiencing a strong, visceral response to its beauty.

The letter read: "Leigh, I know we promised not to be in touch, but I wanted you to have this. I saw it and knew it was for you, that I had to give it to you. The address on the package doesn't exist. It's just some numbers I put there to keep the post office people happy. If you really can't keep it, if it really compromises you, call me at this number, and I'll relieve you of it. I hope you'll want to keep it. I've been thinking a lot about you. All my best, Dan."

Her first instinct was to call and get an address from him so she could return the gift. But her hand didn't seem to want to relinquish its hold on the necklace. And even though she looked over at the telephone on the counter, she knew she wasn't going to call him. At least not about returning the pendant. She wished he hadn't given his number. She could see herself pushing the touch-tone buttons on the telephone face that would connect her with him. To ward off any possibility of this happening, she brought the phone over to the table and called her mother. It had been ten days, time enough.

"Are you still not talking to me?" she asked.

"What sort of condition are you in?" Marietta countered in a voice that said her hair was pinned into place and she was dressed in one of her "working outfits," a simple, belted dress of some lightweight fabric.

"I'm hungry, sober, and sorrier than I can say. If I

drive into town, will you let me take you to dinner? Your choice, anywhere you like.''

"Miles informs me you're returning your advance. Why would you do a thing like that, Stanleigh?''

"Miles shouldn't be representing both of us, as I've said several thousand times before. He loves gossip too much to be completely fair to either of us.''

"You're not answering the question,'' Marietta reminded her.

"Mother, I have no ambition left, no incentive, and nothing I want to say in an illustration. Why can't you accept that it's over? There aren't going to be any more books.''

"It's a sin to waste talent,'' her mother said very seriously. "You don't have the right to abandon a God-given gift. When I think of all you could still do, it's enough to make me weep.''

"Will you let me take you out to dinner tonight?''

"Not tonight, darling, I'm seeing Laurence. Suffice it to say, he has no desire to come anywhere near this apartment at the moment. I'm having to work rather hard to build back his confidence.''

Her mother had called her darling; Leigh knew they were past the worst part. Relieved and grateful, she said, "Tomorrow, then. Or are you booked up for tomorrow; too?''

"Tomorrow will be fine. I'm giving the girls a half-day to do some Christmas shopping. You do plan to be here Christmas?''

Leigh hadn't given it any thought, but quickly said, "Of course.''

"Good. I'm dictating now, Leigh. I'll expect you at six-thirty tomorrow. We'll have a drink before we go out. I'm encouraged to hear your appetite's returned. You've gone gaunt, and it is not you at your best. Tomorrow, darling,'' she said, and ended the call.

While Leigh was filling her shopping cart at Walter Stewart's Market, her fingers toyed with the pendant. When she caught herself doing it, she'd stop. Then two minutes later, she'd be doing it again. She couldn't seem to help herself. Daniel Godard was sufficiently interested in her to go to a great deal of trouble to send her an exquisite, expensive gift. He was willing to take risks— or so he thought—to convey to her his thoughts. And she was impressed.

By the time she'd returned home, put away the groceries, and started preparing a casserole of chicken and braised vegetables, she was holding imaginary conversations with him on the telephone. It was almost too easy to picture herself saying in a low voice into the receiver all she'd been unable to confide yet to anyone else.

Daniel, every time I think about it, they die again. Carl and Stephen and Joel, they keep dying, over and over, and the pain is engulfing. It swamps my senses so that when I open my eyes all I see is the blank gray landscape of infinity; all I taste in my mouth is the fineblown sour ash from the chimneys; I can smell nothing else, feel nothing else, think of nothing else but their deaths. For moments here and there, I forget—I did with you—then I suffocate with guilt at having abandoned them.

She wanted to say, Daniel, I don't know why I'm alive and they're not; I don't know the purpose, and yet I keep on living. Why do you suppose that is? Does it make any kind of sense to you? It doesn't to me. I tell myself I'm alive, and therefore I should attempt to work out some sort of future for myself because if you're alive it's what you're expected to do. It's what my mother expects, and Miles. Everyone becomes very impatient with you if you grieve too long, or too visibly, if you don't ''snap out of it" the way they'd like you to and stop embarrassing everyone with your ungovernable sense of loss and longing.

She thought she'd say, Daniel, I keep thinking of how good it felt to hold you, be held by you. It surprised me. You put your arms around me, and you seemed so very solid. Lately, I expect people to evaporate when I go to hold them; no one appears to me to have any density. But you did. I can still feel you solid in my mind. The touching, joining, was really very good. But best of all was both of us standing fully dressed and having you hold me. You seemed so glad of the shape and size of me, the *me* of me. Was it illusion?

Had it been real? she wondered. Or was she now, and had she then, been embellishing reality, decorating it with her need?

The telephone rang and he snatched it up, fumbling the receiver to his ear.

"Daniel," she said, "it's such an exquisite thing I haven't the heart to refuse it. But I do wish you hadn't done this."

"No hello?" he said jovially, elated because she'd called as he'd known she would. "No 'is that you'? No 'how are you'? Just a reprimand and a backhanded thank-you?"

"I'm sorry." Her voice was pitched so low he could scarcely hear her. He thought her husband must be close by, so she was keeping her voice down. "How are you?" she asked politely.

"I'm a hell of a lot better than I was five minutes ago. I'm glad you called. I was hoping you would."

"You *knew* I would. I was taught always to be mannerly. It's very beautiful, thank you very much. If there'd been a return address, I would have sent it back to you."

"I guessed that, which is why I did it that way. How

are you, Leigh? Did you see your father? How did it go?'' It gave him such a good feeling to know details, facts, about her life.

"I'm fine. Look,'' she said, breaking the rules without having known she would. "I'm coming into the city tomorrow. I could meet you for coffee.''

"Where, when?''

She couldn't think how to answer. "It's a problem,'' she said.

"I understand.'' He figured she was referring to her goddamned husband. "You could come . . . no. Hell! Wait a minute.'' He paused in order to give the impression that the number she'd called him on wasn't located at the place where he intended them to meet. He wanted her to think he, too, was taking risks and making special arrangements to accommodate her. "We could meet in the Village,'' he said, looking around the room. "A friend of mine has a place. I've been keeping an eye on it for him. I stay there sometimes when it's too late to catch the last train.'' That sounded right, he thought.

"I don't know,'' she hesitated. "I won't have much time. I'm sorry to be so dithery, especially during office hours.''

He was very pleased. She'd assumed, as he'd hoped, that she'd reached him on a direct line at his office. "I make great coffee,'' he told her. "We can sit on my friend's only two chairs, have some coffee, and talk.''

"You know talking isn't what you have in mind.''

"Let me give you the address.''

"All right. But I really won't be able to stay long. I have a number of errands, then I'm meeting my mother for dinner. Hold on while I find something to write with.''

He waited, his eyes now on the bed. He'd change the sheets. And maybe, if there was time in the morning, he'd buy a few things to brighten the place up—some flowers, a framed poster, a small rug for the floor.

"Okay. Give me the address."

He gave it to her, then said, "I just knew you'd like the necklace."

"You were right. I do. I could be there by one. How is that for you?"

"Fine, perfect. I have an early meeting, then I'll go directly to the apartment."

She said goodbye, and he put the receiver down gently, as if the instrument actually contained her.

Twelve

He was waiting on the landing, the door to the apartment open behind him. When she got to the top of the stairs he held out his arms, and she walked directly into the circle of his embrace, surrendering to sensation. The world could have stopped right then and she'd have just kept her eyes closed so she wouldn't have to see it go. From the intensity of his embrace and the length of time it was lasting, it seemed he felt the same way. Seconds ticked off an unseen clock while she breathed in his cologne, the scent she remembered, and gave in to small waking dreams with her head against his shoulder, their bodies a single, unmoving line that might be broken only by some ferocious act of nature—volcanic eruption, typhoon—something immense and beyond human control.

He became aware of an insistent little noise behind him inside the apartment and realized it was boiling water splashing over the sides of the pot and hitting the burner.

"The water's boiling over," he said, unwilling to release her. "The water will douse the fire, but the gas'll keep escaping and a couple of days from now when I wake up and strike a match to light a cigarette I'll blow me and everybody else in the building to kingdom come.''

"I suppose you'll have to turn it off," she said drowsily, opening her eyes.

"Still, it'll take quite a while for enough gas to accumulate, what with the door being open and so forth."

"Well, that's all right, then."

"The smell of gas is pretty terrible, though. And the neighbors might complain."

She slid away, saying, "I've been told you make great coffee," and wondered how she could sound so at ease when her mouth was dry and her knees were rubbery.

He allowed her to go ahead of him into the apartment, then went to the stove to fix the coffee, watching as she looked around and then, keeping her coat on, sat down in one of the chairs at the stripped-oak table. She lit a cigarette as he poured the last of the water into the filter and turned to find her eyes on him, the fingers of her left hand toying with the pendant. It caused a quickening inside him, as if her hand were on him.

"Wouldn't you like to take off your coat?" he asked, hand outheld to take it from her.

She stared at him as if the question made no sense. Then she shrugged off the mink, letting it fall over the back of the chair. She was wearing smartly cut black trousers, a white silk blouse with black piping around the collar and cuffs, and a pair of flat-heeled black leather boots. "Whose apartment is this?" she asked.

"A friend's," he answered, returning to the stove to pour the coffee.

"Your friend," she observed, looking around, "obviously doesn't live here. I suspect he brings his lady friends here."

Dan laughed as he put a cup down on the table in front of her before sitting opposite.

"Maybe so," he said. "I've never asked. It's handy, and he doesn't use it very often."

"I quite like it," she said, still turned away. "Minimalist style. I've thought for years I'd like to live with tatami mats and pebbles, several meaningful plants." When she faced him again, she was smiling, holding the cigarette to her mouth. "I shouldn't be here."

"Sure you should."

"No, I shouldn't. And how did you manage to steal time away in the middle of the day?"

"That was my last official buying trip I was on," he explained. "I'm now semiretired, or unofficially retired. Something. I've got more free time than I know what to do with. What kind of lies did you have to tell?"

"Nonspecific ones," she answered, trying the coffee. "This *is* good."

"Godards never misrepresent." *We may lie from time to time, exercise evasive tactics, but we never wrongly present ourselves. Except inadvertently, at times when there's only uncertainty.*

"We're not going to make a habit of this, Daniel."

"Of what? Meeting to drink coffee?"

"Of meeting, period. It could create serious problems for both of us. I don't like the feeling I get, sneaking around . . . making complicated arrangements."

"I kind of enjoyed it myself," he said, tilting his chair so that his weight was balancing on the two rear legs. "Danger gets the old adrenaline pumping."

She looked at him, trying to see if he could possibly be serious. "You don't mean that," she said. "You're just as nervous as I am about this." Again, she looked around.

"All right, I am."

To her relief, he brought his chair forward so all four legs were once more on the floor. It reminded her of the way Stephen had liked to defy gravity, sitting tilted in chairs so that whenever she caught him at it, her heart thumped unpleasantly and she had to ask him please not to do it, fearful he'd tip over backward and be hurt.

She pushed back her cuff to look at the time. One-twelve. Somehow they'd already used up twelve minutes. She still had shopping to do, gifts to find for her mother and for Miles, and something to offer as an apology to Laurence. She hadn't even gone up to her apartment but had merely parked the car in the basement garage before coming directly down here in a taxi. She was here, and it wasn't going at all as she'd thought it might. For one thing, it was broad daylight; sun flooding through the gate-covered windows turned the far end of the empty living room into white, mote-filled amorphousness. She wondered if the bedroom also suffered from such an un-kind deluge of light. If she went in there to discover more of that same harsh illumination she knew she'd keep her clothes on. It was impossible to pretend, or to hide any-thing, in bright light.

"Is it dark in the bedroom?" she asked, taking time putting out her cigarette, in order not to have to see his reaction.

"Dark? I don't know." He got up and walked over to the bedroom doorway and said, "I guess it is pretty dark. This room has vertical blinds. Not much else, but it has vertical blinds."

"Good," she said, and brushed past him into the room.

He hadn't heard her move, but all at once she wasn't out there anymore but inside over here, undoing the but-tons on her cuffs.

"We don't have very much time," she told him, pulling the shirttails free of her trousers.

"No," he agreed numbly, unable to understand why he couldn't ever seem to control the flow of events when he was with her. Somehow, each time, it was she who set things in motion. The strange part was he didn't mind at all. In fact, it pleased him that she was so in charge of her desire and priorities. But her being rather businesslike now did bother him just a little.

He was still standing in the doorway and, seeing this, she became doubtful. "No?" she asked, stopping with her shirt half off one shoulder. "A change of mind?"

He shook his head and went to put his arms around her. "I don't know why it is," he said, his lips against her soft, cropped hair, "but every so often you make me feel so goddamned sad. I care about you. I'm sorry this feels sneaky and complicated. I didn't think about any of that. Knowing you feel that way makes me feel lousy."

"Don't go overboard," she said lightly. "It's not my first trip away from home."

Now he went from feeling sad to laughing. "Know what I think?" he said. "I think we're both a little crazy."

"My mother would be the first to agree with you. We're having trouble again getting started."

"D'you know, I was so busy thinking about you all the way back from Hong Kong that a good half the time I forgot to be afraid? I was actually in the baggage claim at Kennedy when I realized that."

"You shouldn't be thinking about me, Daniel. This really isn't going anywhere."

"Do you have complete control over what you think?" he asked. "It's pretty good, if you do. I haven't figured out yet how to do that. And why do you keep warning me? It's not necessary. But situations have been known to change."

They were going to use up all their time talking. If they talked too much, he'd become too familiar to her, she'd begin developing frames of reference for him, and he'd start spreading through her life like water. She looked down, fitting together the sides of her shirt.

"Don't give up so easily." He put his hands over hers. "Maybe I'm just a slow starter. And the time constraints are pretty inhibiting. Are you going away for Christmas?" He needed to talk with her; they couldn't just lie down together without first having some conversation. Without an exchange of words, it felt too much like a business deal, as if this was her way of thanking him for the gift.

"No. It's a family affair. Are you?"

"I was supposed to be taking Lane . . . our plans got changed." He didn't want her to think he was without options. "Everyone's going to Palm Beach. My parents have a condo there." Maybe he'd go after all, he thought.

"When do you leave?" she asked.

"I'm not sure. The plan is I'll fly down to join them. When hasn't been decided yet." He was intentionally keeping everything vague.

Talking, and more talking. Either they'd go back to the table, drink their coffee and talk, or they'd get on with this. She put her hands on the sides of his face and kissed him, hoping to get him started. She succeeded. He flew into action, taking her out of her clothes as if he were unwrapping a gift someone had unexpectedly given him. He murmured approving sounds as he stripped away her clothes.

I'm too old for this, she thought. I really am too old for games of any nature; and this is just another, somewhat better game. But Christ! He was, as before, making love to her as if it were his first and last time. And she was reacting like dry tinder held to a match, limbs curling, charred, the heat yielding moisture. How could she be concerned with how it might look, when his burrowing fingers and pretty mouth made her squirm and, responding, reach to stroke him? How could she care about anything more than each moment's heightening liquid pleasure? She wanted to open her mouth and devour him whole, nibbling away at different parts of him until she contained him completely. There was always confirmation, reaffirmation—regardless of how temporary—in the proof of a man's response to her. And here it was. She could shape it with her hands, treasure and nurture it, and, finally, hide it deep within the vault of her body.

There was a moment when, his hands guiding her hips as she sat above him, she thought of how she'd seen her mother doing precisely this, and the shock she'd felt at inadvertently encroaching on her mother's cherished privacy. God, the horror of what she'd done! she thought, losing the rhythm. To be caught in an act as arcane and wanton as this was unthinkable. That moment would exist, standing between her and her mother for the rest of their lives. And it needn't have been that way. All she'd had to do was back away, never letting on that she'd seen. But she hadn't done that. She'd taken what she'd seen and beat her mother over the head with it. Christ!

"What's wrong?" Daniel asked, his hands steady on her hips. "Something's wrong," he decided without awaiting her answer. "Is it me?" he wondered aloud, worried. "I don't know what's what anymore. If it's me, for chrissake, say so! I don't want to go charging ahead, playing blind man. I hate people who do that."

She came forward over him, looping her arm under his head. "Daniel," she said against his neck, "it has nothing to do with you. I just lost it for a moment, that's all. Men lose erections all the time."

"Usually because they start thinking. Thinking and sex don't seem to be compatible. I know how that goes."

"Don't you lose it, too."

They rearranged themselves, and she urged him down upon her. He was heavy. Her bones seemed to creak audibly as she tightened her knees, lifting to recreate their rhythm. Locked into silence again, she sought his mouth, her hands on him, guiding. But it was no good. She really had lost it, although the motions were pleasurable, and she encouraged him, watching as if from a distance the changes that overcame him as he got caught at the last in that final, frantic little race out of himself.

When they were dressing, he suddenly stopped her, sat her on the end of the bed, looked for a long moment into her eyes, then pushed open her thighs and dropped to his knees on the floor. His eyes still on hers, he began teasing her with his fingers, watching until she lost her focus and her eyes grew heavy-lidded. Then his hands went under her and he held her to his mouth.

He went on with it until she was no one, nothing, just a quivering parcel of pure reaction. And she wanted to savor the moment, the piercing perfection of it, but he wasn't allowing it. He continued to hold her, going on and on until it was no longer pleasure but a kind of maddening irritation, and when he gave no indication he'd ever stop, when it seemed he intended to go on and on with this, she became frightened, emitting a small scream as she frantically pushed him away, crying, "Stop! Daniel, *stop!*"

And he stopped, but continued to hold her—his hands fastened to the undersides of her thighs in such a punishing grip she was sure there'd be bruises—until the visible heat left her face and chest. Then he put his head in her lap, and she gazed down at him fearfully, whispering, "We can't do this again. We just can't." She felt afraid, didn't want to say or do anything that might provoke him, because he'd seemed as if he'd wanted to burrow his way into the core of her being. But surely, she told herself, she was misinterpreting. She bent over him for a long moment, shielding him with her body, so he could hear the antic beating of her heart and feel the panic in her hands. then, abruptly, she sat up, saying, "I have to go!" and pulled on her clothes, rushing here and there in the room, gathering up her things.

"You could use the bathroom, the shower, if you like," he said, in his trousers and unbuttoned shirt, following her to the living room where she snatched her coat from the chair and pulled it on.

"No," she said. "There isn't time. I really must go. Listen to me, Daniel! I can't see you again. This . . . it can't come to anything."

"You don't know that," he began.

"Yes, I *do* know that. I don't know about your reasons, and I don't want you to tell me because I have no intention of telling you mine. You must take my word, believe that there *are* reasons, and I can't see you anymore."

He didn't believe her. He knew all he had to do was take hold of her and he'd be able to change her mind. He did it now: he took hold of her, and kissed her mouth, then said, "I'd be willing to change things."

"Don't! I'm not capable of changing anything. You've had as much as I can offer anyone." Trying to lighten the atmosphere, she threw in, "There's less to me than meets the eye," and gave him a smile.

"I'm in love with you, Leigh. And I don't give up that easily."

She was becoming frightened again. Not only was he refusing to hear what she was saying but very possibly he *couldn't* hear what she was saying, because he was deafened by the noise of his own arguments. "Give it up! Please! I'm *not* in love with you."

"Then why did you meet me here today?"

"Because I wanted to go to bed with you. What does love have to do with it?"

"Not a thing. Nothing. I'm a jerk, that's all. I know you have to go. It's okay."

He was hurt, and she hated it. *"Daniel!"* she cried.

"Don't try to blackmail me! You're no more in a position to be in love with me than I am with you. My husband, your wife. Remember?"

"Yup. Nothing wrong with the old brain cells. Memory's intact. The Good Doctor. How is he anyway?"

"I'm going." She started toward the door.

"Leigh?"

"What?"

"I don't think I can give you up all that easily. And I don't think I believe you."

"What? What don't you believe?"

"I think you feel it, too."

"Let me tell you something!" she said hotly. "This is an old, old song, and I know the lyrics to every verse. I can sing it backward and in my sleep. In six months you'll have trouble remembering my name. And if you do remember it, it'll be because you happen to be passing the children's department in some bookstore that has a backlist. After the first rush, when it all dies down, you find out you can't stand the sight of each other, you've got nothing to say, and you start thinking about ways to get out of it. Let it go, Daniel." She gentled her tone. "You're very unhappy just now. I can tell, and I'm sorry. Go home to your family, and let me get on with my life." Again she said, "I really am sorry," then opened the door, and left.

He came out onto the landing as she was going down the stairs. "Merry Christmas, Leigh," he called down to her, leaning over the banister so she had to stop and look up at him.

"Oh, hell!" she laughed. "You're incorrigible."

"Probably."

"Merry Christmas, Daniel." She shook her head, then continued on down the stairs.

In the space of a split second, he decided he simply had

to know where she was going. He tore back inside, threw on a coat, pushed his feet into boots, grabbed his wallet and keys, and was out of the apartment and flying down the stairs all in the space of less than two minutes. As he ran he prayed he hadn't taken too long. He hit the street and saw she was just turning the corner onto Fifth Avenue. In a burst of speed, he raced up the street, arriving at the corner in time to see a taxi stop for her. Feeling panicky at the thought of losing her, he leaped into the road, waving his arms to attract the attention of a cab just approaching. The car stopped, Dan jumped into the rear, and told the driver, *"Follow that cab up ahead!"*

"You're kidding!" The driver craned around to look at him.

"I'm not fucking kidding! Keep up with that cab and I'll give you twenty over the meter!"

"You're on!"

His luck held. Leigh's cab hung a left on Eighth Street and another left onto University Place, headed uptown. Riding almost on the bumper of the cab ahead, Dan's driver asked, "Is this Candid goddamned Camera or something?"

"No, no," Dan answered, glad it was a private taxi without the Plexiglas divider. "My wife," he extemporized. "I want to see where she's going."

"Sure." The driver raised his eyebrows, and refrained from further comment.

Leigh emerged from her cab on Park Avenue near Seventy-second Street.

Dan threw thirty dollars at his driver, and climbed out to watch her greet the doorman with a nod as she sailed right inside. This had to be where she lived, Dan reasoned. If it had been her mother's apartment, she wouldn't have made quite the same sort of entrance. How long was she going to stay inside? he wondered, feeling conspicuous. The doorman was giving him the once-over, and anxious not to draw attention to himself, Dan walked past the building to the corner, then crossed to the far side in order to keep an eye on the entrance to Leigh's building.

He walked the length of the block slowly, back and forth, three times before she reappeared. She turned left out of the entrance and started down Park. Keeping half a block behind, he trailed after her, curious to see where she'd go. She cut over to Madison and when she went into a shop, he studied the windows several doors along until she emerged carrying a gift-wrapped package.

She walked, she stopped to enter a total of five shops, and came out each time carrying more packages. She'd been in two antiques shops, a needlepoint place, a jewelry store, and a boutique with handmade lace outfits in the window. He was quite content to shadow her as she headed back to her apartment.

It was four-thirty, he saw, allowing her to get well ahead of him once he'd established she was definitely returning home. He guessed she'd stay inside for a couple of hours before setting out for her mother's. *If* she'd been truthful about her plans for the evening. And what, he thought, if her husband was going to be with her? The last thing Dan wanted was to have to see the Good goddamned Doctor husband. He thought he might be tempted to do something really stupid, like accidentally on purpose bumping into them on the street. No good.

A cab was going past, and he flagged it down. He'd done enough detective work for one day. It was time to go back to the Village, get cleaned up for the final family dinner before Lane and his parents left for Florida. As the cab rocketed down park, he decided he'd have to find out where Leigh's mother lived. If he knew all the addresses, it ought to be possible for him to keep tabs on her whereabouts. Tomorrow, he'd start making inquiries about Marietta Dunne. Right before the holidays would probably be a good time. People weren't so careful at this time of the year.

While he was knotting his tie in front of the bathroom mirror, he had a sudden, alarming, one-step-removed view of his behavior. Jesus Christ! he thought. He was stalking the woman, behaving like one of those psychopaths in thriller novels. No more, he told himself. No harm had been done so far, but if he kept on, letting this thing build into a full-scale obsession . . . no more. And to make sure he couldn't do any more of it, he went directly to the telephone to book a seat on the flight with Lane and his parents. He read out his American Express number, was told to pick up the ticket an hour before the flight time, wished a Merry Christmas, and thanked for flying American.

He didn't want to do it; he wanted to stay in the city in case Leigh changed her mind and called. But he wouldn't. He'd do the sane thing and take her at her word.

He got the tie knotted finally, splashed on some cologne, then went into the bedroom to look at the mess they'd made of the bed. He wanted to lie face down on the sheets and breathe in the smell of her. He *had* to see her again. If he didn't, if she really meant what she'd said, he didn't know what he'd do. The view of the days and weeks ahead with no hope, even of the sight of her, was too devastatingly empty to contemplate.

Thirteen

Leigh picked at the scallops she'd ordered, watching her mother eat with her usual gusto, wondering why this woman's hearty appetites—for food, for men, for life— still impressed her so. Yet each meeting with her mother was like the slight twist of a hugely detailed cyclorama that took a lifetime to view in its entirety. She was never bored in her mother's company, irritated sometimes, intimidated other times, but never bored.

Tonight, Marietta was wearing a wonderful dress of buttercup-yellow heavy silk, with a slashed neckline that offered a tantalizing view of her flawless décolletage. The dress was a minor masterpiece of design, with every last detail lovingly hand-finished. The column of Marietta's neck rose like some exotic stalk, offering itself in all its bared vulnerability to anyone who cared to look. Her hair was twisted into a careless topknot, with wisps escaping down the back of her neck: commas of flame along her ivory nape. The woman composed herself each day like a superb collage, with surprising points of interest here and there: a delicate gold chain with a dainty emerald-

and-diamond pendant; a pearl dinner ring; clear lacquer on her nails; transparent gloss on her lips; tiny pearl earrings.

"You look heavenly," Leigh complimented her.

"Thank you. You're not eating. Is it not to your liking? We could send it back." Her hand was poised to beckon the waiter. Regardless of who might have arranged a dinner and intended paying for it, somehow Marietta was always the one to whom restaurant staff looked for direction.

"It's all right. I want to tell you something."

"Tell me anything you like. Just, please, don't light another cigarette until I've finished my dinner. It's rather too much like having one's food served on a much-used ashtray. What have you been up to?" she asked.

"It's the one from London," Leigh said. "He's married. I don't know why I agreed to meet him."

"You *do* manage to get yourself into things, don't you? Could this possibly have anything to do with your execrable behavior last week?"

"No, not really. Sometimes, when I have a bad dream or I'm afraid, I wish I was a child again, so I could come sleep with you in your bed the way I used to. I get so tired sometimes, of being an adult."

The waiter came to top off their wineglasses. Marietta gave him a smile and the swarthy man blossomed into well-being like time-lapse photography of a seedling shooting through its developmental stages. He moved away, dazzled. Marietta put down her knife and fork to take a sip of wine before saying, "Everyone feels that way from time to time, Stanleigh. I think one especially feels it when someone you love dies."

"They never feel that way in your books."

"Oh, don't be tiresome. We've been doing so well this evening. I know the contempt you have for my work, but

I make no attempt to write about adults. My girls," she said, as if speaking of real people, "are children; they have no pretensions to maturity. That is what makes them so delightful. Every emotion they feel is new; every day is an adventure."

"Even children aren't that naive."

"You think not? My forty-five-year-old child often seems that naive." Marietta sniffed.

"I am at times," Leigh conceded surprisingly, so that her mother regarded her with interest as she popped the last piece of veal into her mouth, then aligned her knife and fork in the center of her plate.

"You may smoke now, if you wish. And perhaps you'll tell me what's happened."

Leigh toyed with her lighter. "It's not that anything's actually happened. I just think I was unwise. Anyway, I told him I wouldn't see him again."

"So what is it that bothers you?"

"Does it ever seem to you," Leigh asked her, "that no one is what he appears to be? I mean, lately I've had the feeling that there's almost nothing that is the way it seems."

"Leigh," her mother began, but was interrupted by the return of the waiter.

"You would have coffee, dessert, Madame?"

Marietta encouraged his recitation of the desserts. Then she wanted to see the dessert cart. The happy little Italian wheeled it over and lovingly pointed out the crème brûlée, the chocolate mousse, the fresh raspberries, the gateaux, the napoleons, the eclairs with mocha cream, and the English trifle. Marietta settled on the crème brûlée topped with the fresh raspberries. The waiter was only slightly crestfallen when Leigh asked just for a double espresso. Marietta's request for cappuccino, however, returned him to his previous ecstasy. He buried the crème brûlée in raspberries, set the overspilling plate before Marietta, then rushed off to the espresso machine.

"He's in love with you," Leigh said with a grin, lighting a cigarette. "You're a shameless vixen."

Marietta flushed with pleasure. "Not shameless," she qualified. "But men do like me. And I do enjoy the attention." Happily, she gazed around. Then, becoming serious again, she dropped her voice, asking, "How *could* you do that, Stanleigh? What were you thinking of? I've gone past being angry with you. But I do feel . . . separated from myself, in a fashion. I thought we understood one another. You were so het up, so enraged. Yet you seemed so very unconcerned with the possibility that *I* might hate *you*. And I did, you know. For a short time, I felt I might never be able to look at you again for creating that vision of me and then forcing it under my nose. How could I be anything but repelled? I know I'm no longer young. I know I must appear ridiculous to you. But I did believe you cared more for me than that. Every morning now, when I'm readying myself for the day, I wonder if I am as ridiculous as you made me feel."

"You could *never* be ridiculous!" Leigh insisted, more ashamed than before. "*I* am, but you could never be. Maybe you were right, maybe I shouldn't have gone to see my father. I don't know. He was very sweet . . . very truthful about what had happened and his feelings. The thing of it is, I believe what you say as well. So, what's true, then? That's what I can't determine."

"Leigh," her mother said quietly, "what I believed to be right at the time may only have been right from my viewpoint."

"What does that mean?"

"Oh," her mother sighed, "I suppose it means that looking at it from your point of view it may well have been a mistake. We all of us make them. If it was a mistake, it wasn't one I made intending to do you any harm."

"I've never thought that was your intention. But I embarrassed you, and Laurence, for no good reason. I love you so much. After the accident, after Carl and Stephen died, I was terrified that something would happen to you, and then I'd have no one. Then, these past three years, with Joel, it's been the same thing all over again. You were my trump card, you were the one who'd be there. When we had that scene the other week, when I went to the country to hide, the only thing I could think, over and over, was that I'd put you in jeopardy somehow. I'd done something so dreadful, and I thought perhaps I'd be the one responsible for losing you. I need you to be alive and well in the world. What I'm having trouble with is caring about being alive and well myself."

"This is frightening," Marietta said, low. "I really don't want to hear you talk this way, Stanleigh."

"Please just forgive me. I'd rather hurt myself than hurt you."

"*I* would rather you didn't hurt either one of us."

The waiter delivered the double espresso and the cappuccino, saw he wasn't going to be rewarded with one of Marietta's smiles, and busied himself relocating the dessert cart.

"I know that," Leigh said, after he'd gone. "I was feeling sorry for the someone I was thirty years ago, and sorry because, no matter how badly I wanted it, nothing I could do would keep Joel alive. But in the past ten days, I've been thinking things through, wondering if it was unfair of me to depend on Joel the way I did."

"I don't think you were dependent upon him," Marietta disagreed.

"To the extent that I wanted to keep him in my life, I was. There isn't anything really wrong with that, is there?'' she asked unhappily. "Is there? I didn't plan my life around him. I didn't keep everything on hold until I knew I'd be seeing him. It was just that I loved him so . . ." She cleared her throat and fiddled for a moment with the coffee spoon.

Marietta looked at her daughter, all at once more afraid for her than she'd been at the height of Leigh's wild behavior. "I wish," she said, "you could see yourself just once, just for a few minutes, as other people see you. You have *everything* to recommend you, but because of your misfortunes you see yourself as a failure. It's very sad, and it's very wrong. I'm your *mother*, Leigh. Don't you know how much I want you to be happy, to have people and things in your life you care about? Don't you know that my one, true fear is that I'd lose you? If I was wrong in what I did, I'm sorry. But it was such a long, long time ago, and you've managed to live through all these years without your father. If you've established a rapport with him, and it gives you satisfaction, then I can only be glad for you. But you really must get back into the world. You've got to pick up and keep going. I meant what I said: it is a sin to waste a talent like yours. And consider this: work could take your mind off everything.''

Leigh shook her head. "It isn't the panacea for me that it is for you. And I'm definitely not in the right frame of mind for painting optimistic visions of fantasy worlds.''

"Then try something else," Marietta counseled. "Why not consider designing the production for *Percival*? You *have* to do *something*! You must!''

Leigh stared at her mother for a long moment, seeing that Marietta was deeply, visibly, frightened for her. It shocked her to such an extent that she knew, in that moment, she was going to have to make every effort to reconstruct her life if only to please her mother. "Marietta," she said with a smile, "my lovely mum. Do you know that when I was little I used to tell my friends you were a princess?" She laughed softly, with welling affection. "I did. I told them you had magical powers and could cast spells. I used to go creeping with them into your bedroom to show them your closet, with all your magical gowns and dancing slippers. They believed me, too. I'm better now," she said, suddenly, surprised. "I am. It feels as if the cloud is passing. Perhaps," she said, tilting her head to one side, still smiling, "you really can do magic."

The balmy weather and humid air made him very aware of a deepening depression he hadn't acknowledged until his arrival in Florida. The only consolation he had resided in the small pocket diary he carried with him everywhere that had Leigh's Manhattan and Connecticut addresses, as well as that of her agent. Several times in the course of a day, he'd flip through the pages, find where he'd written these entries, and gaze at his own tidy printing, lifted just by the sight of her name. It felt as if his knowledge of these two places were something singular and esoteric. He would read her name, look at the street numbers, and feel linked to her.

In his more rational moments—while he sat on a bench with his mother watching his father and Lane play tennis—he told himself he was in trouble, that if he didn't take some decisive, positive position, he'd wind up in a place from which there might be no exit. He reminded himself constantly of all the things he'd done over the years that had been good, selfless, and beyond the call of duty. But he'd get a long-distance call from the Bedford real estate agent with a too-low offer on the house, and whatever morale building he'd done for himself would dissolve. He was having difficulty concentrating on the dinner table conversations that took place each evening; he was struggling every morning with the question of why he should bother to climb out of the guest room bed, put on clothes, and fake his way through another twelve or fourteen hours. He wasn't sleeping well, and awakened three and four and five times a night to tiptoe through the silent apartment to sit out on the balcony, smoking a cigarette and blinking at the night sky, while his insides churned and his brain tripped over itself with colliding thoughts.

At last, he got some stationery and sat down on the beach to write to Leigh. He knew he'd never be able to send the letter because in it he told the complete truth. He told her about Celeste, and Lane; he told her in detail about his mother and father, who after forty-six years of marriage were still in love and still relished each other's company; he told her about how it felt as if his balls had been cut off since he'd sold the company that he'd worked so long and hard to build; he told her that meeting her had been the single most encouraging event in his life in such a long time that he wasn't sure if he knew anymore how to respond to anything encouraging. He told her just about everything and, in the process, covered nearly twenty pages with his closely written script. And when he'd finished, he sat with his arms folded over his knees and gazed out at the foamy surf wishing he'd told her the truth in the first place. But it was too late now to change that.

After a time he scooped out a shallow pit in the sand, threw in the letter and set it on fire. Then he buried the ashes of his confession with sand and got up to go back to his parents and his daughter, knowing he couldn't have told Leigh the truth because he was too goddamned frightened of ever again trusting anyone the way he'd trusted Celeste. He'd always known it was risky, given her penchant for senseless rebellion, her inability to find happiness and sustain it, but he'd gone ahead and trusted her anyway, because she was, after all, his wife and the mother of their child. And he'd loved her. Jesus Christ! he thought, trudging along the beach. If you weren't very fucking careful, love could kill you.

His mother asked if he'd drive her around while she did some shopping, and he agreed, sufficiently distracted not to suspect her of ulterior motives.

They hadn't been in the car two minutes when she said, "Daniel, I think you must talk to me. You are not yourself."

He looked over at this woman, this person who'd always been in his life, and it was as if he'd never seen her before. Petite, dark-haired, wide-eyed; there was a furrow between her eyes, a downturning to her mouth. He thought the frown unbecoming; if she'd only smile she'd be quite beautiful. Then recognition kicked in, she was familiar again, and her expression was a warning to him that he hadn't been doing nearly as successful a job as he'd thought in concealing his anxiety.

He couldn't think of anything to say, and his mother waited until, at last, he admitted to her some of the things that had been troubling him. She listened thoughtfully, interrupting only to suggest a parking spot, and went on listening after Daniel had turned off the engine and sat with his hands gripping the steering wheel, staring straight ahead as the words gushed out of his mouth.

When he got to the end, his mother took a slow, deep breath and said, "I think two things, Daniel. I think first you should discuss these matters with your father. He understands more than you know. And I think secondly you must take your profits and start another business. Find something that has appeal and begin again. You are still a young man, and you have never been someone who could be content being idle.''

"Oh, Christ, Mama! What the hell would I do?"

"Perhaps something different," she suggested. "You are not without resources, and you have an opportunity few are offered. Make a new start with a new enterprise. You *need* to *work*. If you spend all your days and nights thinking only of the past you will drive yourself mad.''

"Maybe you're right," he said, letting go of the steering wheel and turning to look at her. "I'll give it some thought.''

"And talk with your father, Daniel. Don't forget, he too had to begin again. Not perhaps at your age, but a beginning is a beginning.''

He looked again at this woman, marveling at her composure and wisdom. She was the one who'd always taken a hard line with him, insisting he be self-reliant and resourceful, while his father had been the one to philosophize about the vicissitudes of life. Yet it was his father who'd gone into the business world to grapple with the ups and downs of money markets, foreign bankers, devalued currencies, inflated yen, trend-setting deutschmarks, Dow-Jones averages, Standard & Poor's indexes, and the power of the U.S. dollar. Privately, Dan had always believed that his mother, behind their closed bedroom door, had advised his father on every last deal he'd ever made. She might have been fashionable, sociable, and outwardly interested in little more than shopping, but she was also alert, informed, and, above all, vigilantly aware of everything going on around her. Nothing escaped her notice. And he wondered now why he'd thought she wouldn't see through his efforts to appear normal.

"I'll think about it," he said again.

After she'd completed her shopping, and he was carrying her purchases up to the apartment in the elevator, he thanked her. "It's good advice," he said. "I'm glad you got me to talk."

"Men are appallingly bad at talk that has to do with their feelings. You all, every one of you, think you will be made less if you admit to having emotions. Which is why," she concluded with a smile, "you have women. To prod you into confessing."

He kissed her on the top of her head, saying, "I knew there had to be a reason," which made them both laugh.

Christmas Eve, a small group gathered in Marietta's living room for drinks before dinner. Miles was there, resplendent in a black velvet suit, white silk shirt and hand-knotted red silk bow tie. He'd brought with him his latest client, a young man whose first novel Miles was flogging in a simultaneous submission to eleven publishers. Laurence was there, too, periodically casting uncertain glances over at Leigh as if expecting her to stage another unpleasant scene. And when he wasn't inspecting Leigh, he was looking worriedly at the other two unattached males Marietta had invited. One was a wholesale diamond dealer, a distinguished, silver-haired man with penetrating gray eyes and a large hooked nose. The other was a dapper, younger man of about Leigh's age who owned a smart antiques shop on Madison Avenue, which is where he and Marietta had met. Marietta's long-time senior secretary, Alicia, was also present and had, for the occasion, bought a black Albert Nipon dress with huge, padded shoulders and long sleeves, outsized jet buttons, and a very long, full skirt. The garment hung on Alicia's tall, bony frame with startling effectiveness. Leigh doubted anyone shorter than she, or heavier, could have worn it. Alicia had tied her hair back with a thin black velvet ribbon and even put on some makeup.

Leigh, feeling both doubtful and celebratory, had decided to pay homage to Tina Turner and had worn an Ungaro black leather miniskirt, a voluminous white satin shirt, and black shoes with four-inch heels. She'd put a lot of mousse into her hair, fashioned it into a spiky helmet, and then allowed it to dry that way. Marietta had a fit upon seeing her, whispering, "Go directly to the bathroom and fix that crown of thorns!"

With a laugh, Leigh had said, "Don't be silly, darling! It took me ages to get it this way. It's very trendy."

"You look like an offended porcupine!" Marietta had sniffed, before going off to serve more eggnog to her guests.

Feeling Laurence's eyes once again upon her, Leigh made her way toward him, seeing him stiffen at her approach. He was her mother's most frequent companion, and had been in love with her for better than ten years. He'd gone so far as to divorce his wife in the hope of convincing Marietta to marry him, but he'd yet to succeed. He called her daily from his office and saw her as often as Marietta would allow, which was several nights a week. An eminently successful trial lawyer of fiftynine, Laurence never missed an opportunity to give Marietta gifts of jewelry, to take her on trips or to the theater, or to ask her to relent and marry him.

"Laurence," Leigh said quietly, approaching him, "I want to apologize. I was very upset, and not thinking clearly. I know it was dreadful, and I am truly sorry." She spoke very softly so that only he could hear, hoping, as she did, that his patrician profile would soften and turn toward her in forgiveness. "The whole thing was nightmarish, and you have every reason to be furious with me. I simply want you to know I regret it."

His eyes still averted, in an equally quiet tone, he said, "I understand how distraught you've been, Leigh. And we're all terribly sad about Joel. I've had time to think it

over, and I realize you weren't entirely—responsible."
Slowly, he turned to look at her. "It's your mother you
upset, more than me. As long as you've made your peace
with her, then I'm happy. And anyway," his features relaxed and he gave her a smile, "it's Christmas. We'll
forget all about it. Just tell me one thing," he said, eyes
again uncertain. "Who is that?" He nodded in the direction of the antiques dealer. "I mean, I know who he
is. But who is he?"

She patted him on the arm, saying, "Nothing to worry
about, Laurence. You know my mother. She is the way
she is. But she'd *never* give you up." He smiled again,
and she added, "It's the truth." It was. Marietta was all
but addicted to Laurence's style and generosity and at-
tentiveness.

Heartened, Laurence at once made his way across the
room to Marietta's side. Leigh watched him go, feeling
better, lighter. She was actually having a good time.
Miles was dishing up all the latest dirt, and was just in
the middle of a heavily detailed narrative about Jerzy
Kosinski while his very tall, very thin, very fashionable
new young client practically wet himself over the details.
Finishing that story, Miles launched into something he'd
just heard about a middle-aged woman who'd written
three million-plus best-selling romances. "Then," he
said, hitting his stride, "the poor idiot took these two
young thugs up to her hotel room. She had *such* a good
time, she had to cancel out on the conference the next
day because she couldn't find enough concealer to cover
all her bruises."

"The poor thing," Marietta said crossly. "Really,
Miles! I think sometimes you take rather too much pleasure in these sordid little scandals. How *can* you find that
tale amusing?"

Miles grinned, said, "Oops!" and hurried over to give

Marietta a kiss before murmuring an apology only she could hear. The two of them began talking in undertones, and Leigh went out to the kitchen to help herself to one of the hot hors d'oeuvres just being placed on serving trays. She greeted the three women catering the party and turned to go, bumping into her mother who was coming in.

"Just a moment," Marietta said, a hand on Leigh's shoulder.

"What's wrong?" Leigh wanted to know.

"Not a thing," her mother said, and impulsively hugged Leigh to her breast. "Are you having a good time?" she asked, releasing her daughter.

"I am. And you look ravishing."

Marietta lightly pushed her away. "Go talk to people. Talk to Miles, see if you can't get him to stop reciting his party pieces. And slow down on the gin, or you'll be too pied to eat."

"Darling!" Miles called to Leigh as she emerged from the kitchen. "Come hear this! You'll love it. Nothing seamy or sordid," he told Marietta as she reappeared behind Leigh. "Just a stunning bit of skullduggery. Come along, Leigh!" he urged, pulling her close to him.

"Miles," Leigh whispered, "no more stories, please. Mother's becoming jittery."

"Oh!" he said, and appeared suddenly downcast.

"You look most elegant," she told him. "And if you'll be you for a while, I'll stay right by your side and let you whisper all your naughty stories in my ear. But you have to promise to be you for the rest of the evening."

He rolled his eyes, saying, "Only for you. And I don't even know why I *do* these things for you."

"Of course, you do. You know exactly why."

"You know," he said, studying her, "you seem somewhat more recognizable this evening."

"No comments, no observations," she warned him. "just fetch me a fresh drink, then come back and talk to me."

He stood looking down at her for a few more seconds, then reached for her glass and went off to the bar. She watched him, feeling recognizable to herself for the first time in a very long while.

Fourteen

"I was just remarking to myself," Miles said, Christmas morning, "how very like your mother you are."

Leigh groaned softly and accepted the cup of coffee he was holding out to her.

"I always," he went on, folding himself into the armchair positioned near the window of his bedroom, "consider myself more than fortunate when you choose to lavish your sublime attentions upon my unworthy person. I merely wonder how I am meant to interpret this long-delayed return of your interest." He drank some of his coffee and watched her run her hand over her hair, an expression of dismay on her face as her fingers came into contact with the mousse-caked remnants of last night's coif. "The bathroom, complete with all mod cons, is where it's always been," he reminded her, "should you wish to avail yourself of the reviving supply of hot water that comes with this rent-controlled mausoleum."

"How can you talk so much, first thing in the morning?" she grumbled, tasting the coffee. "What time is it, anyway?"

"Oh, early. Just gone eight."

"Why are we *awake*?" she lamented.

"Because prodigal Miles wanted coffee and a quiet read of the *Times*. And then, he wanted company, too. I do hope you're not having second thoughts, regrets, that sort of thing," he said. "It *is* Christmas, and I, for one, have cause for rejoicing. A more perfect Christmas morning I couldn't imagine than waking up to find your lissome form next to mine."

She managed to smile at him and say, "Merry Christmas," while absorbing the picture he made in his burgundy silk dressing gown with the curlicued monogram on the pocket in cream-colored silk. He'd showered and shaved, and had obviously been up for quite some time. In contrast, she felt like something small and dirt-encrusted that had just crawled through a camouflaged hole in the earth, groping its way to the surface. She did not, however, feel at all bad.

"And to you, my raddled poppet."

"Tread gently on my ego, Miles. It's the only one I've got."

"I was observing you last evening, while your inimitable mother juggled those three besotted Lotharios with the grace and dexterity of a Wallenda, and I couldn't help thinking that you have a rather tawdry majesty, especially when you get yourself rigged out in leather wrappings and sport truly wicked-looking high heels. And, observing you further this morning, while you slept, was almost illicitly pleasurable." Abandoning the word play, and with it the terribly tony accent, he said, "You really are very like your mother, Leigh."

She found her purse under the side of the bed, opened it for a cigarette, then sat upright again, asking, "Are you being complimentary? And don't you put any grounds into whatever it is you use?"

"Feel free to brew yourself a stronger version," he told her. "Given my advancing age, flawed ticker, and the rest of it, I've been forced to acquire a taste for brown, coffee-tainted water. I know it's awful."

"It is," she agreed. "I wish you'd come sit over here by me. This feels so confrontational. And I'm honestly not up to having you be caustic and witty at this time of the morning. Come sit with me and be sweet, cuddly Miles, instead of Pinter's unacknowledged half-brother."

With a laugh, he got up from the armchair and positioned himself on the bed, carefully arranging his robe before draping an arm around her shoulders, his fingertips spreading over her upper arm. "You've gone very thin since the last time I saw you without benefit of wrapping. And I don't recall you eating more than a few tidbits last night. Which is a pity, because the dinner was divine. And your mother was in rare form. That gown was a triumph. The only other woman I've ever seen who looked as well in black bugle beads was dear Maggie Leighton at the opening night of *Bye-Bye Birdie* back in London in '61. You're not upset, are you, Leigh?"

She patted his small potbelly and said, "No, anything but. You're one of the few men I've ever slept with who's a genuine, uncomplicated delight."

He beamed, and his fingers stroked up and down her arm.

"What did you mean before," she asked, "about my being like my mother?"

"Aaah! Just that I recognize definite similarities. Physically as well as psychologically. The two of you in one room is a veritable feast for the eyes. Of course, I can't picture Marietta in a leather miniskirt."

"You know," she said, cozy against his side, "when you're not playing to the crowd and giving out with your collected stories, I like you better than almost anyone I can name. Why do you do it? Why do you feel you *have* to do it?''

"Everyone has to do it," he said philosophically. "We all have little hats and little faces we put on to help us play out our assigned roles. Every so often we find ourselves having some difficulty getting the hat off. You spend so much time doing business—breakfast meetings, lunch meetings, cocktail meetings, dinner meetings—you simply forget the hat and the face, or they get stuck on. You do it. Your mother does it. We all do it, Leigh. You're hardly the same person in bed that you are at a party."

"No, that's true."

"Of course it is," he said equably. "Conversely, if you spend too much time away from business, it tends to be rather difficult to locate the hat and the face. Which, recently, has been your problem. Last night, and now, seem like a reunion. I've missed you, missed the late-night calls and your surprise visits. I quite liked it," he admitted, "when you'd stop by here after you'd been to the hospital."

"I always felt guilty, as if I was using you."

"Don't be simple-minded, my darling. There's using and then there's *using*. I was flattered that you'd come here. At the last, I wondered where you went."

"I didn't go anywhere. I just drove for hours, or I'd go home and sit half the night drinking coffee, trying to sleep but afraid to in case the telephone would ring and it would be the hospital telling me to come back."

"I understand," he said, and again stroked her arm. "I've been giving a lot of thought lately to what I'm going to do in my declining years."

"You're hardly declining."

"Whatever. I don't much care for the idea of spending the latter part of my life alone."

"Really, Miles?" She shifted to have a better view of him.

"Yes, really. Last year, after that big Five-O bash, I was more depressed than I've ever dreamed it possible to be. There I was, fifty years old, never married, no family, no one to leave behind. I revised my will and had the devil's own time trying to organize my bequests. I sat in my lawyer's office trying to think who I cared to have benefit from my demise and the two people who figured most strongly were you and your mother. I've shared more with the two of you, spent more time with you, than with anyone else. For God's sake, if it hadn't been for Marietta, I'd never have got the agency off the ground. And then you, my undernourished, neurotic little fantasist, with your Newberys and Caldecotts. You really must get back to work, Leigh."

"I can't," she said flatly. "What would you like for your declining years?" she asked him. "Seriously, what would your perfect scenario be?"

"Aaah," he sighed and looked up at the ceiling. "The perfect scenario. You won't hold this against me, for future use as blackmail?"

"Come on, tell me!"

"All right. Someone in my life to look forward to seeing. A big place, with a wing over here for me, and a wing over there for whomever, and we'd meet Tuesday in the dining room for dinner, or Saturday night we'd send out for pizza and watch old movies on the telly. In between times, we'd be off in our separate wings, doing whatever. Trips together, because we enjoy each other's company; outings to the ballet, and so forth."

She listened, nodding her agreement. "It sounds right."

His arm descended and his hand came around to cover her breast. "It could be arranged," he said soberly. "It is, suffice it to say, highly presumptuous of me."

"No, I'm flattered," she told him, touched. "But you wouldn't want to spend time with me, Miles. I've become a complete bore. All I've done lately is chop wood and go for long walks, trying to wear myself out so I'll be able to sleep."

"You don't think you're being just a little hard on yourself? It's only been a matter of weeks since Joel died."

"But I knew it was coming. I knew for months. That's what I don't understand: it wasn't as if I didn't know, hadn't had ages to prepare myself. But when it happened, it was . . . I couldn't believe it."

"One is never really prepared," he said quietly.

Her cigarette finished, she put it out, then nestled against him once more, reluctant to leave. For almost twenty years, Miles had been her agent and sometime bed partner. They'd gone for as long as eighteen months being platonic friends, and then they'd sleep together for a few months before returning to their platonic friendship. He never changed. No matter with whom, or how, he might be otherwise involved, his interest in her was constant. When she was feeling her best, she enjoyed his passion for gossip, his acerbic wit, his predilection for fancy dress, and she liked his looks. He was very tall, and tending now to be jowly; he had merry brown eyes, and a big brushy moustache over well-shaped lips; his smile was wicked and knowing and tended to show his large, very white teeth. He was highly intelligent, the product of the very best British public schools, and of Oxford; and he was always ticking away, just beneath the surface, ready to come up with some thoroughly libelous piece of gossip, or some spurious bit of knowledge. He was irreverent, disrespectful, and charmingly bearlike in bed. Making love with him was always direct and fairly primitive, but he had an abiding concern for his partner's satisfaction and had never failed to make her feel utterly desirable. On the minus side, he had a tendency to ape people, particularly her mother. And he loved to say outrageous things simply to see what kind of reactions he'd get. Periodically, if he'd just been talking to her mother, or he'd had a difficult day, he'd turn on Leigh in a demanding fashion that had distressed her until she'd learned how to jolly him out of it.

"What are you doing today?" she asked him, her hand going again to his subtle paunch—something about himself he hated but which she liked.

"Childe Harold," he answered, referring to his new young client. "The feast at 4 P.M. Sounds like a horror film," he laughed, fondling her breast. "And you're off to glorious Marietta's, for a Christmas luncheon of flayed pigeons under glass, or something equally bizarre."

"Quail," she corrected him. "I have a gift for you. I'd like to give it to you before I go back to the country. What time do you think you'll be back from Childe Harold's?"

"No later than seven. If you're planning to come back, I'll wait and give you your wee giftie then."

"Are you happy, Miles?" she asked, sitting away to look at him.

"At this moment, excruciatingly. It's always been a mystery and a revelation to me that someone composed almost exclusively of bone and gristle could have such a wealth of breast. I believe I could actually be inspired to devote time creating sonnets to your delectable glands."

"Men are such fetishists," she laughed. "If it isn't breasts it's legs, or asses. Women aren't nearly so stupid."

"They're worse, my darling. Women go about with their heads stuffed full of your mothers addlepated fiction, searching for heroes."

"Shame on you!" she giggled. "Talking that way about your most important client."

"Come back here!" he said, pulling her close to him. "I may represent her, but I've never claimed she was a great literary figure. The truly lamentable fact of present-day life is that the majority of people are so technologically addicted, they are so dependent upon their microwaves, their VCRs, their instant replays, that they've not only succeeded in reducing their attention span to about forty seconds or less, they've also acquired an appetite for trash. We live in an era when everything is disposable—overnight celebrities, fast food that comes in biodegradable containers, and books of no content. A good book requires time, and attention, concentration. No one has time. If it requires thought, it's too much trouble. The quick read, with appropriate amounts of badly described fucking done by no-dimensional characters bent on espionage, treachery, or evil of some sort, brings in the big dollars. Granted, your mother has her own genre, and no one *ever* does the dirty deed between the pages of one of her books. But it is what it is, and it is *not* great writing. It is, however, pleasant enough predigested pap; harmless, innocent, and somehow more worthy than a lot of the stuff I flog in the marketplace.''

"I have to go, Miles.'' She sat up.

"Have I offended you by talking about your mother?''

"No. I just really should go home, wash this jism out of my hair.'' Again she ran her hands over her head while he bellowed with laughter.

"You've got hours yet,'' he said. "Stay and play with Uncle Miles.'' He leered at her.

She sat on her knees and asked, "*Are* you happy?''

"Do you know that I love you, Leigh?''

She shook her head, as if she hadn't heard him properly. "You do?'' she replied stupidly.

"I realized it when you married that insufferable gynecologist. I'd assumed you knew how I felt. Now, naturally, I know it was a ridiculous assumption.''

"Miles! How the hell could you *assume* I'd know a

189

thing like that? You never said a word, not a single goddamned word."

"I thought you knew."

"Well, I didn't!" she said angrily. "And you wait all these years to spring that on me now? I divorced that man more than *eight years ago*!"

"Does it make a difference?" he asked her.

"Of course it makes a difference! How could you assume I knew? I've always had this—this *respect* for your detachment. And now you tell me you're not detached at all. Do you honestly think I'd have married that idiot if I'd known how you felt? I only married him because of Joel. But if you'd told me . . . God damn it, Miles! I could have had my own child, I . . . now it's too late!"

"After the divorce, you stayed out in the country for almost two years," he said, distraught at her tears. "Then, you'd come and go, in and out of my life, and I thought *you* were the one with the astonishing detachment. And just when I was beginning to think perhaps you weren't quite so casual after all, Joel became ill. For the past three years, you've been unapproachable for the most part. Last night was the first time I felt I'd seen you in *years*, Leigh."

She wiped her eyes with the sheet, then crawled back over to him. "I didn't mean to come unglued that way."

"It's all right. I understand."

"I wish *I* did. I really do have to go."

"Would you like me to see you home?" he offered.

"I'll get a taxi."

He watched her fasten on her brassiere before pulling on the glittery pantyhose from the night before. When she was dressed, she came around the side of the bed to sit on his lap and wind her arms around his neck. Her nose touching his, she said, "For an oversized windbag, you really are very sweet. And I love you."

190

"Ah, well. For a malnourished crone, you are quite adorable. I'll see you here at seven."

She stopped in the bedroom doorway to ask, "Miles, did you really propose to me awhile back there?"

"You could say so."

"God, Miles! Why would you want to? I mean, you've seen me without my makeup."

"I've also seen you without your clothes. And vice versa. So what?"

"Well, you've given me something to think about."

"While you're tromping around in the snow out there in exurbia, consider a wing of your own. And pizza Saturday night."

She stood a moment longer, then went on her way.

"Did you spend the evening with Miles?" Marietta asked.

"No, I spent the *evening* with you, and your guests. I went *home* with Miles. He proposed to me."

"He proposed marriage?"

"Yes, he did."

"And I don't suppose you accepted?"

"I didn't say, one way or another."

"Hmmnn." Marietta surveyed the table, said, "Forgot the cranberry chutney," and went back to the kitchen for it.

"How many are coming this evening?" Leigh asked. Every Christmas all Marietta's single friends were invited to a buffet dinner.

"Six all told. I had to invite poor Lucinda. She was feeling terribly sorry for herself because Jeremy has business in Paris and couldn't be home for the holidays. I did warn her not to count on him, but she wouldn't listen. It's such a great mistake for a woman her age to place so much store in a man not only twenty-five years her junior but homosexual to boot. She has the idea in mind that she's going to convert him. It's absurd and depressing. But no one should spend Christmas alone.''

"Aside from that, how is Lucinda?''

"Lucinda wouldn't be happy unless she was miserable,'' Marietta stated. "At times she puts me in mind of you.''

"Oh, nice,'' Leigh replied.

"There is some truth to that.''

"Well, at least I haven't pinned my hopes on someone like Jeremy. He's such an oily little slug. Why, when there are so many really lovely gay men, did she have to choose him?''

"She gave him her Art Deco platinum-and-ruby cigarette case.''

"Christ! Two years ago, she swore she'd never part with it. She just *gave* it to him?''

"It gets worse,'' Marietta said, positioning the roast potatoes between them. "Not only did she give him the cigarette case, but she's also let him have the Cartier tiara for his show. She'll never see it again, the silly cow, and that piece must be worth a quarter of a million. It's an *original*.''

"Don't tell me any more,'' Leigh begged her. "I hate stories about women who get desperate and start doing really stupid things.''

Marietta gazed meaningfully at her.

"I am *not* desperate, and I haven't done anything really stupid.''

"That remains to be seen. Fortunately, you haven't anything monumentally valuable to give away.''

"I've got all those so-called family heirlooms. Why didn't you tell me those were mostly marcasite and crystal?''

"You didn't ask. And there are several quite valuable pieces, too.''

"I know. But what I can't figure out is how pawning those things gave you enough to get started."

"They didn't quite," Marietta said, telltale color in her cheeks. "How do you find the quail? You don't think it's too dry, do you?"

"No, it's fine. How did you do it, then?"

"I took some money, as well as the jewelry. I should have taken more, but at the time I thought it would be enough. After I'd paid our passage and so forth, it was necessary to pawn the jewels. Philip had his solicitor write a filthy, threatening letter, all to do with misappropriation of funds and wrongful flight. I sent a telegram directly to Philip telling him to call off the solicitor or I'd be forced to retaliate. He refused. I took a loan to repay him. And I retaliated by severing his connection with you."

"Why didn't you tell me this before?"

"Because I didn't think you needed to know that your father was someone who would've seen me in prison for taking what was rightfully mine. Five thousand pounds worked out to approximately three hundred and eighty-five pounds a year for every year of our marriage. Secretaries made more! And I had to see to you, and that dreadful house, and those disgusting, stupid chickens, *and* put up with him! I was eighteen when I married that man. He was handsome and withdrawn and I was young enough and stupid enough to mistake his withdrawal for a rare brand of charm."

"You should have told me," Leigh said.

"For what purpose, pray tell!"

"It helps me understand you better."

"You need that, do you?" Marietta asked.

"Sometimes. Understanding you helps me understand myself."

"I see. Have you picked up any nuggets of wisdom from this sordid little story?"

"Yes, I have," Leigh said impishly. "God! I really do love you. What I have learned, by Stanleigh Elizabeth Dunn: I have learned never to entrust my Cartier tiara to a young man of doubtful sexual persuasion with an unctuous manner and big pockets."

Marietta emitted peals of laughter, then had a coughing fit so that Leigh had to get up and pound her on the back.

Fifteen

"Almost every year, for as long as I've known you, you've given me silly little presents that have some rude significance known only to you. And now you give me something like this. You're starting to confuse me seriously, Miles. It's absolutely gorgeous. I love it."

"I thought last year's ashtray was a bit of genius," he said archly. "Nude reclining in bathtub, her feet tipped cunningly over the edge so you'd have somewhere to rest your cigarette."

"Well, really," she said. "That's exactly what I mean."

"At least I *thought* of you," he said, then asked, "You really like it?"

"I've never had anyone give me lingerie before. Are you quite sure you didn't intend this for my mother?"

"Of course not. Hers is yellow." He laughed heartily at his own humor.

"It's lovely," she told him, holding the pale pink silk teddy against herself.

"I confess that until I bought it I always wondered how women managed to do their business wearing one of those things. I shouldn't have worried. But don't those little snaps tend to irritate?''

"I'll report back to you."

"Perhaps you'd care to model it for me."

"What? Now? I've got to get going. But next visit, if you like."

"I would like. What's so urgently awaiting you in the country?"

"Snow, quiet, room to pace. I need time alone just now."

He sat for a moment stroking the leather of the attaché case she'd given him. "You'll listen to the tape, read the book of the show?" he asked.

"I told you I would, and I will."

"You can't pace for the rest of your life, Leigh."

"I know that. I'm parked in a tow-away zone, Miles. I have to go."

"What about New Year's Eve?" he asked. "What have you got on?"

"Nothing."

"Good. You'll come out with me! Wear something fabulous that you can move in. We'll go dancing."

"You're joking!"

"I am not. Get yourself tarted up, and I'll collect you at seven-thirty."

"Miles, I really don't . . ."

"There's the elevator. I will not take no for an answer. I'll ring you during the week. Drive carefully!"

She stopped at the mailbox at the top of the driveway, leaving the car running and the door open as she cleared the box, then climbed back, dumping the letters and magazines on the passenger seat. Only magazines and occasional bills came to the apartment. The bulk of her mail was delivered here. More snow. And the man with the snowplow still hadn't come. The car crunched through the frozen-over surface of the thick snow, its headlights catching and somehow magnifying the falling flakes. The effect was hypnotic. The night was very quiet, except for the faint whirr of the wind. She closed the garage door and, carrying her bag and the mail, walked back along the tire tracks to the house. She stood for a moment, her hand poised to open the door, listening. Nothing.

Her boots off and her coat hung away, she carried the mail to the kitchen and left it on the table while she plugged in the kettle for coffee. Then she quickly sorted through the mail, tossing the junk ads and solicitations directly into the trash. The magazines to one side, bills over there, and letters here. A large envelope of fan mail forwarded from her publishers; mostly letters from kids. They were, those letters, the best, most rewarding aspect of her work, and she always answered every last one of them by hand. A couple of statements from Miles's office notifying her of royalty deposits made directly to her bank account, with scrawled greetings penned by Miles across the bottom. Something from the Authors Guild, a dozen or so Christmas cards, and a letter postmarked Florida. She knew at once it was from Daniel and wondered, looking around, how he'd managed to get her address. She hadn't given it to him, but he'd obtained it somehow. And that bothered her. Thinking again of the frenzied way he'd made love to her, she was almost afraid to read the letter, and put it off until she'd started a fire in the living room, drawn the curtains, and sat down with her coffee and the fan mail, reading everything else first.

Finally, she slit open the envelope.

"Dear Leigh," he'd written, "I can't stop thinking about you. I meant the things I said, the way I feel. I have to see you again. We have to talk. I've been trying to concentrate on getting a tan, playing some tennis, but somehow everything makes me think of you. Please call me once Christmas is out of the way. Hope you have a good Christmas in the meantime. All my best, Dan.''

She had no idea what she'd done with the number he'd sent along with the pendant. And right then, all she felt was upset at his having discovered her address. The letter served to add to the reservations she'd had at their last meeting and to strengthen her resolve not to see him again. But his asking her to call reminded her of the telephone and she went to the kitchen to see that the red light was flashing on the answering machine. She hesitated, reluctant to hear the messages for fear of learning that Daniel had also managed to get her unlisted number.

"Don't be ridiculous!" she told herself, and hit the PLAY button.

Three hang-ups, another call from *TV Guide*—didn't those people ever give up?—a message from her old school chum, Dolly, berating her for being such a rotten friend and ". . . How come you never call me? Seriously, I'm very sad about Joel, and imagine you must be down in the dumps. So, call me, okay? We'll get drunk and reminisce. Happy Christmas, Stannie, and please call when you get home. It's been too long, and I miss you."

The tone. Then Miles saying, "New Year's Eve, you unreliable strumpet. Be sure to write it in your diary. And let me know at any time if you're interested in having a wing of my estate. Call me in the interim if you're bored, or out of sorts, or in the mood to hear the latest, a positively juicy item I've only just heard. Be a good little tartlet, and don't forget to listen to the tape and read the book." His voice changed, and he said, "Forget all that, and call me when you get in, will you?"

While she was waiting for the machine to reset, she wondered about the recent spate of hang-ups, hoping they had nothing to do with Daniel.

"You took your sweet time," Miles said. "I was beginning to think something had happened."

"I was looking through my mail. I simply forgot to check the machine. Are you going to start keeping tabs on me?"

"Not at all. I just wanted to tell you last night was very nice, Leigh. And I'm absolutely serious about New Year's Eve. Don't disappoint me. I'm planning a fantastic night."

"You're serious about all of it, aren't you?" she asked him.

"I believe I am, yes."

"Why, suddenly?"

"Because I don't want you rushing off getting yourself involved with yet another fool without at least knowing how I feel about you. That way, if you do get involved elsewhere, I'll have stated my case. And *please*, look over the *Percival* material."

"I will consider everything," she told him.

Dan truly had intended to stay the full two weeks, but by the end of the first week he was so agitated, so restless that when the call came in from the real estate agent with a decent offer, he jumped at the opportunity to go back and deal in person with the negotiations. He told the agent he'd counteroffer by that evening, and quickly booked a seat on the afternoon flight to New York. He told Lane and his parents that some business had come up, as well as an offer on the house, packed his bag, kissed everyone goodbye, and got a cab to take him to the airport, refusing his father's offer of a ride.

Once on his way, he felt infinitely lighter, less antsy. And on the flight back, he several times got out his address book to look at the listings he'd made for Leigh. It amused him to think that, with the glut of mail over the holidays, he might actually get there in advance of his letter. She'd really be surprised.

One problem he could foresee was his apartment telephone. He'd have to get a machine so he wouldn't miss any calls, although the only call he cared about was the one he was sure to get from Leigh. Turning to the blank pages at the back of the little book, he started a list. He put "answering machine" at the top, followed by "moving company" with a question mark. If his counteroffer was accepted, he'd have to do something about clearing the house; he'd also have to start looking in earnest for another place. That meant trekking around with real estate people, and he didn't even know what he wanted, except to be nearer to Leigh. New Canaan had a number of advantages, not the least of which was that Connecticut had no state income tax. All the signs were positive.

Thinking about her and that house on Moonstone Lane, he had to wonder if she wasn't lonely there, out on such an isolated piece of property. The nearest neighbors were at least a quarter of a mile away. He hadn't been able to get a full view of the house, so it was possibly larger than it had looked, with only its side and part of the front visible from the main road. The garage was at the end of the long driveway, separated from the house by about a hundred yards. It was a two-car garage, but he'd seen only the Mercedes. The Good Doctor had probably dropped the second car off at the station when he'd taken the train to his office in the city.

She didn't have any kind of a marriage, he thought. Not only did she seldom refer to her husband, but she seemed to come and go when she chose, without consulting anyone. Look at the way she'd come to meet him. And the way she'd made love with him! No one with a good marriage did the things she did.

Christ! he chided himself. Since when had he become

an expert on women and marriages? His only firsthand experience was his own fucked-up marriage to poor fucked-up Celeste. He closed his eyes and saw her, and the panic started pounding in his chest. For a second or two he couldn't seem to open his eyes and he thought he might start screaming. Then his eyes shot open and he gasped for air, frantically filling his lungs as he tried to erase that view of her, all the blood, so much of it; that blood like screams without volume.

He dried his hands on his handkerchief and gulped down the drink he'd ordered, a double vodka on the rocks. Why was it getting to him now? That's what he couldn't understand. He'd been just fine at the time. He'd handled the whole thing dispassionately, proud of himself for not coming unglued. What a jerk he'd been, to think he could get through something like that without turning a hair!

Neither his parents nor Lane knew all the details; he'd spared them that. And Celeste's father had passed away more than a year before, so he hadn't had to know. The only people he'd talked to had been the police, and that hadn't, strictly speaking, been talking. It had been a case of responding to questions, reciting facts. He hadn't really *talked* to anyone, and maybe that had been his big mistake. Maybe if he'd discussed it with his father or his mother, maybe if he'd told some people what it had really been like, it wouldn't have kept coming back at him now, giving him night sweats, making him feel so constantly on edge.

But there was Leigh. She was the positive side to all this, and thinking of her gave him a lift. He knew she cared. She was afraid to admit to it because of her doctor husband. But they'd work it out. Maybe he'd drive out, see the real estate agent, and then go by and look at Leigh's house. If only he had her number, he'd be able to call her up and they'd talk. They had a lot of talking to do. There had to be some way to get her number. But how? He went back and forth over ways and means, and suddenly, there it was. It was tricky, but not impossible.

"You *cannot* back out!" Miles said. "I knew, left to your own devices, you'd change your mind. But I won't have it, Leigh. If I must, I'll come out there and get you. This is pure, divine inspiration, and under no circumstances will I allow you to deprive either one of us. *Leigh!*" he implored her. "I've wanted for the last hundred years to live out this particular fantasy."

"My God!" she said, impressed by his pleading. "Just what is it you've lined up?"

"It's a delicious surprise. I guarantee you'll have the best time ever."

"You've got me so curious, I suppose I'll have to come."

"Oh, wonderful! Wear your frothiest creation. You have my word, it won't be out of place. I'll collect you at seven-thirty sharp. It's going to be such fun!" he crowed, sounding years younger and breathless with excitement.

She hung up and wandered back to the living room to open the curtains. The room smelled of last night's fire, and cigarette smoke. It looked shabby and she thought she really should get new carpeting and have the furniture re-upholstered. Nothing had been done in here in fifteen years. The sofa and armchairs were all saggy-bottomed, the fabric worn right through in places. Maybe that would be her New Year's resolution: to do over this room. She'd have the house spruced up, and very possibly she'd do the production design for the musical.

She'd been prepared to hate what had been done, but the dialogue was spare and right in keeping with the original. And the songs—sung on the tape by the composer and lyricist—were cheery but not saccharine, and pretty catchy. For the past couple of days she'd been going around the house humming fragments of the melodies, Percival's theme in particular. She had, the previous evening, gone to the bookcase to get a copy of the book, studying the illustrations with an eye to how they might translate into stage sets.

In the bedroom, she looked through the closet. Nothing suitable here, but there was an evening gown in the city she'd worn once, about ten years before, to a charity ball the Good Doctor had wanted to attend. The dress had been hanging in a fabric bag in the closet ever since. And if she remembered correctly, the matching shoes were there, too. It was starting to feel like fun, and she unearthed the box with the jewelry her mother had given her to see if there was anything that might go well with the gown.

By two, she was ready to go. She carried her overnight bag to the car, thankful the snow had finally stopped so she wouldn't have to worry about road conditions. While she waited for the engine to warm up, she decided she'd tell Miles that evening she wanted to do the production design.

Dan couldn't believe it! She came out of the house carrying a small suitcase, opened the garage door, disappeared into the darkness inside, and five minutes later reversed the Mercedes and drove off.

He was torn between wanting to follow her and his need to get her telephone number. A few seconds and the decision made itself. Her car was out of sight. She drove very fast, and he made a mental note to talk to her about that. It was dangerous to drive too fast on these back roads, with so many blind turns.

He made himself wait fifteen minutes before he got out of his car, checked to make sure no one was around, then ran down the driveway to do a quick tour of the perimeter of the house. Through the kitchen window he could see the telephone and answering machine on the far end of the counter. But he couldn't read the printing on the dial.

All the doors and windows were locked. The mud room door was a snap, though. He just pushed his MasterCard in between the lock and the frame, jiggled the knob a couple of times, and the door opened. Perspiring heavily, he ran to the side of the house to see that the driveway was still clear, then he raced back and let himself in.

It wasn't at all the way he'd thought a house of hers would be. The kitchen wasn't, anyway. He'd have loved to take a good, long look around, but it was too risky. He left his wet shoes in the mud room, then went into the kitchen and looked at the phone. The center circle of the dial was blank except for the area code; 203 in large print, and then nothing. He was stunned with disbelief. Maybe the number was on the extension. He ran into the bedroom, spotted the extension on the table beside the bed, and got to it to find this dial, too, was blank. "Shit!" he muttered, returning to the kitchen. He stood, the kitchen clock ticking very loudly, trying to think. She wouldn't have her own number listed in her address book. And he couldn't see any address book around. He stared at the telephone and the answering machine beside it. Then, on impulse, he went over and pressed the outgoing message button on the machine. Her voice came on giving the number, followed by a message. Quickly, he noted the number in his book, reset the machine, made sure the signal light came on, then rushed back to the mud room.

There were different-sized coats and jackets hanging from hooks on one wall of the room. Above them hung a variety of hats. Opposite were a washer and dryer. And a stack of freshly done laundry, folded and waiting to be put away. Without thinking, he snatched the first item from the top of the stack, pushed it into his pocket, stepped into his shoes, and let himself out.

He was about to run back up the driveway when he stopped and looked to see his footprints disappearing around the side of the house. Breaking into a sweat, he realized he was going to have to do something about them. There was a shovel leaning beside the front door. He grabbed it and made a circle of the perimeter of the house, smoothing fresh snow over the impressions he'd made, following his tracks all the way to the cleared walk. Then he returned the shovel to where he'd found it, looked again to be sure the footprints had been erased, and fled back to his car, amazed at how easy it had been.

Someone really ought to talk to her about those locks, he thought, as he drove off. If he could break in so easily, anyone might. Checking his watch, he saw that the whole thing had taken less than seven minutes, although it had felt like hours. But he'd done it. He'd been inside her house, got her phone number, and something else—what was it he'd taken? he wondered, reaching into his pocket.

Some kind of slip, he decided, taking a hasty look. He'd examine it more carefully once he was out of the area. He was due at the real estate office in New Canaan in twenty minutes. The Bedford house was sold, pending the usual inspections and mortgage approval, and at an excellent price.

It seemed as if the broker wanted to know everything. Before she'd even consult her book of listings, she had to have information, specifics, so she could narrow down the number of places she'd show him. He was annoyed and overheated, and reached into his pocket for his handkerchief, almost pulling out Leigh's slip before he realized what it was. He glanced at the agent, hoping she hadn't noticed. She hadn't. But things were getting out of hand. What the hell was he doing, breaking into someone's house and stealing her undergarments? Did he really think Leigh wasn't going to notice the thing was missing? Or that someone had gone to the trouble of smoothing out the snow around the entire perimeter of her house? Had he moved anything, touched anything she might notice? Jesus! He was getting so worked up he could hardly concentrate on what the agent was saying.

"I have two very special condominiums I think might suit you," the woman said. "We'll go in my car."

They *were* very special, Daniel had to agree. Where had his mind been when she'd asked all those questions and he'd supposedly given answers? Special to the tune of nearly half a million for one, and just under four hundred thousand for the other.

"These are a little out of my price range," he told her. "But you're headed in the right direction."

"What is your ceiling, Mr. Godard?" she asked him a bit impatiently. "Perhaps I misunderstood."

She was such a bitch, Dan thought; she was acting as if she didn't believe he could afford anything in this town. Why was she being so miserable?

"I don't want to go higher than three," he told her. Three hundred thousand for a goddamned apartment was a lot of money, by anyone's standards. And six percent commission on a sale like that was a sweet eighteen thousand. Not a bad day's work for someone who only had to drive around town and show her listings. There was no need at all to be bitchy. Especially when, these days, you couldn't tell how much money anyone had by the way he dressed.

"Fine!" she said, flashing a quick, icy smile. "I have three other listings in that range that are also very special. Slightly older buildings, but lovely."

They drove through town, and he found himself becoming increasingly disturbed. By the time she was showing him through the last of the apartments, he was so distracted he could barely feign an interest in seeing the master suite and the two-and-a-half bathrooms. He said, ''I'll have to think it over,'' and suffered while she drove him back to the office. He promised he'd be in touch, then jumped into his car and nearly rear-ended someone by starting to reverse without first checking the rearview mirror.

He was driving, but he didn't know where he was going. All at once he was so exhausted he knew he couldn't make the trip back into the city. He needed to stop, to lie down and sleep. Resigned, he turned the car around and headed back to Bedford. He'd sleep on the sofa bed in the den, he decided, his hand in his pocket, buried in the silk teddy.

Sixteen

Miles stood, his hands clasped in front of his chin, his breath held as he gazed at her, momentarily lost for words. He had never seen her look as heart-stoppingly beautiful as she did that night. The dress, of black taffeta, was strapless and ran in a line just below the tops of her breasts. Beneath the line were two rows of wide ruffles. Then the fabric wrapped itself tightly around her torso just to the waist, where it descended from dozens of tiny tucks into a full, sweeping skirt banded at the bottom with two more rows of ruffles.

Her hair was completely concealed beneath a close-fitting black net cap covered with sequins and beads in a feather design. With her hair covered and her high forehead bare, her eyes looked very large and very bright; her cheekbones were prominent; the shape of her face had startling definition.

"Leigh," he said at last, "you're simply beautiful."

"Oh, no," she tried to push away the compliment.

"You are," he insisted.

"Miles," she said, smiling, "you're very sweet." She began to turn, and he stopped her, his hands on her arms.

"Just once," he told her, "believe that it's you, and not someone being kind. Now," he released her. "Are you all set?"

"I borrowed Mother's evening cape," she laughed, caught up in his excitement. She grabbed the floor-length black satin cape from the chair and shook it open to reveal its brilliant egg-yolk yellow lining, then fastened it on at the neck and pushed it back over her shoulders so that the lining showed. The cape framed the bare expanse of her pale skin above the black gown. Her only jewelry was a large citrine pendant in a Victorian setting of curling silver leaves and flowers.

He couldn't stop looking at her, admiring not only the very flattering outfit, but this new version of the woman he knew. "I've never seen you in party gear. You realize that? We'll have to do this often. When I think of all the parties we could go to . . . this is going to be even better than I'd hoped."

"Where are we going?" she asked him.

"It's a surprise. No questions, please."

He'd hired a limo. The liveried driver snapped to attention as they came out of her building and, with a bit of a bow, held open the door.

"I'm getting very curious, Miles. You do look most elegant. Even black patent evening pumps. I've never seen *you* all rigged out in a tuxedo. You look edible." She leaned over to nuzzle her nose into his neck, then sat away to light a cigarette. It surprised her to discover she felt very strongly about him. Until Christmas morning, when they'd had that conversation, neither of them had attempted to put words to their relationship. Since then, intermittently, she'd found herself thinking about him. And now, all at once, it seemed she cared far more than she'd suspected. She wasn't sure of herself, or her timing, and so tried to put her emotions to one side. "Mother's going to the Plaza," she said, "with Laurence."

"Yes, I know."

"You do?" She looked around at him.

"I do have occasion to talk to her."

"Fairly often, from the sound of it."

"Almost daily, as it happens. Recently, we've talked rather more than usual. She's been, to say the least, rather concerned about you."

"I've started feeling better, since Christmas."

"That is undoubtedly because I've taken you under my amply endowed wing."

"It is, is it?" She smiled at him.

"I have decided you need guidance out of that slough of despond in which you've been mired."

"And you are my self-appointed tour guide?"

"Until such time as I am directed otherwise. Put that out!" he told her. "We're arriving."

As she pushed the cigarette into the ashtray, she looked out the window, asking, *"Where?* I don't see a thing."

"Paradise on the second floor," he replied. "Roseland."

"How fantastic! I've always wanted to see what it's like."

"You will love it," he declared.

The mirrored ball in the ceiling revolved, sending shards of white light over the dense, whirling crowd, while the big band onstage played Glen Miller classics.

"I do love it!" she laughed, as he moved her about the floor.

"My secret passion," he confided, leading her with effective ease. "I was the too-tall, too-thin—if you can imagine it—out-of-place youth who hung about the local *palais-de-danse* and won the hearts of every young female within a fifty-mile radius. Every weekend while I was at Oxford, I polished up my shoes, slicked down the hair I then had in abundance, and went to loiter with intent while I eyed the likelier of the ladies. There are times when, if I close my eyes, I can see those girls in their best frocks, and hear the music. Those are some of my happiest memories."

"I'll want to come here all the time. It's like a time warp, Miles. All the beehive hairdos and crinolines, anklestrap high heels. And the makeup; so much bright-blue eye shadow."

"Forgive me," he said, "but are you not the same woman who came out disguised as Billy Idol a short time back?"

"Point made."

"All of us here are devoted to the dance, and to the music."

"Thank you for bringing me," she said seriously. "I'm having a wonderful time."

He kissed the tip of her nose, then said, "This city is the most terrifying and the most fabulous on earth. I know of places that simply couldn't exist anywhere else. Yet you risk your life to get to them. Twenty-seven years I've been trying to make sense of why I'm here. But every time I think of living anywhere else, I start traveling down a mental list of the things I'd miss, and I know it isn't time yet for me to leave. Undoubtedly, I'll wake up one morning to find there's no list at all. Then, I'll retire to the country."

"To the estate, with the wing over here, and the wing over there."

"It does exist," he said. "I have some property, with a dilapidated farmhouse on it."

"I didn't know that."

"Don't be naive, my darling. I don't blurt out everything. And I'd remind you the two of us have only very recently begun to communicate again in any reasonable sort of fashion. A drink?''

"I'd love one."

Everything seemed extraordinary. He led her by the hand off the dance floor, and she felt secure and cosseted simply because he had hold of her hand and was leading the way. She wondered if making love with him would be different now, and experienced twinges of excitement at the prospect.

"Who was the old friend, by the way?" he asked, after their drinks had been served.

"What old friend?"

"The one who rang me, then sent along the insured package."

"Oh! Someone I met on the flight to London."

"I see," he said.

She thought he looked hurt as he turned to watch the dancers for a minute or two.

"You didn't give him my address, did you, Miles?"

"Shame on you!" He turned back to her. "You know better than that. There is no one on my staff who'd give out any personal information at all about any of my clients. Why?"

"I had a letter from him, at the house. It bothers me. I can't think how he got my address, and I don't like the idea that people could easily find out where I live, start pestering me."

"You wanted to dip in and out of this chap's life like some convenient pool. But he's smitten, and he's pursuing you. Have I got it about right?"

"Why are you so angry?" she asked him.

"I'm not angry at all," he said, with an exaggerated lifting of the eyebrows and widening of the eyes that only served to underscore the fact that he was indeed angry.

"You are," she insisted.

"Never mind that. Why are you so concerned that this chap's managed to get your address? Have you done something foolish, Leigh?"

"I don't think so. I slept with him twice."

"Bestowing your favors at random again."

"Miles! You're being unpleasant and peculiar, not to mention insulting. If you want to know the truth, the only other person I've slept with in the last two years is you."

Hearing this, he softened and became apologetic. "Is that the truth?" he asked, reaching for her hand. "Honestly?"

"Honestly."

He held her hand to his mouth, and gazed at her. "You're my only one, too," he admitted.

"Why?" she asked him.

He kissed her knuckles, then her palm. "No one else interests me."

"I think I want to design the production, Miles. I love the songs. I can't stop humming the melodies. And they've been very clever and sparing with the dialogue."

"That makes me happy," he said, smiling now. "It really does make me happy."

"Why have you never married?"

"Why?" he repeated, closing both his hands now over hers and holding it captive on the table in front of him. "Why?" He looked around, listened for a moment to the band, then returned his eyes to hers. "Come dance with me," he said. "We've only got another forty minutes before we move on, and we can just as easily talk while we dance."

He directed her back onto the floor, wrapped his arm around her waist, put his cheek to hers, and said, "Twenty-five years ago, you were Marietta's fractious, married daughter. The first time I saw you is as clear in my mind as if it were yesterday. I'd stopped by the apartment for a drink with your mother. We were sitting in the living room going over the terms of a contract, and you came flying in, all full of yourself and vibrating with energy. I remember looking up thinking, 'What the bloody hell?' and feeling my stomach drop at the sight of you. You were what, twenty? Didn't look more than fifteen or sixteen. And you had that astonishing mane of burnished copper hair, and those great calf's eyes of pale green. You were long and skinny and electric, and couldn't have been anyone but Marietta's daughter. I'll never forget it. Your bell-bottom trousers and a paint-smeared sweatshirt, dirty fingernails. You were in and out in five minutes.

"When your mother told me you were married, I couldn't believe it. For one thing, you didn't look old enough. And for another, it simply wasn't *fair*. But that's the way things were. There was nothing to be done about it.

"A couple of years after that, you had the first book done and I offered to represent you. And a couple of years after that, you invited me, and I quote, 'to reaffirm your desirability.' "

"God!" she laughed softly. "I really did say that, didn't I?"

"You did indeed. And I was only too happy to oblige you. So," he took a breath, "we embarked upon our curious affair. Now you see her, now you don't, for the next six or seven years. Until the accident. Then, when I should have stated my case, I didn't, and you married that overpaid vagina inspector. Mercifully, that didn't last too long. But by then, I'd decided to take things as they came because it seemed fairly clear I'd left it for too long. And anyway, I thought I'd become adept at being a bachelor. No shortage of invitations, no shortage of company. And when the mood suited you, I'd be available. I've only ever thought of *you* as someone I'd consider attempting to live with, and you seemed—after that last go-round—to prefer being on your own.

"Then, as I told you, after that depressing bash last year, I started thinking about my life and came to the conclusion that I'd probably blown it for good and always. But if I ever again had the chance to state my case, I would, and in no uncertain terms. Soooo," he wound down, "finding you there in my bed on Christmas morning, I decided to play fast and loose with my own poor shriveled ego and tell you that you still excite me, in all kinds of ways, and that despite all the nonsense, I adore you, you cantankerous little hen." He lifted his head to look at her, and asked, "Was it that bad a story?" as he put a finger to her cheek, caught a tear and licked it from his finger.

"I remember you that first time," she told him. "You were sitting on the sofa with Mother, and your legs were so long that your knees were up almost to your chin. And I thought you were far too young to have that great big moustache; I thought you'd probably grown it hoping it made you look older." She sniffed and smiled up at him. "This great oaf sitting there in his three-piece suit, with his terribly upper-class accent, and his excruciatingly good manners. You jumped up and shook hands with me. Remember? And I started laughing. I don't even know why, really. I just thought you were trying so hard to be mature and competent, and underneath all that, you weren't really sure what was going on. I guessed right off you'd been to bed with Mother. You had such a guilty look. I liked you, Miles." She rested her head on his shoulder. "You made me wish I'd met you, and not Carl, first.

"I'll tell you a secret not even Mother knows. No one but the Good Doctor knows. Because it was part of the agreement." She raised her head and met his eyes. "The reason I got so upset when we talked the other morning

. . . I agreed because of Joel, you see, because Jacobson had him and categorically didn't want any more children. But I thought it wouldn't matter. I'd have Joel. So I agreed, and he had one of his colleagues do it. He claimed it was unethical to perform surgery on one's own wife, but he had a colleague who would take care of making sure there'd be no possibility of my having any more babies.

"It was supposed to be a simple, little procedure. But it went horribly wrong. Infection set in, and they had to take me back into surgery. By that time, the infection had spread so far the only thing they could do was remove everything. I told myself I didn't mind. Because I'd be going home to Joel. Well, as we both know, Joel is no more. I'm not really sorry, Miles. Not about Joel. But when you said what you did, and I thought about how different things might have been . . ." She left the rest unsaid, and returned her head to his shoulder. After a few minutes, she said, "I cared far more for you than I ever did for Erik Jacobson."

"What about now, Leigh?" He'd stopped moving, and they'd become an island around which the other dancers eddied. "What about now?"

"Maybe," she allowed. "Maybe. But I need time. It's still too soon. I still cry without warning. I'm still finding things of Joel's in the apartment, and at the house. I do love you, and part of it is because I know you now. It probably wouldn't have worked back then. But I do know you now. Give me a kiss, Miles."

Dan couldn't sleep. He lay on the sofa bed in the den in the dark, his eyes open, his brain almost audibly clicking and whirring. At last, he turned on the light, got up, and went through each room of the house, turning the lights on as he went. Years of history crowded in on him as he recalled all the birthday parties at which Lane had sat there, at the head of the table, in the dining room. Paper hats and party horns, gaily wrapped gifts, triangle sandwiches, ice cream, and cakes with candles. Family dinners of silent, epic duration while Celeste sat and glowered at him and Lane, defying them to choke down their food in her presence.

Her anger was like a coating that lay heavy on the walls of every room. If he put out his hand, he was sure he'd feel it, hot and sticky, like her blood. He was aware of her presence as he pushed past the swinging door into the kitchen and stopped with his hand on the light switch, blinking in the fluorescent brightness at the white appliances, the bare counters and polished floor of black and white tiles. The plants on the windowsill had long since died, but no one had thought to dispose of them. He stalked across the room, opened the cupboard under the sink, found a large green plastic bag, and dumped the desiccated plants into it; knotted the top, opened the back door to admit a burst of gelid air, and heaved the bag out beside the bin enclosure. The raccoons and neighborhood dogs wouldn't bother with this particular trash.

He slammed shut the door, locking it, then marched out of the kitchen leaving the lights on. Into the living room to glare at the furniture, wondering how they could have called it a ''living'' room when neither he nor Lane had ever voluntarily set foot in the room for fear of disarranging the magazines so artfully positioned on the table behind the sofa, or of inadvertently pushing a chair or a pillow out of place. This was Celeste's showpiece, with the needlepoint fire screen, and the never used tuxedo sofa, the polished brass candlesticks, the standing brass lamps and crystal ashtrays. Jesus! All these years and no fire had ever been lit in that fireplace because the smoke might have discolored the pale-green walls, or an ember might have burned a hole in the pale-green carpet, or the smell of burning wood might have buried itself in the draperies. He hated this room.

Upstairs, he stood in the middle of Lane's bedroom, studying the rock posters on the wall, blow-ups of last year's superstars—Boy George, and Frankie Goes to Hollywood, and Cyndi Lauper. Stuffed toys surveyed the scene from the top shelf of the bookcase to which they'd been relegated some years earlier. The lower shelves were crammed with old school textbooks and paperback novels. *To Kill a Mockingbird, There Must Be a Pony, The Catcher in the Rye,* volumes of Shirley Jackson and Raymond Chandler, and *A Separate Peace; Your Turn to Curtsey, My Turn to Bow*—all books he'd read years ago himself, titles that had the warmth of familiarity.

This was the only room in the whole fucking house that had experienced a life, that had shaken with music and telephone conversations and crowds of girls giggling together over the school yearbook, with its muzzy class pictures and cute comments.

He turned off the light, shut the door gently, and moved along the hallway to the master suite. This was where he'd been headed all along. This had been his destination for twenty-one years. And had he only known it, he'd never have said yes, never have said I'll be honorable, I'll be responsible, I'll do the right thing, the supposed only thing. He'd have locked himself into his boyhood bedroom and refused to come out.

Barefoot, he padded across the carpet, sucking in his breath as he went, his shoulders rigid with tension as he arrived at the bathroom and stopped, gearing himself up. Fear like bile rising into his throat, he reached inside and flicked on the light. Of course it was immaculate. The place had been completely scrubbed and repainted. But he could see it all nevertheless, just the way it had been, the way she'd intended him to see it. The blood pooled on the floor by the sink, splatters leading over the floor to the tub.

His eyes moved across the room and came to rest on the tub. He was folding inward, trying to contain the horror. Right there, that was where she'd abandoned herself finally, leaving the remnants behind for him to find, knowing—she'd had to know—she'd at last succeeded in attaining the reaction she'd been seeking all her life.

Sliding down, boneless, he sat on the floor, trying to understand what she must have been thinking while she did it. No "hesitation marks." The police, the officials had spoken so knowledgeably, as if they'd dealt with similar scenes of carnage so often they'd lost their capacity to react. Long, purposeful cuts, they'd told him. The length of both inner forearms, around both ankles. And then, as if dissatisfied, it appeared she'd gone berserk, slashing at herself; she'd left the fouled single-edged blade on the edge of the sink before lifting her lacerated limbs into the tub, to immerse herself in the water that overflowed, spilling down the porcelain to inch across the floor. All tucked into herself, as if shielding those torn arms, the ravaged breasts and belly and thighs, she'd closed her eyes and gone dreaming while the blood ceased its humming in her veins and swam outward in thick, swirling strands to blend with the water; an embryo returned to its liquid medium. They'd never, the cool officials admitted, seen quite such an *angry* suicide; never seen anyone so *flayed* by her own hand. Which was why they had to ask so many difficult questions.

He wept, great shuddering sobs, and crawled out on his hands and knees, to collapse on the bedroom carpet until his body ceased its spasm. He shouldn't have come here, no matter how tired he'd been; he should have gone back to that safely impersonal little apartment where he had no difficulty sleeping, where the bedclothes still bore Leigh's

219

scent. This place no longer belonged to him; it had never been his. In sixty days it would be overrun by the new owners' three small children; their ebullience would kill off Celeste's ghost. Arrangements would be made for movers and packers to come here and deal with the collection of worldly goods Celeste had so avidly acquired. But then what?

He sat up. There was no point in wrapping and packing when he wanted none of this, and only Lane's things had a future. He'd get rid of it all, sell it. He never wanted to see any of it, ever again. He and Leigh would get their own things, new things, comfortable things, things without prior history. They'd shop together, mutually agree on their selections.

Back downstairs, he closed up the sofa bed, returned the pillows and bedding to the den closet, then went into the hall bathroom to shower. He steeled himself to return upstairs to the closet where he stripped his clothes from the hangers and dresser drawers, packing everything in suitcases and some cartons he brought up from the basement. Then he carried it all out to the car, filling up the trunk and most of the back seat.

When he was done, and he'd taken everything—the photo albums and framed pictures, income tax papers from the desk in the den, and the Braun electric coffee mill from the kitchen—he was so dizzy from lack of sleep he was seeing double. But he wouldn't stay in this house. He put on his coat, wound a scarf around his neck, went out to the car, and started to drive.

A knocking sound awakened him. Jerking upright, completely disoriented, he turned, and opened the car window.

"See your driver's license and registration, sir?" the police officer asked politely.

"Sure." Dan wet his lips and popped open the glove compartment for the registration, then got his wallet from his hip pocket to pull out the license. While the officer went back to his patrol car to check the documents, Dan looked through the windshield to see, with a start, that he was parked on Route 124, opposite Moonstone Lane. Jesus! he thought. What if she'd come home and seen the car, called the police?

The officer returned, passed the papers back to him, and bent down with one hand on the roof of the car, asking, "You all right, sir?"

"Oh, I'm fine. Just felt too tired to keep driving, so I thought I'd pull over, grab a little shut-eye for a few minutes."

The officer's eyes went to the boxes on the back seat. "Moving, huh?"

"That's right. Shifting some stuff from the old house."

"Helluva way to spend New Year's Eve," the officer said. "Drive carefully now. And don't forget to buckle up. Good day, sir."

Dan got the car started, remembered to fasten his seat belt, then pulled cautiously off the shoulder onto the road. A glance in the rearview mirror confirmed that the officer was standing by the patrol car, watching him go. Dan drove on, checking the mirror every few moments, until he'd gone a good five miles and the road was deserted in both directions. It was six-forty. He'd slept for almost four hours out there on the road where anyone could have seen him. What bothered him, when he remembered as he was taking the on-ramp to the Merritt, was that he'd forgotten to do what he'd gone there for: the damned silk thing was still on the passenger seat. The cop must've seen it and wondered if Dan was one of those creeps who liked to masturbate into women's underwear.

"Jesus!" he said aloud, easing his foot down on the

accelerator. Not only hadn't he put the thing back when he'd had the chance, but a goddamned cop had seen it. He was going to have to be very, very careful from now on.

Seventeen

"I really wish I knew why you insist on fleeing back to the country every time, without fail, just when I'm enjoying your company most. We have before us a four-day weekend. What is so urgently awaiting you out there, in the hinterlands?"

"Nothing, especially. Why don't you come with me?" Leigh said. "We could go over some of my ideas for the production. I've made a few notes, some rough sketches."

Miles sat, silently contemplating the logistics. "I suppose," he said at length, "I could bring my car and follow you there."

"You could also drive up with me. I'll put you on the train Sunday night."

"No good. It wouldn't be so bad if it was a direct run, but I loathe making that change in Stamford, hanging about on the platform, hoping the express is going to be on time. And it never is. I will come, but I'll bring my car."

"You're an elitist snob," she teased. "The truth is, you don't like being mistaken for a lowly executive."

"I see nothing wrong with elitism," he said loftily. "Some of my best friends are members of the elite."

"I'll give you Joel's keys, and you can meet me at the house."

"Perfect."

She found the keys in the kitchen drawer and gave them to him before they went down to the garage to get her car. She dropped him in front of his apartment on Fifty-ninth Street, explained that she'd stop along the way for some groceries, then headed across town. The traffic was light, the day mild and sunny. She felt really very well as she played with the dial on the radio until she'd located Joel's favorite station. The old show tunes connected her to Joel, and she was able to think about him without feeling bereft. Nostalgic, lonely for him, but no longer anguished. She had, with Miles's help, taken another small step away from the darkness of her grief.

Since she knew none of the stores in New Canaan would be open, she took the thruway instead of the Merritt, in order to stop at one of the markets she thought would likely be open in Darien. It was a minor but necessary inconvenience. With Miles in the house for four days, she was going to have to offer him something more substantial than coffee and burned toast.

Because there was so little traffic, she couldn't help noticing the dark-blue BMW that seemed to be keeping pace with her. She looked into the rearview mirror every so often to see that it was still behind her, and wondered idly why it didn't pass. Then she got caught up in the music and forgot about the other car until she was leaving the thruway at the Darien exit. When she put on her turn signal, so did the BMW. The car stayed behind her right through town, keeping a short distance back. It was there when she turned toward the shopping center after passing under the railroad bridge, but when she pulled into the parking lot, the BMW drove on past, and she promptly forgot all about it.

She filled a cart, actually enjoying herself. These new moments of all but mindless pleasure seemed remarkable to her; they were proof of her slow but steady return to life, and when she recognized the moments she became increasingly optimistic, as well as mildly guilty at leaving her sorrow behind. Yet she knew this was the way it had to be, and she accepted it.

Miles had already arrived. His car was in the garage, and he came out of the house as she pulled in, to help carry the bags inside. As she was about to open the trunk, she noticed a dark-blue car going past on the main road. She thought to mention it to Miles, decided it was nothing more than coincidence—Connecticut was crawling with BMWs, Benz's, and other imported cars—and said nothing.

"Very domestic, this is," Miles commented, helping to put away the groceries. "Very suburban, and very twee."

She leaned against the counter, lighting a cigarette. "Good or bad?" she asked him. "Sometimes I find it hard to decipher your cryptic little observations."

He closed the refrigerator door, saying, "It's a pleasant change. I always forget how quiet it is outside the city. It's also been quite some time since I've seen you in your alternative environment. While I was waiting, I had a look around."

"Snooping!"

"No, merely a look around. In view of the deplorable condition of the rest of this place, I have to assume Joel did over the kitchen. It's the only room that's had any attention paid to it. Speaking of which, your light's flashing." He indicated the answering machine, and stayed by the refrigerator as she walked over, carrying her cigarette, to push the PLAY button. He liked the way she moved, the way she held her cigarette; he liked it that even the smallest things captured her attention, so that the directness of her movements led to periods of stillness while she studied an object, or listened to something. She'd sail purposefully across a space, then halt all motion while she concentrated her attention. Now, for instance, she stood with one hand on the counter and the other, with the cigarette, in midair, her eyes on the machine as the tape rewound. He was also perennially intrigued by the kinds of things that caught her attention. He attributed her eye for the unusual to her being an artist, but unlike other artists he'd known, Leigh could be highly articulate about how the things she saw and heard affected her.

He was so taken by the look of her in this setting that it was a few seconds before he homed in on the voice on the tape. Then, his focus shifted to her face, to see she looked agitated and confused.

"I decided," the voice said with a forced little laugh, "that you must've lost my number. Which is why I haven't heard from you." A change of tone, the voice going deeper: "Leigh, I have to see you. Please call me as soon as you get in. There are things we really have to talk about; important things." He gave a number, then said goodbye.

The tone signaled the end of the message.

Then, "It's me again. I forgot to wish you a happy New Year. Please don't forget to call me as soon as you get in."

The tone, followed by five short beeps, signified the last of the messages.

"Jesus!" Leigh said, and hit the RESET button. "Now he's got my number. How the *hell* did he get it?"

"I take it," Miles said, "that's your airplane playmate."

"It's *not* amusing!" she said sharply. "First he manages to get my address. Now he's got my telephone number. I feel as if I'm under siege. Obviously, I'll have to get a new listing.''

"Why don't you simply tell him, nicely, of course, that you're not interested?''

"I've already done that. Clearly, it's made no impression whatever. Do you want a drink, or some coffee?''

"You want a drink,'' he could see. "Why don't we have coffee instead? It's still a bit early to hit the sauce.''

She held the cigarette under the faucet, doused it, then threw it into the garbage bin under the sink. "Could your ticker handle a decent cup of coffee?'' she asked, grabbing the kettle to fill it.

"My ticker is capable of handling any number of things.''

"Yes, but what about real coffee?''

"Even real coffee.'' He gave her a smile, but she didn't notice.

She opened the cupboard over the stove, got the Chemex pot, threw a paper cone into the filter, then half-filled the filter with the fresh-ground dark roasted coffee she'd just bought. Her movements were now jerky, jagged, reflecting her irritation.

"Is there something wrong with this guy?'' he asked, curious.

"I don't know *what's* wrong with him! He certainly doesn't understand a 'no' when he hears one. I want to change clothes. Come keep me company.''

"I'd like to remind you you did promise to model a certain undergarment.''

"The fashion show's scheduled for later on,'' she told him, trying not to take her upset out on him, but having trouble holding it in. It gave her the jitters to think Daniel had somehow managed to secure both her address and telephone number.

He sat on the side of the bed while she threw open the

closet doors, watching as she collected a pair of jeans, a plaid shirt, a heavy sweater, and a pair of wool socks.

"I'm sorry to go on and on about it," she said, tearing off her clothes as if they were contaminated, "but I'd dearly love to know how he got this number. I mean, what's the point to being unlisted if just anyone can get hold of your number?"

He let her talk, thinking she'd run herself dry on the subject if he simply listened without commenting. She kept on, speculating on the possible ways in which Daniel might have obtained her number, while she hung away the outfit she'd been wearing, then pulled on the casual clothes. By the time she was dressed, rather than running dry, she'd worked herself into a tight-lipped state of near-hysteria. She went quiet very abruptly and stood gazing at the framed picture of Joel on the dresser top.

"We could take a drive later, go to see the 'estate,' if you like."

"What?" She turned to look at him.

"It's not too far, over near Brewster. I thought you might care to see my dilapidated holdings."

"The coffee," she remembered, and went shoeless back to the kitchen.

He got up to follow and arrived in time to see her lighting another cigarette, before lifting the kettle to pour water into the filter. She seemed, at best, only peripherally aware of him, and he told himself the wise thing to do would be to take himself off to the living room with one of the manuscripts he'd brought along. No point to crowding her, he reasoned; if she wanted to talk, she would. He opened the new attaché case she'd given him, got a manuscript, then stretched out on the sofa with his head propped on the arm, and started to read.

A few minutes later, she came in carrying two mugs of coffee, the cigarette clenched between her teeth. She placed one mug on the coffee table within his reach, and the other on the mantel. Then, squinting against the cigarette smoke, she pushed crumpled newspapers under the grate, positioned three logs, and struck a match to get the fire going. It was something he'd seen her do many times, but he watched her over the top of the manuscript, trying to keep up with her mood swings. She was no longer as visibly agitated, but deeply pensive, as she reached for her coffee, at last removed the cigarette from between her teeth, and sat cross-legged on the floor to keep watch on the fire.

As had happened not infrequently during the many years he'd known her, he found himself moved and softened by her upset. "Are you feeling sad, Leigh?" he asked.

She gave a slow nod of her head, allowing almost a full minute to go by before saying, "I did warn you. I'm not the best company just now, full of unpredictable ups and downs."

"I don't require entertaining," he said, and went back to his reading.

She drank her coffee and chain-smoked, from time to time poking at the fire to rearrange the logs. She liked the heat, and smell, and noise, of the fire; it soothed her, made her drowsy. Like a poultice, it drew at her anger and apprehension and sadness, until her shoulders relaxed and she felt calmer. She gazed into the fire, appreciating the many different colors it produced, almost mesmerized by the glow. When at last she shifted to look over at Miles, she saw he'd fallen asleep. The manuscript was in danger of sliding off his chest.

She got up and put the pages on the coffee table, then watched him sleep, feeling her affection for him returning. He was too long for the sofa, and didn't appear especially comfortable with his head and feet propped on the shabby arms. His presence, though, altered the room, made it look less neglected, less abandoned.

Redirecting her gaze to the window, she saw odd snowflakes drifting down, and the sun casting blue shadows on the undisturbed snow coating the lawn; its surface was so smooth it looked lacquered. Her mood lifting, she thought she'd get the teddy and put in on to show him. She went to the mud room for the laundry and carried it to the bedroom. No teddy. She was sure she'd put it through the delicate cycle with the other undergarments. Maybe it was still in one of the machines. She went to check. Both the washer and dryer were empty. She double-checked, then went back to the bedroom to search every drawer in case it had been put away with the socks or the shirts. It hadn't.

Puzzled, she reviewed the teddy's whereabouts since Miles had given it to her. She'd brought it here along with her other Christmas gifts. She remembered setting it to one side; she preferred to launder anything new prior to wearing it, in order to get rid of any sizing the manufacturer might have put in to keep the item from losing its shape. She could see herself setting the wash cycle, adding the Woolite; she saw herself timing the dryer and setting the dial to air-dry the lingerie; she knew she'd taken care to fold the garment and set it on the top of the pile. So where was it?

She went again to the mud room, looking around, even craning far over to look down between and behind the machines. Nothing. Was she becoming forgetful? she wondered, making a slow tour of each room of the house, even looking under the beds and checking all the wastebaskets.

"The damned thing's simply disappeared," she told Miles, sitting on the coffee table and patting him on the arm. "I've been over every inch of this house, and the teddy's gone. You haven't seen it, by any chance, have you?''

He roused himself, turning to lean on his elbow. ''You can't find it?'' he asked dopily, not quite awake. ''Did you leave it in town?''

''I brought it here. I washed it. It was with the other laundry, right on top. Now it's gone.''

''What about your cleaning lady?''

''I haven't had her for months. I didn't want anyone around.''

''Well,'' he said, ''that *is* odd.'' He sat up and smoothed his hair with both hands. ''Undoubtedly, you'll find it at the apartment. Miles has to go to the loo.'' He gave both her knees a squeeze. ''Why don't we go for a drive?'' he suggested, on his way to the bathroom. ''Get some fresh air, see how the old estate's faring.''

''Only if we take my car. You can drive it. I'm really not up to a long ride in a vehicle with no springs, hundred-year-old shocks, and a heating system that's equivalent to having someone lying on the floorboards breathing on one's ankles.''

''We'll take your car,'' he laughed.

Abstractedly, she set the fire screen into position, then carried the mugs to the kitchen. It niggled her that she couldn't find the teddy. She knew damned well she'd washed it; she knew exactly how she'd folded it so that the embroidery on the front was uppermost.

''Just going to put on a sweater,'' Miles called from the bedroom. ''Won't be a tick.''

She simply couldn't stay up, and was peeved at herself. How long was it going to take before she could sustain her moods? Pocketing her cigarettes, she found her keys and bag, then went to the mud room to pull on her old Frye boots and Joel's sheepskin jacket, all the while looking around, hoping to spot the teddy.

231

Miles reappeared wearing a pale-blue pullover and a pair of loafers. "It's about thirty minutes from here," he told her, noticing she'd slipped into a different frame of mind. "Thirty minutes there, thirty to look around, thirty back, should make it around six. Then a nap before dinner, perhaps a cuddle with Uncle Miles. You'd rather not go."

"It'll be dark soon. Why don't we wait and go tomorrow? Would you mind very much?"

"I do not mind." He helped her out of the jacket and returned it to the wall peg while she got out of the boots.

She turned and wound her arms around his waist, hiding her face against his chest.

"Poor old Leigh," he commiserated, resting his chin on the top of her head. "Why don't you tell me about this Daniel person. You have my promise I won't be judgmental. I think perhaps you should talk about it."

"I'm such a mess," she said, her words muffled. "Driving home today I really was smug, thinking what terrific progress I'd made. Stupid, stupid."

"Rubbish," he said fondly, and looped her arm through his as they went back to the living room.

While she added another log to the fire, he dropped into the armchair nearest the fireplace. She went to sit on the floor before him, with her back against his legs, her eyes at once drawn to the fire. "His name is Daniel Godard. His father teaches French at NYU. His mother was formerly a fashion buyer for Bloomingdale's. He had some sort of mail-order business, but it was bought out two years ago. He has a daughter, Lane, who is evidently a big fan of my books, which is how, he said, he knew who I was. His wife, Celeste, has, from the sound of it, every problem known to man, from alcoholism to frigidity. He's forty-two, very good-looking, and terrified of flying. And that is how we got into conversation. We hit some turbulence and he turned positively ashen.

"Once we landed, I thought I'd seen the last of him. But he'd spied on me while I was filing out my landing card, and came to Brown's that afternoon. To make a long story short, by six we were in bed." She twisted around to cross her arms on his knees, her expression apologetic. "I was in appalling shape, Miles."

"Go on," he said. "I told you, I'm not going to judge any of this."

"Well, there I was, sitting alone in the lounge, quietly going to pieces, and he arrived to save the day. So, we had our little what-have-you, and I said very firmly I wouldn't see him again, but back he came the next day. Finally, he left to go on to Bangkok, I believe. And that, I thought, was the end of that. Except, he ferreted you out, and sent along the gift, with his number. It was not the sort of gift one could ignore. At least I couldn't. So I rang up to thank him and before I knew what I was doing, I'd agreed to meet him."

"And you slept with him a second time," Miles filled in. "And again, you told him you wouldn't see him. And again, he didn't believe you."

"That's exactly right."

"I don't suppose I'd have believed you either, my darling."

"I did *not* give him my address or my telephone number. I told him categorically I would not see him in future. He frightened me," she admitted.

"How?"

"Sexually. I won't go into the lurid details. Let's just say there was an undercurrent that alarmed me, and I decided I really didn't want to risk seeing him again."

"Risk? Kindly go into the lurid details. *How* did he frighten you? You're fairly intrepid, you know, my hedonistic little love slave. When you confess to being alarmed, I think it's very significant.''

''Are you mocking me, Miles? I swear I'll do you an injury if you are.''

''I'm completely serious,'' he assured her. ''You know I can't resist coining endearments. Do tell me. Seriously.''

''He didn't want to stop. That's all. It was as if he intended to keep on with it until one of us died. And I thought it might be me.''

''Literally?''

''Oh, I don't *know*, Miles! I'm talking about a feeling, not anything tangible or literal. There was something about him that was just—desperate. I felt terribly sorry for him because he seemed, at moments, so dreadfully unhappy. But there was more to it than that. I had the sense,'' she said slowly, thinking it through, ''that as close to the edge as I thought I was, he was very much closer. As I say, it was simply a feeling.''

''But a frightening one.''

''Yes.''

Miles thought for a time, automatically running his hand up and down her arm. Whenever they were together, he was drawn to touch her. ''I think,'' he said, ''Monday morning you should make arrangements for a new listing. It might even, you know, Leigh, be wise to consider staying in the city for a time, until he's given up hounding you. You don't think he has the New York number, too, do you?''

''I don't know. I'll go check that line, see if he's left any messages.'' She went to the kitchen and returned inside of two minutes to say, ''No messages.''

''Inconclusive,'' he said, thinking aloud. ''Perhaps he knows you're here.''

''Don't!'' Her eyes widened. ''I don't need you to alarm me further, Miles.''

"Sorry." He looked at his watch. "Time for a drink. Gin and tonic?" he asked, rising to go to the trolley by the dining room door.

"Uh-huh," she answered. "Christ, Miles! All the men I've known over the years, not one of them's ever kept on after me. Why now? I'm not up to this. I'm really not."

"So, don't stay here," he said, carrying the ice bucket out to the kitchen. "Come back into town and stay with me, or with your mother. Wait it out. He's bound to quit eventually."

"It's so damned irritating!" she railed. "I can't imagine a woman doing this sort of thing."

"Oh, no?" he said calmly, returning with the full bucket. "Obviously, you've never seen a minor masterpiece Clint Eastwood did called *Play Misty for Me*. Women most certainly do do things like this. I wish you'd stop believing unpredictable behavior is the exclusive domain of men. I've had women hound me after I've tried, in the nicest possible fashion, to break off with them. There was one who persisted for an entire year before she finally gave it up. For twelve long months I didn't dare answer my telephone at home. I screened every call through the answering machine. And, suffice it to say, I had to tell Diane not to accept any calls from her at the office. In the end, she did quit. But I promise you I found it every bit as unpleasant as you're finding this. He will stop in time. It may take a while before the penny drops, but he'll stop. They always do." He gave her her drink and a smile, saying, "These things happen, Leigh. It's a fact of life. And, actually, you've been bloody lucky it hasn't happened to you before now. You'll get a new telephone number; you'll spend some time in town; and he'll give it up and leave you alone."

"What happened in the movie?" she asked, then tasted

her drink. "Come sit with me by the fire. Bring the sofa pillows, if you want to make yourself a nest."

He laughed. "Strike you as an oversized bird, do I?"

"Only sometimes."

He stretched out on his stomach, his chin propped on one hand, and tried to sketch in the details of the film. "It's been ages since I saw it, so I don't remember it all that well. Eastwood was a disc jockey with a late-night show. And this woman kept calling to request 'Misty.' Somehow, they meet up and go to bed. Next thing anyone knows, she has a full-fledged obsession. I recall it got very gory at the end, and she was carted off after running amok with a knife or scissors or somesuch. The point was, he got involved because he entered into what he thought would be nothing more than a one-nighter. Interesting, rather Gothic, morality tale, that illustrates quite well that women cannot lay exclusive claim to the role of victim. Not," he added, "that I see you that way."

"I should hope not." She shivered and moved closer to the fire. "I never dreamed it would get so out of hand. He was there when I needed someone . . . something. And I suppose I did give him mixed signals. Let's not talk any more about it."

"Well, you're welcome to come hide out in the mausoleum with me." He rattled the ice in his glass, then said, "I can't for the life of me think why I'm down here in this horribly unnatural position." He pushed himself into sitting position, took another swallow of his Scotch, then set the glass on the coffee table. "Fancy a cuddle? Why not come over here and let Uncle Miles drool all over you?"

She laughed, set aside her drink, then knee-walked over the carpet to give him a kiss.

"One of the things I like best about you," he told her, draping his arm around her shoulders, "aside from your truthfulness, is your brain." He tapped his finger lightly against her temple. "You are a truly intelligent being. What I never cease to wonder at, though, is how someone so truly intelligent can be so naive about the implications of her actions. I promised not to judge, and I'm not going to. I think this happened because you were, and are, having the devil's own time trying to stay steady. And I know how that is. You think you've come out of it; you're actually able to laugh, and hold a rational conversation. Then, wham! You're up to your eyebrows in pure blackness and it's hard to breathe, let alone talk, or laugh, or do any of the dozens of everyday things you've got to do."

"How do you know that?" she asked.

"Luckily," he said, "I was young. The young are so much more resilient. I believe the older you are, the rougher it is."

"But what happened? How young were you? Miles! What haven't you told me?"

"Nothing alarming," he said, giving her a kiss on the forehead. "Don't overreact," he said kindly. "I'm not going to tell you a horror story. It's not even a terribly uncommon tale. I was nine, the youngest in the family, and was evacuated to the country. A raid wiped out the rest of them, mother, father, and two older sisters. I was old enough to suffer, and young enough to be able to go forward."

She shook her head sadly. "How old were your sisters?"

"Sixteen and eighteen. I was one of those 'surprises' that came long after they thought they were done with nappies and feedings and so forth. For a time I had three mothers, really, not counting various aunts, and a lovely gran. Perhaps that's why I've always liked women so much, having my early years surrounded by them. Believe it or not, there are times when I still feel lonely for them. Lovely girls, my sisters.''

"Somehow I've always thought your family was all over there. Miles, I am sorry. How very sad for you."

"It wasn't so bad, really," he said. "I lived with my Uncle James and Aunt Caroline, my mother's sister and her husband. It wasn't in the least Dickensian. They were very good to me. Their son Geoff and I attended school together. We've stayed in touch." As he talked, he drew her gradually closer until she was seated in his lap. "There was a fairly sizable estate. Uncle James was the executor." He was about to go on when something—a movement?—caught his eye, and he looked over at the window.

"What?" Leigh asked, at once aware of the sudden shift of his attention.

"Nothing." He told himself he must have imagined it. "I've lost track of my narrative thread. It's difficult to concentrate with you purring away here like a great, tawny cat."

"I'm too warm now," she said, and sat away to pull the sweater off over her head.

"I interpret that as an invitation," he warned her.

She didn't say anything but simply kept her eyes on his.

"Well," he said, "since there's no objection . . ." Lazily, he began to undo the buttons on her shirt. "I suppose it must have something to do with all the fresh air and country quiet."

"What does?"

"My renewed interest in your anatomy."

"I think it has more to do with opportunity, which is something you've never been able to resist."

"Whatever." Adroitly, he unhooked her bra and, with a sigh, closed his hand over her breast. "Lovely," he murmured approvingly. "Give us a kiss, love. We'll have a bit of a cuddle, then see to dinner."

Made serious by his persuasive hands, she tilted her head back to kiss him. His mouth brushed back and forth against hers, lips grazing, before coming to rest. She liked the way he kissed. He was never presumptuous, never invasive, but always progressed gradually toward the heart of a kiss, and its expanding potential.

His mouth moved to her throat, then to the rise of her breast, and then to her nipple. Her body gave a small responsive leap, and she laced her fingers over the back of his head to hold him to her, as she extended her legs in a pleasurable stretch, her eyes closing.

Eighteen

Dan unloaded the car, dumped all the bags and boxes in the middle of the apartment living room, then went downstairs intending to return the car to the garage. He found himself headed uptown instead. He badly wanted to see Leigh. He had left her a couple of messages, but it was too soon to expect her to call back. He parked halfway down the next block on the same side of the street as her building, and settled in to wait. He couldn't even be sure she was there. But her car hadn't been at the house in New Canaan, so the chances were better than even that she'd come by the apartment at some point—assuming she planned to head back to Connecticut. Of course, she might be spending the entire weekend in the city. He hated not knowing her plans. It made him feel left out, and diminished in a way, as if he wasn't important enough to be told what she was doing. Naturally, she was in no position to do that, what with the Good Doctor probably hanging constantly in the background, keeping tabs on her. Once the doctor was out of the way, neither he nor Leigh would have to go through any more of this crap. In the meantime, he thought he'd keep watch for a while, on the off chance she turned up. He felt purposeful, and quite comfortable, waiting. He had the radio turned on low, and every half hour or so he started up the engine to warm the car's interior.

While he waited, he ran down all the possibilities: she might already have made an early start back to the country; she might not emerge from the apartment—if she was in fact in there—for several days; she was probably with the Good Doctor—a notion that bothered the hell out of him. He wanted a look at this guy, wanted to see what kind of man could take a woman like Leigh for granted; what kind of man didn't bother with good locks on his doors to ensure his wife's safety, didn't bother to be aware of his wife's comings and goings.

He smoked a cigarette, cracking open the window to keep the air circulating in the car, his eyes on the building entrance. Good thing it was a holiday. The streets were pretty much deserted. Wednesday, but it felt like Sunday. Quite a few offices in town were staying closed right through Monday. All in all, it was very damned fortunate he had so much free time now to devote to Leigh. Any other time in his life he'd have been too busy—with the business, with trying to keep Celeste on an even keel, with keeping his parents up-to-date, and with making sure Lane had everything she needed. The timing couldn't have been better.

At twelve-ten, he saw the Mercedes nose out of the garage entrance on the side of the building. With bursting excitement—glad he'd thought to keep both the side and the front of the building in view—he put the BMW into gear and pulled out, getting close enough to see there were two people in the car. Seeing this started an electric buzzing in his chest. He was finally going to get a look at the Good Doctor.

The Mercedes headed down Park to Fifty-ninth and pulled over in front of an older, medium-rise building with a number of doctors' offices on the ground floor. The passenger door opened, and Dan saw the Good Doctor climb out. The man bent to say something to Leigh, then shut the car door and went into the building.

So that was the husband. There wasn't time now to think about it. He had to pay attention to tailing Leigh. It was a cinch, really. Once he figured out that she was headed over to the East Side he fell back, letting a few cars get between them. He stayed maybe a quarter of a mile behind, noting she drove fast and well, signaling without fail every time she changed lanes. He admired the way she handled the big sedan. She was a decisive driver, maintaining her speed, obviously relaxed behind the wheel. Celeste, when she'd been sober enough to drive, had been the worst: easily rattled, lacking a sense of direction, frightened by the power of the car. "It's *you*!" she'd accused regularly. "I drive just fine when I'm by myself. I know you're watching every last thing I do, and it makes me so edgy I can't do anything." The truth, of course, was she was simply a lousy driver.

He kept up with Leigh along the Bruckner, all the way to the New England Thruway exit. He was not far behind when she left the thruway at Exit 11 in Darien, and let his speed fall under the limit as they took the Post Road through town. He expected her to keep going to the start of 124, but she turned right immediately under the railroad bridge, and he had to cut over from the left lane—fortunately no one was on his right—to make the turn.

It would be too obvious if he followed after her into the shopping center parking lot, so he kept going, reversed in the driveway of the outdoor market—closed for the winter—and went back to cruise the lot until he spotted her car. He parked a couple of aisles over, then hunched down in the seat to wait, feeling even more purposeful and keyed up. He was doing things he'd been seeing all his life in movies and on television, but until now it had never occurred to him that he'd absorbed a hell of a lot of information on how to play sleuth.

Half an hour later she came out of the market pushing a cart. She unloaded the bags, returned the cart to the market entrance—he gave her points for that; it was something he always did, too—then got back in the car. He tailed her, staying a half mile or so behind, right the way to her house, and cruised past the top of the driveway just as she was about to open the trunk of the Mercedes. He hadn't timed that too well, and hoped she hadn't spotted him. He'd seen the second car in the garage, which meant the Good Doctor had decided to spend some time at home for a change.

He was anxious for a closer look at the doctor, but that wasn't going to be possible in daylight. After sundown, though, he'd be able to sneak up to the house and see what was going on. Only a few hours until dark. In the meantime, there were a couple more things he wanted from the Bedford house.

In the light of day, the house didn't bother him so much, and he even wondered, for a few minutes, if he wasn't perhaps making a mistake getting rid of it. No going back now, though, he reminded himself. And he'd made one hell of a profit on his initial investment. Besides, there was no way on God's earth he could ever bring Leigh here. No. The two of them would start fresh, with someplace new.

He got his toolbox from the garage and stowed it in the BMW's trunk, then let himself in the side door, surprised to hear the telephone ringing. He wondered if it could be Leigh, remembered she didn't have this number, and thought maybe it was the real estate agent with the latest news on the sale. Or maybe it was Lane, or his parents. He hesitated, reluctant to speak to anyone. He'd just spent a week with his family, and right now the only person he wanted to talk to was Leigh. Besides, the agent wouldn't be calling him on New Year's Day, would she? He hesitated too long, and the ringing stopped. Relieved, he went to the den to get several items from his desk.

Sitting behind the desk, he considered Leigh's husband. The man was not what Dan had expected. He was big, over six feet, and solidly built. Expensive black topcoat, no hat, moustache; he'd moved with authority, giving the doorman a slight nod as he'd gone inside. Big stupid bastard didn't know what he had, and it was too late to change anything. All Dan had to do was get her off somewhere quiet where they could talk, and he could make her see she was wasting herself, wasting time and potential and emotion. He'd make her see.

He thought about things she'd told him, about other affairs she'd had, about the look and feel of her in bed, and knew she'd understand there was no need to do any of that anymore. He'd keep her happy, keep her satisfied. It was what she wanted. She was just afraid to make the break. He knew how that was. But once the decision was made, things became very easy. Making the decision was the big step. All right, so maybe Celeste had made that decision for him, in a way. It didn't matter; what mattered was his making that decision now, for Leigh.

All at once, he remembered the piece of lingerie in his coat pocket; he fished it out and laid it on the desk top, with his fingertip tracing the embroidery on the bodice. He laid his head down on the cool silk and closed his eyes. Then, reluctantly, he sat up and opened the top drawer for the scissors. It was a shame, but he really had to destroy it. He couldn't go around with the thing in his pocket.

When he was finished, he folded the pieces into a sheet

of paper, and dumped it into the garbage in the kitchen. Before he left, he'd put the garbage in the bin outside. Tired and hungry now, he fixed a can of soup and ate it out of the pot along with a handful of crackers. Then he rinsed the pot, put it in the dishwasher, wiped the crumbs off the counter, and, yawning, decided he'd take a nap. He opened the sofa bed in the den, got the bedding from the closet, pushed off his shoes, and lay down.

When he awakened, it was dark; almost five. He'd slept longer than he'd thought he would, but felt better as he went into the hall bathroom to shower and shave.

By six, he'd parked about a quarter mile past Moonstone Lane, on a gravel shoulder at whose apex sat a row of mailboxes. There wouldn't be a mail delivery, so it was a good place to leave the car. There were no outside lights on at her house, but the living room windows glowed invitingly. He ran quickly, lightly—he felt unbelievably weightless, and somehow powerful—down one of the tire tracks in the snow on the driveway, dropping low as he left the track and cut diagonally across the lawn. He crept to the side of the house and, with extreme caution, raised his head until he could see through the window, instantly jerking out of sight when he spotted the two of them sitting on the floor near the fireplace. He'd unwittingly placed himself directly in the Good Doctor's eye line. Luckily, he hadn't been seen. Ducking below the window, he inched along to the second of the three windows, that would allow him to take a peek inside without placing himself in view.

Pressing tight to the wall of the house, he rose up on the far side of the window, then inched forward until he had an unimpaired view of that portion of the room. Immediately, he was livid at having to watch that son of a bitch in there pushing himself on Leigh. Dan could see she didn't care for it. She gave in though, took off her sweater, and lay across the bastard's lap like a rug, closing her eyes so she wouldn't have to see. Poor Leigh. He had to get her out of this situation; it was rotten.

He knew he shouldn't be watching, but he couldn't look away, a twisting spurt of anger overtaking him at the sight of that oversized, heavy-handed prick mauling her, sucking on her like some immense infant. Jesus! It was so goddamned wrong! She was being forced to perform. And he had to give her credit, he thought, the anger robbing him of much of his lightness; she was playing it out very damned convincingly. He had a moment or two of doubt, wondering if she really was acting. But no. He could tell it was a performance. Still, performance or not, he had to restrain himself from smashing through the window, or running over to kick in the door when the son of a bitch pulled her jeans halfway down her legs and then worked his hand between her thighs. He had Leigh half-naked in his lap. The two of them were going to do it in front of his eyes, and he had to drag himself away from the window because if he saw one more second of what was going on in there, he'd kill the bastard.

He raced back up the driveway, panting hard, his arms and legs pumping, fists clenched. He had to put a stop to this, get Leigh the hell out of that situation. He threw himself into the car, got the engine going, then floored the accelerator, sending gravel rattling against the undercarriage as he flew halfway across the road, reversed in a fury, then shot off, shifting from first directly into fourth, back toward Bedford. His temples were pounding, his lungs heaving, his eardrums vibrating noisily. *No more of this!* he ranted silently, hitting sixty, then seventy, when the road straightened. He'd get her out of there; they'd talk; he'd rescue her.

He had a great deal to do, a tremendous number of things to do, and not a lot of time in which to do them.

Most likely it would take the better part of the night to get everything done. But that was all right. He felt huge, bursting with untapped energy, his brain busy ticking off details on a mental list.

Even in the country, without the clanging of delivery trucks and garbage cans being emptied at 5 A.M., Miles couldn't hang on to his sleep. It eased away, leaving him alert and ready for the day. It had always been that way, but he didn't mind. He used the time in the city to get paperwork done before leaving for the office. He was able to wander at a leisurely pace around the apartment, doing this and that, having breakfast and a read of the paper while the noise on the streets gained in volume. He liked mornings. They made him feel young, for some reason. He'd always been able, in the light of morning, to make sense of things that had seemed somewhat indecipherable during the night; he found a clarity to the world and to his life with the advent of each new morning that often was just beyond his reach in the dark.

For a time, he watched Leigh sleep, liking the sight of her at rest equally as well as he enjoyed visually measuring the economy or generosity of her movements when awake. Altogether, he liked her. He doubted that would ever change. No one else he'd known, male or female, was such a blend of contradicting qualities; no one else could be as painfully serious, or give herself so wholeheartedly over to sheer nonsense. He found her entirely irresistible, as much now as twenty-five years before. And his being here now was the most encouraging thing that had happened since Joel had taken ill, when she'd cut herself off from everyone and everything but the death that was taking place inside of someone who, by rights, should have had a long, rich life. It wasn't surprising that Leigh was having such trouble coping with the loss of Joel. Joel had been a rare and remarkable young man, one it was impossible to dislike. He'd had a natural zest, a limitless enthusiasm that embraced all things, new and old, as well as people and events, and most especially Leigh. She'd been his staunchest ally, his devoted mother, and his willing friend; she was the only mother Joel had known, and there'd never been a moment when he'd minimized her importance. She'd been his anchor, his confidante, his greatest admirer. And he'd rewarded her, in his unique fashion, with a filial regard and a comprehension of her complexities that was nothing less than outstanding in one so young. They'd understood each other perfectly, even when they'd disagreed. Joel had accepted her infrequent criticisms, her brief-lived affairs, and her advice, with an intuitive recognition both of his own good fortune and of her wisdom. That Joel had died was a true tragedy. But that he, Miles, was being received back into her life was, perhaps, a result of that tragedy. And he thought, not for the first time, how very odd and convoluted were the paths along which one's life could lead.

He would surprise her, he decided, and prepare breakfast. While the bacon was spitting under the broiler, he went to open the front door on the off chance she was still having the *Times* delivered. No such luck. He was about to close the door when he noticed footprints in the snow; two sets of them cut across the lawn. Leaning out, he saw where the snow had been trampled between two of the front windows. Bemused, he closed the door and went into the living room to look out at the impressions in the snow, then turned around to study the interior of the room, first from the near window, and then from the far one. Both afforded a clear view of the fireplace end of the room. He *had* seen something last evening. That very slight movement hadn't been his imagination. Someone had stood outside and looked in at them. The hair on his arms rose, and he rubbed his forearms.

Returning to the kitchen to check the bacon, he decided not to mention it to Leigh. What he would do was increase his effort to persuade her to spend some time in the city. Obviously, it wasn't a good idea for her to remain alone here. But if he didn't point out the footprints, or tell her he'd seen a shadow in the window, wouldn't he be doing her a frightful disservice?

He filled the kettle and put it on to boil, becoming progressively angrier at the idea that someone had been watching when they'd made love the night before. What kind of man sneaked around looking in people's windows? Bloody disgusting! he thought, opening the refrigerator for the eggs. Once the breakfast was ready, he'd wake Leigh, they'd eat, then they'd drive to Brewster. And he'd broach the subject somewhere along the route.

She came in, belting her robe, as he was buttering the English muffins. "The bacon woke me," she said, pouring herself some coffee. "Miles?" She leaned over the counter to look at him. "Is something wrong? You look a little peculiar."

He should have known her special radar would pick up on his mood. "I *feel* peculiar," he admitted, wiping his hands on the dish towel. "At first, I wasn't going to say anything. But then I saw that would be sheer bloody negligence, to say the least. Leigh, you cannot stay here on your own. I'm going to *insist* you come back to the city with me. You can stay at your place, or with your mother, or even with me if you like. But I absolutely will not allow you to remain here."

"Why, for heaven's sake?"

"I want to show you something." Taking her by the upper arm, he led her to the front door, opened it, pulled her over the threshold, and pointed. "What do you make of *that*?" he demanded.

It wasn't possible to overlook the footprints. She followed their trail to the windows then back to the driveway. It could have been an oil delivery. The tank was buried somewhere over there. But the company didn't make deliveries on holidays, except in emergencies. And besides, they'd filled her tank the previous week. She recalled taking the delivery slip from the mailbox at the top of the driveway. Those prints in the snow hadn't been there yesterday when she'd arrived. She'd have noticed them. Which had to mean they'd been made sometime last night.

"You've got a peeping Tom!" Miles declared, pulling her back into the house. "I *thought* I saw something last evening but I told myself I was being fanciful. Clearly I was *not*. Someone stood out there and looked in at us. Think about this for a moment, Leigh! You could scream your heart out in here and no one would hear you. If I have to *carry* you out to the car, if I have to bind you hand and foot, I am not leaving here without you."

"I need a cigarette," she said, and freed herself from his grip to go get one.

"You *need* an *alarm system*," he called after her, "and some *protection*! Not a bloody cigarette!"

"Stop bellowing at me," she said quietly, returning from the bedroom with her cigarettes. "It's hardly *my* fault that someone's decided to start looking in at my windows. And I'm not stupid, Miles. Do you seriously think I'd *want* to be here alone, knowing someone's watching me? You're fighting all by yourself. I wouldn't dream of spending any more time here than necessary. In fact, I'll pack and leave with you this afternoon. I'll call Tom in town and get him to look after the place while I'm away."

"Call the local police, too, and have them start patrolling the house. Breakfast is ready," he said curtly. "I'll dish up."

"My God! You really do think I'm stupid!" she accused.

He stopped, pulled himself together, and turned back to her. "I don't think anything of the sort, actually. I'm taking it out on you because I opened the door to see if you were having a newspaper delivered these days, and what do I see but tracks in the snow! You're anything but stupid. But you *are* very damned vulnerable here, and that makes me edgy, which in turn makes me angry. I apologize for my less than gracious way of displaying my concern for you. I love you. The very *idea* that any harm might come to you . . . well."

The telephone rang. They both started, then turned to stare.

"I'll let the machine answer," she said, with the feeling that things were suddenly closing in on her.

They waited until the machine clicked on, followed by a silence while the outgoing message played, then Marietta's voice said, "Leigh, you can't have gone out this early in the morning. Are you there, darling?"

Leigh went to pick up the receiver, at the same time pressing the RESET button. "I'm here. How are you?"

"I am perfectly well. How are you? Is Miles with you? I rang both your numbers and concluded you'd gone off together."

"You should try your hand at detective novels," Leigh laughed. "He's here."

"Well, that's lovely. It's high time the two of you started taking each other seriously. I have nothing of significance to say. I simply wanted to know how you are, and if you had a good time last night."

"We had a wonderful time. Did you?"

"The Plaza," Marietta said sadly, "is *not* the splendid

hotel it once was. It's gone downhill, and badly, I'm sorry to say. But it was a most pleasant evening. I won't keep you.''

"Miles has talked me into coming into town for a while. I'll call you this evening when we get back.''

"What a good idea! Are you going to do *Percival*?''

"I think so, yes.''

"Better and better! I couldn't be more pleased. I'll ring off now. My love to Miles.''

Leigh hung up to see Miles had put the food on the table and was waiting for her to join him.

"How is your mother?'' he asked.

"The Plaza has gone downhill.''

"Poor Marietta's always the last to know,'' he said, and laughed.

Leigh drank some of her coffee, thinking. It had to be Daniel who'd come looking in the windows. What a bizarre thing for him to do! And it really did have to be him. It was exceedingly unlikely that anyone else would take such a risk. It irked her that he'd violate her privacy in that fashion, but mainly she felt sorry for him. Something was dreadfully wrong in his life and whatever it was, it was driving him to do things that were, she was certain, very out of character. No matter how she turned the pieces, she couldn't see him as a particularly menacing figure.

"You're not eating,'' Miles said. "I'm becoming terribly bored by your not eating.''

"We can't have that, can we?'' she countered, and dutifully picked up her knife and fork. "I think it was Daniel, Miles.''

"I must say you're being very damned calm about it. It doesn't *bother* you that he's got your address, your telephone number, and now he's started peeping through your windows?''

"Of course, it bothers me. But . . . I don't know. I'm

not sure what I think, or how I really feel. There's something so very very sad about him."

Miles reached over and stole a strip of her bacon, then sat munching it while she ate some of the scrambled eggs. He was about to offer his opinion on the matter when there was the sound of a car pulling into the driveway. He craned around toward the door as Leigh got up and went to the window to see a dark-blue BMW pull to a stop at the foot of the walk.

An alarm went off inside her head at the realization that it had been Daniel following her from the city yesterday. She said, "Oh, no!" as he now got out of the car and came striding up the walk.

"Who is that? Is that this Daniel person?" Miles asked from the table.

"Damn it all! What is he *doing* here? This is ridiculous!" She backed away from the window and looked over at Miles as the doorbell sounded. "Let me handle this, please. I'll get rid of him." She cracked open the door and said, "Daniel, what do you think you're doing?"

"I want to see you, Leigh. We have to talk."

Miles got up from the table, saying, "What the bloody hell is this?"

Leigh turned, her hand upheld to stop him, as she said, "Daniel, please leave. This is difficult and embarrassing."

"What the hell do you want?" Miles thundered, pulling the door fully open to confront the younger man.

"She doesn't love you!" Daniel informed him.

"Oh, for God's sake!" Leigh interjected.

"Are you out of your mind?" Miles pushed forward, attempting to shift Leigh to one side, out of harm's way.

"Don't touch her!" Daniel exploded, and drove his fist solidly into Miles's middle.

Leigh screamed.

Miles gagged, and bent double. But Dan wasn't finished. His fists began pounding into Miles, delivering up-percuts, crosscuts, body blows, as he shouted out Miles's unworthiness, reviling him for forcing himself on Leigh.

"STOP IT!" Leigh screamed, pulling at Daniel. "STOP IT! *He has a bad heart! You'll kill him!* WHAT DO YOU WANT?"

"I want to *talk* to you!" Daniel huffed, letting up on Miles. "I want you to *come* with me!" He panted, hanging over Miles, who was on his knees now, struggling to catch his breath, his face purple.

"Don't hit him again!" she begged. "Let me get my coat. I'll come with you, and we'll talk. Will you just let me get my coat? Please, don't hit him anymore! Miles?" She moved to go to him, but Dan pushed her away.

"Get your coat!" he ordered. "I'm taking you out of here, away from this son of a bitch."

She ran to the closet for her coat, keeping her eyes on the two men, terribly afraid Daniel would actually kill Miles, who had sunk all the way to the floor now, his face still dark as he drew in wisps of air. Pushing her bare feet into the first available pair of boots, she got the coat on and ran back, anxious to help Miles. But Daniel took hold of her arm and dragged her out of the house and down the walk toward the BMW.

Upon arriving at the car, he became apologetic and strangely formal, saying, "I'm sorry, Leigh, but I'm going to have to ask you to ride back here."

She didn't know what he was talking about, didn't even want to hear him. She was too worried about Miles, and turned toward the house, afraid he'd been seriously injured.

Dan was opening the trunk of the car. She turned to gape at him, suddenly, finally, afraid. Was he actually telling her he wanted her to get into the *trunk* of his car? She took a step away. "I'm not getting in there!" she said, and took another step, looking again over at the house. She'd thought she'd sit with him in the car for a few minutes, they'd talk, she'd convince him he was behaving irrationally, then she'd go back inside and see to Miles. But he was actually coming after her, determined to get her into the trunk. He put his hand on her arm and she flung it off. "I am *not* getting in there! Don't be ridiculous!"

"Please don't fight me, Leigh," he said quietly. "If I thought I could trust you not to try to jump out of the car, there'd be no problem. Normally I wouldn't dream of asking you to do this, but I'm very afraid you'd try something, and I wouldn't want to risk your getting hurt. Please." His hand closed around her wrist. She yanked futilely against his grip.

When he saw she intended to go on resisting, he said, "If you don't do as I ask, I'll kill the son of a bitch. I really don't care, Leigh." And as if to prove the weight of his threat, he lifted his other hand to reveal the tire iron he'd just removed from the trunk and had been keeping by his side, out of her view. The sight of it stopped her.

"All right," she relented. "Just promise me you won't harm him any more than you already have."

"I give you my word. Now come on." He drew her to the rear of the car and she looked into the trunk, her heart giving a frenzied leap as she saw he'd placed a blanket and some pillows inside. It looked to her like a coffin.

"What *is* this?" she cried, pulling back.

"I only want you to be comfortable. Come on. Climb in. I'll give you a hand."

Unable to believe this was actually happening, that she'd get inside, and he'd shut the lid on her, she lifted one leg over the rear bumper—surely to God something would happen to put a stop to this lunacy!—then the other. She looked around. Maybe a car going by on the road . . .

"Lie down, Leigh," he told her. "You'll be all right."

She didn't want to lower her head. As long as she kept looking around, there was the possibility of someone coming to help, something . . .

"Lie down!"

She had to turn on her side and bend her knees in order to fit into the space.

"Don't worry, Leigh," he said. "I'll drive carefully."

Oh, Jesus! He was really going to do it. Gently, he pushed closed the lid, and she was trapped in the rubber-smelling, pitch-black, cramped space. She heard the car door slam, then felt the vibrating roar of the engine as it started. Then the car was moving. Even though she knew it would do no good, she put her hands flat on the lid and pushed hard. Useless. She was locked in. And he was driving away. What about Miles? God! He had to be all right. Where was this man taking her? What if he intended to kill her? What if he meant to trick her by making it seem as if he was driving away when what he was actually planning was to go back into the house and murder Miles? *God!* Nothing must happen to Miles. He gave his promise he wouldn't harm Miles. But what if he decided to kill *her* if she didn't do what he wanted?

Nineteen

He knew the contents of the note by heart. They recited themselves to him when he least expected it. Her voice, sounding sixteen or seventeen, read the words she'd written on that piece of her expensive stationery. She'd had to have paper from Tiffany's, with her monogram in the corner, supplies for letters she never wrote—except for thank-you notes now and then to his parents or hers, for some nightmare of a dinner or some gift they'd given her.

"Dear Danny"—her voice filled the car's interior—"I'm completely sober right now. It's not my favorite thing, but that doesn't matter. I feel so sad, Danny. I've been feeling this way for so long that I don't know how anything else feels anymore. I don't really blame you. It's just that you've always had such high ideals, such impossible expectations. You set standards and because you could meet them, you wanted all of us to meet them, too. But I was never you, Danny. I was always just me, but you wanted me to be you. I never liked being me, it was hard, so hard, especially when you didn't seem too happy with the me I was, either. We agreed on that, didn't we? Neither one of us was happy with me. I'm just so tired. It'll be better this way. I'm sorry. Celeste.''

He hated it! He didn't want to have to hear this. He turned up the volume on the radio. His foot pressed down on the accelerator. He made as much noise as he could, but it was like a loop, and he couldn't stop it playing. ''Danny, it'll be better this way.'' She'd had to blame him, had to blame his standards, his expectations. Christ! He'd given every last thing he had to the effort, to making it work. But she'd never be clear, never say she wanted or needed this or that; she'd never give him a clue to help him find out what would turn her around. It was his fault. Hers too. But his fault. Not now. Not now.

He upped the volume even more on the radio, but kept an eye on the speed.

Gradually, she came to believe she was suffocating. The darkness, the smell, the vibrations, enveloped her until she wondered if this was going to be how she died, locked into the trunk of a car driven by a man out of control. The space was getting smaller and smaller, and she closed in on herself, bringing her knees up to her chest and winding her arms tightly around them as if this might make her physical self more manageable.

Claustrophobia. That was the name of this feeling. The word now had a dreadful new meaning. She'd scoffed once upon a time at hearing of people who grew panicky in confined spaces, in elevators, for example. She was appalled to think she'd disbelieved, doubted the truth of so foolish-sounding a concept. She had no doubt about it now: it was an absence of light, and tainted, diminishing quantities of air, and a monstrous confinement. She kept her eyes open, blinking repeatedly, as if this might clear the darkness and bring light. She examined with her hands the walls of her cage, looking for something, anything.

There was nothing. Daniel had removed even the spare tire from the trunk. Her hands moved over the rough, prime-coated metal, touching every ridge, every die-stamped indentation. Then she tucked her hands between her thighs, listening to her heartbeat in her ears. The vibrations were making her nauseated, as was the rubber smell, underlaid with traces of gasoline and carbon monoxide. Where was he taking her? The ride was going on and on interminably. Each time the car slowed, even fractionally, she thought perhaps now they'd stop. But they went on, the engine noise rising to a higher note as the revolutions became faster, and music from the car radio seeped in through minuscule crevices, bass-heavy and pulsing.

The car was tightly sprung, taking every bump and pothole with a hard snap of its taut suspension. And she felt all of it right through to her bones as she was shaken and thumped in direct correlation to the condition of the road. A large pothole. The wheels sank into it; her body lifted, then fell on the hard metal bed of the trunk. Fluid kept filling her mouth; she swallowed repeatedly; her throat worked nonstop as she swallowed the bitterness. She tried not to smell the odors or taste the metallic air, but her fear of being smothered kept her mouth open wide. She prayed the motion would stop soon because she was going to be sick. The coffee and eggs she'd eaten were threatening to gush from her throat. She had to close her eyes at last, to concentrate on holding down the nausea. Her fingers laced together between her thighs, eyes closed, she tried to focus on controlling the sickness. But it was gaining, and hours, days, were passing as every last pebble, pothole, and wrinkle in the roadbed made its direct impression on her body.

This would be what hell was like. You didn't know you were going there; you simply spent eternity in the process of transit; confined in reeking darkness with only your dissociated thoughts to comfort or confuse you. Maybe she was already dead.

The car left the highway, and she could hear street sounds, cars honking; there was the stop-and-go of an intersection. The music from inside the car was turned down. Sudden accelerations and decelerations. It was the abrupt starts and stops that destroyed her best efforts. Her stomach overturned and she retched, frantically turning her head toward the rear of the trunk in order not to soil herself. But in turning so suddenly, so blindly, she struck her head sharply on the trunk lid and helplessly vomited all over herself, collapsing back on the pillows with involuntary tears leaking from her eyes and blood oozing from her scalp. She was so thoroughly, unremittingly ill that, for the present, she was incapable even of thought. All she wanted was an end to the punishing entrapment.

He pulled up in front of the building on West Tenth, locked the car, then hurried to open the trunk, stopped cold by the sight of her. Her face, under trickles of blood, was dead white with a greenish tinge around her mouth and nostrils. Her hair was sticky wet and clung to her skull. Her eyes had sunken into dark hollows. And she'd been sick all down the front of herself. The robe hung open under the fur coat, leaving her all but naked. She stared so fixedly, she lay so still, he thought for one horrific moment she was dead. Then, her pupils dilated, and she blinked against the light.

He glanced up and down the street. No one around.

"Jesus, Leigh," he whispered, maneuvering her to a sitting position, trying to think how best he could lift her out of there. "I'm sorry. I never thought . . . Jesus!" Leaning forward, he got his arms under hers and around her back, and pulled her out, her legs dragging painfully over the metal lip. He had to hold her upright while he got the trunk closed because if he let go of her, she'd collapse. She shoved him away, and he grabbed for her, thinking she'd been faking him out, but she staggered to the curb and, holding on to a lamppost for support, vomited into the gutter, then stood hanging on to the post, her head lolling.

"Let me get you inside," he said, draping her arm around his neck and getting a firm grip around her waist. "We'll get you cleaned up. I'll make you some tea to settle your stomach. Come on now, Leigh. Try to walk."

Drunkenly, she wiped her mouth with the back of her hand, trying to get her legs to function properly. They wanted to buckle, and she thought she'd like to sit down on the stairs and stay there until the dizziness went away and her stomach stopped leaping convusively. She'd never felt so sick. It was so dreadful, so absolutely complete, that it preoccupied her utterly, rendering her temporarily unconcerned with her whereabouts. Tea. He'd said something about tea, and it sounded right. Tea, and someplace to lie down; perhaps a bathtub filed with tepid water. She reeked of vomit; the smell of it caused her to start retching again when they were halfway up the inside stairs. He stopped, waiting. But her stomach was empty now. Her body shuddered its way through a series of dry heaves that left her incapacitated. She started to slide away, but Dan kept hold of her, turned her around and slung her over his shoulder. The motion heightened her dizziness, and she shut her eyes in order not to have to see the stairs behind them telescoping mountainously.

Inside the apartment, he set her on her feet, a steadying arm around her, while he locked the door.

"I want a bath," she got out. He heard, picked her up, and carried her through to the bathroom, sat her down on the toilet then stoppered the tub and got the water going. As the tub was filling, he took her out of the coat and her boots, saying, "It never occurred to me it'd make you sick. You have to believe that. You'll take your bath and I'll fix you some tea. It'll calm your stomach. Okay?"

She didn't answer, but simply gazed at him from her sunken eyes. He could not believe an hour or so in the trunk had had such a devastating effect on her. Daunted, he took refuge in practicalities. "I'll sponge off your coat and the robe. They'll be as good as new. I've got some cleaning stuff in the kitchen." He busied himself putting her things just outside the bathroom door; he tested the water and, satisfied, turned off the taps. "Come on. I'll help you in."

Lacking the energy to question or protest, she allowed herself to be lifted into the tub. She sank into the water—hotter than she'd have wished—and watched him inspect her robe before folding it over his arm. "Try to relax," he told her. "I'll be back in a couple of minutes. There's shampoo, and soap. And I put a fresh washcloth there, on the rim. Everything you need."

It registered: he'd planned for some time to bring her here. This was his apartment, not that of some friend who was out of town.

Her eyes seemed all she was able to move. They turned to take in the details of this bathroom she hadn't seen on her previous visit. There was no shower curtain or hooks. The mirrored door to the medicine cabinet had been removed. The shelves held a plastic container of Johnson's baby powder and one of baby oil, several bars of soap, two toothbrushes and a tube of Crest, roll-on Ban, and alone, on the top shelf, a bottle of Vol de Nuit, her perfume. The sight of it disturbed her; it symbolized something. What? Did he think she'd dab perfume in the bends of her elbows and knees in some fantasy performance? Did he think the perfume would make her feel at home here? What the hell *did* he think? She hadn't the remotest idea. Her stomach ached; her throat burned; her mouth tasted foul. She lay unmoving in the water, still feeling the motion of the car. Her eyelids kept wanting to close, and she had to force them open. She needed her wits about her, but her attention span had suffered and been abbreviated severely by that ghastly ride.

Dan reappeared carrying a white mug. "Here's your tea, and some aspirin." He approached the side of the tub and squatted to be at eye level with her. "Drink this, and take the pills, then soak for a while." When she failed to respond, he said, "Poor Leigh. I guess you need a hand." He rolled up his sleeves, reached for the washcloth and the soap, began lathering the cloth. And then he bathed her.

She was both eased and offended by his casual control of her. She told her body to reject his hands; told herself to get hold of the soapy cloth and fling it in his eyes, blinding him, so she could get the hell out of there. But her circuitry seemed deadened, as if someone had thrown a master switch somewhere. She couldn't do a damned thing but watch as he washed her the way he'd undoubtedly washed his daughter a hundred times or more in her childhood. He had that parental way of holding her, of applying the lathered cloth to the parts of her body, and then efficiently rinsing away the soap. He even slid his arm under her neck, supporting her head while he gingerly shampooed her hair and inspected the gash in her scalp. He did it all in no time flat, then eased her down into the water, stood up and dried his hands, saying, "Try to drink the tea. I'll be back in a couple of minutes to help you out of there."

He went away. She didn't care. She managed to lift the mug, managed to get it to her mouth and swallow some of the now lukewarm tea. Her stomach received it, accepted it, seemed to be subdued by the liquid. He'd added sugar, and almost immediately she felt a degree of energy returning. She sat up slightly higher in the water, holding the mug to her mouth with both hands, sipping steadily until the tea was finished and her belly seemed obscenely swollen from the several ounces of liquid.

Returning the mug to the side of the tub, she held very still, listening intently. Only a clock ticking—the same one she'd heard the last time. Where was he? Maybe he'd gone to move the car. He'd double-parked. He couldn't just leave it that way. He'd have to move it. That was likely what he'd gone to do. With newfound strength, she got herself out of the tub, took a towel from the rail and, wrapping it around herself as she went, tiptoed out of the bathroom. Glanced into the bedroom. Empty. He'd gone out. Her coat had been sponged clean and was draped over the back of one of the two chairs, her boots standing to one side. Throwing off the towel, she pushed her feet into the boots, pulled on the coat, then rushed to the door. It wouldn't open. She turned the deadbolt, twisted the doorknob, but still it wouldn't open. Why? What? She looked over the door and saw, about eighteen inches above the deadbolt, another lock, of a variety she'd never before seen. It had an odd-shaped keyhole. She ran her fingers over it, bewildered, trying to think how to open this smooth-faced cylinder, defied by its unusual keyhole. This had to be a lock that opened from either side, and he'd gone off after securing it from the outside. He'd imprisoned her in this apartment. She couldn't believe it, and whirled around to search for an alternative exit. There were two windows in the living room, with the gates she'd noticed on her earlier visit padlocked over them. Same in the bedroom. Beneath the vertical blinds was another window, another padlocked gate. The bathroom had no window. Knowing it was useless, she nonetheless went to each of the windows to yank on the padlocks. Thick, solidly locked. She stood there, trying to think what to do when she heard footsteps on the stairs. Thinking it might be Daniel returning, she returned the coat to the back of the chair, positioned the boots as she'd found them. The footsteps went past.

Picking up the towel, she padded back to the bathroom, her sugar high dissipating. She moved to pull the plug in the tub, but stopped. Let him do it! For spite, she threw in the aspirins, and then the mug. It hit the surface of the water, tipped, slowly filled, and sank to the bottom, striking the porcelain with a small clunk.

The telephone! She went through the place—which took only a minute or two—finding jacks, but no phone. Not in the closets, or the kitchen cabinets, or the refrigerator. He'd removed the telephone. She was so frustrated, she wanted to start screaming. And thinking of screaming, she remembered Miles saying she could scream her heart out and no one would hear. God! What if Daniel's beating had triggered a heart attack? What if he were lying there at her front door, dead? Damn Daniel! What the hell did he think he was doing? This was insane! He'd locked her into this goddamned apartment, taken out the telephone. She didn't even have any cigarettes.

Neither did he. Another search showed he had plenty of food and liquor, but no telephone, no cigarettes, and nothing sharper than a butter knife, not even a pair of scissors or a razor blade. The place had been cleared, as if in anticipation of a suicide. There wasn't even a pot or frying pan that weighed more than a few ounces. What did all this mean?

He'd been gone at least half an hour, she estimated, unable to locate that clock whose ticking could be faintly heard everywhere in the apartment. There was a ghetto blaster, and she wanted to find a news station, but first she was cold. She was also feeling dizzy again, and sick to her stomach. She opened the closet in the bedroom.

Slacks, rows of suits, sports jackets, shirts, but nothing casual. She put on one of his shirts, a pair of his boxer shorts she found on the closet shelf, and a camel's hair sweater. Then she sat down at the table with the ghetto blaster, wondering if she was about to hear of herself as a news item. Woman abducted by stranger. Author kidnapped from breakfast table. Agent murdered by unknown assailant; author sought.

Keys fitted into the locks; she froze. The door opened, and Daniel stepped inside. His face was masklike for a moment. Then he smiled, and said, "You're feeling better. Good. You're probably hungry. I picked up some stuff at the deli on my way back from the garage. I have a place over on the pier where I keep the car. It's very reasonable, even if it is a little out of the way." He chatted, as if she'd just dropped in for an impromptu visit, while he hung up his coat, then carried the bag from the deli behind the counter that separated the kitchen from the living/dining room.

She turned off the radio. "I need a cigarette."

He stopped what he was doing and looked over at her. "You really don't, Leigh. I've been meaning to talk to you about it. You smoke way too much. It's very bad for you. So, we're both going to quit. I got rid of all the cigarettes, including the pack I found in the pocket of your robe. I'm afraid I had to get rid of the robe, too. Never mind. I'll replace it. It'll be easy. You'll see. The nicotine's out of your system in seventy-two hours. After that, it's only a matter of kicking the psychological addiction. The cilia in your lungs actually become activated after seventy-two hours; they start working again, clearing out the garbage. Three days, that's all. It's pretty incredible, when you think about it." He'd never been able to convince Celeste. And she'd made such a fuss, finally shouting at him, "I'm *not* you! I'm not filled with endless purpose. I *like* smoking.

At least it's something that's all mine!'' He carefully folded the brown paper bag, then put it in one of the drawers, saying, ''We'll kick it together. Just don't think about it.''

''You are out of your goddamned mind,'' she said quietly.

His eyes when he looked at her were, for only the briefest moment, filled with madness. For that moment, he looked capable of rage, and of the violence she'd seen him inflict on Miles. ''Don't say that, Leigh,'' he rebuked her, his eyes normal again. ''I adore you. I'm not out of my mind. I *had* to do something. I couldn't stand you being with someone who doesn't treat you properly, someone you don't love. It's so obvious you don't care about that man.''

The words were right there in her mouth. All she had to do was explain who Miles was, confess she'd lied about being married. Although she wasn't quite sure why, she decided it would be best to allow Daniel to go on believing Miles was the Good Doctor. ''What is your plan, Daniel?'' she asked him. ''Do you even *have* a plan? Or are you merely intending to keep me locked up in here forever?''

''Plan?'' He seemed muddled. ''No, I don't have a plan. I mean, I wanted to see you. I wanted to bring you here. I had to get you away from him. I couldn't stand seeing the way he . . .'' He stopped, unwilling to admit he'd spied on her.

''You stood outside the house last night and watched us,'' she said, trying not to think about how much she wanted a cigarette. ''How could you do that? Have you any idea how it makes me feel to know you watched us making love? When I *think* of it . . . my God! It's such an offensive thing to do, Daniel. *All* these things you're doing, they're such violations. Can't you *see* that? Surely you can't want me to feel as invaded as I do.''

He watched her lips move, hearing Celeste say, "I could have been someone decent, Danny. But I've never been able to be the way I thought you wanted me to be. Danny? Are you even listening?" He shook his head, and smiled. "You look kind of cute in my things, Leigh. I wish I could let you keep them on."

He came out from behind the counter and stood close to her. "I really can't let you do that." He held his hand out to her. "Come on, Leigh. Come with me."

"Where? Why?"

"We're going into the other room."

"What if I say no, Daniel? What if I say, to hell with you? What if I say, I'm not going to do one damned thing you want me to? What then?"

He regarded her with an expression of infinite sadness. "You don't want to fight me. I've got the Good Doctor's address on Fifty-ninth. And your mother's, too," he lied. "I don't want to hurt anyone, but if I have to, I will."

It chilled her. She took another tack. "What about your wife? And your parents, your daughter? Isn't someone going to be wondering where you are?"

"I'll be in touch with them," he answered, some doubt touching his features. "I'm away pretty often, traveling. They're used to it." His hand was still extended to her. When she remained stubbornly seated, ignoring his hand, he said, "You have every right to be pissed off with me for the ride I gave you. I'm sorry, and I mean it. But you've got to come with me. Please don't fight me. I hate fighting all the time. I'm worn out from it."

"Just answer one question. Tell me what you hope to gain from this."

"You. I want you. I know you care for me. It was there, right from the start, on the plane. I intend to convince you to make the break, get yourself out of that marriage. Once you see that, then we'll be on our way."

"And if I don't see it, you'll harm my family. Daniel, can't you see that threatening my family won't make me care for you?"

"You *already* care for me. The way you let me . . . the way you . . . I know you care. Whatever it takes, I'll do it. *Whatever* it takes."

There it was again in his eyes, that madness. It made her skin go cold, seeing it. How much proof did she need? she asked herself. She'd already seen him use his fists on Miles. All she had to do was picture Marietta unwittingly opening the door to this man . . . she got up and brushed past him. Once inside the bedroom, she waited to see what he'd do.

"Take off the clothes, Leigh."

Oh, no! she thought. But could she refuse? Perhaps if she made love to him, played it out, she'd get him to trust and believe her. Then she'd been able to get away from this place. She could see no alternatives. So she removed the clothes, and he returned them to the closet. He opened a box he got down from the shelf, saying, as he did, "Lie down."

When she saw what he meant to do, everything in her protested. While she didn't doubt what he'd said about going after Miles or her mother, until this moment, she hadn't thought he'd actually harm her. She could only wonder at her stupidity. And if she struggled with him over this, he'd subdue her; she hadn't the strength to protect herself.

She couldn't help it. She began to cry when he took hold of her wrist and fastened a long, institutional-looking canvas restraint around it. She tried to sit up, her limbs rigid with resistance, and he said, "Just lie still, Leigh," while he fastened the other end of the canvas to the leg of the bed frame. One wrist, then the other. She held herself stiff, but it did no good. One ankle, then the other. She gazed at the ceiling, swallowing against the fear, the indignity, the excruciating inhumanity of this act he'd committed against her, strapping her to the bed frame like a sacrificial victim in some grotesque, demented ritual. She was spread on the altar of his choosing, agonized at being so gapingly on display, at this nonphysical rape. The humiliation robbed her momentarily of her ability to speak, or to look at him. She shut her eyes, but it didn't help. The humiliation sang in her ears, pumped in her lungs, churned in her belly. How could this be happening?

"Daniel," she whispered, forcing herself to look at him in the hope that he'd see and comprehend her suffering, "don't do this, please. I'm not young. I don't have the strength for this. Please!"

He didn't see, didn't comprehend. She could read the desire overtaking him, and had to wonder what substance in him craved this kind of power, this degree of control. Even her tears failed to affect him. He undressed, put away his clothes, and left the room. She heard the shower go on, and even though she believed it was useless, she began to rock back and forth against the restraints, encouraged when the bed moved slightly. The frame was on casters. The bed could be rolled. With every last bit of her energy, she threw her body from side to side, succeeding in moving the bed somewhat more to the left. She rested a moment, listening for the sound of the shower. Still going. A deep breath, and she began again. The bed rolled a bit more to the left. Then a bit more. And suddenly, miraculously, the tension of the bindings on her left wrist and ankle eased. He'd wrapped the canvas around the legs of the frame and her rocking had freed her. Two seconds and she was up, pulling wildly at the restraints. Ten more seconds and she was in the living room, snatching up her coat as she flew to the door, her hand reaching out to the key that was now in the lock.

The impact when he landed on her was so tremendous it knocked the air from her lungs as he sent her crashing into the door. He grabbed her by the back of the neck and threw her halfway across the room, then came after her as she scrambled on her hands and knees toward the door. His hands in her armpits, he lifted her to her feet, kicking the fur coat aside. She saw his arm pull back but had no time to defend herself. His fist approached with almost invisible speed, made stunning impact with her jaw, and there was an instant of utter silence before the blow registered, and she felt herself falling.

Twenty

He hit her. There was an audible crack as his fist connected with her chin. Her eyes rolled back into her head, and she fell. He was so jolted by his own actions that for a time he seemed to become disconnected from himself and from her, and could only watch as she fell, her body bonelessly toppling. She lay in a heap on the floor; he was rooted, immobilized. *Danny, why don't you give it up, go out and find yourself someone who'll be the way you want her to be? It'll never be me. Don't you know how that makes me feel, Danny? I'm always going to fail. So what's the point to trying?*

His vision seemed to clear, enabling him to see all at once the bruises on her back and legs, the scrapes on her shins where her legs had dragged as he'd lifted her out of the trunk. He was inflicting injuries on this woman; he'd actually struck her with his fist, when all he'd wanted was to be with her, to be close to her, to show her how very much he cared for her. Why couldn't it ever be right? Why did things always get so screwed up?

He picked her up and carried her to the bedroom where,

very carefully, he positioned her on the bed before going to the kitchen for ice. He took half a dozen paper towels, folded them over a handful of ice cubes, then returned to the bedroom where he stopped to think.

He deeply regretted using force on her, but he couldn't see he had any alternative. If he didn't bind her in some fashion, she'd keep on battling him, keep on trying to get away. And he couldn't let that happen, not before he'd had any reasonable kind of chance to make his points. There came a time when your voice just had to be heard. You couldn't keep on indefinitely, hoping gestures, displays of kindness and thoughtfulness, would make an impression. All he wanted her to do was try to see things as he did. It wasn't such a lot to ask.

He lifted each corner of the bed and removed the casters. Then he returned her wrists and ankles to the restraints, before testing the bed to make sure it no longer rolled.

She came to, knowing instantly he'd tied her up again. He had, however, undergone some minor form of metamorphosis in the interval, because he was stretched out beside her on the bed, holding an ice pack to her jaw as he told her, over and over, how shocked and sorry he was.

"I've never hit anyone, ever, before today," he was saying. "None of this is the way I wanted it to be, the way I pictured it. You have to believe that. I care so much for you, and seeing you last night, having to see that bastard touching you . . . I knew it was all wrong to watch, but I couldn't . . . I . . . there are so many things I want to tell you . . . why is it always so damned hard to get the timing right, to get in everything that has to be said?" He lifted away the ice pack to see the condition of her jaw. It didn't seem bruised. Letting the pack fall over the side of the bed, he moved closer to her. "They're not so tight this time. There's enough slack so you can turn on your side to sleep. I had no idea you were so badly thrown around in the back of the car. You should've said something. But I'll try to make you feel better." He sat up and reached for something. It was the baby oil. "This'll help," he told her, and poured out some of the oil on his palm, put aside the bottle, and coated his hands.

Her eyes followed his every move, as she tried to find some thread of logic in the things he said and did. He seemed to alternate between differing aspects of his personality, as if feelings he'd suppressed for a lifetime had all at once started fighting for precedence in their right to expression. In order to try to deal with him, she kept having to put aside her attempts to make sense of this situation. Despite the fact that there were only the two of them here, it was hard to keep track of the many and varied themes that appeared to worry and distract him.

Starting at her right foot, he began massaging the oil into her skin, all the while keeping up a rambling monologue that didn't entirely divert either one of them from what he was doing with his hands. She couldn't get a fix on her feelings; couldn't sustain her fear, or her anger, or her confusion. Nor could she prevent herself from responding on a purely primal level to certain of his acts—first his bathing her, now this very sensual laying on of hands.

"It's late in the day, everybody tells me, to be reacting. And I keep telling them I can't help it. I think of all the things I did wrong, and part of me believes I was responsible; it was my fault. Another part of me says, no. It was fifty-fifty. I don't know." He reached for the bottle, poured more oil into his palm, then went back to work, on her thigh now, lifting to get to the underside of her leg. "She was angry the whole of her life. Nobody ever knew why. We'd get together and talk about it, her parents and me.

But we couldn't figure it out. It was as if cylinders in her brain were constantly misfiring; or maybe she kept short-circuiting. Whatever it was, the most she could manage, ever, was a day or two when she'd be up and happy and involved. Then, down she'd go, and she hated everyone and everything, and most of all herself. Christ, how she hated herself! Hated her face, her hair, her legs, the shape of her breasts, her hands, her feet, her teeth. Consuming, lifelong hatred. It was her full-time occupation, hating herself. And when I came along, what could possibly have been more natural than hating *me* for *not* hating her."

More oil, then his hands rubbed, stroked, rubbed, her belly, her waist, her buttocks; rubbing, stroking. "When Lane was born, I thought maybe that would be the magic. Someone new, someone perfect. Celeste couldn't possibly hate her own baby. But she did. Hated her. The baby cried; the baby messed her diapers; the baby was hungry; the baby had colic. Celeste hated her. 'Here's your child!' she'd say, furious, and practically *throw* Lane at me. How can she hate an infant? I wondered, and looked at this perfect little girl, trying to understand. But I couldn't. I just couldn't. Lane was beautiful; she was our child. So, I took her over. The minute I came through the door in the evening, I was busy with Lane, getting her fed, getting her bathed, getting her ready for bed, getting up for her night feedings; first thing in the morning, I was up to put her into a clean diaper, heat her formula—and later on, the little jars of cereal—feed her and put her back into the crib before I left for the office. Most of the time there was some babysitter from the service with the baby when I got home from the office. And Celeste would be up in the bedroom, on the bed with a drink in her hand, watching the soaps, or some old movie, just waiting to recite this long list of grievances she had. I decided it was post-partum depression; she'd get over it; just give her time and room enough, and she'd get over it. But she managed to go from the postpartum depression into general depression without missing a beat. And from there, it was Celeste's state of being: she was depressed." *Danny, how can you talk about me this way, to someone who doesn't even know me?* "I'm sorry."

Leigh watched and listened, willing herself to disappear, to evaporate.

More oil, and gently he shifted her onto her side to smooth the oil into her back and shoulders, down her arms, rubbing, rubbing; his hands curving over her buttocks, down the backs of her thighs, her calves, then up again to ease her onto her back once more, with a pause for additional oil so he could knead it into her breasts and the length of her throat, then down between her breasts and over her belly to her inner thighs, where one hand stayed while the other spread itself over her breast, and he stared first at his hand on her breast, and then down at the hand wedged between her thighs, and he lost track of what he'd been saying and thinking because he was so completely captivated by her glistening body that he had to come nearer to see close-to every last detail of her construction—the deep-blue veins that traversed her shoulders and ran beneath the bluish-white skin the length of her arms and surfaced on her breasts like tiny, irregular roads leading to the delicate buds that collected at the tips. Her breasts were, to him, as soft as the dreams he'd had as a small child, and as tantalizing. Her belly was flat but cushiony, bisected by that thin scar that disappeared down into her groin, down, to hide behind silken red-brown hair that contrasted so startlingly with the milky flesh coating her bones. He had to rest his face on that inviting cushion of flesh, pressing his lips against the promontories of bone that sheltered it, dipping his tongue into the hidden knot punctuating that too-tempting expanse. He longed to sleep with his face pressed into her belly, his one hand covering her breast, his other curved into her groin. But it was a fleeting desire, of no significance; he was driven to touch her, to slip his fingers into the heated elastic interior of her body, to withdraw to investigate the secrets contained within the folds of her flesh; pushing, probing, until the body beneath his hands shifted in response, lifting, spreading.

Hadn't he known? he thought deliriously, leveling himself between her thighs to touch and taste, to submerge himself in sensation, ecstatic at proving once again, to both of them, how strong was the bond between them. Here was the proof: she was dissolving in undulating invitation, her thighs tensed, her belly quivering. He'd prove to her how well he knew her, how right they were together; he'd make her see that the balance could be attained, that the sense lay not solely on one side or the other but precisely in the middle.

She listened attentively to all he said, hoping for some inadvertent clue that might provide a way in which she could deal with him. But he seemed so genuinely infatuated with her that he was unable to sustain his thoughts. He'd hit her; he'd actually knocked her unconscious. Now her head hurt terribly, the dizziness had returned full force, the massage had evolved into a full-scale lubricious assault on her body, and she was not free to reject him. She was tied to a bed—granted, the restraints were looser than before, but she was a captive nevertheless—and this man could do anything he fancied to her; he'd deprived her of her right to consent, he'd deprived her of her freedom, and now he was depriving her of control over her own body.

She steeled herself, determined to remain detached; she would be stone, she would feel nothing. She would not react. This man had beaten Miles, dear, dear Miles. This man had abducted her from her home and forced her to ride in the trunk of his stinking car; he'd physically harmed her; he'd strapped her down and humiliated her to her very soul; she would feel nothing. He put his mouth on her, his hands and tongue played over her, and she told herself she would remain cold; she would feel nothing. The last time they'd been together, he'd made love to her in this same manner, and had refused to stop; he'd gone on until the pleasure he'd given her had devolved into a gruesome form of pain, but still he'd refused to stop. She would feel nothing. Yet, if she didn't contribute actively, didn't play out an affectionate charade with this man, he would strike her again, hurt her in ever more serious fashion until she ceased to exist. He would kill her. She trembled. From fear? Reaction? She would not feel. She would not. But, God! Here he was again, making love in that heartbreakingly doomed fashion, a supplicant worshiping at a shrine of his own creating, and he was causing her to feel a grating mix of base sexual pleasure, mounting fear, and pity; she could not prevent herself from feeling.

He laid himself upon her defenseless body, he slid his hands under her and held her open like a book he might read; he sighed and pushed himself fully into her in one rending motion that made her heart pause; and then, like a lone shipwreck survivor clinging to a fragile bit of wreckage, he pressed kisses on her lips and throat, he licked her eyelids and her chin, as he rode the outgoing tide and sang hymns of his own composing in the hope of salvation.

His body remained heavy on hers, motionless, still solidly lodged within her. She turned her head aside, overcome by sudden loathing for him, and for herself. Had she not been tethered, she'd have thrust him away; she might even have tried to hurt him, to inflict some small measure of retaliatory pain. There were excuses for his behavior, perhaps; but she had none. He'd invaded her, and her odious body had betrayed her, had gone over to the enemy like some avid, independent camp follower. He'd abraded her senses, forcing her—physically, at least—to feel. And she'd felt everything, *everything*; she'd even been aware, during an instant of sudden stillness, of his release within her, that deluge of additional heat blanketing her interior. She'd been momentarily awed, and then bludgeoned by dismay and thoughts of death. He might not be intending to kill her, but he might, inadvertently, succeed in causing her death. Just now, she had an almost indecent yearning for freedom of any kind, even death. To have this confinement continue, to suffer through more of his sexual forays, would make her despise herself so totally she'd have no desire left to live. He was compelling her to look at herself from his critically disseminated viewpoint, and she knew now, too agonizingly well, what her mother had meant when she'd spoken of feeling separated from herself. Leigh had thought she understood at the time. She realized now, laboring to breathe under this man's weight, that she hadn't understood in the least. And, seeing this, she began to weep again, wishing she could right the terrible wrong she'd done her mother. It was far more than having had a firsthand viewing of her mother's still strong sexuality. It was far more significant than the one-step-removed beauty that the artist she was had perceived—there was, without doubt, an ethereal beauty to a voluntary act of love, especially when engaged in by a lovely, willing woman and an eager, caring man. No, she'd have been in safe territory, they all would have been, had she hoarded her private image instead of flinging it back at her mother. Very few people, if any, could withstand the shock that came with having their most intimate, most voluptuous moments infringed upon by outsiders. She'd done it to her mother. Now Daniel had done it to her. And, like a child, she wanted her mother, wanted the comfort and forgiveness and sympathy only her mother could give her. Perhaps she'd never see her mother again. This thought accelerated her weeping.

Daniel became aware of the change in her breathing, the cadence of her sadness. He withdrew from her, and was taken aback by the way his departure appeared to cause her pain. Her body seemed to shrivel, her flesh rippling as if he'd slowly pulled a long knife from her interior; her nipples tightened; the hair on her arms rose; the tendons in her throat gained alarming definition; she shivered, and tried to shield herself with her elbows and knees but because of the canvas ties she could only bend inward slightly.

"Daniel," she said, her voiced deep and cracked, "you must listen to me." Her eyes when she turned them on him, were hollowed and dark. "If you don't untie me, if you don't trust me, at the very least, not to try to run out of here without any clothes, I will lose my reason. I truly will go mad. You don't want that, do you?"

"But there's slack, you can move some. And it's warm enough in here, but if you're cold . . ."

"*Daniel, listen!* You're taking away everything I need, all the things that allow me to have any feeling for myself. If you strip me of *everything*, I can't live. Surely you can understand that. It's not so very complicated. You have my word I'll stay with you. I won't fight you. But you've got to untie me. I feel ill. I have to use the bathroom. Please, undo these things and let me go to the bathroom. Please!"

Without another word, he went around the bed, kneeling to release the restraints. Then he took them from her wrists and ankles, and stood rolling the strips, asking, "Do you need help?"

"No, thank you. I can manage."

"You'll have to leave the door open," he began.

"I will close and lock the door," she said firmly. "I must have *some* privacy. Do you intend to witness my every last act?"

"You can close the door, but don't lock it."

"Thank you. May I wear one of your shirts?"

He shook his head. She didn't push it, but stood up unsteadily and walked out to the bathroom. The dizziness rushed back with being upright, and she had to keep her hand on the wall to prevent herself from falling. Being on her feet also caused a gush of fluid down her thighs, and the feel of it, the smell of sex, nauseated her. She got inside the bathroom, reached automatically to lock the door only to discover he'd removed the locking mechanism. Hopeless. Her stomach rose, and she vomited the tea into the sink, then hung over the basin, quaking. She really was too old to sustain much more abuse; perhaps she would die, after all. She rinsed her mouth and the basin, then sat on the toilet feeling as if some frenetic aging process had overtaken her and was racing through her system, burning out nerve endings, dimming her vision, dehydrating her cells. More fluid left her body. Her interior felt battered, scalded. She got the shower going, then climbed into the tub and sat beneath the water, hoping to God Miles hadn't been seriously hurt, that his heart was strong enough to withstand the beating Daniel had given him. She wanted him alive; she wanted her mother alive. If they were out there, beyond that locked front door, she had an objective: to get back to them, and to make good on every last error or omission she'd ever made. She'd find some way to erase from her mother's mind that dreadful image Leigh had forced her to see. And she'd tell Miles, finally, how deeply, how long-lastingly, she cared for him.

Dear God, but she'd been a fool! All those years of coming and going, arrivals and departures, in and out of his life; she'd been waiting for him to make some declaration of caring and intent, as if it mattered who instigated the making of declarations. Anyone looking at her life would have interpreted it the way Miles had, would have withheld whatever pronouncements he might have rehearsed dozens of times. She'd lived for years and years on the surface of situations, taking flight at the slightest hint of anyone's need for more of her than she was willing to give. She'd elected to show the very best of herself only to her two sons, because her two husbands, and the many lovers in between, hadn't displayed the elusive qualities she'd sought without actively knowing of her quest. And all that time, if only she'd stopped to look, she would have seen that he'd been there all along. Miles was the one who'd accepted her from the outset precisely as she was, without qualification, without hidden plans to alter her to suit more closely his specifications; he'd been happy to have however much of herself, her body, her thoughts, her emotions, she cared to offer. And instead of giving him the most and the best, as he deserved, she'd played out the game, on and on, bedding strangers, investigating strangers, even caring for strangers. And why? Because men were not to be trusted. They left you in your childhood, abandoned you for mysterious, never-stated reasons; they died and left you to try to find ways to fill the emotional gaps; they elicited frightful promises and made you put your mark on the agreement in blood and tissue ripped from your insides; they used you for purposes so vague, so muddled and indeterminate, that the only possible defense you had was to remain a stranger yourself, offering only inadvertent glimpses of what lay beneath your misleading surfaces. But Miles had been constant; Miles had been faithful in his heart; Miles had offered pleasure, and protection, and even a home. Christ! What did it take to make her see and value what had been there for so long?

And now that she thought about it, it was likely she was the only one *not* to see it. Certainly her mother had known for ages, had made numberless references to the very unique qualities Miles had. And Joel. Joel had teased her, saying, "Give the poor guy a break, Leigh. He sees pure gold when he looks at you. I sure as hell wouldn't pass on someone who looked at me the way Miles looks at you. That doesn't happen too often in a lifetime." And what had she replied? Something flip, something silly, something witty, to cover the hesitation underneath, the fear not quite buried, of investing one more time in one more man.

The door opened and Daniel was there, looking in at her, with his hand on the knob.

"GET OUT OF HERE!" she shouted at him, covering her breasts with her hands, drawing her knees up. "YOU GAVE YOUR WORD YOU'D LEAVE ME ALONE IN HERE!"

"Just wanted to make sure you're all right," he defended himself.

"LEAVE ME ALONE!" she screamed, her eyes and mouth and nose filling with water. "JUST LEAVE ME ALONE!"

He backed away. The door closed.

She sat under the stinging spray and cried noisily, her hands still clasped protectively over her breasts. She really didn't want to die.

"They have absolutely nothing to go on," Miles was saying. "There is no French professor at NYU by that name; nor has there ever been a buyer at Bloomingdale's of that name. Undoubtedly, there is a daughter, at some college somewhere. But it could take *years* to check every college roster in this country. The message he left on Leigh's machine was erased by your call. We did find a sketch of the man that Leigh made. The police are circulating it throughout New York, Connecticut, and New Jersey. There's also a bulletin out on the car. The snag is we don't have a license plate number. There are a fair number of Godards in the Manhattan directory, and they're all being canvassed. I think," he said slowly, "we have to make some sort of statement to the press. It may be the only hope we have of getting anyone who's seen or heard anything to come forward. I can't think what else we can do." He raised his hands in a defeated gesture, and waited to hear what Marietta would say. He'd never seen her in a condition remotely like the one now. There was a furrow between her brows that seemed to have materialized overnight. Her natural pallor now appeared waxy, even unhealthy. She hadn't bothered with her hair and it hung to her shoulders, which had an uncharacteristic slump. She'd found a package of cigarettes someone had left behind, and was smoking one as she listened to what Miles had to say.

For her part, she winced inwardly at the varicolored bruises around his eyes and along his jaw and cheekbone. His face was lumpy with swelling on one side, but he'd declined her offer to have the housekeeper fetch him some ice. He had repeatedly beat his fists together over the past two hours, furiously blaming himself for his failure to keep Leigh safe. "Gone to bloody seed," he'd insisted. "I was useless, a damned great bag of wind, puffing and blustering. He ran right over me like a train."

"It is not your fault," Marietta had several times absolved him. "*No one* could have anticipated anything like this."

She smoked the cigarette, made queasy by the inhalations, trying to come to grips with the facts. "If you believe it might do some good, I don't think we have any choice. Perhaps you could write a press release, handle this for me. I couldn't possibly deal with reporters *en masse*. Or even individually. I simply want to stay here, close to the telephone. You don't think he'll harm her, do you? Why is he doing this? Is it money he's after? And if he is, why hasn't he made any demands? I simply don't understand the purpose of his taking her.''

Miles closed his eyes for a moment, biting back on his instinct to state unequivocally that he would kill the man if he harmed Leigh in any way. His eyes open, he said, ''He seems to care for her. One can only hope.''

''Miles, more than anyone or anything else, I love my daughter.'' She extinguished the cigarette, then said, ''Until two days ago, I never fully appreciated just what Leigh's been through, her losses, the anxiety, the pain of grief, the protracted mourning. I'm ashamed to admit there were times when I was most impatient with her; I was convinced she was being self-indulgent, wallowing in her sorrow, anointing herself in it. The deaths I've experienced have been appropriate, somehow, or not directly connected with me. My mother, my father, they were well into their eighties when they died. There was a naturalness, an inevitability to their passing. I was fond of Carl; I was devoted to Stephen and to Joel. But they were *Leigh's* connections, *her* bonds, and only incidentally mine. This loss is mine, entirely mine. The dread, the speculations, the fear . . . I cannot *bear* the thought that I might never see her again. And I simply cannot stop thinking of all the occasions when I failed to praise her, or to compliment her; when I failed to work harder to understand her, to display all the love I've always had for her. Please do whatever has to be done. In the past two days, I've come to see that nothing, really, will ever again have any value without Leigh. In two days, I've come to recognize how very well, in fact, she handled those losses. I have nothing like her resilience. I have nowhere near her degree of courage. I'd prefer to be alone now, Miles," she said regretfully. "You'll ring me later?"

"Of course."

"You'll forgive me if I don't see you out."

"Of course."

He got up, crossed the room to press a kiss on her cheek, then made his way to the foyer, hearing behind him Marietta's deep, painful-sounding sigh. He really would, he vowed, kill that man if he harmed Leigh.

Twenty-one

She wordlessly refused his offers of food and drink, and lay on the edge of the bed, her eyes to the wall. He gazed at the knobs of her spine, at her naked haunches, then went to cover her with the blankets. He thought about tying her up again, decided it would be all right for now; he wasn't going anywhere, and neither was she. She was giving him the "silent treatment," but he was used to that. It never lasted very long.

She didn't want to talk, had nothing it was safe to say. If she said anything at all, it would lead to more attempts on her part to determine some logical course to his actions, and logic had nothing to do with what was happening. She wanted to go home; she wanted her mother; she wanted to be assured of Miles's well-being; she wanted the familiar safe haven of Miles's embrace. She could feel Daniel's eyes, but would not acknowledge him. She shut him, and this place, and her entrapment, out; she closed her eyes.

He went to the kitchen to make coffee, then sat at the table with a mug and listened to the radio with the volume very low so as not to disturb her. When he looked in again on her, she was asleep. Periodically, he went to check on her, but she hadn't moved. Finally, he ate. Then he climbed in on the far side of the bed and, after watching her for a time, went to sleep.

She slept right through until the afternoon of the next day, and he thought she'd probably go on sleeping if he didn't rouse her. He sat on the side of the bed and put his hand on her arm, softly saying her name. She didn't stir. It alarmed him. He shook her, spoke her name loudly, and her eyes opened. She looked at him blankly, without recognition.

"You have to eat, Leigh. I've made you something. Don't go back to sleep. Come on. I'll put the food on the table."

He got up and went to the door. Her eyes tracked him. Nothing had changed. She was still here. She reeled into the bathroom, used one of the toothbrushes to clean her teeth, then went to sit at the table, drawing her knees up against her chest, and wrapping her arms around them. Her vision was blurry. She felt strangely distanced from everything. "I want a cigarette," she said, ignoring the coffee he put in front of her.

"Drink your coffee and don't think about it. Food'll be ready in a minute."

She reached for the mug, and had to use both hands to lift it. She couldn't believe how weak she was. Her body felt as if it was going to topple off the chair. She drank some of the flavorful coffee and, keeping hold of the mug for its warmth, she watched him, busy in the kitchen, radiating health and energy as he put food on two plates. He was dressed in navy slacks and a pink shirt with white collar and cuffs; he was clean-shaven, his hair damp-combed. She was naked. She felt like an animal, and despised him for making her feel that way. How dare he treat her like some uncommon form of house pet! Putting the mug down, she got off the chair, went into the bedroom to snatch one of his shirts from its hanger. She buttoned it on, then returned to the chair and her coffee.

"You can wear it for now," he relented. "But I can't let you keep it on." He spoke most temperately, as if what was taking place was in no way out of the usual. It ignited a fuse in her chest.

"Why don't you kill me now?" she said with cold rage. "You must have a knife hidden somewhere, or a blunt object, something you could use. Why don't you just do that, Daniel? Get it over with quickly. It would be infinitely kinder than doing it by inches, the way you are. Here," she held out her wrists. "Get a razor blade and open my arteries. I'd prefer to die fast than go through any more of this."

His eyes went round. He dropped the plates. He began to shake as if palsied. His head vibrated back and forth, back and forth, in some form—she thought—of denial. Tears streamed down his face. As she watched, her anger shunted off to one side by this astounding display, he lost control.

"How did you know?" he asked, between gulping sobs. "You knew! Did you know? You didn't know. How could you know?" He put his head down on the counter and wept like a child. She'd never seen anything like it. But she recognized the emotion, and the recognition drew her out of the chair and around behind the counter.

"Daniel, I'm sorry," she told him, a sympathetic hand on his heaving back. "That's what happened, isn't it? I'm so sorry."

"I told myself it was good, it was over, it was better, we weren't going anywhere, not for years and years, it was better. *It wasn't better!*" he cried. "I tried so hard, I did, I know I did, I tried but nothing was ever right or good, she couldn't be happy, and I tried so hard, *I tried*, but she did it, it was my fault, my fault!''

She tried to transmit her sympathy through her hand on his back. But he raised himself abruptly, his arm flying out, catching her across the face. "DON'T PATRONIZE ME!" he shouted. "DON'T THINK I'M SO STUPID I CAN BE CONNED!" A second blow drove his fist between her breasts and sent her colliding with the refrigerator door. Slipping in the spilled food on the floor, her feet went out from under her, and she fell, her lungs in spasm. She couldn't breathe. If she let her panic take precedence over her common sense, she knew she'd asphyxiate. Hold on, hold on! she told herself; don't struggle, don't try to breathe, just concentrate on getting your throat to open; don't panic; wait for everything to right itself. It'll be okay, okay. She let what air remained in her lungs escape slowly, slowly, and at last there was an inner relaxing; she was able to draw in tiny sips of air. She took shallow breaths, overcoming her instinct to pant, her eyes never leaving him. His stance was simian; his shoulders were hunched forward, his fists held tightly at his sides. He looked ready to administer more blows. If she said the wrong thing now, he'd almost certainly go on striking her. Oh God! What was the right thing to say to him? What would keep him from delivering more blows, further injuries?

"Daniel," she whispered, "how can you treat me this way when you know I love you?"

He grunted, and wiped his face on his shirtsleeve, his eyes red-rimmed.

"I love you," she whispered.

He made a disbelieving noise, but his eyes stayed on her.

"I love you, Daniel," she told him again.

He threw back his head and roared at the ceiling. It

made her skin crawl, but she changed neither her expression nor the tone of her voice. His eyes returned to her.

"You know I love you," she repeated, breathing slowly, steadily; each inhalation bringing pain. Something in her chest felt broken. He'd struck her so hard; it had been like a brick thrown at her at great speed. "I love you," she insisted. "You've been right all along. I can't deny it."

He fumbled with his trousers. She wanted to, but didn't dare close her eyes. He fought his way out of the trousers and his shorts, then he threw her down and fell upon her, tearing the shirt out of the way, stabbing blindly against her until he located where he wanted to be and pushed into her, oblivious to everything but his need.

She didn't struggle; she didn't help; she tried not to cry out, tolerating the pain of dry flesh driving within dry flesh. If you fight him, you will die, she told herself. Whatever he does, whatever happens, don't fight him! You can live through this; you can. It hurt. He wanted to rip her to shreds; the knowledge transmitted itself through the ugly thrusting, the grinding of his bones against hers.

It was over. He rested for a moment, then pulled abruptly out of her. She gasped, feeling her eyes bulge at the pain. God oh God God! As if nothing extraordinary had happened, he put his clothes back on, went to the sink for the sponge and began cleaning the floor. She sat up slowly, trembling hands trying to cover herself with the shirt. Her eyes never left him; she feared doing anything that might provoke him. There were fragments of broken crockery all over the floor, several splinters were embedded in her feet and the backs of her legs. She looked at her legs, then at Daniel scooping food up with both hands and dumping it into the garbage. His lips were moving; they shaped inaudible words.

"I have to go to the bathroom, Daniel."

"So go!" he snapped without looking at her, busy setting the kitchen to rights.

"I wouldn't leave you if it wasn't necessary."

"Go on!" he said impatiently. "And get that fucking shirt off, the way I told you to!"

Without a sound, she pulled herself upright, hesitated long enough to pull shards of porcelain from the soles of each foot, then limped off to the bathroom, leaving a trail of blood.

She kept looking over at the door, expecting him to come bursting in, but he left her alone to catalogue her injuries and sort through her thoughts. She could only be grateful now that he'd removed the bathroom mirror. She didn't have to see herself. It would have heightened her fear, she knew, to see the bruising she could feel with her fingertips on her jaw and cheek, the healing gash on her head. The area between her breasts was already starting to turn blue; breathing was agonizing, as was any but the smallest movement of her arms and shoulders.

Fortunately, none of the cuts was deep, but several of them didn't want to stop bleeding. And inside, dear God! Inside it was as if he'd taken rough-grade sandpaper to her. She was swollen and raw. Using the toilet brought tears to her eyes. *I want to go home go home want to go home.* Soundless litany; soundless tears. Eyes traveling over the walls, the ceiling, searching for something, anything. She was taking too long; Daniel was bound to come after her. Pull back the tears; push away the little girl's recitation; prepare to deal, to do whatever has to be done in order to get through this.

She almost forgot to take off the shirt, remembered just as she was about to open the door, and removed it. Naked again.

She went to sit at the table, knees tightly together, feet flat on the floor, hands in her lap: a portrait of obedience and contrition. He was at work, preparing more food. She sat very still, thinking how far away and long ago it was since Christmas. And Miles, who knew most of her secrets and all her imperfections, quirks. Miles, whom Daniel had struck so hard half a dozen times, with such rage. Miles with the tricky heart, and the periodic EKGs, and the cautionary lectures from his internist. Had Daniel killed him? She told herself no. You couldn't kill someone so easily. Yes, but you could; if Daniel's blows, his assaults on her body were anything to go by.

He brought her a plate of food, and she thanked him. He was calm again as he sat opposite and poured two glasses of red Mouton Cadet. She gave him the best smile she could manage as she picked up her knife and fork, then looked at the food. The smell of it repelled her. Some kind of frozen fish filet in a white sauce, with bright green frozen peas, and frozen hash-browns shiny with cooking oil.

"Eat, Leigh," he said, back again in his reasonable mode. "You really must eat." He held out his glass, said, *"Salut!"* and tasted the wine.

She murmured, "Cheers!" and took a sip. She would eat, and drink, and then, she was certain, she would be sick. Setting down her glass, she cut into the fish, raised the fork to her mouth, inserted the fish, began to gag, stopped, waited, chewed, and swallowed. The fish fell into the well of her stomach to swim on the shallow surface of the wine. She cut, chewed, swallowed, drank more of the wine. She would not think about how much she craved a cigarette, or about her nakedness, or about his eyes taking bites out of her exposed flesh; she would eat the oily potatoes, the slimy peas, the fish that tasted faintly of iodine.

He looked over at her midway through the meal, and found himself disconnected again, and profoundly frightened by the situation he'd created. Poor, lovely Leigh; he'd taken away her clothes; he'd made those bruises on her face and chest. He'd subdued her, and she'd at last admitted to her true feelings for him. But why the hell did it have to be such a contest? Why did they have to go through such turmoil?

As he gazed at her, she seemed suddenly foreign, and he wondered who she was. Who was this woman sitting so quietly, eating the food he'd made for her, drinking the wine he'd poured into her glass? Her hair was short instead of long; she was very thin, not rounded and billowing; her eyes were green, not brown. *You never see me the way I really am, Danny. If you could just once see me, really see me, maybe then you'd let up a little on both of us.*

Well, he could hear that, all right. He wasn't crazy. He knew damned well this wasn't Celeste. Celeste was where she'd wanted to be, where she'd taken herself. Christ! Goddamned mind games. It annoyed the hell out of him.

But who was this woman? Sure, he knew her name. She just didn't look all that familiar. She wasn't young. Maybe he hadn't been aware of it before, but he could see it now. Her skin wasn't as tight to her bones as he'd thought, and her breasts had undoubtedly been higher even a year or two earlier. The texture of her skin lacked the elasticity of youth. Yet she'd been created wonderfully well, and he craved her softness, the feel of her under his hands. Having her there, being able to look at her, was wonderful, just wonderful. And she'd at last declared her love for him. Everything would be all right now. He adored the shape of her head, the breadth of her shoulders, the symmetrical bounty of her breasts; he loved her accessibility, and the knowledge that she was there for him, solely for him. And she loved him.

* * *

After the meal, he said he had to go out for an hour. "You can listen to the radio, if you like. Do you want me to get anything for you?"

Inspired, she said, "I need Tampax. And some cigarettes?"

"No cigarettes. Are you expecting your period?" he asked, looking fascinated. "I hadn't considered that. Do you take birth control pills or something?"

"Pills," she fabricated smoothly. "They're at the house."

"Well, if you're expecting a period, it's not likely you're going to get pregnant. But that would be okay, too." His eyes turned vague for just a moment. "Anything else?"

"Some sort of antiseptic, for the cuts."

"Okay. I won't be long."

"Oh!" she called after him. "Perhaps a newspaper?"

"Sure," he agreed, and went out, locking both the deadbolt and the strange mechanism above it.

While he was gone, hoping to appease him, she cleared the dishes and loaded the dishwasher. Then again she limped through the apartment looking for something she might use on the locks, or the padlocks on the window gates. The butter knives were no good, too thick to insert between the door and the frame. She tried the foil containers from the frozen food but they were too malleable, useless. In the midst of her searching, her stomach gave stabbing warning signals and she had to run to the bathroom to be sick again.

Chilled, she put on her fur coat, guessing she had perhaps thirty-five minutes before he got back. She went over every inch of the apartment, but found nothing. At last, she peeled a banana and gagged it down while she sat at the table and went from station to station on the ghetto blaster, hoping to hear some news item about herself. Nothing.

Hearing footsteps outside, she hurried to put her coat

back in the closet, then sat again at the table to play with the tuning dial, looking for Joel's favorite station. It distressed her that she couldn't find it. She turned off the radio and went to push aside the verticals, looking out at the windows of other apartments across the way. She felt invisible. Maybe she could find something to smash the glass; she'd stand there and scream until someone saw her; they'd call the police. The key turned in the deadbolt and she moved back to the table, her heart beating too quickly, as if he'd almost caught her in the act of screaming.

Dan put down a brown paper bag containing Tampax, a small bottle of iodine, and the day's final of the *News*. He hung away his coat, then carried what looked like a toolbox into the bedroom. While she skimmed the paper, he began banging and hammering. In the fifteen minutes it took her to go through the paper twice, he completed whatever he'd been doing in the bedroom and came back out carrying the toolbox. He unlocked the padlock on one of the gates, slid it aside, opened the window, put the toolbox outside on the fire escape, then closed the window and the gate, and secured the lock. The keys went into his briefcase which he snapped shut. The case had a combination lock, she saw. But it was something that could be opened even with a dull butter knife. Hope shifted in the pit of her stomach. Or was she about to throw up the banana? She sat listening to WQXR, maintaining her pose of external calm. The banana stayed down. But she was exhausted. She'd only been awake a few hours, yet she was ready to sleep again.

"I'd like to lie down, Daniel," she told him.

"Sure," he said, and got up to go with her to the bedroom. "There's a slight change," he told her, indicating the metal loop he'd fastened to the exposed-brick wall. "We'll let the leg restraints go for the time being, but I have to make sure you stay in one place." With that, he bound her wrists with one of the canvas straps, and secured it to the loop in the wall. He left her plenty of slack so she could turn over, but not enough to allow her to go beyond the foot of the bed.

Again, she lay facing the wall. He sat and stroked her, smoothed her hair back from her face, then stroked her some more, his gestures becoming bolder; he fondled her breasts with greedy possessiveness. She couldn't believe he wanted more sex, but it appeared he did. "Daniel," she smiled at him, "I can't just now. I'm feeling very crampy."

"When are you due?" he asked.

"I've lost track. Anytime, I should think."

"Well, we'll try again later," he said, and to her enormous relief, he covered her, turned out the lights, and left.

Being trussed up this way wasn't quite the indignity being spread on the bed had been, but it was ignominious nonetheless. Fine points. The freedom to close her legs, to shut some part of herself away from his eyes, restored a tiny portion of the self-respect he'd stolen by tying her legs apart. Just thinking of the way she'd been strapped to the bed made her begin to perspire, as the heat of degradation merged with her anger and fear.

She told herself she couldn't afford to waste time or energy on being angry. She needed to think how to handle this. He'd "collected" her, as if he'd read the Fowles novel. Now he was rewriting the book, adding twists and sexual variations, while she was preoccupied with thoughts of the death of the captured butterfly.

Well, she was no goddamned butterfly, and she had a fully functioning brain. There had to be certain advantages she could claim—recreating a menstrual cycle for herself was one. She'd insert a tampon first thing in the morning. While it didn't guarantee he wouldn't devise other ways and means of using her, it might give her some time to mend internally.

Oh, *God*! she thought, for the moment losing her ability to think calmly and rationally. She wanted to be out of this place, away from this man. People had to be looking for her. Unless Daniel had killed Miles. If he had, it might be some time before Miles was found. And then no one would have any idea what had become of her. Perhaps Miles was dead, and it was assumed that she was, too. If Miles was dead . . .

Daniel appeared in the doorway, silhouetted against the light from the living room. He'd lost all trace of the simian stance he'd had earlier in the kitchen and seemed more like the Daniel with whom she was most familiar.

Seizing hold of the opportunity, keeping her voice hushed, she said, "Daniel, on a purely practical level, there are things I'm going to need." He remained in the doorway, listening. "Much as I hate to admit it, I do have my vanity, and there are all sorts of creams and lotions I use. If I *don't* use them, I'll start to look like a used tea bag."

She gave a little laugh, and wondered at herself, at her resources. He laughed with her. Encouraged, she went on. "My electric shaver and my cosmetics. *Tweezers,*" she laughed. "I don't think you'll care very much for the sight of me dried out and hairy."

He stood thinking, then said, "I can fix that," and left the doorway.

If he went out—perhaps to buy a few things for her— she'd have a go at the screws holding the hinges of the gates to the window frames, using the edge of the butter knife. She examined the hinges in her mind, reaching three of them, with three screws in each. It wouldn't be very difficult, or take very long, to remove nine screws. Then she'd be able to push aside the gate, open the window, and get away down the fire escape. Her coat and boots were in the closet. She'd find a taxi, have the doorman at her building pay the fare. God, God! She was fifteen minutes away from home, if she could just get out of this small-scale prison, away from this frighteningly disturbed man.

He came back, carrying something. She couldn't make out what. Then he turned on the light and she saw he had a towel over his arm, and in his hands a basin of water, soap, a sponge, an orange Bic disposable razor, and the bottle of Vol de Nuit.

"Stand up a minute, Leigh," he instructed. Afraid to refuse or to question him, she did. He spread the towel over the sheet, as she watched with mounting apprehension. "Okay," he said. "You can lie down again now."

Keeping her hushed tone, she asked, "Daniel, what are you doing?"

"Don't worry," he told her. "I'm not going to hurt you. Come on. Lie down."

Jesus! Her pulse speeded up. There was no way on God's earth she was ever going to be able to anticipate the circuitous turns of this man's thinking. She stretched out on the towel while he put down the basin, then freed her hands. At once, she rubbed her wrists where the canvas strap had impaired her circulation, her eyes never leaving him. Maybe he intended to pry the blade free of its plastic casing and do as she'd suggested: open her veins. She could only hope he hadn't succumbed quite that thoroughly to his madness.

He sat two thirds of the way down the bed and lifted her legs across his lap. He lathered the sponge, soaped one of her legs, then picked up the razor. Working slowly, deliberately, he began to shave her leg. She wanted to laugh; she didn't dare.

By the time he'd sponged and dried one leg and started on the other, she'd relaxed. He really wasn't going to hurt her. If anything, this was somewhat more bizarre, but equally as comforting—at the outset—as the massage had been. He had moments when he seemed acutely aware of the more esoteric aspects of femaleness.

He derived such pleasure from attending to her, from his responsibility for her well-being, that he never wanted this time to end. When he'd shaved clean each leg, he smoothed the baby oil into her skin, from her ankles to the tops of her thighs; he applied dots of the perfume to the insides of her ankles and at the backs of her knees. Then he sat with her legs resting across his lap and looked at her groin, then at her arms. She didn't shave her outer arms. Fine, golden hairs. Celeste had despised her body hair, had shaved her arms as well as her legs. Her body had always been smooth as a baby's. He looked again at Leigh's groin, a stirring in his belly. He said, "Open your legs, Leigh." Her eyes widened. She didn't move. "Open them," he told her.

"What are you going to do?" she asked, aware of the pulse beating hard in her throat, and at her temples. So quickly, in an instant, she felt once more imperiled.

"Just relax, and don't worry," he crooned, urging her knees apart.

"Jesus Christ!" she whispered, putting both hands between her legs. "Daniel!"

"You'll like it," he told her, and plucked away her hands. "I'll be very careful. It's something I want to do."

"Daniel!" her voice was pleading.

"You have to trust me," he insisted.

It was true; she did. She had no choice.

"Lie back and close your eyes," he told her.

She did as he wished, feeling the perspiration collect and trickle down her sides. It lasted an eternity, while she kept motionless, her fists pressed into her eyes, terrified he'd slip and slice into her with the razor. He scraped and lathered, paused to clean the blade, lathered and scraped some more. He told her to bend her knees. With reluctance and dread, she obeyed. More lathering, more scraping. She tried to control the shaking that started somewhere in the center of her body and spread outward in waves.

He lifted the lower half of her body and removed the towel. The sheet felt refreshingly cool. She exhaled with relief and was about to open her eyes when his bare, oily hands began the subtle attack she'd known all along was coming.

His fingers slid over her. He used both hands, watching himself, then glanced up to see her biting the side of her hand as he succeeded in gaining access to every part of her. And then, with her caught, impaled upon him like a glove of flesh, he had to bend his head to taste and explore her.

He delivered her a new brand of pain, then placed a layer of vile sexual stimulation on top of it, causing her to writhe impotently, which heightened the pleasure as well as the pain. He didn't overextend it this time, but took her right to the limit, nudged her over, then played witness to another loss of herself, keeping her impaled until the last of her tremors had ended. Then he withdrew his hands, and gently straightened her legs, and she thanked God it was over, feeling, in the aftermath, agonizingly distended by his acts. She also felt emptied, wrung dry. If he'd just leave her alone now, she'd sleep—possibly for days. But when she opened her eyes, it was to find him at her side, expecting her to perform. And if she didn't do as he wished, he'd either strike her again, or worse, force his way inside her and do further damage. So she got down on her knees, and she did it. He caressed her hair, and said over and over, "I love you." She did it, and forgave herself for wanting to survive so badly that she'd set aside her pride, her dignity, any and all caring she'd ever had for herself. She did it. And gagged. Then ran, still gagging, to the bathroom.

After that, he allowed her to sleep.

Twenty-two

"Are you all right? Would you like me to come?" Miles asked anxiously.

Marietta sounded just a little older every time he talked to her, and that was on an average of half a dozen times daily for the past four days. This afternoon her voice was weary as well as older. "I can't do a thing," she confessed, as if her inactivity were a crime. "I've asked the girls not to come in for the present. Except for Alicia, who's been so good, screening the calls, keeping people away. Did you find anything?"

"I went through everything in the house and the apartment. Luckily, I had Joel's keys, so I didn't have to bother with the manager at her building. Marietta, I went through every pocket of every last garment she owns, her handbags, her luggage, the studio, her desk, every last drawer and cupboard in both kitchens; even the wastebaskets. I've looked *everywhere*. Either she destroyed the letter he sent her, or he managed to get it back from her when she saw him. I don't know. It's maddening. I know I saw a return address on the package I forwarded to her, as well as the letter with it. Diane doesn't remember, either. Federal Express, of course, only has our address on the label. I was so hoping . . . I can't think what else to do. And the police, well, it's simply laughable. Every department points at some other department, insisting it's their jurisdiction. The general assumption is she's been taken out of state. However, since there's no *proof* of that, the Connecticut police are spinning their wheels and the FBI can't be called in. And the New York police argue that since no one can be certain she's in New York State, let alone the city, they can't do anything more than they've already done—which is bloody little. No one has anything to go on. When they ran the computer check on the flight manifest, it turned out Mr. Godard had paid for his ticket in cash. Therefore no credit card number, therefore no mailing address. They've asked Scotland Yard to try to track down his landing card, but evidently it's a process that can take as long as ten days. It's as if the man never existed. I *imagined* him. And since I didn't actually *see* him force her into the car, there's even the possibility that she went with him voluntarily. The pendant is untraceable, of foreign origin. It's been two days since we gave the release to the press. I thought by now perhaps there'd be something. I honestly don't know what to say. It's the most frustrating . . . I don't have to tell you. I'll stop by later. I have a meeting out of the office at four. I'll be with you by six.''

''Oh, good,'' she said, sounding dazed.

''Have you slept?'' he asked, concerned.

''The odd hour. I'll see you at six, dear,'' she said, and put down the phone.

He hung up, wishing he hadn't any business demanding his attention. Every hour he spent away from his effort to locate Leigh added to his guilt and his fear. Four days. It seemed like months, years. He looked repeatedly at his watch throughout each day, confused and bothered by how slowly the minute hands moved. He'd collected all the items Leigh had given him over the years and sat examining each one in turn, recalling the occasion of its presentation, and what they'd said to each other, what they'd done before and after. For hours, he'd retrieved near-lost moments, to study and treasure them. And then he'd returned the gifts to the places where they normally resided, with the sudden fear that he had, perhaps, held some sort of private memorial service in advance of the end of her life; perhaps he'd been wrong to look at and hold those items she'd once looked at and held; perhaps, by his actions, he'd sent mistaken messages into the atmosphere that might find their way to her. Everything felt wrong, smelled wrong, tasted wrong, looked wrong.

He tidied his desk top now, dreading this last meeting of the day, with a good, young editor whose inscrutability would, Miles knew, be insufferable. Tolerable at any other time, but not today. But he couldn't postpone. He'd sold the man a book, he'd accepted his commission, and he had a moral obligation to the author to stay in the ring and keep bobbing and weaving.

He sat with his head in his hands gazing at the blotter, trying yet again to come up with something he might have missed. The package and its accompanying letter had been the only clues he'd so far come up with, and his disappointment at failing to find either the wrappings or the letter was so acute it made him feel ill. He kept going back in his mind to New Year's Eve, and the way he and Leigh had danced at Roseland, when he'd achieved a state of happiness it seemed he'd anticipated all of his life. They'd been inches away from a commitment. He'd believed utterly that another few days or weeks, and she'd have been willing, at the very least, to make alterations in their living arrangements. Perhaps she'd have agreed to sell the New Canaan house and move her belongings to his place outside Brewster. He couldn't think now why he'd described it to her as dilapidated when, for more than eight years, he'd been going up on weekends and holidays to oversee the kitchen renovations, the installation of two new bathrooms, the replacement of the roof, the repainting of the exterior, the double-glazing of the windows, the decorating of the interior. He'd gone to garage sales, scouring the local papers for ads, picking up odds and ends, occasional antiques in good condition; he'd shopped for months to find just the right sofa, the most comfortable chairs. Every spare cent he had had gone into the house. And it was very near to being the way he'd envisioned it at the outset. All along, it had been his intention to show it to Leigh, to offer it as a lure, to induce her to take up residence in the far bedroom with the onetime lean-to he'd had converted to a north-light studio. He'd created his version of the perfect environment for her, with a refinished and lacquered brass double bed, an Edwardian dressing table and matching chest of drawers; there were flowing white curtains on the windows and dusky rose carpeting on the floor that complemented the flower pattern of the white-ground handmade quilt he'd bought for the bed. He'd left the brick floor of the studio as it was, merely having it scrubbed before putting down a large square straw mat. Bamboo shades on the studio windows and over the sliding doors to the garden, as well as on the skylight he'd had cut into the roof; there was even a small sitting area with a white wicker rocker and matching table.

The house was the surprise he'd planned for her ever since the day she'd announced to him she was divorcing the Good Doctor, having finally legally adopted Joel. That very same day, after leaving his office, he'd gone to the garage for his car and made the drive out to the country to look at the house, picturing her in it. Not once during those years had he ever considered it a fruitless enterprise.

He'd always believed a time would come when she'd stop skipping out of reach every time matters threatened to turn serious. She wasn't a frivolous woman, he'd told himself; she'd been badly burned, and was fearful of being burned again. To her way of thinking, it was less hazardous to indulge in casual affairs. What had never failed to bemuse him was her inability to see that she was every bit as enticing to men as her mother. They seemed to spot her from a distance and gravitate toward her, perhaps sensing her singular gift for giving. Because even at her lowest ebb, she always gave far more than she took away with her. Yet in all the years he'd known her she'd never accepted as truth his compliments, his praise, his eagerness to show to her her own beauty. She just couldn't see or believe it. But she cared. Marietta was spot-on on that score: Leigh's greatest talent, and greatest weapon against herself, was her ability to care. She'd cared about some man on a flight across the Atlantic, and it had detonated in all their faces. Hell! he thought miserably. She *had* to be all right. He'd come to pieces—he could feel it, incipient as a cold—if any harm came to her. He, too, had spotted her from the distance and been drawn to her. But unlike the others, he'd placed his faith in time and circumstance and the conviction that she'd turn one day and realize he'd been patiently waiting. Patience did not necessarily provide rewards. And time now felt like an enemy.

He swiveled his chair around to look out the window, remembering the costume party he'd had one year. Joel had been fifteen, he recalled, starting to smile as the details of the occasion came back to him. What a splendid party that had been! Joel, in a long, dark wig, his makeup perfect, had come as Hedy Lamarr, rigged out in evening gear with high heels. He'd been the hit of the party. And Leigh. He reached for his handkerchief. Joel had done

Leigh up as a French courtesan, with a white, powdered wig and a rented gown; powdered cleavage and decorative beauty patches. She'd been so lovely, Miles had found it hard to breathe, looking at her. White, the dress had been. And white the stockings and the shoes. And later on, after she'd sent Joel home with Marietta, she'd showed him the corset. Laced down the back, and white, too. Ruffled white pantaloons. He'd sat and gazed at her, dazzled.

Lane was sprawled on her bed trying to study for a psych test when Cath came charging in without even bothering to knock.

"Wait till you see this!" Cath told her, waving a newspaper. "I nearly *shit* when I saw it."

"What?"

"I was at the chiro's this afternoon, for my back, you know. And there's always hundred-year-old *National Geographics* and shit like that in the waiting room, or weird magazines like *Runners' World*; stuff you'd never read if you weren't stuck there. Anyway, there's this whole stack of old newspapers, right? So, if it's a choice between *Runners' World* or the old papers, I'm going for the papers. So, anyway, I'm sitting there, just looking at the pictures, about to turn the page, and that's when I saw it. *Look!*" Cath had folded the paper to the article and scrunched on the bed beside Lane, tapping her finger to point it out.

Lane took the paper and read the short AP piece, feeling weird. She knew in her bones her dad had something to do with this. She didn't want to believe he could do anything so warped as kidnapping someone, but she did believe it. The last couple of months he'd been getting stranger and stranger, and every time she saw him he was so kind of out of it that it made her want to put her arms around him and hold him, as if he were a little kid, and promise him everything was going to be okay. He made her feel like crying all the time because she could tell he'd lost his center.

"Your dad met her, right?" Cath was saying, taking the paper from Lane and rereading the story. "Didn't you tell me he got you her autograph?"

"Right," Lane said quietly. "He did."

"And now she's been abducted! That is just too amazing!" Cath declared. "Don't you think?"

"Yeah," Lane agreed. "Amazing. Can I keep that?" she asked, reaching for the paper.

"What? Oh, sure. Bet you'll want to show your dad, right? God! Won't *he* freak?"

Lane didn't respond. It was her turn to reread the piece.

"I thought you'd be totally amazed," Cath said, frowning at Lane's subdued reaction.

"I am. It's just that I've got this psych test day after tomorrow, and I've really got to study."

"Right," Cath said, getting off the bed. "So, fuck off, Cath. Right?"

"Yeah. Okay?" Lane gave her a smile she didn't feel. "I absolutely have to go over the stuff, or I'll blow the course. Thanks a lot for showing me this. It's pretty amazing, all right."

"Call you tomorrow," Cath said a bit doubtfully, at the door.

"Okay, Cath. Thanks a lot. Really."

"Yeah." Cath went out and shut the door.

Lane read the story a third time. Then she got her wallet, put on her coat, and went out to the pay phone down the road. She didn't want to call from the phone in the hallway, where anybody could hear. She felt shaky as she punched out the number for the Bedford house, then gave the operator her dad's AT&T credit card number. The phone rang and rang. She let it go twenty times before hanging up. Then she punched out the Palm Beach number, recited the credit card to another operator, and worked out what she wanted to say.

Her grandmother answered, and Lane had to get herself together and sound cheery as she said hello and how are you, then listened to her grandmother say she was fine, and so was her grandfather. And how was she?

"I'm fine," Lane told her. "Have you heard from Daddy lately?" she asked, trying to keep it casual.

"He hasn't called you?" her grandmother asked, at once sounding disturbed.

"No," Lane admitted, "and I'm getting kind of worried. I was hoping maybe you'd heard from him."

"Not a word since he left us. It seems to be becoming a habit: he vanishes for days, and then reappears."

"Not for this long," Lane said. "It's eight days tomorrow. The longest he's been gone before this was six days. I'm worried about him," she allowed. "If you do hear from him, will you call and let me know? Sometimes it's hard to get hold of me here, I know."

"Of course," her grandmother said, sounding shocked that Lane would think she wouldn't. "You are all right, *petite? Tu as besoin de quelque chose?*"

"No, I'm okay, Grandmother. Give my love to Grandfather. And *please* call me if you hear anything."

"Of course," her grandmother said again.

It didn't feel right. Nothing felt right, and hadn't since her mother had killed herself in the upstairs bathroom. It creeped her out even to think about taking a razor blade to her veins. She'd always known her mother was a borderliner, but she'd never thought Celeste would actually kill herself. And Lane had a hunch she hadn't been told the half of it. Because if her father was anything to go by lately, it'd been a major number, her mother's last act. Lane just knew it'd been so bad it'd thrown her father totally for a loop.

He'd seemed okay at first, when he'd called to break the news. She really hadn't felt much of anything except sad for her father because despite the fact that Celeste had been a major bitch forever, he'd loved her. The woman had been a boozer, a bitch, a total embarrassment—Lane had stopped inviting kids to the house when she was twelve—and nothing like a mother. If it hadn't been for her dad, Lane would probably have run away when she was fourteen, because the woman just would *not* get off her case. There wasn't one single thing Lane had ever done in her whole life that her mother had liked. Lane couldn't make the slightest move without setting her off. Her mother hated Lane's hair, her clothes, her friends, the way she sat, stood, walked, talked, ate—every last thing about her. Lane couldn't remember even one time when her mother had hugged her or kissed her or even smiled at her. All the hugs and kisses and smiles Lane had ever received had come from her father and her grandparents. Back when she was little, she used to try to do things to please her mother, to make her happy. But by the time she was eight, she knew it was a total waste of time. And she decided it wasn't her fault if her mother didn't like her, because everybody else did and told her so, which meant it had to be something about Celeste, and not anything that was wrong with Lane. So, she'd stopped trying, and did her best not to rise to it when her mother had a fit about something or other; she'd ignored Celeste or pretended she didn't hear. And when her dad asked if she'd maybe like to go to boarding school for grade nine, Lane had said, You bet, for sure, absolutely, but I'll miss you, Dad. And he'd said, 'It has to be better for you than this, sweetheart,' and she'd known what he meant. He didn't have to say any more than that, because he'd always known how things were. What she'd never been able to understand was why he'd stayed married to Celeste, how he could claim to love her even when she turned into a total slob and was blotto by eleven in the morning. But he did, and he stayed, and he wouldn't hear one bad word about his wife, not from anyone. And by the time she was seventeen, Lane thought she had a fix on both of them, and it made her sad. Because it really was as if her dad was in love with this girl he'd known in high school who'd gone off and left this other woman behind in her place, and he was spending his entire life trying to find the girl from high school inside this other woman. And Celeste, in one of her rare, lucid moments, had really rocked Lane by saying, "He can't see that that girl was never real. He made her up, then wanted me to become her. I tried, but how do you turn into someone else? I did try. It was just too hard."

That first year in boarding school, Lane had come home during the school breaks. But after the second time, when Celeste threw a fit because Lane talked on the phone too long with Cath, and pulled the cord right out of the wall before starting to pound Lane over the head with the receiver and her dad had to pull Celeste off, Lane spent all her school vacations with her grandparents. And aside from that afternoon the summer she was seventeen when she'd sat out on the terrace with Celeste, watching her mother smoke one cigarette after another, her hands trembling, while she eyed the drink on the glass-topped side table and tried not to go for it because she wanted to have some kind of sensible conversation with Lane, and actually managed to be a real person for a couple of hours, the next time she'd seen her mother was at graduation, and Lane had made a major effort to be nice and polite and everything, but Celeste was so bombed you could smell it from six feet away and everybody was staring at her because she could hardly stand up straight. She'd looked years older than Lane's dad, and Lane had felt so sorry for the both of them that she'd stuck with them the whole time, right up to when they left to go home. Then Lane had gone back to her room and cried until she threw up because she'd hated the whole scene so much, and she didn't want to feel sorry for her mother, but she did. That whole afternoon was the first time—maybe it was because Lane was eighteen, and sleeping with Steve by then, and not a kid anymore—that she could see the walking, talking tragedy that her mother really was, that her dad had helped Celeste become. Looking at Celeste—which was what Lane had always called her, never Mother—was like looking into this big, dark tunnel that had no light at all, not even a hint of it at the other end. If you went into that place, you'd never come out again. It was scary as hell. And if it hadn't been for her dad, maybe Celeste would've been someone else and okay; or maybe she'd have been locked up somewhere a long, long time before. But nobody ever did lock Celeste up, and she never did get a fix on things, so she went and offed herself. And it blew her dad's brain. The past couple of months he'd been like someone dangling from a high wire, afraid to hang on and afraid to let go. He blamed himself for Celeste, and Lane knew why, and knew there was never any way to do the right thing every time, not for anybody, and he was taking on too much of the blame because even Celeste had known that the things he'd always said and done were from the heart and never out of meanness or spite. He just didn't have any of those things in him. Which was why Celeste worked on him the way she did—because it was the only area where she had a fighting chance of coming out even. They were two people who shouldn't ever have been together. But they were. For twenty-one years. And if Celeste hadn't finally ended it, they'd have been together forever, with her dad trying and trying with no hope ever of succeeding, and Celeste resisting and resisting, with even less hope.

Back in her room, she went through the article one more time, deciding a whole lot had intentionally been left out. The story hinted that the police knew who'd abducted the author, but weren't releasing all the facts. They quoted comments by the guy who'd been with her, her agent, and gave his name as well as that of Marietta Dunne, who was the mother.

Lane sat on the bed, holding the newspaper on her lap, touching her fingertips to the kind of blurry newsphoto of Stanleigh Dunn that didn't really give you any idea what the woman actually looked like, and tried to think what to do.

Miles was on his way out the office door on the afternoon of the sixth day, when he overheard his receptionist saying, "I'm sorry. He's not available at the moment."

Miles signaled to her, mouthing Who is it?

Diane said, "Just a moment, please," into the mouthpiece, and put the caller on hold as she referred to the name she'd jotted down on her pad. "Lane Godard?"

Miles reacted as if he'd touched a live wire. "I'll talk to her!" he said. "Put her through." He flew back to his desk to grab up the telephone. "This is Miles Dearborn," he said breathlessly.

"Mr. Dearborn," a young voice said, "you don't know me. My name is Lane Godard. I just yesterday saw the story in the paper. The thing is, my father told me he met Miss Dunn on one of his flights."

"Yes, I know that," Miles said urgently.

"Well, when I saw the item in the paper . . ." She hesitated, then went on. "Mr. Dearborn, I think maybe my dad has something to do with this."

"He most definitely has something to do with this,"

314

Miles said, keeping his voice steady. "I'd very much like to see you, talk with you."

"I'd like that, too. I'm calling from Vermont. I go to college here," she explained. "But I've got a car, and if I leave now, I could make it to New York by about eight or nine tonight, depending on the traffic."

"I'll meet you. Tell me where."

"Mr. Dearborn, do the police have to be involved in this?"

"We can discuss that."

"Okay. My grandparents have an apartment on Fifth Avenue. That's where I live when I'm home from school."

"Fine. Give me the address. I'll meet you there, let's say at eight-thirty."

She gave him the address, then said, "I don't really know if I can help you. Nobody's heard from my dad in a week and a half."

"Drive very carefully," he told her. "And we'll talk this evening."

Excited at this break, Miles quickly called Marietta to tell her. "It may come to nothing, and it may be something. I'll keep you posted."

"Come here directly after you've talked to the girl," Marietta told him. "I don't care how late it is."

Lane made another call to her grandparents, to let them know she was taking some days off from school and was on her way to New York. She didn't mention anything about her father or Stanleigh Dunn. She didn't want to say a thing to them until she'd spoken with Mr. Dearborn and heard the whole story. Once she knew the facts, then she'd have some idea what to do.

* * *

"You've got to understand," Lane said. "Whatever my dad's done, it's because he's been totally wrecked since my mother committed suicide almost seven months ago."

Miles sucked in his breath and sat back, stunned.

"Would you like something to drink, Mr. Dearborn?" Lane asked. "There's everything in the bar. My grandparents entertain a lot."

"I would, actually. Scotch and water would be lovely. Thank you."

She went to fetch his drink and he tried to relate this very forthright, obviously distraught young woman to the man who'd erupted into Leigh's house and begun using his fists. She was wholesome, in a low-key punk fashion that was uniquely well suited to her. About an inch or two over five feet, she had long, glossy brown hair fastened to sit askew on top of her head; round, questioning eyes; olive complexion. She was dressed in skin-tight black trousers and what looked to be combat boots, a man's dress shirt with a pleated front, and over everything was an outsized burgundy wool cardigan festooned with a variety of rhinestone brooches. One of her ears sported three pierced earrings, the other merely one. The effect was most pleasant. He thought she looked like nothing so much as a feisty little elf. She was tiny enough to look good in the gear. And she had an effervescent quality that even her present distress couldn't disguise. This young woman had a natural exuberance coupled with visible intelligence. Her eyes challenged; she listened closely to whatever was said; and she had no fear of silences. Miles liked her. He simply couldn't connect her to her father, except for her eyes. They both had the same brilliant blue eyes, ringed darkly around the irises. In the case of the father, the eyes had been most disconcerting. The daughter's eyes were a triumph of sheer beauty.

She came back with something clear for herself and

Miles's Scotch, sat close by on the footstool that was the partner to the chair Miles occupied, and went on with her explanation. "My dad told me he'd lied to Miss Dunn about my grandparents, about what they did. My grandfather retired two years ago. He was in international banking. And my grandmother has never worked. He told me he didn't know why he'd said those things. But I knew, kind of." She looked down at the glass in her hand, then raised it to her mouth. From the way she drank, Miles knew the beverage was nonalcoholic. "He's always told basically harmless lies. It was sort of his protection, his camouflage; he told people things that were meant to make everything look okay. My mother was crazy," she said flatly, turning those exquisite eyes once again to Miles. "From what I've heard over the years, she was always crazy, right from the time she was a kid. But she was the only woman Dad ever knew. They started dating in high school. She got pregnant, and he married her. I was the pregnant part," she said with a little smile. "Anyway, she started hitting the sauce when I was born, and she just never stopped. The couple of times she tried drying out, she was so totally insane that it was actually better when she was drinking. The booze kept her kind of vague. But sober. Boy! I mean, she'd pick a fight with me, or with my dad, over absolutely anything. When she was on the sauce, she'd be so out of it that the fights never lasted long. Sober, they went on for days. I mean *days*. She'd start in on Dad the minute he walked through the door and keep it up all the way through dinner. I'd hear them still at it when I went to bed. And next morning, she'd be following him down the stairs, still shrieking away at him. I don't know how he stood it. I honestly don't. But he put up with it. It was like he came home every night hoping for miracles. He'd come through the door with a big smile, ready for things to have turned around. Naturally, they never did.

Because neither one of them could hear what the other one was saying. And that was the whole problem, right there. They were in love with two different people, these dream images they'd made up for themselves back in high school when they were kids. He was okay, because he had control over every other area, you know? But all she had was the house, and me. And she couldn't control me, she couldn't make me into the way she wanted herself to be. Because I wasn't like her. I don't know if you can follow that. Celeste thought she could say what she had to say through me, and if I said the words, then maybe Daddy would finally hear. The problem was she'd forgotten a long time ago what she was trying to say. And anyway I didn't want to be *her*, I wanted to be me. Dad, at least, always knew who I was. He could see what was going on with Celeste and me, and he could tell she was totally disconnected from me; like she didn't have any parental switches anybody could turn on, so I was either going to be her alter ego, or I was competition. When she stopped trying to program me, I became the full-time competition. Until Dad sent me away to school. That was when I was fourteen. Until then, it was a war. Mostly between the two of them. Really, between Celeste and Celeste. You know? Nobody understood her. So she had contempt for everyone, and especially Dad. Jesus Christ! He was this jerk who didn't have the brains of a pineapple; he was weak; he was stupid; he was worthless. She even, this one time, made insinuations about how maybe the two of us, me and my dad, had something sexual going on. I went totally berserk. I was going to kill her. Dad had to drag me out of the house and walk me up and down the road for an hour to get me cooled down. Imagine *saying* a thing like that!'' She looked at Miles, seeking confirmation of the horror of the accusation.

"I can't imagine it," Miles said quietly.

"Right! She was out of her fucking mind. Sorry for swearing. But you can imagine what it was like for me, trying to figure this whole thing out for years and years. Well, what happened was, back last June I finished up my first year at college and went on a cruise with my grandparents. I like to spend as much time with them as I can. They're pretty elderly, you know. So anyway, we sailed on the twelfth. Dad came to see us off with champagne and flowers, the works. Then he went home and found her. I know it had to be pretty bad, and that he didn't tell me or my grandparents anywhere near all of it. It *had* to be bad, because the whole bathroom had to be done over, the walls, the floor, all of it. We got a ship-to-shore call from him and flew home from the next port for the service. Closed casket, and then a cremation. I thought he was taking it really well. You know? I mean, I kept looking at him, waiting to see cracks. But he seemed okay. He went back to work—he had six months left of his contract with the big company that bought him out—and made his buying trips; went away and came back all right. The only thing different was he wouldn't go anywhere near the house. He stayed here with us, then he'd take another trip for two or three weeks, and back he'd come.

"Then, at the beginning of November, no, wait, it was Thanksgiving, that's right, we were in the middle of dinner with the turkey and the rest of it when suddenly I could see Dad was all choked up. He was sitting there, holding his knife and fork, staring at his plateful of food, and he started to cry. I felt like dying," she said, her voice gone small. "I love my dad, Mr. Dearborn. He's the best father anybody could ever have. I mean that. He's decent, and kind, and good to people. He was good to that poor crazy woman for twenty-one years. I can't believe he'd ever hurt anybody, not on purpose. And if he's done this, the way you say he has, it's because he doesn't know what he's doing. He's not who he's always been. And it's because of what my mother did, not because he's a sicko or anything like that. You *have* to *believe* me.''

"I do believe you. But—forgive me—he beat me stupid and kidnapped someone I love very much. It's rather difficult to be as sympathetic as I might under other circumstances.''

She stared at him, taking in the bruises on his face, her eyes filling. "My dad did that to you?'' she asked.

"I'm afraid so.''

"Oh, shit!'' she whispered. "I'm getting so scared. I feel like I'm going to wet my pants. Excuse me a minute,'' she said, put down her drink, and ran out of the room.

When she returned a few minutes later, she said, "If anything happened to my father, I don't know what I'd do. I really don't. I can't even *think* about it.''

Miles reached out to put his hand on her arm. "I feel precisely that way about Leigh,'' he told her.

"But she's married.'' Her brows drew together in confusion. "Dad told me that was the big problem: she's married.''

Miles shook his head. "No, not for many years.''

"I don't get it. None of this makes sense.''

"Your father told Leigh *he* was married. You're right: none of it makes sense. There's someone I'd like you to meet. May I use your telephone?''

"Oh, sure. It's over there.'' She pointed out an extension on a table near the living room door.

Marietta had pulled herself together for the meeting. She'd pinned up her hair and, for once in a very rare while, had applied a bit of makeup to relieve her pallor. She sat very quietly, smoking a cigarette, and heard Lane out.

Lane repeated what she'd told Miles, unable to take her eyes off the woman seated opposite. She was kind of old, and she looked really upset, but she was the most beautiful woman Lane had ever seen. And all the time she was talking, Lane kept wondering what Stanleigh Dunn must look like—that newsphoto was nothing, a dud—if her mother was this beautiful. The whole thing was getting to Lane really badly now that she'd heard Mr. Dearborn's story, and she'd told both him and this amazing woman all about her mother and father. She felt as if she was on the verge of losing everything in the world that had ever mattered to her, and she didn't know what she could do to prevent it happening. She told all of it, even some things she hadn't told Mr. Dearborn, because she didn't want to disappoint this woman who paid such close attention and seemed so incredibly sympathetic. Lane couldn't imagine having a mother like this. It would have to be like the miracle her dad had always hoped for.

"I'll do anything I can," she promised them both, winding down. "I know it's probably hard for you to see from your side of it, but I'm as scared for my dad as you are for Miss Dunn."

"I'm able to see that," Marietta said kindly, very taken with this outlandish child with the extraordinary eyes. It seemed inconceivable to her that a man who could foster such loyalty and love in his child would do harm to Leigh. "I think," she said judiciously, "your father's very fortunate to have a daughter like you."

That tipped it. Lane covered her face with her hands and started crying. She felt sorry for absolutely everybody. Here her father was a kidnapper, of all things. And these people were being so decent and understanding. She accepted the handkerchief Miles offered, blotted her face, and stood up, saying, "I'll keep this and send it back to you clean. Okay?" Then she went over to where Marietta was sitting and before she knew what she was doing, she was on her knees with her head in the woman's lap, crying all over again, and saying, "I'm sorry. I'm really sorry. He's not a bad person; he's really not. He's just had *such* a bad time; it's been *so hard* for him. If you knew him, the way he really is, you'd know he'd never intentionally hurt anyone."

Marietta put her hands on Lane's face, looked into her eyes, and said, "You are not responsible for what your father's done. Whatever happens, remember that. Will you remember that?"

Lane nodded dumbly.

"If you don't wish to stay alone in your grandparents' apartment, you're more than welcome to stay here."

"I'll be okay," Lane said, thinking she should probably feel embarrassed at making such a total Gumby of herself, but she didn't. These two people weren't about to blame her for her father's actions. Somehow that made matters worse. Maybe Celeste had taught her to expect blame, she thought; also it was the one thing she knew really well how to deal with. She got up, again mopping her face with Mr. Dearborn's handkerchief. "I want to go up to Bedford and look through the house. The thing is, if I find anything . . . what I mean is, I'll help any way I can, but I can't stand the idea of bringing the police in on my dad. So maybe"—she looked first at Miles and then at Marietta—"we could try to do this without involving them. I mean, I know maybe they'll have to get into it in a big way, but maybe they won't. You know?"

"I understand," Marietta said. "It would suit everyone if this could be resolved privately."

"Right. So, I'll check it out and let you know if I get anywhere."

Marietta got up to see her to the door, waiting while Lane shook hands with Miles.

"I meant what I said," Marietta told her in the foyer. "You are *not* responsible. The people we love very often do inexplicable things. Those things don't necessarily reflect on *our* actions. You're a lovely girl, and your mother was something of a fool. Anyone would be proud of you.''

"You're so nice!" Lane cried, and gave Marietta a hug. "I've got your number and you've got mine. I'll call you either way, and if I don't find anything at the house, we'll get together tomorrow and try to think what to do next. Right?''

"Right," Marietta agreed, returning the hug. "You've had a very long drive. Go home now and try to get some sleep.''

Lane stepped away out of the woman's embrace. And maybe it was because of all the emotion and talking about things she'd never before had an opportunity to tell anyone outside the family, and maybe it was the scariness of the whole situation, but she looked into Marietta's terrific green eyes and said fervently, "I'd've given *anything* to have a mother like you!" Then she bounded off down the hall, and Marietta closed the door.

Twenty-three

Leigh had lost track of time. Days became nights, became days; and the more time that passed, the likelier it seemed she might never again see her mother, or Miles, if he was still alive. Daniel's blow to her chest had been more damaging than she'd thought initially. The bruise between her breasts was a deep purple-red area, from which threads of livid color traveled outward. While externally there was no particular tenderness, internally she ached. And it was most acute when she attempted to eat. Daniel presented her with food. She swallowed as much as she could. Most often, within minutes, her body rejected what she'd consumed. He prepared cups of tea and coffee, swimming with cream and thick with sugar. She drank the liquid, gaining temporary energy from the sugar, then becoming dizzy and weak-limbed after the sugar high ended. Daniel believed she was faking it. He didn't actually say it; his actions and facial expressions did. Because his own health was unimpaired, he couldn't see that anything occurring could possibly make her ill. Therefore, it had to be a ploy, a sign of her weakness like her less frequent requests now for cigarettes.

She remembered, with rekindled hope, the letter Daniel had sent with the pendant, giving his telephone number. Surely, if Miles were all right and found that number, the authorities would be able to trace the address. But her hopes collapsed when, alone and unfettered for an hour while Daniel went out on one of his mysterious errands, she put on her fur coat and found the letter in the pocket. She sat on the floor of the unfurnished living room, huddled inside the coat, and wept with frustration and despair. Then, pulling herself together, she returned the letter to her pocket, went to the kitchen for the butter knife, and began working at the screws threaded through the hinges of the steel gate over the far window. It was slow going. Only the very tip of the knife was thin enough to fit the slot on the screw face. The knife slipped constantly out of the groove, but she kept at it, finally managing to loosen all three screws in the bottom hinge. Then, because Daniel was due back at any moment, she quickly gave each screw several turns back into the wood of the frame so her efforts wouldn't be noticeable. The knife rinsed and returned to the drawer, her coat back in the closet, she shut herself into the bathroom to sit in a tubful of hot water, the heat drawing some of the hurt out of her cuts and bruises.

Several of the cuts had become infected, their perimeters inflamed and red. She applied the iodine, tears springing to her eyes as the brown medication seared the liquid rims of the cuts.

On her first try, she couldn't insert the tampon. She was too swollen. She needed some sort of lubricant, but she couldn't find the baby oil. Perhaps Daniel had used it all during those sexual preambles. For her second try, she accidentally managed to tip over the bottle of Mazola cooking oil he'd left on the counter. In the bathroom under the pretext of washing her hands, she coated the applicator tube with the oil, and was able to position the tampon inside her. While she was washing her hands, she wondered at the degree of madness in this apartment, and its contagion. Surely to God, what she was doing was every bit as deranged as the majority of Daniel's actions. And if she ever did get away from him, was she going to be rational? What was rational? She was no longer certain. She simply knew she had to do anything and everything in order not only to keep whatever grip she could on her sense of herself, but also to discourage Daniel from surrendering to his unpredictable spurts of brutality.

She believed now one truly could die in captivity. But she had no intention of giving up her life without using every last resource she had. So she went about the apartment, slowly pacing the living room back and forth at Daniel's urging—like a convict in the yard—trying to keep her body functional, trying to hold on to the last shreds of her dignity, parading naked, back and forth, back and forth, with the damned Tampax pushed inside her like a bullet in a gun chamber, the string dangling irritatingly between her thighs. She hated him; she hated herself. She felt increasingly capable of murder.

Daniel had stopped bringing newspapers; he'd removed the batteries from the ghetto blaster and stored them in his briefcase. More tantalizing than anything else was her discovery of the telephone, sitting out there on the fire escape, wrapped in a plastic bag, beside the toolbox. She stared and stared at it, thinking she could reach through the gates to smash the glass, but it was beyond her range. There was no way for her to get to it. So it sat, inches away, with a steel gate and a sheet of glass between her and the freedom one call would bring. She wasted perhaps ten minutes hanging on to the gate, staring out helplessly, all but shattered by her mounting frustration. Then she went back to work, and as she struggled with the unyielding screws on the second hinge, her eyes went repeatedly to the telephone. She could feel the instrument in her hands, could see herself plugging it into the jack in the living room just over there, could hear herself speaking quickly into the mouthpiece, summoning help. But she couldn't get to it.

On the evening of the second day of wearing the tampons, he came into the bedroom and said, "Take it out, Leigh!"

For one dreadful moment, she thought he'd somehow discovered her lie, and couldn't think what to say or do.

"Take it out," he said again. "Don't be embarrassed. I really don't mind. It's not so bad; it's even kind of warm. We'll have a shower after. I want to be inside of you."

"Daniel, I can't. Please, don't ask me to do this."

"You're being silly."

"No, truly, it is embarrassing. It's very private. I'd prefer not to. Come lie down, and I'll make love to you."

"I don't want to be in your mouth," he said petulantly. "I want to be *in you*. Just go and take it out!"

"Daniel, I'm not up to it. I don't feel well. Let me make love to you now, and tomorrow I'll be well enough to do it properly."

"Take it out!" he insisted, his eyes darkening.

All her resolve to be cautious, to play by his rules to keep him appeased, vanished. She simply broke. It was as if something inside her head had been stretched too thin, and it snapped. "FUCK YOU!" she screamed, and smacked his face hard, first with one hand, then with the other. Scrambling onto her knees on the bed, she struck him as hard as she was able with her fists, screaming all the while. She wanted to kill him.

For a moment, he was so taken aback he could only sit there, with his arms raised to ward off the blows. Then he realized someone might hear her; he had to shut her up. He caught hold of her wrists, hissing, "Shut up, shut up!" but she was shrilling at the top of her lungs, face bright red with the force of her screams. He slapped her. She broke free and slapped him back, still screaming. He was beginning to sweat, panicky at the thought that someone might be home in one of the other apartments and hear the noise and come pounding at the door demanding to know what the hell was going on in there. And he couldn't have that. So he dragged her forward, put one hand around her wrists, and clamped the other over her mouth. But she didn't stop, the volume was merely reduced. "Shut up!" he warned, forcing her down, his knee across her midriff. "Shut up, shut up! You'll spoil everything!" She went quiet; he relaxed his hand fractionally but kept it over her mouth. Then her teeth sank into the side of his hand, breaking through the skin, biting deep and hard until the pain was excruciating. Her legs thrashed, her knees banged against his ribs, her whole body was fighting him, while her teeth threatened to meet in his hand. He did the only thing he could think of: he wrapped his free hand around her throat and pressed down on her windpipe, harder and harder, until her jaws unclenched and he could get his hand free, until she stopped thrashing about, until her eyes were bulging from their sockets, until she went limp, and her eyes closed.

Absently, he wiped his bleeding hand on the sheet as his breathing quieted. Then he saw she didn't seem to be breathing, and a new panic exploded inside his head as he pressed his hand under her breast, unable to feel any heartbeat. "Oh, Jesus!" he cried, and pinched together her nostrils, pulled open her mouth and began breathing into her, mentally counting. He pushed air into her lungs, then pressed his joined hands into her heart, counting, counting, tears dropping from the end of his nose, terrified to think he'd killed her when all he'd been after was to stop her screaming. She *couldn't* die. Not Celeste and Leigh, too. *Breathe!* he begged her. Breathe! And then her lungs seemed to flutter, and he heard the air rushing into her mouth. It made a whistling sound as she drew it in, in, then slowly out; a rhythm was established. He held his shaking hand under her breast to feel her heart beating slowly, steadily, and cried loudly, open-mouthed, unaware that he was making almost as much noise as she had.

Unable to stop shaking, he covered her with the blankets and lay down, holding her tightly, terrified at how close they'd come. What was he doing? What? He no longer knew. She shouldn't have defied him; she shouldn't have attacked him that way. Why couldn't she allow him to love her without feeling the need to do battle every inch of the way? There was no need for it. Why wouldn't she see that? If she'd just do what he wanted her to do; if she'd just eat and let him take care of her; if she'd just stop trying to direct him away from where he wanted to be, it would all be perfect. But she couldn't do anything the way he wanted her to, and she kept challenging him. She could eat, but she refused merely to get back at him. And she could've taken out the goddamned Tampax, but she wanted him to beg. When was she going to stop all of it, and give in? What difference did it make if she had her period? It was nothing, nothing. He loved her, but she was making everything so goddamned, unnecessarily complicated. Maybe it was because she had nothing to do here, and she was bored. He'd taken the batteries out of the radio, but couldn't remember now why. There was no TV or newspapers. He hadn't even thought about getting her any books or magazines to read, or maybe some pencils and a sketch pad. Sure, that was it. She was putting up such a fuss because she was bored. He'd go out and get her some magazines over on Eighth Street, some drawing supplies, maybe some candy or something. And, for a change, he'd bring back a pizza, make a salad and some garlic bread, open a bottle of the Chianti. A change of pace would do the trick, give her something to do, something to look at, something different to eat.

When she woke up, she knew she was alone. She'd come to recognize a certain stillness to the apartment when Daniel wasn't in it. Even sitting motionless in a chair, his presence sent electric currents into the air. She lay, feeling deadened. He might as well have tied her up again because she was as shackled by exhaustion as she was when he bound her wrists with the restraints and attached the canvas to the loop in the wall. Her legs felt numb. The ache was still there in her chest and she could scarcely swallow. Her hands were battered from their brief fight, and her head throbbed, her eardrums hurt. She'd fought him, and he'd choked her until she'd blacked out. Why, when she knew how incendiary he was, had she put herself so at risk? Stupid. Bloody stupid. He wanted complete capitulation. She'd have to give it to him, or next time she really might die. She'd come too close this time. She could still feel again the undiluted terror of being unable to breathe, of his hand bearing down down down, closing her throat. God! The fear, the utter agony of having no air to breathe, the protesting shudder of starving lungs, the disbelief and panic causing every bodily system to shut down. She couldn't quite believe she'd actually lived through it, that she'd been as near to death as she had without going all the way over into the darkness on the other side.

She was profoundly aware now of her breathing, of the action of her lungs with each inhalation. It seemed miraculous that her heart continued to beat, that she could flex her fingers if she wished to, or even turn her head. She hadn't died after all, and she would take no further risks.

She would obey him absolutely, regardless of the nature of his requests. She would not disagree, or defy, or argue, or strike out at him; she would be precisely what he wished her to be: an obedient slave. She would loathe it, but she would save herself. He wanted her; she would find the strength to go to the bathroom and remove the tampon. If he questioned her, she would supply some credible lie. She would permit him access to any part of her he cared to claim; she would allow herself to be used. This would not last forever. Common sense dictated her time of entrapment would be limited. It wasn't possible to hide out in the middle of Manhattan with a captive indefinitely.

She could, of course, start a fire. But in the event the fire went out of control, she might suffocate, or be burned alive. No good. She could smash the windows through the gates in the hope of attracting attention. But being Manhattan, it was likely no one would pay any attention. She could take a couple of cans from the kitchen cupboard and pound on the front door with them. But there was little traffic in and out of this building, almost none during the day. The other tenants were nine-to-fivers, and Daniel now went out only during those hours. In the evenings, he remained with her, insisting she sit at the table and keep him company while he fixed a meal, or changed the bed linens, or acted out his sexual fantasies upon her body wherever they happened to be when the urge overtook him. The most she could do was keep on working at the screws on the gate hinges. If she could get them all loosened, she'd only have to wait for him to go out again, then put on her coat and boots before pulling the gate free of its moorings, opening the window, and climbing away down the fire escape. But for now, her first priority was to return her body to a state of accessibility. How he could derive satisfaction from using her in the ways that he did, she couldn't comprehend. It had to do, as she'd first suspected, with power, and his lack of it with his late wife. And, in a peculiar way, it had to do with her old favorite pastime, reaffirmation. She didn't want to understand him, but in many ways she did. It was both a useful tool and an extreme disadvantage, because understanding of what had tipped him over the edge made her more sympathetic than she should have been. Even locked into combat with him, she sensed the disbelief he felt at his own actions. It was as if the Daniel she'd met on the flight to London was also locked up in some small place, struggling against the Daniel who had, for the time being, taken charge of his thoughts and actions.

She was able to sit up, but had to remain on the side of the bed for many minutes until what felt like vertigo ebbed. It was the same when she gained her feet. She had to lean against the wall for support, then take many small steps around the perimeter of the room, groping her way to the door, until she was out and working toward the bathroom.

He had bought more aspirin, at her request, and she tried to take some but couldn't swallow. She was obliged to crush several on the rim of the sink with the bottom of the bottle, then lower herself painfully to lick up the acidic powder before washing it down with handfuls of water. She felt ninety years old. Even the slightest movement required concentration and involved some degree of pain. After removing the Tampax, she sat on the toilet with her hands resting on her thighs, very aware of the bones beneath her palms. She was shrinking, her tissues dissolving. After—what?—seven days, eight, locked up here, she'd eaten practically nothing—sips of tea and coffee, bites of unbuttered toast, half a banana. Her stomach was becoming distended; the knobs of her knees had hideous prominence, as did her hipbones and elbows. And, feeling about with her hands, so did her shoulder and ribs. Back rushed her terror. She had to do something, take in some nourishment, or her body would cease to function. She was in far worse condition than she'd thought. Perhaps she'd been here not just days, but weeks. She couldn't recall.

What to do, what to do? She thought of Joel, closed her eyes and saw him, her wonderful son, tall and handsome and smiling. Stephen stayed forever young. But Joel had grown to manhood, with wide shoulders and great, long legs. He'd shaved; he'd worn cologne; he'd known love; he'd given love. He'd had style, and humor; he'd had kindness and wisdom; he'd had the best sense of fun and occasion. His father had despised him, had refused even to see him when he knew Joel was dying. "He wouldn't come, would he?" Joel had guessed from the look on her face when she'd come back from the pay phone in the hospital waiting room. "Oh, well," Joel had said. "It's his loss. Right, toots?"

Joel. He'd been everyone's favorite waiter at the restaurant where he'd worked nights. He never forgot anything, delivered food and drinks with a flourish, never intruded but gave special service. And everyone adored him, gave him huge tips, and returned asking to be seated at his station. He'd looked very smart in his black tuxedo trousers, white shirt, and black bow tie. He'd played out his role with pleasure and effectiveness. "Just don't, please, come eat here," he'd begged her. "They put the leftovers back into the pots. They use the pieces of bread you leave on your plate to make croutons. The kitchen floor would turn your stomach. There are mice under the fridge. And they use whatever's left in the wineglasses to make their salad dressing. If you or the Grand Duchess"—which is what he'd called Marietta for years—"ever show up here, I won't be able to *save* you. You'll be eating recycled food."

Joel. He'd been her model for *Percival*, and for *Doll-*

dance. He'd been her best and closest friend, her cheerer-upper, her lovely boy, her grown-man son. She could almost hear him telling her what to do, whispering into her ear.

She heard the front door open, but didn't move. She continued to sit on the toilet, shivering with cold, but unable to get up. She listened to Daniel bustling about, putting away his coat, doing this and that, then his footsteps crossed the living room floor to the bedroom. A pause. She waited. The bathroom door opened.

"Why are you just sitting there that way?" he asked, not sounding angry, only confused.

"I can't get up. I'm sorry. I can't." Her eyes and nose had started to run. Her head hung. Talking hurt her throat. Her voice was no more than a whisper, barely audible.

He thought she looked like a skeleton somebody had propped up in the bathroom for a joke. He wondered why he hadn't noticed it sooner. "Are you doing it on purpose?" he asked from the doorway. "Are you starving yourself to get back at me?"

"No," came her all but disembodied reply. "I can't eat."

He wasn't sure. Yet he could feel himself leaning toward her.

"You have to help me," she whispered, turning sunken eyes on him. "Help me."

He could see every last vein in her body, especially across her chest, and in her lower arms. She looked like some kind of anatomical chart, with even the capillaries visible in the bends of her elbows and around her ankles. She was completely without color, blank white, except for those alarming dark-blue veins that seemed too close to the surface of her skin, and the intense bruising between her breasts. Her eyelids, and beneath, also looked bruised. Her lips were cracked and split. The flesh beneath her cheekbones dipped into hollowed shadows. The shape of her skull was clearly discernible under her matted hair. And along her jaw, and around her throat, were more discolorations; cuts and scrapes on her legs; fading, yellowed areas down the length of her back. He went over and lifted her, most alarmed by her lightness. She seemed to weigh nothing, as if her bones contained only air.

He carried her to the bedroom, saw that the sheet was wet, and had to set her down on the floor while he stripped the sheet, got a fresh one, and put it on. After he'd encased her in the blankets, he was about to go when her hand reached to stop him. Curious, he looked at her. This was all very strange.

"Daniel, listen to me." She wet her lips, tugging on his sleeve—a small, ineffective gesture, but one that made him sit down beside her. *"Listen!"* her wispy voice pleaded. "Daniel, I know you're in there somewhere, and I know you care about me." She had to stop for a moment. Speaking was agony. "Daniel, are you listening?"

He nodded, his eyes on hers.

"I'm dying, Daniel. If you don't help me, I'm going to die. Is that really what you want?"

He didn't say anything, but she thought she saw his eyes relenting.

"When Stephen was an infant, he was very ill with bronchitis, got dehydrated and weak, nothing would stay down. The doctor had me give him an electrolyte liquid. Go to the drugstore, Daniel, tell them you have a sick child, ask for something with electrolytes." She stopped again, swallowing in an effort to ease her throat. "Even Gatorade," she whispered. "Joel used to drink it when he ran. Ask the pharmacist. Please! Don't let me die, Daniel. You can't want that. Please?"

"Oh, Leigh," he said unhappily, his eyes glossy with tears. "I *don't* want that. I'll take care of you. I will.

Please don't die. What is it? Electrolytes? I'll get it for you. I'll go right now. I'll hurry.''

He got up and ran out without bothering to stop to put on his coat. He locked the door, then took the stairs three at a time, to hurry over to the drugstore on Eighth Street; back where he'd just come from. Oh Jesus! he thought, pounding along the icy, slippery pavement. Don't let her die! I really don't want that. Electrolytes electrolytes. Christ! What if they'd never heard of the stuff? What if it was some kind of coded message, and they'd hear it and know he had her locked up in the apartment? No, that was nuts. Electrolytes. Had to be real. Who was Joel? He didn't remember her mentioning anyone called Joel. Maybe it was the Good Doctor's first name. No, she'd called him Miles. But, wait a minute. He slowed to a walk. That agent, *his* name was Miles. It hadn't been her husband at the house. It had been the agent. The son of a bitch he'd seen her with, the two of them half-naked on the living room floor, it hadn't been her doctor husband, but her *agent*. So where the hell was her husband?

What does that matter? he asked himself, turning the corner on Tenth. So she had other men. None of that had a thing to do with right now. *She's going to die if you don't bring back this electrolyte stuff. How about two dead women on your conscience? That'll be good, Godard. Two of them, and you'll never sleep again; there won't be anywhere you'll be able to go. Is that what you want?* No! No!

Danny, you're not a bad person. I've never said that you were. But maybe I am, Danny; maybe I'm the one; and maybe this is never going to work because no matter how much you love me, no matter how well I know that, you only love the person you think I am. No one could ever love the person I really am. Let me go, Dan. Just let me go. Do us both a favor.

He began to run again, got to the drugstore, and raced to the back counter where the pharmacist was busy typing a label.

"Be with you in a moment," he told Dan.

"Listen!" Dan couldn't wait. "My baby, my daughter's very sick. I talked to the pediatrician. He said to come in and ask for an electrolyte liquid. She's got bronchitis, can't keep anything down. My wife's scared silly because we're from out of town, just passing through, and don't have a doctor here. *Please!*"

The man stopped typing and peered at Dan over the tops of his bifocals. "Hang on," he said, and went over to the shelves to pick up a quart-sized brown glass bottle. "Take it easy," he told Dan, giving the bottle a shake, then setting it down while he looked up the price. "How old's the baby?" he asked, running his finger down what looked to be an inventory list.

"Three months. She's so goddamned *little*." It was the truth. Leigh was disappearing, dwindling away.

"Four times a day, couple of tablespoons."

Dan paid, thanked the man profusely, then clutched the bottle to his chest and went running out, back along the ice-slick streets, afraid he'd fall and smash the bottle and Leigh's life liquid would drain away; he ran as fast and as carefully as he could to get this stuff to Leigh, so she wouldn't die.

And Celeste's voice, he could hear it, clear and young, told him, *It's a good thing to do, Danny; the right thing. I know you've always tried your hardest.*

Twenty-four

Lane didn't say anything to her grandparents about what was going on. She didn't want them to know what her father had done, and she had the idea that they might not ever *have* to know if she could be the one to find her father. She had to admit it was a pretty remote chance that, even if she did find her father and Miss Dunn, the police wouldn't be involved. But she believed that if she could be the one to locate them, the entire matter might be resolved without either her grandparents having to know or the police being dragged into it. It was pretty iffy, but she believed it. She'd find them; then she'd take care of her dad, look after him, make sure he got glued back together.

The problem was, she couldn't find one single thing that was of any help to her. She drove up to the Bedford house to discover a note on the kitchen counter from a real estate agent begging Mr. Godard to call immediately. Lane phoned the woman, who explained that the sale was all set, the buyers' mortgage had been approved, and she needed Mr. Godard to sign various documents. Lane promised to have her father call, then went to the den to go through the desk.

It looked as if her dad had cleared out a lot of his papers. And the ones he'd left behind were mostly old tax returns, paid bills, business correspondence, birthday and occasion cards she'd given him; and a big brown envelope full of drawings and stories and stuff she'd done when she was really little. He'd saved all her funny stick-doll drawings, and pages of printing. "You're the marshmallow, Dad," she said aloud, returning the stuff to the envelope, "not me."

There had to be a clue somewhere. He couldn't've just vanished without leaving something, even unintentionally. And that's when it hit her. She opened the bottom drawer of the desk again and pulled out all the files, piled them on the floor, and began to go through their contents.

He had to hold Leigh's head up to give her the liquid. Then he fed her some mashed bananas. She could only get a small amount down, but it was a start. And she was so grateful that it made him feel the way he had when Lane was a baby and he'd spooned cereal into her tiny pink mouth; when he'd bathed the baby, and dried and powdered her, before pinning on a clean diaper. He'd had a sense then that came back to him now of the singularity of his responsibility to this other being who was so completely dependent upon him for her survival. He'd cherished both the infant and his responsibility. Lane had established for him his sense of his own worth. It was very similar now, attending to Leigh.

After he'd fed her, he brought a basin of water and gave her a sponge bath, then patted her dry. Already he thought she looked better. He brought in the things he'd bought earlier—the hyacinth plant whose blossoms were just opening to emit their pungent perfume, the half-dozen magazines, the art supplies, and the now-cold pizza. He set the plant down on the floor near the bed so she could see and smell it; he positioned the magazines and art supplies nearby so she could reach them. Then he sat on the floor with his back to the wall, and ate wedges of the cold pepperoni-and-mushroom pizza while he talked to her.

She could see a change. It was as if her approach to the entryway to death had shocked him back, at least part way, to his senses. He was nowhere near as in control of himself as he'd been at their first meeting, but he was less angry, and overwhelmingly upset and apologetic. What struck her most strongly was the impersonal way in which he was describing what had to have been a true horror, and she understood that only by distancing himself verbally, and in his visual recall, could he even approach thinking about it.

"I couldn't let Lane or my parents see her," he was saying. "Not in that condition. *No one* should've had to see her." His eyes were opaque, as if he were reviewing the details from the vantage point of many miles and many years away. "You don't," he went on, "think about death in that context. I mean, we all think about getting old, dying someday. You read stories in the newspapers, or you turn on the network news, and there's the latest atrocity. But it has nothing to do with you. You react to the sight of body bags, and the closeups of shattered glass and blood spills. Television really removes you from things, and it shows you so much gore that it loses its impact. It's such an ongoing part of everyday life . . . it comes to you live at five, or from the Eyewitness News Team at six, or from Tom Brokaw or whomever, at seven . . . that the news doesn't seem like the news unless there's a story in there somewhere about the latest skyjacking by lunatic terrorists with causes nobody knows about, or hundred car pile-ups on some expressway, or an earthquake in some remote country, or some outspoken deejay who's gunned down getting into his car. You become inured to it. It's like Stallone and Bronson and Eastwood and Norris; all those guys playing 'might is right' and blasting people to shit if they come up against resistance. Bodies right, left, and center, and everybody buys that. The kids line up for days to see these 'good guys' kill off their enemies with submachine guns. As if that's the way to handle people who get in your way. The thing is, you just get used to death as a form of news or entertainment. So, when you come home and go upstairs to your bedroom and you happen to look over and see through the bathroom door that there are what look like puddles all over the floor, and you very slowly put down your briefcase, and very slowly walk over to the door to look inside, and you see what you see, you want to believe it's another news item. But you know goddamned well it's no movie, and not the network news. It's for real, and it's not some foreign diplomat, or five hundred strangers on some airplane, it's your thirty-nine-year-old wife. It's this person you've known since she was fifteen. It's this woman you had a baby with, this someone you've been trying to know for more than twenty years who never *wanted* to be known because the only thing she believed was her own was the secret to her identity. That's who it is. Except that she's not there anymore. She's gone away and left behind this body she's eviscerated; she's ripped this body to pieces with a razor blade, then cut its throat, and left it curled up in the bathtub, floating in thick, dark red liquid, for you to find. And a note.'' His mouth remained open but no more words came out. He stared and stared at that faraway scene, as his hand put down the half-eaten wedge of pizza, then came up to hover for a moment before covering his eyes.

He cried like a small child locked out of his house. It was terrible to see, and terrible to find herself reaching out in sympathy to him. But how could she not seek to console him when she knew that pain so well? She whispered, "Daniel," and held out her arms to him, and he huddled against her, and wept so desolately that she had to weep with him, aware of the wrenching irony of the situation, but momentarily unconcerned. She was incapable of ignoring his suffering, even if it had driven him over the brink of the madness that resulted in her being there. She even regretted having exaggerated the extent of her physical disability, despite its having been the key she'd needed to unlock him.

She held him and tried to kiss away the hurt the way she'd kissed Stephen's boyhood cuts and scrapes, the way she'd tried, at the outset, to console herself in this man's arms. The human touch, fundamental and necessary as water, was the most and best she could offer him. And she wondered at herself, at her capacity to disregard, even temporarily, what had gone before. But she could; she did. People would think *she* was the mad one. But what did anyone know, really? It all came down to losses, one way or another, and trying to find some way to deal with them. And it helped, it did help, as she well knew, to hold on. So she held him, and mourned for Stephen, and for Carl, for Joel, and for Daniel's dead wife. She applied herself to the task of amelioration, consoling him with kisses, with the touch of her hands, with her mouth, with the length and depths of her body, enveloping him in her sympathy in order to ease the pain. She directed him to where he'd wanted all along to be, then rocked him in the cradle of her thighs, whispering assurances that everything would be all right, he'd see. It would. "You'll see. It will. You'll see, you'll see."

Lane finally manage to get through to Cath.

"Where *are* you?" Cath wanted to know. "*Everybody's* been looking for you."

"I'm home. Listen! I don't have much time. You know that friend of Davy Kaye's, the guy he knows who's a major hacker?"

"Right. What about him?"

"You've got to get me his number. I have to get in touch with him."

"Why? What's going on?"

"Cath, I can't go into it now. You've got to get me his number, or get him to call me. I'm at the house, in Bedford. I'm gonna stay right here by the phone. I don't care what you're doing, drop it and get Davy to call the guy and either get me his number or ask him to call me collect. Will you do it, please?"

"Well, I guess."

"Cath, it's so important! It's probably the most important thing you're *ever* going to do. Call Davy right away, then call me back. Okay?"

"Okay."

"Leigh, who's Miles?"

She shifted a bit to one side to have a better view of his face. "Why?"

"Who is he, Leigh?"

"Miles is my agent."

"And he was the one with you at the house."

"Yes."

"Not your husband."

"No."

"And who's Joel?"

"Joel was my stepson, actually my adopted son. He died two days before you and I met."

"I didn't know you had a stepson. How come you never mentioned him before?"

"I wasn't aware that I hadn't."

"You *never* mentioned him."

343

"I was very distraught, Daniel."

"That's okay. But if Miles is your agent, and Joel was your stepson, then who's the Good Doctor, and where is he? Why was your agent with you at the house?"

"The doctor is Erik," she answered, not sure if telling the truth now might not set him off again. He seemed more himself than at any time since he'd taken her out of the house. "Miles was with me," she said carefully, "because I asked him to be there."

"Am I stupid? Is there something missing?"

"Daniel, I've been divorced for more than eight years."

"So why the hell did you tell me you were married?"

"Why did *you* tell me *you* were married?" she countered.

"I don't know. I was scared."

"I can't say that I was scared, but I was extremely upset. I loved Joel dearly. I was having a terrible time accepting his death. You, of all people, should have no problem understanding that. I didn't want to become involved, so I simply told you I was married."

He rolled away from her and lay on his back looking up at the ceiling. She kept her eyes on him, wondering which way he'd go.

He let out a long, long sigh, then, with disbelief, said, "We didn't have to go through one bit of this, not a bit of it. Jesus! We both lied. And *look* where it got us! *Jesus!*" He sat up, asking, "Why do you sleep with so many men? Why do you do that?"

"I don't know. Perhaps because it makes me feel attractive."

"You need to sleep with a lot of men to know that?" He looked dumbfounded. "You don't know it any other way?"

She couldn't give him an answer; she didn't have one.

He dropped back down, and turned to look at her.

"You're the only other woman I've ever made love with, except for Celeste."

"Oh, Daniel, it was *all* lies, wasn't it?"

"Why did you say you had your period when you didn't?" he wanted to know.

"Think for a minute about what's been going on here, and then ask me that question again."

"You didn't *want* me?" he asked, childlike once more.

"You didn't give me a choice."

He stared at her, and in the silence she thought she heard that clock ticking somewhere. Where was it? He brought up his hand to look at it. It was obviously infected.

"We should clean that," she whispered, "Put some iodine on it."

"Doesn't matter." He lowered his hand, for a few moments aware only of its throbbing heat. "I can't let you leave," he said finally.

"Of course you can," she said calmly.

"No, I can't. You'll have me locked up; they'll throw away the key."

"Daniel, whatever happens, you have my promise I won't do that."

"I'd be a cluck to buy that, Leigh. I just *can't* let you leave."

"You also can't keep me here forever. I'm already ill. If this goes on very much longer, I won't make it. Look at me, Daniel! Take a good look!"

He did. And, as before, it was impossible to argue with the reality. He'd abused her in many ways, and it showed. He shook his head back and forth.

"Have you been in touch with your family?" she asked.

Another shake of his head.

"I imagine they must be very worried about you. Don't

you think you should get in touch with them, let them know you're all right?''

There had to be a catch in it somewhere, but he couldn't spot it. What she said made sense. And he felt guilty as sin for neglecting Lane. She was probably worried sick about him.

''You should at least telephone and talk to them,'' she suggested. ''And then perhaps you could let someone— my mother or Miles—know that I'm all right, too.''

''No,'' he said, the recognizable Daniel starting to recede. ''You'd better have some more of that electrolyte liquid.''

''All right,'' she agreed, and gave up for the moment.

''Hi! Listen, thanks so much for calling me back. I really appreciate it. Look! I've got this major major problem and you're the only person I could think of who maybe could help. See, what it is, I've got this telephone number. Right? What I need is for you to find out the address for me. No, no. It's nothing like that. Look, can I be straight with you? My dad's in some trouble, and I'm trying to help him. The number's his, see. And if I can get an address to go with it, then I'll be able . . . what? No way. I've got the phone bill right here in my hand. I wish it *did* have the address. No, my dad's having this other number billed in on our regular phone. So, like in with all the other stuff on the bill, there's a separate account for this other line. I swear, it's the absolute truth. It's *very* important. Ask Cath. She'll tell you I don't mess with weird shit. *Please!* . . . Oh, sure. Like I can see me calling up the phone company business office and laying this on them. They'd buy it about the same way you are. No way. Listen, I *know* you could get into major trouble. I'll *pay* you. Whatever you want. Well, I don't know. What's fair? Sure, okay, fine. A hundred's fine. How long will it take? Really?

Shit, that's fantastic! No, okay. No, right. I'll wait right here. Thanks so much. Really. Thanks."

"There's no reason why you shouldn't stay with me," Dan was saying. "None. Not one single reason. If you care about me, what difference does it make?"

"The difference comes back to the matter of choice. And there isn't any involved in this. Can't you see that?"

"No. No, I can't. No husband, no wife. No reason not to stay with me. I need you here. I *need* you, Leigh. I'm looking after you now. You're already starting to look better after just a day and a night on that stuff. A couple more days and you'll be feeling stronger, and then maybe you'll want to look at some of these magazines, or maybe do some drawing." He could see he wasn't winning her over. It gave him an ache in the gut, because he was trying so goddamned hard to convince her. Or was it himself he was trying to convince? Things were very mixed up. "If you love me, if you're telling the truth, then what does any of it have to do with choice? I just can't trust you. I mean, I know if I leave the door unlocked, if I open the gates on the windows, and then go out for half an hour, when I come back, you'll be gone. I don't want to *lose* you."

"You won't lose me," she told him, hating being forced to be so dishonest, and trying to ignore the cloying fragrance of the hyacinths. "I don't see why, after all we've been through together, you don't even trust me enough to let me sleep one night without tying me up. Do you plan for me to sleep this way forever? You can't imagine how dreadful it is, Daniel. You'd be miserable if I did it to you. You'd be miserable if I came bursting into the bathroom when you were in there, or if I took away your clothes while I kept mine on. What will make you trust me? Tell me, and I'll do my best to prove I'm worthy of your trust. Just tell me what you want."

"Stop pushing at me!" His voice rose. He glared at her, holding his injured hand in the palm of the other like an earthbound sparrow. "I can't stand it, being pushed at constantly! This is the way it has to be! Don't back me into a corner where I have to make my points by hurting you! I *can't stand* hurting you, but you force me into it."

"All right," she sighed, and turned away from the sickening perfume of the hyacinths she didn't dare ask him to remove.

"Hi! You *got* it? Oh, Christ, that's amazing! What? I've got a pen and paper ready. I'm all set. Okay. Yeah. Right. No, I've got it. The minute I get back to school you'll have your money. Thank you *so much*. You'll never know what this means to me. What? Well, sure, I guess. No, okay. That'd be cool. Wait a minute, I'll write it down. Right. I'll call you for sure, first thing. We'll get together. Great. Thanks again, Ralph. Really."

She put the phone down, then said, "No way, asshole. The money's *all* you get. What an amazing nerve!"

She dialed the Manhattan number, and let it ring twenty-five times before she hung up, confused and disappointed. She'd been so sure her dad was there, that he'd pick up and she'd be able to talk to him. Had she made some mistake? Was this number a new office her dad had opened and hadn't told her about? No way. An office wouldn't have an unlisted phone; it would have a company name, not just her dad's. It had to be where he was. She wanted to get in the car then and there and drive into the city, but it was too late. By the time she got there it would be close to midnight and no way was she going to go playing detective in the Village at that time of night, not to mention the problem of parking the car, or the creeps who only seemed to come out after dark. What she'd do was keep trying the number until midnight. Then, if there still was no answer, she'd try again first thing in the morning. And if no one answered she'd drive into town and go to the Village. It was possible he was there and just not answering the phone. Maybe he'd unplugged it. If he had Miss Dunn with him, he wouldn't want people calling, or maybe he wouldn't want Miss Dunn to have a chance to call the police or something.

Shit! She didn't want to think he was capable of stuff like that, but she had to believe what Mr. Dearborn had told her. And she'd seen how beat up he was. It was all so scary, so totally Twilight Zone. She couldn't imagine her dad hitting anybody, but Mr. Dearborn wasn't someone who'd lie. You could tell that about him; you could tell a lot about him by the way he'd talked about Miss Dunn—Leigh, he'd called her—he'd said her name so sort of sadly, as if the worst thing he could think of was that he'd never see her again.

And Miss Dunn's mother, she'd been ready to hate Lane at the beginning, and all because of Dad. But she'd been so incredibly fair, offering to let Lane stay there with her, and even being so nice about Lane crying all over her lap. The whole thing was one gigantic, scary mess, but it was going to be over soon. She absolutely knew it.

She went upstairs, going past her own room to her parents' bedroom, to put on the light and then go to look at the bathroom where it'd happened. In a way, she almost wished she'd seen it for herself. Maybe if she had it would've been more real to her than it was, because she just couldn't picture it, couldn't come up with any kind of an image of her mother to put into the frame. The whole thing was such a major waste—Celeste spending her entire life being miserable and taking it out on everybody; her Dad breaking his ass to turn it all around and make it into a fairy tale with everybody happy; and her growing up being her own mother, and sometimes being mother to her dad, too. She'd tried forever not to be resentful about the fact that she'd never had anybody play mother to her, except for Grandmother who was really kind and generous and everything, but not a mother. She just couldn't stop thinking how amazing it would be to have a mother like Marietta Dunne.

She tried the Manhattan number once more before she went to bed in her old room. She let it ring thirty times. No answer. She set the alarm for eight. That way, she'd get back to the city, stow the car in her slot in her grandparents' garage, then go downtown to that address on West Tenth Street.

"I have to go out for an hour," Dan told her. "So, if you have to go to the bathroom or anything, go now."

"Why? What do you mean?"

"Do you want to use the bathroom or not?" he asked impatiently, finding the situation very heavy going for some reason this morning. He felt tired of it, tired of having to keep track of everything.

"Yes, I do."

"Okay. Make it fast."

"Daniel, what's so urgent?"

"I've got things to do," he said, standing with the canvas strip in his hand, waiting for her to stop wasting his time and go to the bathroom. He'd suddenly remembered he had to sign the sale papers for the house, and he wanted to call the real estate woman and get her to courier them down to him. It was risky, having someone come to the door, but he figured he'd just put some tape over Leigh's mouth or something, keep her out of the way and quiet until the coast was clear, and then that matter would be completed. He'd considered driving out to Bedford to get it all done, but he didn't want to take the chance of leaving Leigh alone in the apartment for the three or four hours that would entail. He'd use the restraints to keep her out of the way and quiet now for the hour or so he'd be gone. He'd go out and call the agent, then he'd zip up to midtown to his bank. He wished he hadn't resisted getting a bank card all these years. With a card, he could've got money out of some local machine. But he didn't have one, so he was going to have to hike up to his branch on Madison and Forty-sixth. Christ, but she took ages in the bathroom! Just like Celeste. What was it with women and bathrooms and the amounts of time they could spend in them? Back when he and Celeste had first been married, she used to sit on one side of the basin with her feet on the other while she put on her makeup. She'd stopped it after Lane was born. And, in a funny way, he'd missed the sprinklings of powder and eyeshadow that had tinted the backsplash.

"Come on!" he called from outside the door. "I've got things to do, Leigh. I can't wait around all day out here."

"Then why don't you go?" came her muted reply.

"Come on!"

She opened the door asking, "Is there some reason for your waiting?"

"I want you in the bedroom." He turned on his heel, the canvas unfurling from his hand.

"You're not going to tie me up and leave me alone here," she protested. "What if there's a fire? What if something happens? I'll be completely helpless, Daniel. I can scarcely make myself heard. I'd be incinerated if there were a fire. I wouldn't be able to scream."

"Nothing's going to happen." He grabbed her wrists, threaded the long end of the canvas through one of the reinforced slots, made sure she had just enough room so her circulation wouldn't get cut off, then secured the end to the loop in the wall. "I'll be an hour, an hour and a

half tops. Nothing," he repeated, "is going to happen."
Christ, but he was fed up with this whole thing!

"This is cruel, Daniel," she reproached him. "I thought
you were going to look after me."

"I am. But for now I want you to stay in here. I'll make
it up to you," he promised, with no idea, as he spoke the
words, how he'd ever be able to do that.

Resigned, she turned her head away. She felt his eyes,
felt his desire to say something more, but he didn't. After
a few seconds, he left. The front door opened and closed;
the cylinders turned first on one lock, then on the other.
She wondered if he'd discovered that she'd loosened the
screws on the window gate and that was why he'd left her
tied up. Dear God! Was this *ever* going to end?

Twenty-five

After he left, Leigh lay looking at the metal loop fastened to a steel plate, through which four screws penetrated into the brick wall. She tugged experimentally, then yanked hard with the full weight of her body. Nothing. She got up off the bed to sit on the floor directly in front of the loop, thinking it wouldn't be too hard to free herself. The canvas strip was elaborately knotted into and around the loop, but if she used both her hands, she'd be able to undo the knots. Since he'd previously only tied her up this way while he was present in the apartment, she'd had no opportunity to examine the setup at close range. Now that she did, she saw, with a darting excitement, that all that was involved was untying the strip. She positioned herself even closer to the wall and extended her hands, then stopped. If he returned to find her free, he might suffer another enraged spasm and strike her, or choke her again.

She didn't know what to do, and tried to guess how long it might take her to get loose. Ten or fifteen minutes perhaps. Another fifteen or twenty to work on the final screws on the iron gate. It could be done. She might actually be out of this place within as little as half an hour. She had to try.

As Lane expected, no one answered when she dialed the number first thing the next morning. She hurried to dress, then ran out to the car only to find that it wouldn't start. When she turned the key in the ignition the engine groaned like someone trying to lift a big rock, then went dead. "Shit!" she cried, pounding the steering wheel with her fist. She had to get to the city. Of all the times for the battery to die! Knowing it was useless, she waited a couple of minutes, then tried the starter again anyway. This time, not even so much as a groan. Why had she left the car outside instead of putting it in the heated garage for the night? The garage. She looked over at the closed double doors. Her mother's car was still in there. Her dad kept talking about selling it, but hadn't so far done anything about it. Its battery was probably dead, too, after all this time. But it was worth a try.

She had to go through the house because she didn't have either the automatic garage door opener or the key for the manual one. She entered the garage through the kitchen door, switched on the overhead light, and stood looking at her mothers dust-covered white Lincoln. Celeste had practically never used it, even though she'd always liked to drive and was a pretty decent driver when she was sober. It kind of bothered Lane to touch something of Celeste's, but her sense of urgency overcame her reluctance, and she opened the driver's door to see that the keys were right there in the ignition. Crossing the fingers of her left hand, she reached out and turned the key. The engine coughed a couple of times. She gave it a little gas, the engine caught, she eased off the accelerator, and the car sat idling. "Great!" she said. "Great!" and felt a totally surprising burst of warmth toward Celeste.

* * *

The real estate woman sounded overjoyed at hearing from him. "I was beginning to wonder," she said, with a giddy little laugh. "But then I heard from your daughter, and she said you'd be in touch."

"You what?" Dan asked her, his grip tightening around the receiver.

"Your daughter saw the message I left for you, and called me yesterday. She said she'd ask you to contact me."

Dan couldn't think for a moment. What was Lane doing at the house when she was supposed to be up in Vermont?

"Mr. Godard? Are you still there?"

"I'm here."

"We need your signature . . ."

"I know that. I'll give you an address. Send everything down by courier. I'll sign the papers and get them right back to you. Don't worry," he added, before she could object. "I'll pay for the courier."

"That'll be fine. Now hold on just a tick while I get something to write with."

She actually put him on hold; he couldn't believe it. What the hell was *wrong* with everyone? And why wasn't Lane at school where she belonged? He listened to the static on the line, growing more and more annoyed, while better than a minute went by before the woman came back on the line.

"Sorry," she said. "Another call came in. Now, what was that address?"

Jesus! he thought. He felt like telling her to forget the whole thing, but he couldn't do that. So he took a calming breath, then gave her the address. He had to repeat everything, and by the time the call ended, he'd worked himself into a temper and wondered if he should put off going to the bank until Monday. But, checking his billfold, he saw he was almost out of cash. He flagged down a cab, noting the time. Twenty after ten. He figured he'd get back down to the Village by eleven.

Lane made it to her grandparents' apartment by nine-fifty, was out on the street looking for a taxi by ten, and in front of the brownstone on West Tenth Street by ten twenty-five. She paid the driver, then stood on the sidewalk studying the building, getting up her nerve. Maybe her father wasn't even here. But she had nothing else to go on, and nothing to lose. She walked up the front steps, looked at the row of bells on the outside of the door. One bell's name slot was empty. She pressed that button, and waited. Nothing. She pressed it again, and waited. Still nothing. She gave the door a push and, to her surprise, it opened. She passed into the hallway and stopped at the foot of the stairs, listening. Not a sound. Burglars' paradise, she thought. Six bells, one without a name, second from the top. The place had a garden entrance as well as this one. If the bells were in height order, that meant second from the top had to be on the second floor in a three-story building.

She started up the stairs, checking the doors as she went. No numbers. Two doors on the second floor. She went to the far end of the hall. Blank. She came back to the door nearest the stairs. A handlettered card in a brass slot. She turned and went back to the door at the far end.

Leigh heard the buzzer go; her head jerked up; her heart lurched. The buzzer went a second time. She got up and walked as far as the restraint would allow, which was to the foot of the bed, to stop, straining forward. There was the sound of light footsteps coming up the stairs. God! Someone was coming here! Had they finally found her? She strained further against the canvas strap, trying to get closer to the door. There was a quiet knocking.

"I'M IN HERE!" Leigh gave her shout as much volume as she could muster. "CAN YOU HEAR ME?"

The knocking grew louder. "Oh, God! They can't hear me! I'M IN HERE!" The tendons in her throat felt as if they'd break from the effort she gave to making herself heard.

Lane thought she heard something, and put her ear close to the door. *"Is somebody in there?"* she called.

"YES! YES! CAN YOU HEAR ME?"

Lane pressed closer to the door, her hands flat either side of her head, able to hear what sounded like whispering from inside. *"I can just barely hear you!"* she called back. *"Is that Leigh?"*

"YES!" Tears came to Leigh's eyes. "YES!"

"This is Lane! I'm going to go call Mr. Dearborn, then I'll come back. I'll be back as fast as I can. Did you hear?"

"YES!"

"Okay! I'm going now."

The light footsteps ran away down the stairs. Leigh sat abruptly on the foot of the bed. The girl was going to get Miles. Miles was all right. The two of them were going to get her out of here. It was over. Over.

Lane rummaged through her bag for the paper with Mr. Dearborn's number; found it, dropped a quarter in the slot, pushed out the numbers. Busy. Busy? She disconnected, dropped the quarter again, redialed. Busy. No way! She jiggled the arm, threw in the quarter for a third time, got the operator and asked her to try the number.

"You can dial that number direct," the operator droned.

"I know. I want you to check it."

"One moment."

Silence. The number tones. Busy signal.

Then, "That line's busy."

"It can't be. It's a business phone. Could you *check* it please, to make sure it's really busy and not out of order?"

"Just one moment, please."

The line went vague and fuzzy, the way it did when you got put on hold, and Lane waited, tapping her foot, her body feeling as if it was going to start jumping up and down, jiggling around.

The operator came back. "There's a problem on that line."

"Oh, hell! Thanks." Lane hung up, then dialed again, just once more, on the off chance it was a mistake. No mistake. Busy busy. She fingered her quarter out of the slot, ran to the curb and scanned the street for a cab. Nothing coming. She started to run toward the intersection. The subway would be faster than a cab. She'd hop on a train, go to his office, get Miles, bring him back down here. But what if he wasn't there. He *had* to be there! No way was she going to call the police on her dad, no way.

There was a long line at the bank. Daniel looked around at the other customers—businessmen, secretaries, a woman in a fur coat. His eyes stayed on the woman for several moments, then moved on. Tellers behind the counters, special service people, a guard, a woman in a fur coat with high-heeled black boots. The line inched forward. The woman was over at the counter, talking head to head with a young woman behind the counter. So many people, so many. Everyone on this side of the counter in heavy coats and boots, scarves wound around their necks. The floor wet with tracked-in slush, brown muck. The guard stood by the door, hands folded in front of him. The line moved forward another foot. And it seemed, all at once, as if all these other people were performing in different little scenarios. They were all very separate, very distinct. Again he looked at the woman in the fur coat, her back to him. He, too, was separate, and visible, alive. It shook him to think of his state of being, of his validity as a unit, a man, a person, someone independent and autonomous. Until that moment, he'd lost sight of something very basic: that every last creature stood alone, and was allowed the right to function alone, or in concert with others, at his choosing. It seemed incredible. Yet, standing there in the bank, looking at the woman in the fur coat, he was all but overwhelmed by guilt at the realization that he had willfully, abusively, deprived another person of that fundamental license. Down in an apartment in the Village that no one else knew about, was an important woman whose importance had been taken away from her—by him. What he'd done in forcibly removing her from her home and installing her in that small secured fortress was an offense of such epic proportions that it actually stunned him as he waited in the queue, inching closer to the person who would provide him with the funds that he'd come for in order to perpetuate the crime he was committing against Stanleigh Dunn. It was so wrong, so monstrously wrong, that he simply couldn't think why he'd done it, or what he'd hoped to accomplish.

Standing there, holding his withdrawal slip, with only two other people left in front of him in the line, he felt so much a criminal that he was sure the other customers had to be able to see and smell it, like some foul aura he radiated. Standing there, patiently waiting while the female customer now at the counter engaged in what looked like it would be a lengthy transaction, it occurred to him that he was in terrible trouble. And if he took action, he could prevent the trouble from becoming worse. He looked again to the front of the queue, then at the broad, overcoated back of the man ahead of him, and asked himself what he was doing. It wasn't too late to set some of it to rights.

He broke out of the line, shoved the withdrawal slip into his pocket, and hurried out to the street. A taxi would take too long. He started running along Forty-sixth Street, toward Lexington and the subway. He had to get back down to the Village and set Leigh free, end this crazy thing he'd done. He sprinted along the sidewalk, darting around people, fused on reaching his destination. He had to return to Leigh all, or at least part, of what he'd taken from her. A stitch in his side, he breathed through his mouth, maintaining his pace, ignoring the pain, seeing—with each yard he covered—more of the scope of his actions. And the more he saw, the more convinced he became that he was out of his mind; he'd gone completely crazy. Maybe he was coming back from it now, or maybe this was merely a temporary remission. It didn't matter. The only important thing was getting back to the prison he'd created, to free his prisoner. He wanted it so badly that his throat worked and his eyes swam; his fingers pressed tightly into his palms; his heart pumped deliriously; and his head felt crammed with the broadening ramifications of his mad acts. He was out of his goddamned mind. He'd probably be spending a fair portion of his future in a jail somewhere, while Lane and his mother and father tried to deal with the facts of what he'd done. He saw himself being carted off in handcuffs; saw himself being incarcerated, interrogated. He deserved it. Christ! He'd tied her up and gone off without even bothering to give her any more of the electrolyte drink. If she died, he'd be a murderer. He felt as if his bowels had turned to ice water. A murderer. Maybe somebody had come while he'd been out, kicked in the door to find this dead woman, naked and restrained, in the bedroom. Christ, Christ! He'd never wanted anyone dead, not Celeste, and not Leigh. He didn't want anyone to die. And Lane! What would she think, finding out that her father had done something so completely insane? He got a token, pushed it into the turnstile slot, and paced back and forth on the platform, his eyes on the tunnel, willing the train to hurry.

The sound of the door opening awakened her. She sat up, using both fettered hands to keep the blankets around her, and was taken aback by the sight of Daniel, red-faced and out of breath, rushing into the room to begin undoing the canvas from the loop in the wall, while declaring, in highly agitated fashion, the shame he felt at his actions.

"I'll get you out of here," he told her. "This is crazy. I don't know what the hell's been going on, but I'll get you out of here before I do any more of it. I don't have the right, *nobody* has the right to do something like this. I know you'll never forgive me, and you shouldn't. I'm just so goddamned glad you're still alive, that I haven't really hurt you badly. Leigh," he cried, struggling with the knots, breaking into tears. "I never *meant* any of this to happen. Honest to Christ, I didn't. I'm not in love with you, Leigh. I don't even know who you are. And I know you've only been saying the things you have to protect yourself. The things I've done to you! Jesus! It's like I keep sliding in and out, and I've got to get you out of here before I slide back again." He finally got the knots undone, then bent to release her wrists, stopped by the sight of her abraded skin, his tears proliferating. "I'm *sorry!*" he wept. "I'm so goddamned sorry!" Gently, he put her hands down, saying, "I'll get your coat, your boots, and take you home."

He went out to the living room and was about to open the closet when there was a knock at the front door. He went rigid. More knocking. And then he heard Lane call out, "Daddy? Are you there?"

Lane. He took a step toward the door, then stopped.

"Daddy?"

Ah, Lane! He lowered his head, swamped by misery and self-disgust. Too late, too late!

"Are you in there, Daddy?"

He began moving to the door. Leigh came out of the bedroom, her eyes on him as she reached into the closet for her coat and pulled it on. He undid the top lock, then the bottom one, visibly shaking from head to toe. His hand went to the knob, and he turned it.

The door opened and there was a moment of silent tableau. Miles saw this man and, beyond him, Leigh. The sight of Leigh, her condition, ignited Miles. He threw himself at Daniel, prepared to beat him to a pulp.

"Miles!" Leigh begged, running over. "Don't hurt him! Please, don't!"

Miles let go of the man, and looked uncertainly at Leigh. He wanted to take hold of her, to get her out of there, but something else was happening, and she was compelling him to see it. She took hold of his hand and clung to it, but her eyes were not on him. And he turned to see what it was that had her so in its grip.

Dan looked at Lane, who was standing out in the hallway staring wide-eyed at Leigh. Her hand came up to cover her mouth as her eyes turned questioningly to her father.

Leigh let go of Miles's hand and moved forward. Daniel shrank out of her way, flinching in anticipation of curses or blows.

Lane couldn't move. Her feet and legs turned to cement, she watched, weighted down, as the woman with large, sunken eyes in a face that, beneath the bruises, was almost gray, came toward her. Lane took it all in: the marks on Leigh's throat, the rubbed-raw areas on her wrists, and all she could think was that her father had done those things to this woman. *Her father.* It was so much worse than anything she'd imagined; way worse. Her dad had hurt this woman, hurt her badly, hit her, and done God only knew what else.

The two men stood apart, both of them watching Leigh.

Leigh went to the girl and wordlessly drew her close. The girl came willingly, burying her face in the luxurious fur, quivering, afraid. Leigh held her tightly and whispered, "Don't hate your father for this. Help him, but don't hate him." Her arms brought the girl closer still, and Lane burrowed against her, eager for her words, for her forgiveness. "Nothing will happen," Leigh promised. "Nothing. Thank you," she said inadequately. "You've been very brave; I'm so grateful."

Miles nodded in agreement, not at the words he couldn't hear, but at this display of Leigh's instinctive knowing and generosity. Then he put his hand on her shoulder. "I'll take you home, Leigh."

"Don't hate him," Leigh whispered fervently. Then she released the girl and let Miles take her out of there.

"Should I take you to your mother's?" Miles asked in the taxi. "A doctor? Perhaps I should get you to a doctor."

She shook her head, reluctant to turn away from the window and the exceptional scenes of life on the streets. Even the freezing rain seemed remarkable. "Take me to my place," she whispered, turning inside the circle of his safeguarding arm. "I can't let Mother see me this way."

"Oh, Leigh, are you sure I shouldn't get you some medical attention?"

"I'll be all right," she insisted, pressing herself closer to him, very cold. "I thought you were dead. I didn't know. Will you stay with me?"

"Sshhh. Of course I will." He held her hand in silence for the duration of the ride, trying to quell the frantic action of his heart.

* * *

She looked around, finding everything different, altered. Miles reached to help her out of her coat, emitting a shocked gasp at finding her naked under it. He made angry noises in his throat at seeing how emaciated she was, and how battered. He scooped her up, declaring, "I'm putting you straight to bed," and carried her to the bedroom.

He pulled back the blankets, set her down, then stared, exclaiming, "What the bloody hell!"

"What?"

"Did that sick bastard do that to you?"

"What?"

"*That!*" He pointed at her groin, indignation and outrage making his ears ring.

"That," she repeated, and raised up on her elbows to look down at herself. "That." She looked at him, then again at herself. "It makes me look much younger, don't you think?" She fell back laughing so hard that tears came to her eyes. And then she broke.

He held her, while sobs throttled her, wrenching their way from her throat, and she tried to tell him how she felt. "I was so afraid he'd killed you. I couldn't think how I'd go on if he had. I was so afraid for you, so afraid."

"It's over now," he told her. "Over."

After a time, calmer, she said, "I keep thinking perhaps I won't know how to be free anymore, Miles. Nothing looks or feels quite right. I'm so frightened." She began to tremble, and it so unnerved him that he said, "If you won't have a doctor, then you must have your mother."

"Please, don't call her! I don't want her to see me this way!"

"Leigh, don't you realize she'd rather see you 'this way,' than dead? *We* were so afraid *we'd* lost *you*. I'm going to call her. She'll know better than I what needs to be done here, Leigh. I'm out of my depth. The most I can do isn't good enough."

"He said if I didn't get into the car, if I didn't ride in the trunk—he made me ride in the trunk, Miles, it made me so ill—if I didn't do it, he said he had your address and hers, he'd come after you. I'm so glad you're alive, Miles!"

Keeping hold of her hand, he picked up the telephone on the bedside table and dialed Marietta's number, spoke to Alicia, then waited while Marietta came to the phone.

Miles said, "Hold on a moment, Marietta," and put the receiver into Leigh's hand.

Leigh got the instrument to her mouth, and said, "I need you. I . . ." She couldn't say anything more.

"I'll come at once," Marietta said, and broke the connection.

"She's coming," Leigh told him wonderingly.

"I know." He replaced the receiver and touched his hand to her cheek. "I'll get you a nightgown."

She watched him open the drawer and select her favorite long-sleeved granny gown. He held her, got the gown on her, then tenderly eased her down again.

"Thank you," she whispered, clutching his hand. "I do love you so, Miles. I think," she said, then paused to moisten her lips. "I think we've been very foolish, you and I."

"No," he began to disagree, but her eyes were closing. "With all my heart, I love you."

Her eyelids lifted, and she smiled at him. "You're so romantic," she teased. Then, growing serious, her eyes beginning to close again, she said, "I'm not going to die, after all." As sleep overtook her, she wondered if she'd actually spoken the words aloud.

After

It was a perfect spring day, pleasantly warm. The sun shone unimpeded through a cloudless blue sky. There was an easy breeze with a soft edge that held the scent of newly cut grass. Leigh sat in a wooden lawn chair in the rear garden, her hands resting on the arms, her head supported by the broad back slats. Her face turned to the sun, she breathed deeply and slowly while mentally taking stock. All in all, she felt physically well. The damaged ligaments in her chest had taken the longest to mend, and with each breath she drew she still expected to feel the protesting soreness in her chest. But it was no more now than a faint echo. She wasn't yet accustomed to the loss of pain, and thought how very strange it was that one could come to rely on discomfort, as if its existence were proof one was actually alive.

She was also unaccustomed to living without cigarettes, and often dreamed of smoking. When she woke up, she looked around guiltily for the evidence, not completely certain dreams couldn't transcend sleep. Of course, there was nothing to be found, except the lowgrade, continuing longing she had to hold a cigarette to her mouth and fill her lungs with pungent smoke. Daniel had forced her to give up cigarettes, but she didn't want to take them up again. She thought more often, with more yearning, about cigarettes, than she did about anything or anyone except Joel. And Daniel. There was no fear attached to her thoughts of Daniel, but rather a sense of wonder coupled with disbelief that those ten days had, in fact, been real.

It was strange to think of that time and to relate it to the way she was occasionally startled by sounds or shadows, by the recreation in her dreams of certain scenes that caused her to surface with her heart pounding and sweat soaking into the bedclothes. There were moments in the dark when she was suddenly convinced it wasn't Miles with her in bed, but Daniel. She even came to, some mornings, to find she'd slept on her side with her wrists pressed together, as if bound.

At random moments, heat would overtake her, and she felt again the humiliation she'd suffered at being tied to the bed. These were the bad times, when she'd mourn for the woman she'd been prior to the experience, because she doubted she'd ever again feel one hundred percent free, or safe. There would always be some part of her brain that stubbornly held on to the experience, arbitrarily pitching images at her. She didn't take them well. She cringed, and sought distraction. She despaired of the grating anxiety that turned her lungs to punctured sacs unable to contain sufficient air; of the shame of having been seen, and examined, and used.

Everyone was kind. Miles paid close attention, waiting for signals, encouraging her to talk, controlling his reactions so there'd be one less thing with which she'd have to cope. Marietta was attentive but not overly indulgent. Once satisfied Leigh had sustained no debilitating injuries, either psychic or physical, she took to treating her in the

367

old, accustomed way—exhorting Leigh to get to work, to get up and get out, to stop being so indecisive. "It was nasty; it was sordid and hateful, but it's over," Marietta told her. "But if you dwell on it, it will *never* be over."

Leigh felt fairly confident that externally she revealed a little less of her feelings about the incident each day, while internally she tried to deal with those feelings. She was working on the production design for *Percival*, had already completed the scale model of the stage, with the flats and the revolve, as well as watercolor sketches of the finished set and the costumes. She'd been attending rehearsals, to study the cast as they moved about the rehearsal hall on the West Side, in order to keep the designs appropriate to the individuals who would have to perform in them. And after this weekend she'd be staying in the city to oversee the making of the costumes, as well as the preparation and painting of the sets—which were, in most cases, large-scale reproductions of the original illustrations. She wanted to be present as all the pieces came together, in case there were problems with the lighting, or the way the costumes fit against the flats. She was enjoying it. As her mother had said, there was pleasure in work; there was progress and satisfaction, and a sense of ineffable rightness. Work was good; work preoccupied her; work kept her darker thoughts at bay for long periods of time. Miles was also good, and with him, as well, there was progress and satisfaction. He was attentive and loving and, of course, still the old Miles, with his passion for lurid tales and for gossip. And when he and her mother and she were together, Miles and Marietta bickered and fussed, and she sometimes thought that if one hadn't known of certain events, one would have been unable to perceive any alteration in their behavior. But everything was subtly altered. Marietta continued to see Laurence and her other men friends, but was spending more evenings at home alone. She claimed it was because she was overworked, or desirous of her own company, or had a need for thinking time. Leigh thought the truth was that Marietta had looked into an abyss, and it had badly frightened her. She could no longer dance with her previous abandon. None of them could. And it was sad to think that Daniel's actions had wider-reaching effects than anyone could ever have dreamed. Marietta's new stay-at-home policy was one example. Miles's tendency to be overly solicitous was another. He kept on asking Leigh did she need this, or want that, until she had to say, "Miles, I'm not crippled or impaired in any way. And if you don't stop treating me as if I'm made of glass, I swear I'll go stark raving mad. I liked you far better as a bear." He frowned, then said, "Well, in that case, I have things to do. So, I will see you later," and off he went, smiling, to make a number of telephone calls.

It was all slightly odd and anticlimactic, as if, had she suffered more extensive injuries, they'd each have been better able to cope with her. But the damage was primarily inside her head, in her thoughts and feelings, her hesitations and reactions, and that was an area she was able to keep out of sight. So, with a sigh and a slight shake of the head, the three of them picked up and went on with their lives.

Some nights she dreamed of Daniel; she saw again his astonishing black-outlined irises, and heard his laughter or his sobs, and felt a new emptiness inside herself, as if some vital organ had been removed without her knowledge. No matter how she tried, she couldn't get to the root of this particular emotion. She knew it had, in some measure, to do with the dependency he'd compelled her to feel and to display; it also had to do with his inability to be responsible for his acts, and her understanding of that. In all her thoughts of him, he was an abandoned little boy, caught up in a bewildering emotional circus the exits from which always seemed to close before he was able to reach them. And she couldn't help wondering if the Daniel who emerged, ultimately, would resemble either of the other Daniels to whom she'd been exposed, or if he'd be someone completely different. Certainly, *she* was different as a result of her prolonged and intense exposure to him. Locks on bathrooms had to lock. Yet even when they did, throughout her time in the tub, or the shower, or at the sink, she kept expecting the door to fly open. Her bed had to be well away from the walls of the room. And she'd removed the frame from beneath it. The sight of an innocent towel loop in the ladies' room of a restaurant disturbed her so much that she ran from the place. Small things: like driving through the city and glancing out the car window while stopped at an intersection to notice police gates across a pair of windows beneath which was a fire escape; like the scent of hyacinths; like a man coming out of an office building wearing a pink shirt with white collar and cuffs; like a nude mannequin in Bendel's window, awaiting clothes with a fur coat draped around its shoulders. Things no one else would take notice of caused an interior clutching, dried her mouth, made her nervous.

She lowered her head now, and looked around. She felt drowsy with the heat of the sun soaking into the wool of the cardigan she'd put on over one of Joel's favorite shirts. She looked at her hands: dark smudges of soft lead pencil, several nicks from the mat knife, flecks of dried paint. She returned her hands to the flat arms of the chair, and raised her feet to look at the old Bass loafers she'd found while they'd been packing up the New Canaan house. Teenaged feet. It amused her to think that if she were viewed from the knees down, she might pass for someone young. She let her feet return to the grass, her eyes caught by the forsythia bushes, their tips full to bursting, ready to reveal the yellow flowers within. The land sloped gently downhill to the gravel driveway and then rose again, cutting off the view of the road. At night, the silence was like an additional blanket she pulled over herself; it was thick and soothing, without secrets. More often now, she slept long nights, to find the morning spread sumptuously in every direction. She could slide open the glass doors of the studio and walk barefoot across the chill damp grass to see what new growth had occurred overnight; or she could stand and marvel at finding that some small internal area had healed itself while she slept, leaving her fractionally safer and less fearful. Some mornings she thought perhaps her time with Daniel would, one day soon, like her periods of mourning, lose its sharp edges and become just a vague interlude, a time between times; an experience bracketed by other, equally if not more important experiences. She would never forget it, however. And it sometimes surprised her that she'd survived, because Daniel had given her such a craving for her own death, such hunger for an ending. But she'd chosen to fight and to survive, because she'd had enough of death, and wanted life. She'd chosen not to press charges, and it had been a good choice. Daniel had committed himself for treatment, had temporarily signed away his freedom. The act seemed to Leigh singularly appropriate.

They'd traveled together to such extremes, to such remote regions of human experience, that it didn't seem likely that anything would ever again be quite so terrifying, or so personally revealing. There were times when she placed the experience under the microscope of her analytical skills and saw, with a shudder both of revulsion and fascination, that her brain and her body had been induced to suffer seismic convulsions, not all of which were without pleasure. It was hateful to acknowledge the pleasure, but it had existed. She could only view it as some sort of flaw in her psychological makeup that she could have derived pleasure from one single moment of her imprisonment, yet she had. So what did that make her? And what did it make Daniel? She wanted to know. She thought that if she did know she might be able to respond more fully to the many good moments in her present life.

She heard the car turn into the driveway before she saw it. Tires on the gravel. She got up from the chair and walked over the grass along the side of the house as the car came to the top of the driveway and stopped. The engine was turned off and the silence, like a lid, closed over the space where its noise had been. The door on the drivers side opened, and Leigh descended the slope to the driveway, breaking into a smile, her arms swinging open in welcome. As her body hurried forward to make good the welcome, her arms closing around this dear, eccentric, lovely young woman, she thought perhaps she knew, after all, what her time with Daniel had made her.

"I'm so happy to see you!" she laughed, reveling in the moment.

"You look amazing!" Lane exclaimed. "Your hair's getting so long! And I love that shirt!"

"Come inside!" Leigh took her by the hand. "Mother and Miles are waiting to see you. But first I want you to see the 'amazing' studio Miles had made for me. And I want to hear about your father and your grandparents and school."

"This place is incredible!" Lane said, marching along at her side. "I love it. It's huge. Did you finish everything, the sets and costumes and everything?"

"All but the last-minute changes." Leigh stopped. "How is your father?"

"Way better," Lane said soberly. "Really way better. But he doesn't think he's ready to come home yet."

"He will be," Leigh said, putting her arm around Lane's shoulders as they began walking again. Suddenly, she felt very much better herself, because she had an answer of sorts. And it suited her reasoning.

"Are you going to marry Miles? You really should you know, Leigh. He's just gonzo over you."

"Gonzo?" Leigh laughed. "I'm carefully considering all the pros and cons. They tend to weigh rather heavily in his favor." Stopping again, she turned Lane toward her and looked her over. Ribbons and vests and a T-shirt under what had to be one of Daniel's shirts, a gypsyish brilliant-red skirt; odd clips in her hair, bracelets halfway up her arm, and army boots. "Will you let me take some photographs of you?" she asked.

"Oh, sure. D'you love this? Check it out!" Lane did a turn on the grass, the skirt ballooning around her legs. "Come on!" She pushed her arm through Leigh's. "Where's this amazing studio?"

"Just over here."

Her time with Daniel, Leigh thought, going arm in arm over the grass toward the back of the house, had been the long, attenuated labor that had returned her to motherhood. And here was the end product, the living, lively child. It made sense, really, if you thought about it that way.

About the Author

CHARLOTTE VALE ALLEN is the author of several novels that have been bestsellers and of a nonfiction book, DADDY'S GIRL. She has one teenage daughter and divides her time between Toronto, Ontario, and Norwalk, Connecticut.